ELLIOTT BAKER (b. 1922) was born and raised in Buffalo, New York. He graduated from Indiana University, after which he had a brief career in professional baseball as a pitcher for the Cincinnati Reds, followed by service as an infantry rifleman in World War II. After winning a playwriting competition for servicemen, Baker became interested in the theater, and then in television, for which he wrote a number of plays in the 1950s.

His first novel, *A Fine Madness,* was completed in 1959 and was turned down by several publishers before it was finally accepted by one of the original rejectors. It then went on to become a national best seller and an international success. In the meantime, Baker's career in television and film continued to flourish, and he wrote many more screenplays, alternately living in California and England. Since the publication of *A Fine Madness,* Baker has written and published five novels, *The Penny Wars* (1968), *Pocock and Pitt* (1971), *Unrequited Loves* (1974), *Klynt's Law* (1976), and *And We Were Young* (1979). He currently resides in Los Angeles.

AVAILABLE FROM SHORELINE BOOKS
Twentieth-century fiction

Death in the Woods & Other Stories
by Sherwood Anderson
A Fine Madness by Elliott Baker
Good Morning, Midnight by Jean Rhys
The Narrow House by Evelyn Scott
Testimony & Demeanor by John Casey
Tin Wedding by Margaret Leech

ELLIOTT BAKER

A Fine Madness

an imprint of
W · W · NORTON & COMPANY · NEW YORK · LONDON

Library of Congress Cataloging-in-Publication Data
Baker, Elliott.
A fine madness.
I. Title.
PS3552.A424F5 1986 813'.54 86–12673

ISBN 0-393-30395-0

W. W. Norton & Company, Inc., 500 Fifth Avenue, New York, N.Y. 10110
W. W. Norton & Company Ltd., 37 Great Russell Street, London WC1B 3NU

1 2 3 4 5 6 7 8 9 0

The pure products of America
go crazy—

WILLIAM CARLOS WILLIAMS

A Fine Madness

Chapter One

WHEN Samson Shillitoe stepped off the subway the beginning of the poem brushed against his brain. As he mounted toward the late afternoon light the exact words pranced across his teeth, tickled his left lung and tweaked his colon. Reaching the street he almost had them, the magnet of his concentration pulling them up, up, up. Then the clump of rags and whiskers held out a hand.

"Fifteen cents ta' get me home?"

Shillitoe looked up, the grip of his mind relaxed for a fraction of a second and the words scampered away. His eyes tried to snag them back, from the pyramid of apples at the fruit stand, from the dusty insides of the Double-Deuce saloon, from the pockets of the shiny checkered suits hanging in front of Manny's Savile Row. For a moment he stared at Manny's sign, GOING OUT OF BUSINESS! EVERYTHING MUST BE SOLD! flaked from two winters and three summers. Then, realizing his perfect words were gone, he grabbed the panhandler by the shirt and started to shake him like a fixed slot machine. But the lack of any resistance made him stop.

"Fifteen cents so's I kin get home."

"Home" on such puffed and purple lips was a blasphemy. What foul typhoon could blow from the crib to this?

"Just fifteen cents, buddy?"

"Fifteen cents," said Shillitoe. "And if they hadn't raised the fare you'd be settling for a nickel."

"No kiddin', buddy. I gotta' get to a hundred'n twenty-fif' street."

"No imagination," said Shillitoe. "Because you're standing near a subway you can't think beyond Harlem. Come on. Stretch that mind of yours. Ask me for ninety cents to get to Newark or ten bucks to go to Baltimore."

"Baltimore stinks!"

"Ah, a critic. Not a thought in your life, but a critic. Typical." Shillitoe tapped him on the forehead. "Try it again. Think! Imagine something. Make yourself give it form. Go on. Feel it! See it!"

The derelict face squeezed in concentration.

"That's the way," encouraged Shillitoe. "Now name it and state your price."

"Thuddy cents fer a shot a' rye."

"Ask for imagination," said Shillitoe, "and all you get is candor." He pushed the bum aside and walked away.

The hall, as usual, smelled of cooking cabbage; Fireman Fitzgerald's sole nourishment. As Shillitoe passed the door on the third landing it opened and the fumes poured out. It was *himself* wearing his full hook-and-ladder regalia.

"Just wanted to see who it was," Fitzgerald said.

"Is Mrs. Fitz' *that* hot?"

"Keep your dirty mind to yourself," snapped the fine broth of an idiot.

Shillitoe stared at the raincoat and helmet, searching for the simile. Like a gangrened turnip? Like an ebony juice squeezer on a swart totem pole?

"What you looking at?" asked Fitzgerald.

"Like the erection of a black whale," said Shillitoe.

Plaster fell throughout the building when Fitzgerald slammed the door.

Though the rooms on the top floor had been baked by the sun all day their barrenness was cooling. Shillitoe unstuck his clothes, kicked two wandering cockroaches back down the drain and stepped optimistically under the shower. But it groaned out the same old begrudging trickle. Rhoda still hadn't fixed it. And she'd again put too much starch in the white shirt she'd hung out for him. He growled at the door through which she'd soon enter, then took it back when he found the refrigerator newly stocked with beer.

Rhoda had also sharpened his pencils and arranged them like freshly cut flowers in a tumbler on the table. The yellow ruled pad she'd placed next to them presented its challenge. He sat down, grabbed his hair with both hands and tried to recapture the words the panhandler had chased away. But his thoughts kept returning to the girl on the forty-third floor.

He'd been pleased at being sent on the office building job. Shampooing the carpets in private apartments had taken too much out of him. Not that it happened every time but often enough for him to conclude that the East Side was generally more priapistic than the West Side, and that he should be especially wary of those who have pallet-knife paintings and marble coffee tables. At first he'd shown an admirable amount of self-control. But as the weeks went by he'd weakened. That last chirpy yo-yo showed just how much so. He wondered if Moscowitz suspected anything. Probably not, but his employer's timing of the new job couldn't have been better.

Starting on the office building Monday had been like entering a Benedictine monastery. Everything in it was scientifically designed to prevent distraction. As he worked on the thick carpets of the engineering firm on the fortieth floor he began to regain his energy. It continued to accumulate in the cubicles of the advertising agency on the forty-first and forty-second. Shillitoe felt he would soon have back the old vigor that enabled him to stay up half the night writing. But today he'd started on the forty-third floor, the Trust Company, the stodgy, money-grubbing Trust Company with the pouty-mouthed receptionist. Why hadn't he ignored her as she had him? Or, if he had to say something, why not a line appropriate to a carpet shampooer? "Don't I know you from someplace?" Or, "You doing anything tonight?" and she would have flounced away. But no. He had to drag out the quotation.

"Alone and palely loitering."

It had been appropriate, the way she stood to one side while he worked round her desk. But that was no excuse. He should know better by now. The rest of the day pouty-mouth was bumping into him every time he turned round.

"Why did you say what you did? Tell me."

Still, that was as far as it went. He knew he should be glad of that, the alcoholic with another twenty-four hours under his belt. But she had been munchy, in an embalmed sort of way, willowy, not more than twenty-three or four, with tangerines under the organdy blouse and a nice flat abdomen. And that small office in the back with the leather couch obviously wasn't being used. And it did have a door that locked.

Seeing Mrs. Fitzgerald on the front stoop, Rhoda tried to minimize her limp. She didn't want to hear any more friendly suggestions that she might have a blood clot. Every time Mrs. Fitzgerald said it, her leg hurt more.

"Still haven't seen a doctor about it," said Mrs. Fitzgerald as soon as Rhoda was within earshot.

"It's much better today," said Rhoda.

"Diseased bones can fool you," said Mrs. Fitzgerald.

The leg throbbed painfully.

"Maybe I'll have somebody look at it tomorrow." Rhoda hoisted the bag of groceries to emphasize its heaviness and inched toward the front door. She knew she had to make it before Mrs. Fitzgerald started on her own state of health. Mrs. Fitzgerald, who'd been a nurse's aide before her marriage, was always describing gruesome things that were going on in her insides. Samson said, asking her how she felt was like uncorking a vat of entrails.

"I want to talk to you about Mr. Shillitoe," Mrs. Fitzgerald said. "He insulted my husband again."

"He don't mean nothing."

"How would you like your husband to be called a whale's . . . ?" Mrs. Fitzgerald stopped all of a sudden as if her tongue had found a filling missing.

"I'll tell him to lay off," said Rhoda.

"Little good that will do. I worked in hospitals long enough to see plenty of his kind. One of these day's he'll turn on you."

"I'll tell him to leave your husband alone," said Rhoda.

"Believe me, Bellevue's full of writers. Not that I'm convinced he's really a writer."

"Aw, shut up!" Rhoda said and went inside.

"I'm just saying it for your own good." Mrs. Fitzgerald's parting shot followed Rhoda up the stairs. "He's a case for a psychiatrist if I ever saw one."

Samson was asleep, his cheek resting on the back of one hand, the ends of his black hair feathered across the yellow pad. She lowered herself onto the arm of their one upholstered chair to ease her leg and watched the steady billowing of his breathing.

Rhoda could never quite reconcile his face to the fact that he was a poet. Not that she still believed they were all sissies. She'd looked up pictures of some of the famous ones and had decided that no real poet looked like a poet. Walt Whitman looked like a cowboy, Oscar Wilde a headwaiter, and the lawyers in English movies were all spittin' images of Shakespeare.

The same went for the real poets she'd met through Samson. Not the phonies trying to grow beards. But the *real* ones.

Like that Dylan who kept pinching until she'd hauled off and smacked him one. All the time he and Samson were drinking and singing those dirty songs she kept thinking that Dylan looked just like a used-car salesman.

As for Samson, her first impression had been that he was a prizefighter. Herschel had his lunchroom on Eighth Avenue then, near Stillman's Gym, and a lot of the boxers used to come in. As Herschel would say, one thing they never ran out of was cauliflower. That was why she thought Samson was a fighter; that and his nose being swollen and blue from the chair that someone hit him with in the Double-Deuce. He'd come in three times before he said a word, but she felt him eying her. Then the fourth time he breezed up to the counter like they were old friends.

"Black coffee, Catherine."

"The name's Rhoda."

"You *look* like Catherine Blake."

"Rhoda."

"We'll see."

She'd been positive he was punchy then. Imagine her not even knowing who Catherine Blake was. She'd sure been ignorant before she knew Samson.

She looked at his face again. His high forehead and big chin placed him in the prow of a ship with the ocean spray hitting his eyes. Or he could be a prairie scout, always up ahead, alert for the first sign of the enemy. That was it, the same look that made her think of Whitman as a cowboy. Like Samson always said, poets were first pioneers.

Rhoda leaned forward to peek at the yellow pad. Seeing the paper blank she almost sighed aloud. It had been eleven weeks now since he'd written anything and she knew how it was eating him. Living with Samson when the poetry flowed was an experience. First there was the feeling that she wasn't there at all. He would just look right through her. Then, suddenly, the place would be alive with words. Rhoda felt sorry for any woman who didn't know what it was like. But then there was the other extreme like these last eleven weeks, the awful silence with Samson pacing around as if any minute he'd break the few things they owned. Then he'd go down to the Double-Deuce and drink too much and start arguing with everybody until someone conked him good.

To make matters worse, Samson had promised Rollie Butter a long poem, an allegory he called it, for the October issue of *Moot* and Rollie paid him in advance. That was over a month ago and last week they ran into Rollie on Third Avenue and he started yelling for the poem in that high voice of his. She'd butted in and said that poetry wasn't something you can just turn out by the yard. But Samson told her to mind her own goddam business.

He still hadn't written a word of the allegory. Why didn't he just sit down and write it? She tried to remember if there was any one thing that took place before he wrote other poems. But it had happened in all kinds of ways in all kinds of places, during a meal, out walking, at night, in the morning, before love-making, after love-making, once even in the middle and she'd blown her top. If only she could do something to get him started. But Rhoda knew that, whoever was Samson's inspiration, it wasn't her.

She sighed and stood up, then grabbed the chair to keep from falling. What a leg cramp! Only fear of waking up Samson kept her from letting out a yell. But enough was enough. Besides, Mrs. Fitzgerald could be right about blood clots. Rhoda made up her mind. The next morning, after the breakfast mob cleared out of Herschel's, she'd go see one of the million doctors in the neighborhood.

Chapter Two

DOCTOR Posmanture's hands were shaking so much the thermometer kept rattling against Mrs. Tupperman's lower teeth. Finally he got the silver tip under her tongue and went over to the window. It faced the Hudson and directly across the river the huge sign advertised Spry. Doctor Posmanture concentrated hard on this to keep his mind off the other thing. Then he remembered that he hadn't looked at his watch when he'd inserted the thermometer.

Almost noon! His wife would be waiting in the lobby with the suitcases this very minute. No matter how much he hurried now, he'd be late. And she'd complain about it every mile of the drive to The Concord. It was his own fault. She'd told him not to go to the office today. But there'd been a few odds and ends and last-minute instructions to give the nurse and he'd sworn he wouldn't take any phone calls. In a way, though, it was lucky he had. The call from Leonard Tupperman had saved him from the most embarrassing moment in his whole life as a physician.

Doctor Posmanture tried to recall anything worse. No, he couldn't count errors in diagnosis like when Rebecca Shapiro's allergy to strawberries had appeared to him as chicken pox and he'd quarantined the whole family for ten days. Then that glutton of a Rebecca had to go and eat strawberries the very day the yellow sign came off the door.

But this? This common *shikseh* with her pug nose and curly red hair daring to question him. Imagine! After almost forty years of practice to be spoken to in such a way. Who did she think she was, limping into his office without even an appointment, *chrexing* about her leg and giving him a story about working in a lunchroom around the corner and being on her feet all day. All night was more like it, in some ten-cents-a-dance hall.

He was going to tell her that he was just leaving for his vacation and that she should go to one of the other doctors in the building. But she looked in so much pain, and there was enough time for a brief examination.

So, what had he done any different? Nothing. He had helped her up on the table, turned his back as he started filling out her card and said, like he always said, that she should disrobe to the waist. Last name—Shillitoe, first name—Rhoda, age—thirty-two, married, no children, home address, place of employment; he printed the information slowly in big block letters to give her plenty of time to take off the man's shirt she wore with the sleeves rolled up and to slide down the slip if she was wearing one and remove her brassiere. It was a good three minutes later that he turned around. And she hadn't moved an inch! The shirt was still buttoned.

"Disrobe to the waist, please," he repeated good and loud, assuming she was hard of hearing.

"What for?" she shouted right back.

"My dear lady, I'm a doctor."

"Then you oughta' know that my leg ain't above my waist."

"I have to begin with a thorough examination."

"The pain's in my foot and leg."

"But I . . ."

"I ain't insinuating nothing," she said, "but when I scalded my arm, every time I went to have the bandage changed I got examined for breast cancer. I ain't putting up with any more of that."

Such an accusation! Still, it served him right for taking a woman patient while his nurse was out to the bank. It served him right for taking her at all. But once he'd started, he shouldn't have stood for any back talk. Then he wouldn't have been so upset that he'd picked up the phone when Leonard Tupperman called about the tranquilizers not doing any good and Mrs. Tupperman carrying on more than ever. And if he hadn't been upset he wouldn't have said he'd come right over and be standing here now instead of on his way to The Concord.

Still, he'd had the presence of mind to tell the Shillitoe woman not to come back until three o'clock. By then he'd be far away from the city. There was nothing unethical in his doing this, either. She only cared about her foot and leg. She didn't want anybody to look at her above the knee. Okay. He'd have his nurse make an appointment for her with Doctor Gordon the podiatrist.

Mrs. Tupperman moaned at him, pointing to the thermometer until he pulled it from her mouth. Ninety-eight point six. What else? Doctor Posmanture quickly prepared to check her heart and blood pressure, but he knew they'd also be normal like they always were. Meanwhile, she had started raving again, blaming her condition on her mother and her son and, most of all, on her husband.

Mrs. Fish tiptoed to the bedroom door again and stood listening. Still not a sound. What was Posmanture doing so long? She went back to the living room. Leonard sat there like death warmed over. Man of the house! A strong breeze and he fell apart.

Mrs. Fish, on the other hand, was perfectly calm. It was all very obvious. Evelyn was pregnant again. Surprise? Mrs. Fish had to admit that it was. Sixteen years between children was a lot. But, she'd never fully accepted having only three grandchildren, especially with Norma and her twins being all the way out in South Bend. And she'd always told Evelyn that Dana needed a sister.

She looked at Dana now and wished he'd go outside so she and Leonard could talk openly.

"Dana, you look so pale."

"I'm okay, Gramma'."

"Doesn't he look white, Leonard?"

"He looks like he always looks."

"My linens should look so white. All we need now is for him to come down with something. Dana, go get some fresh air. Stand in front of the building for a while."

Dana screwed up his face into a silent whine. Whenever he did this Mrs. Fish's heart melted.

"Do I have to go outside?"

"Stop arguing with your grandmother and go outside!" The way Leonard yelled at him.

Dana dragged himself away. When the hall door closed, Mrs. Fish waited for Leonard to speak first. But he just sat there, gripping his hands together like he was Indian-wrestling with himself. It was probably the closest thing to exercise he'd had in years. How bloated he was getting, and he'd been such a skinny little runt when Evelyn married him. Now only the slightest indentation showed where his chin left off and his neck began. His hair was seeing its last, too. And without his coat on, he had no shoulders at all. Some physique, like a scoop of ice cream.

"So?" sighed Mrs. Fish.

"So?"

"So she'll be pregnant again."

His head popped up.

"Who?"

"Who?" repeated Mrs. Fish. "Not me."

"Who says she's pregnant? Is that what she told you?"

"Of course not." Mrs. Fish posed for the Christmas cover of *The Saturday Evening Post*. "A mother is always the last to hear. Hasn't she dropped any hints to you?"

"She'd better not drop any hints. If she's pregnant, I've got grounds for divorce."

"What kind of language is that? Your own wife's in there, dying for all you know, and you sit plotting."

When attacked, Mrs. Fish always took the offensive. Not

pregnant? The web of her mind unraveled and lay waiting to be restrung. Before she could do it, the bedroom door opened, and Doctor Posmanture came in like a pall bearer.

"Well?" asked Mrs. Fish.

"I've given her a strong sedative. She'll fall asleep soon." He motioned Mrs. Fish to the sofa and stood between her and Leonard. "It's the pace," he said, "the confusion, the stress of the times we live in. You know, after all, she's a mother, concerned about the welfare of her child. And with hydrogen missiles and the Russians such maniacs . . ."

Mrs. Fish turned helplessly to her son-in-law.

"Do *you* know what he's talking about?"

"Please bear with me a moment," said Doctor Posmanture. "There were some statistics recently in the Medical Journal. It's more common than you think."

"What's more common?" asked Leonard.

"Right now, one person out of every ten needs mental help."

"Mental!"

Mrs. Fish and Leonard were both on their feet.

"Now, now, no cause for alarm," soothed Doctor Posmanture. Then, remembering another statistic, "One out of every two hospital beds holds a mental patient."

"Evelyn, a mental patient?" Mrs. Fish prepared to deny it with her last breath.

"Let's just call it a nervous breakdown. It's nothing to be ashamed of," said Doctor Posmanture, walking backwards as Mrs. Fish advanced toward him.

"I never heard such garbage," she said. "What do you know about it? You're not even a surgeon!"

"If you wish to consult someone else . . ."

"A mental patient," she scoffed. "Did you hear him, Leonard?"

"Let him talk," said Leonard.

"For what? Evelyn's a mental patient like Rebecca Shapiro had the measles."

Doctor Posmanture gave her a look like he wanted to kill her.

"The first thing is for her to have a good long rest," he said. "And the best place to rest is in a hospital."

"If you think so, she'll go," said Leonard. "That's what I've got the Blue Cross for."

"I'm afraid your hospital insurance doesn't apply to an illness like this."

Mrs. Fish wasn't listening. Her mind had started projecting scenes yet to come, on the street, in stores, at the Hadassah luncheons. She heard questions from all her friends. "What happened to your daughter?" "What's the matter with Evelyn?" All right, if Evelyn had to be sick, let it be gallstones, an ulcer—even a hysterectomy and she'd settle for three grandchildren. But mental illness? Pictures floated past the end of Mrs. Fish's pointed nose, straitjackets and people who thought they were Theodore Roosevelt and wild-looking women in sackcloth moving aimlessly around a cold, stone room with bars on the windows.

"You can keep her here," conceded Doctor Posmanture. "But you'll need a daytime nurse."

"No nurse," piped Mrs. Fish. "What's a mother for?"

"The only thing is," said Doctor Posmanture, "she has to see a psychiatrist. It's expensive. But say, so's an operation."

The comparison hit home. A specialist was required and who was more specialized than a psychiatrist. Mrs. Fish knew them from the movies, all Gregory Pecks. Or was he the patient? Her thoughts stumbled momentarily, then raced on. Anyway, *that* type, with a voice full of knowledge, telling patients to count backwards from one hundred. Quickly, she twisted humiliation into a new triumph. After all, what broke down? She looked at Leonard. A mind like his you couldn't unbalance with a sledgehammer. But Evelyn's was like the inside of a Longine watch. Doctor Posmanture was absolutely right. It was the lunatic Russians.

Leonard was beginning to fight back.

"Maybe she'll get over it in a few days."

"Mr. Tupperman, she won't get over it unless she has help."

"How can you be sure she's got what you said?"

Mrs. Fish sailed between them.

"You know more than a doctor, suddenly. He says Evelyn needs a psychiatrist. Listen to him and learn something."

She let her momentum carry her on to the hall. The telephone squatted before her. She dialed the operator and asked for Western Union. Norma wouldn't be able to complain that she wasn't told immediately. Mrs. Fish mapped out the message.

"Evelyn very ill. Come at once." Or maybe "*desperately* ill" would be better. The longer word was substituted.

Leonard and Doctor Posmanture were still haggling as she entered the bedroom. Evelyn lay on her back under one sheet, staring at the glass chandelier like a corpse. Mrs. Fish pinched off the tears before they could ripple her voice.

"How do you feel, darling?"

"Awful."

"You'll be all right. Everything's going to be fine."

"Let me sleep, Ma."

"Sure, darling. Sleep. Sleep." Evelyn's eyelids started down. "But let me ask you first. Leonard's going to be a problem. He's still living in the Middle Ages. But you want to see a specialist, don't you?"

"Do I have to be operated on?"

"No, no. You've just got one of those nervous upsets that are going around. Doctor Posmanture says ten percent of the people have it. And a lot walk around without even knowing. The only thing is, Leonard's afraid it will cost him a few dollars."

"Tight bastard," mumbled Evelyn.

"So you insist, you hear?"

"I insist."

"That's right. Now go to sleep."

When Mrs. Fish got back to the living room, primed to rejoin the battle, Doctor Posmanture was saying he knew a very good psychiatrist and he'd have his nurse give them the name and address and make the first appointment, all in the strictest confidence.

Chapter Three

THE lament was creeping into Alben Parker's voice again. Oliver Wren waved aside the jab of impatience he always felt when a patient slipped back and splashed around in the bog of self-pity. Parker was still his most absorbing case. Any blocked writer was a challenge to a psychoanalyst. And Alben Parker, who had won both the Pulitzer Prize and Drama Critics' Award, wasn't just *any* blocked writer.

It had been almost two years since Parker first came to him, his self-confidence shattered by unanimously unfavorable reviews of his last play, convinced that he could never write another. For a while, Oliver wasn't sure the block could be overcome. Then there was the breakthrough and after that, line by line, scene by scene, he had prompted and goaded the playwright until the new script was finished. It was pure Alben Parker; the fiery, headlong rush of words, the metallic scraping of human emotions. But Oliver knew he had made a definite contribution to the script. He found himself anticipating its première performance when he would sit next to Lydia and know that part of her applause belonged to him.

"But what if it doesn't play as well as it reads?"

Oliver didn't answer, afraid that his irritation might be detectable. If only therapy included an occasional grabbing of a patient's shoulders, a sharp "Dammit! You're too sensitive!" But if it had been said to Emily Brontë, would she have despaired any the less? Time, time. What had someone written about Art being long and Life being short? Not that Alben Parker was an artist exactly. Facile, yes; certainly very talented. But too "box office," too opportunistic with none of the consuming passion that always marked the true artist.

The muted buzzer on the side of his desk sounded. Miss Bueler was signaling that the next patient had arrived. He let Parker finish a long explanation of why the critics had a grudge against him, then stood up.

"We'll go into this in more detail the next time."

Parker sat up slowly. The expensive suit was wrinkled across the back, the light hair pressed flat by the headpiece of the couch. As he gained his feet their relationship changed, from the patient and the analyst to the celebrity and the unknown. It was a subtle accomplishment, but Oliver had been quick to observe it.

"Do you like musical shows?" asked Parker.

"Usually."

"I have two tickets for *Troika,* if you could use them."

"*Troika?* Which one is that?"

"It's based on *Dead Souls.* You know, Gogol's."

"Oh yes." Oliver refrained from adding that he'd read the book twice. "I know Mrs. Wren wants to see it. But I'd like to pay for the tickets."

"No. They're house seats."

"Well, thank you very much. Which night is that?"

"The nineteenth."

"Oh. I'm sorry. The Parapraxes Society has its banquet on the nineteenth. It's our big night."

"No call for tears." Parker hesitated at the door. "Did you say 'Parapraxes Society'?"

"Yes. It's a national organization of psychiatrists."

"Unless my Latin teacher deceived me, a parapraxes is a slip of the tongue."

"That's right."

"Isn't it an odd name for a society representing your profession?" Parker put a scathing inflection on the "your."

"It's kind of an inside joke. Doctor Holland, one of the founders, thought of it. And most of our members didn't have Latin teachers as thorough as yours."

"Oh." Parker's smile was as slight as possible. "Bye."

Oliver went to his desk and buzzed Bueler. She would wait sixty seconds before ushering in the next patient. Who was it? He looked at his desk pad. A new name. Good. "Referred by Doctor Abraham Posmanture." And who the devil was Dr. Abraham Posmanture? Oliver concentrated on memory association; first and last syllables, Pos . . . ture. Posture brought nothing to mind. First and second syllables, Pos . . . man. No. Say it fast, posman, postman. The bald, plodding mail carrier he'd watched from the parlor window when a boy in Lowell, Massachusetts, metamorphosed into the bald, plodding doctor who'd attended one of his lectures at Columbia and hung on his elbow afterwards asking banal questions. Yes, that must have been Abraham Posmanture.

Bueler's knock. He stepped to the center of the room as his secretary entered. The woman behind her had a round face and bright eyes. Another manic one. He censured himself immediately. He was getting as bad as Bueler with her one-word descriptions of patients.

As if aware of his criticism, Bueler stopped suddenly and the woman almost leapfrogged over her. Then the curt introduction. He tried to offset his secretary's stiffness with a casual indication of the chair facing his desk. The woman plopped onto it ungracefully as Bueler went out and closed the door.

Oliver leaned back in his swivel chair and took a deep look at his new patient. This was one of the most exciting moments of all; a face, a personality, a collection of millions of moments completely unknown to him. He was about to embark on another safari into the dark interior of a solitary mind. First step, the establishment of a bit of common ground.

"And how is Doctor Posmanture?"

"What a dope."

"Oh?" He smiled gently. "Do you really think so?"

"I know so."

Antagonistic, even on this simple level. He wondered if she was now choosing a derogatory label for him. But her face appeared relaxed enough. He watched her surveying the room, his dictation machine, his books, Lydia's painting. She frowned at this and he almost got ready to defend it. Then, without comment, she turned and pointed to the couch of green fabric poised on its wrought-iron legs.

"You want me to lay down on that?"

"Not now. Eventually."

She threw him a questioning look, then shrugged and bent over. What was she doing? He leaned across the desk to see.

Her shoe was off!

"Well, aincha' goin' to look at it?"

"At what?"

"The swelling."

"It is swollen a little."

"A little?"

Again that questioning look. He felt uneasy. He should have telephoned Posmanture and found out a little about the case in advance.

"Suppose you just relax and place your confidence in me."

"Okay."

Initial contact at last. She sighed and sat back.

"But I ain't got forever."

Now he knew the way. They all began with a similar remark. They had acquaintances who were in the third or fourth year of analysis. But not them. They'd give him up to six months and no more.

"Then let's try to make as rapid progress as we can."

"Right!" She held her foot up. For a moment he thought she was going to rest it on the desk top.

"It's real agony, you know, standing on my feet eight hours a day."

"It started with headaches?"

"What started with headaches? It started in my leg and it's still in my leg."

"Your leg?"

"And I ain't strippin' to the waist."

Did she think he was a Reichian?

"I haven't asked you to," he said, not letting it sound defensive.

"Well, that's an improvement." She leaned forward confidingly. "Whenever I stand awhile the pain's like a hot iron, right up my leg."

"Your leg?"

"My leg. My leg!"

She was waving it at him. What had that old fool Posmanture got him into?

"And what did Doctor Posmanture say about your leg?"

"Nothing."

"He must have said something."

"When I went back at three, his nurse said he told her to give me this."

She handed him the prescription blank. No mistake. His name, address and telephone number were scribbled across it.

"The nurse didn't say anything else, anything at all?"

"Nope. Except that she'd make this appointment for me. It sure was long enough in advance. You that busy?"

"I'm afraid so. But . . ."

"I wouldn't of waited but I don't know any other podiatrists."

"Podiatrists?"

"What's the matter? Didn't I pronounce it right?"

Podiatrist. He almost laughed with relief. So that was it. A nurse's misunderstanding. Did Posmanture have an accent? He couldn't remember. What guttural speech would make psychiatrist sound like podiatrist? Lydia would have hysterics when he told her about this woman taking off her shoe and waving her leg like a chorus girl.

He hastened to explain, soberly apologetic, expecting her to hide her embarrassment with indignation. But instead, when his explanation finally dented those round eyes, she let out a long howl and doubled over in delight.

He buzzed Bueler and she came in.

"Miss Bueler, please give Mrs. Shillitoe the address of Doctor Huddleson. No. Suppose you call Doctor Huddleson and make an appointment for her. Tell him, as soon as possible. And Bueler." She stopped at the door. "Don't call another psychiatrist by mistake."

The woman roared again and Bueler threw her an impassive glance before going back to the reception room.

"So you're one of them." Mrs. Shillitoe winced as she squeezed her shoe back on. "Bet you don't get many people like me coming in here."

"No. You're the first podiatry case I've had."

The laugh he expected didn't come.

"I mean people like me. You know, working people."

"You'd be surprised at the range of my practice."

"Even working people?"

"Even working people."

"I thought you just got mixed-up screwballs who were rich and successful."

"Those too."

"And they think they got problems."

"Some of them do have, Mrs. Shillitoe."

"Like what?"

"Many things."

"Like what?"

Her stance was almost pugnacious. He realized she wouldn't turn toward the door until he'd cited an example.

"Well . . ." It was natural to remember his last patient. "Well, it might be a writer who suddenly finds himself unable to write."

"And you can help him?" Her interest seemed greatly out of proportion.

"I've had success with that particular problem."

Then Bueler was at the door. If Mrs. Shillitoe could go directly to Doctor Huddleson's office, he'd take her right away.

She thanked him heartily. He was afraid there'd be a stammering moment when she'd ask if there was any charge. But the thought didn't seem to occur to her. As she went out, though, she did look back at him as if there was something more she wanted to say.

He returned to his desk. Forty-five unexpected minutes ahead of him. Time to take care of some of the dictation which was piling up on him. He opened Alben Parker's folder and stared at the transcript of a visit three weeks back. Podiatrist? Psychiatrist? No accent, however thick, could make them sound very similar. Then he noticed the prescription blank the woman had given him. Didn't she say that Posmanture had left it with his nurse? Was it possible there had been references for two patients and that the nurse had mixed them up. If so, the woman who was supposed to come to him might be pouring out her emotional problems this very moment to some baffled foot doctor.

He reached toward the buzzer to tell Miss Bueler to call Doctor Posmanture. Then his hand stopped. No. Even a psychiatrist should be allowed a little joke once in a while.

Chapter Four

"EVERYTHING's red," said Shillitoe, "coquelicot sun, annatto sand, fuchsine sky, merely different shades of red. Even this spongy cerement you call a skin is a kind of washed-out morbidezza—derivation obvious. Venetian red, Indian red, Southern Slovakian red, scarlet, cardinal, cinnabar, every blood type from rose to rust. But teacher tells you you're looking at a rainbow so it never occurs to you that you're in hell. Cochineal! There's a tasty red, made from dried-up bodies of female insects. Why don't you volunteer yours?"

"The way you talk slays me," said pouty-mouth and shimmied out of her girdle.

He'd managed to resist for seven working days, all the way up to the fiftieth floor. But that morning the elevator had made a stop at the forty-third and he'd had a glimpse of her at the reception desk, cheerless and bored. Before the elevator door wiped her away his willpower sprang a leak. Even so, he'd held out another hour before carrying the cylinder and applicator hose down the service stairway.

She'd looked as if nothing he could possibly say would be of any interest as he explained there'd been a complaint about his shampooing of one of the carpets. Strictly a professional call. He knew which office it was. Would she lead the way? Following her down the corridor, watching the boom-bang-boom under her skirt, he'd decided she was crated for a life insurance salesman and three and a half rooms on Staten Island. Then what was he doing in her wake? The question had slowed his steps. There'd still been time to change direction. But he remembered the flicker of hope when he'd quoted her the line of Keats. Perhaps the well of dreams wasn't completely dry. Rationalization swiftly set in. The least he could do was talk to her for a few minutes, just to assure her there was more and sweeter music than her allotted prothalamium.

How the hell had he got on the subject of colors? And who had locked the door? He couldn't recall having turned the key. And what did she think she was doing now? A million coolies trudged up his spine, a blanket of greed and a quilt of sin, suspended black widow hanging on a slow crane, lowering her hickey, hills of home, mint-polluted saliva, vermilion, crimson, damask, coral, up from the bubbling casserole of chunky memories seasoned with delight. Seventeen fierce blue seconds, then the fire ebbed to red again.

"Christ! I'm a poet, not an oil well."

Mr. Bingham, Assistant Vice-President in charge of Credit Ratings, was the first to notice that the reception desk was empty. He duly dispatched Miss Hogan to the ladies' room to summon the truant Miss Walnicki. When Miss Hogan reported that Miss Walnicki wasn't there, Mr. Bingham insisted that she must be. Miss Hogan, frightened by his tone, began to recite a roll call of the occupants of the sinks and stalls. Mr. Bingham blushed and scurried away to peek into the cubicles of the junior officers. Soon Miss Walnicki's name was being relayed from Mortgages to Loans to Foreign Exchange and the small posse began to form. Within twenty minutes, all of the forty-third floor had been covered except for the Conference Room, the President's office and the small office of Mr. Solotrance, Safe Deposit Boxes. The Conference Room yielded half a dozen sleepy trainees watching a series of slides tracing the history of the company, the President's quarters were off limits even in emergencies such as this and Mr. Solotrance's office was locked.

The locked door struck Mr. Bingham as odd. Mr. Solotrance had been out more than a month with his heart attack. Certainly the door couldn't have been locked all that time without it being noticed. Were some of the lazy girls like Miss Walnicki using the room for catnapping? Mr. Bingham rapped his fist against the door.

"Miss Walnicki! Are you in there?"

Complete silence, then whispering and a thud. Something or someone had fallen to the floor. Mr. Bingham pressed an eager, gleaming eye against the keyhole and hot lava churned his stomach until he realized he was staring at the round tip of the key. By then other members of the search party had arrived and they all exhorted Miss Walnicki to come out.

After the first rap on the door tumbled pouty-mouth off the couch, Shillitoe gauged the width of the ledge outside the window, envisioned himself spread-eagled on one of the tiny yellow taxi tops below and told himself he couldn't die with a total output less than Poe's. Pouty-mouth was fastening her stockings and hissing at him to do something. He thought of how unattractive women got when terrified. Fear turned men to slobbering baby boys but drove maidens straight to hagdom. A point to be made in the allegory he would write, but meanwhile he did have to do something.

The position didn't seem as grave as pouty-mouth was making out. He need only spread some cleaner on the carpet, stick to his original story about having received a complaint and add that the receptionist had stood by to make sure he didn't rifle the desk. Simple enough. He opened the cylinder valve. But he wasn't as unnerved as he had supposed or he wouldn't have opened it all the way. The chemical foam gushed out and before he could get a firm hold on the slippery valve the foam was a foot deep in the room. Pouty-mouth let out a bloodcurdling scream and unlocked the door. And the fools rushed in.

Breughel would have appreciated the scene; pin-striped bankers and bunned stenographers skidding and sliding, whooping and squealing, arms semaphoring frantically like clock hands riding a broken spring, then a ker-plunk and another one would be spitting out lather and trying to scramble back to his feet. But even the mixed bathing didn't break the protocol. Every shouted name was preceded by a Miss or Mister. Shillitoe called to them to stand still, that they were working up the suds. But no one listened. A Mister Bingham lifted a Miss Hogan for one chivalrous moment before both went down in the now knee-deep foam. The others, pulling skirts and trouser legs higher and higher, pranced around like peasants pressing grapes. Then Mister Bingham managed to crawl to the desk and bellowed into the intercom for help.

Shillitoe waded to the door, stopped only long enough to wave good-bye to pouty-mouth somewhere in the melee, and made the service stairs before the first rescuers arrived. He wanted to get back to the shop and tell his version of the story to Moscowitz first. But as soon as he opened the door he knew he'd come in second.

"Out!" yelled Moscowitz, hopping up and down on his stumpy legs. His eyes were bulging and he kept slapping the top of his bald head with alternate hands. "Out! Out! No rapist works for the Acme Carpet Cleaning."

"My dear Mr. Moscowitz . . ."

"Never mind the salutations. Never mind the two men I had to rush over to clean up after you. Never mind the hundred and forty-eight dollars and odd cents I advanced you in pay. Out, Samson, out!"

Shillitoe was fond of his employer. It wasn't often one encountered such a simple and clear-cut vision of the world. To Moscowitz there were only three groups of people, Jews, a small twilight fringe of good *goyem* and fascists. Shillitoe suspected he had been temporarily hung on a peg, dangling over the latter two. He hated to catalog himself. But, as Moscowitz would say, an emergency isn't something you can put off.

"Mr. Moscowitz, may I at least know why you're acting like this?"

"I ain't acting. Out! Out!"

"Won't you even listen to my side of it?"

"I know your side." Moscowitz ran to the door and pointed the direction he wanted him to take. "Out! The girl supplied all the details. You're lucky that Mr. Bingham who called wants to avoid publicity. Thank God it was a bank and not the *Daily News.* Twenty years you could get."

"And you believed Mr. Bingham? You disappoint me, Mr. Moscowitz."

"Out! Out!"

"As you wish," said Shillitoe. He stopped at the door, mingling innocence and pain in his gesture of farewell. "But I never thought you'd take the word of an anti-Semite."

Moscowitz hauled him protesting back in from the street.

"What, Samson? Who? What happened?"

"Mr. Moscowitz, did you ever hear of any bank hiring someone of Jewish faith?"

Moscowitz shook his head sadly, before bouncing back.

"But why should you care? You're a *shagetz.*"

"One of my great-grandfathers wasn't. Moses Shillitoe."

Shillitoe thought this name would carry more weight than several others that came to mind. Moscowitz looked at him as if seeing him properly for the first time. He started to spread his arms to welcome him, but suspicion held them down.

"So what were you doing locked up with the girl?"

"I'm not going to demean our relationship with explanations," said Shillitoe. "You can accept Mr. Bingham's word or mine." As Moscowitz hesitated, he thought he'd better play it extra safe. "The one thing I'll say is, I couldn't get twenty years for what I did, except under a Nazi regime."

The hated word did it. Moscowitz dunked himself in apologies and promised never to mention the incident again. Shillitoe felt a twinge of self-reproach when his employer insisted he take a week off with pay until the next job was ready to begin. He even refused to accept the week's pay in advance. But Moscowitz shoved it into his hand and scampered out of reach so he couldn't give it back.

On the way home he made up his mind to dedicate the allegory to his new patron. A full untrammeled week ahead to concentrate on its form and substance. Kind, generous, lover of the arts, Wolf Moscowitz. "All happiness and that eternity promised by our ever loving poet." He would give Mr. Wolf Moscowitz the same immortality Shakespeare gave to Mr. W. H.

Rhoda found him in the Double-Deuce at six o'clock. Rollie Butter was with her, blond, floppy and loose-mouthed like a Scandinavian marathon runner on the home stretch.

"How much you drank?" started Rhoda.

Shillitoe shoved her aside and held Rollie at arm's length.

"Don't have the goddam poem yet."

"You promised me, Shillitoe."

"Stop hounding me. Devery, you let pederasts annoy your customers?"

"Huh?" Devery, behind the bar, turned to Rollie and pressed his hands together to make his biceps bulge.

"It's okay, Devery," said Rhoda.

"It's okay. It's okay," mimicked Shillitoe. "The slogan of womanhood as man is beaten into the ground. Itiosis, okiasis, sigillum. In sperm we trust."

"Watch your language," said Rhoda. "Mr. Butter's got good news for you."

"*Mister* Butter? When was the operation?"

"I'm not here about the poem, Shillitoe. But we do go to press in two weeks."

"No got," snarled Shillitoe. "Do the next best thing. Paraphrase a piece of 'Paradise Lost' or some of that crap. Break up the lines, throw in a couple of teats and twats and everybody'll call it modern. 'The broad circumference hung on his shoulders like the moon.' Milton meant Galileo, but your readers will think it's a new position."

"Ought'a wash your mouth out," said Rhoda.

"Listen you two," said Rollie.

"Listen to Mr. Butter," said Rhoda.

"If you can get off from work Thursday afternoon," Rollie said, "you can read some of your work at Da Vinci Hall."

Shillitoe coughed his half-swallowed drink back into its glass.

"Mr. Butter ain't kidding," said Rhoda, pounding his back until the coughing stopped. "It's some fancy woman's organization. They're gonna' have a guy playing the harp and an art critic and you."

"Fiend!" He threw a roundhouse right, but she stepped inside it.

"You don't have to do it," peeved Rollie. "They just asked me to suggest one young poet and I thought . . ."

"Young? I'm nine years past the last day Jesus ever saw."

"And I thought you could use the hundred dollars."

The last sober outpost within Shillitoe dug a foothold.

"A hundred bucks," verified Rhoda. "And you only gotta' recite for fifteen or twenty minutes."

Tumblers were clicking numbers in his head. One hundred dollars for twenty minutes, three hundred per hour, twenty-four hundred for an eight-hour day. The poet as capitalist. How big would the tax bite be? He could get around some of it by investing in breeding bulls.

"Nothing doing," said Shillitoe.

"Samson, there was a letter today," Rhoda rammed it home gently, "from Daniel K. Papp."

Papp! Leech! Bloodsucker! Dragon draining his strength! He could shampoo every rug in Persia and the revenue wouldn't satisfy Daniel K. Papp. He knew what the letter said. He had no choice.

"Okay," said Shillitoe, "provided I follow the harp player. Devery, I'm going to read poems to housewives and mothers. Nothing like hyperbole to sooth the aching crotch."

"Why do you always have to talk so dirty?" blushed Rhoda.

"A good question," said Shillitoe. "Explain it to her, Rollie. You're a healthy, normal, typical American fairy."

"Never mind, Shillitoe. I'm more acceptable the way I am than you are."

"True, true. A pertinent comment on democracy."

"He don't mean anything, Mr. Butter," said Rhoda.

"Don't tell me what I mean!" The edge of his hand just missed her nose as he tried a downward chop. "Poet's first duty is to be unpatriotic. Had to liquor Tennyson up before he'd sing to the Union Jack. Ever hear about when he tried to leave a party by climbing up the chimney flue?"

"Some other time," sighed Rollie. He took out a leather-bound notebook and a gold pencil. "Before I go, they want some information about you for their program."

"The biographer begins his index with 'ablutions' and the giant melts away."

"He's from Indiana," supplied Rhoda.

"Good place," nodded Shillitoe. "Feel about Indiana the way Mister Butter feels about Mister Universe."

Rollie made a note. "And who were your early literary influences?"

"Penrod and Sam," said Shillitoe.

"Didn't John Greenleaf Whittier come from Indiana?" asked Rhoda helpfully.

"Whittier!" Rollie's eyebrows almost touched the ceiling.

"It was somebody with three names," said Rhoda ducking Shillitoe's left jab.

Shillitoe ordered another drink, courtesy of Mr. Moscowitz, while Rhoda and Rollie arranged Thursday's schedule. He had to be at Da Vinci Hall at three-thirty, so Rollie would call for him at three sharp. As part of the drink dribbled down his chin, he felt Rollie eying him with misgiving.

"Maybe I ought to have Lalage Churchill do the reading."

"Good body," Shillitoe said.

"Her stuff don't hold a candle to Samson's," bristled Rhoda.

"All right, all right." Rollie held up his hands in surrender. "But Shillitoe, you've got to promise to be absolutely sober Thursday, understand? Absolutely sober!"

Shillitoe thought again of Daniel K. Papp and promised.

After Rollie minced away, Rhoda went to a chair by the window and sat down. Her new orthopedic shoes were stiff and uncomfortable so that now both her legs ached.

"Good old Catherine." Samson waved at her. "Dependable as a fire hydrant. When you sit down the earth is flat."

Rhoda waved back. His words hadn't stung because she knew why he was being nasty. When she'd got home the floor was littered with wadded-up pages of the yellow pad. Each, as she pressed it flat, yielded a few words in his heavy scrawl, and she had filed them all away with the others in the bottom dresser drawer. He'd made an attempt at the allegory. That was better than nothing. And the fact that it hadn't flowed was why he was drinking so much.

Rhoda remembered what Doctor Wren had told her. A writer who wasn't able to write had a real problem. For some reason, thinking of Doctor Wren saying this made her feel better.

Chapter Five

MRS. FITZGERALD was sitting on the front stoop, holding a sheet of aluminum foil under her chin and poking her face at the sun. As Shillitoe came out he patted her shoulder.

"Have a nice *coup de soleil,* Mrs. Fitz'."

It was a half hour before Rollie Butter was due to call for him. But Shillitoe's nerve ends were sputtering and he thought that walking the seventy-three blocks to Da Vinci Hall might deaden them enough for him to go through with the reading.

The thick tweed suit was suffocating. The thin copy of *Hel-*

lebore in the pocket banged its forewarning against his hip. The shirt collar, appropriately enough, felt like a noose. If that lunkhead didn't stop starching everything, he'd starch her. He tried to pile other grievances on Rhoda, to build a case against her so he could blame her for what he was about to do. But he had never been able to volley responsibility for his actions over to others and the poetry reading was no exception. He had been conscious when he agreed to do it. He could even recall being titillated by visions of high finance. He deserved everything he was about to get.

This might, he realized, exceed his most hideous expectations. Shillitoe had never read one of his own poems aloud to anyone. Once transferred from him to paper and complete they held little interest for him. As for reading to an audience, that was for the octogenarians with their fluffy white crowns making personal appearances to prove that one could have a soul and still survive. But, in a little while, it would be he who was on the stage, staring at a room full of "kulcher" chasers, clearing his throat and . . . And what?

What would he do? How would he begin? He could tell a joke, except he hated jokes and never remembered any. He could let loose a few metaphors that would creep up their skirts. That's what they really wanted. But why should he give them what they wanted? They'd like him to wear a black turtle-necked sweater. That was why he'd put on the starched collar and his one and only suit even though it was Harris tweed and stunk of naphthalene. They'd also like plenty of exhibitionism. So he'd open his book, read for twenty minutes in a monotone and scram as soon as he collected the hundred bucks.

This decision strengthened his steps for another few blocks. Then, gradually, he became increasingly aware of the bars he was passing. As the heat shortened and slowed his stride, the cool, dark doorways beckoned more seductively. Shillitoe gritted his teeth and trudged on. He might have made it all the way if Gaye Litmus hadn't come around the corner.

"Shillitoe!" she rasped happily.

"Hello, Gaye. How's the whoring?"

"I got a problem, Shillitoe. Let's have a drink and I'll tell you."

"No thanks."

"Jesus, that's a good one."

The nearest place was a cocktail lounge. The round cushions of the bar stools gasped as they sat down, Vikings pitchforked mermaids on the frosted mirror and muted dance music seemed to come from the cash register. The bartender approached them suspiciously.

"Beer," said Shillitoe.

"I'm paying," said Gaye.

"The best Scotch you've got," said Shillitoe.

"That's my Samson." Gaye pounded him on the back. "I still got that poem you wrote for me. I framed it and hung it right over my bed. It got lots of laughs."

"Which poem's that?"

"You know. 'Up lad, when the journey's over there'll be time enough to sleep.' "

"Not me," he said. "Housman."

"I never worked in a house, you pimp!"

"Forget it," he said. "Tell me your problem."

"It's this guy. He does certified public accounting. He's got me paying income tax." Gaye's laugh sounded like it was being sucked through a straw. Shillitoe looked her over. She was developing the hump on her shoulders that so many women raised in their forties. Her features had spread as her face had become more bloated and her heavy makeup didn't completely hide the pitted skin. When she raised her hands to smooth her fluffy bleached hair he saw the dark splotches under her arms. Simultaneously, the odor hit him.

"Christ, haven't you taken a bath yet?"

"Destroys the natural oils."

"I don't know how in hell you make a living."

"Applegarth doesn't complain."

"Who's Applegarth?"

"I told you. The accountant. It's been steady with him now for almost two months."

"Love?"

"Yeah. I really got it for him."

"And how does he feel?"

"He don't say. He just likes to do a certain thing. You know."

"Urolagnia?"

"What the hell's that?" She nodded as he put it into more colloquial terms. "Yeah. That's my Applegarth."

"Sounds like the basis of a happy marriage."

"That's the problem," said Gaye sadly. "I think a girl should only go so far before she's married."

"Popular ethics," said Shillitoe and ordered another two drinks.

"The only thing is, he's got three sons and a crummy wife. She don't appreciate him."

"Maybe he's never experimental at home."

"Don't be such a wise-guy," she snapped. "This is important to me. What am I supposed to do?"

Shillitoe pondered the question for several seconds. "For one thing, stop doing what Applegarth wants."

"And what if he starts looking for somebody else? I really got it for him, Shillitoe."

"The rules of free enterprise distinctly state that no man shall pay for what he receives free. Nobody knows this better than the maker of poetry. But he has no choice."

"Aw, shove the sermon."

Shillitoe signaled the bartender again. "What do you want me to do?"

Tears began to extend her mascara. "I don't know. But I thought you'd do something. I thought at least you were my friend."

"I am your friend."

"I kept you going, how many years?"

"About six months."

"And I never asked you any favors, did I?" Shillitoe agreed

that she hadn't. "So when I finally ask you for one thing, one pimpin' little thing . . ."

"What thing?"

"I told you. I really got it for Applegarth. I ain't getting any younger, Shillitoe. It's time I got married again. If you were so smart you could think of something."

"I'll think of something," said Shillitoe.

"The hell you will."

"I told you I'll think of something. That's a promise. Now have another drink."

When the mermaids on the frosted glass began to wiggle their tails, Shillitoe asked the bartender the time.

"Three-thirty."

Three-thirty? Where was he supposed to be at three-thirty? The dance music from the cash register kept repeating the same four notes, dum-dum-de-dum, da-dum-de-hall, da-vinchi-hall.

"Gotta' beat it," he said to Gaye, wavering off the stool.

"Where's the fire?"

"Gotta' read poetry."

Gaye clung to his arm, telling him how much she liked poetry, especially, "Up lad, when the journey's over there'll be time enough to sleep."

The sun had stretched the street and tilted it at a crazy angle. Hundreds of automobiles blockaded every crossing but they squeezed by, swearing back at the bilious faces and skipping arm-in-arm to the next barricade. Then they were in a booming stone entrance hall and groups of women in peacock and sunflower dresses were huddling around and conspiring against them.

"Your invitations, please?"

It came from a mouth like a mail slot. Shillitoe felt in his pockets for tickets to drop between the even rows of teeth. All he could find was his library card.

"Oh, Mr. Shillitoe. The chairman was just looking for you. And is this person with you?"

He explained that Gaye was the literary editor of *The Manchester Guardian.*

"The Manchester Guardian," squeaked the teeth. "Do you know Alistair Cooke?"

"Sure," said Gaye. "Up lad, when the journey's over . . ." She finished the line over her shoulder as Shillitoe dragged her inside.

"Find yourself a seat," he said. "I gotta' report to somebody."

"Anything I can do?" asked Gaye.

"Just keep out of the way. And when they introduce me, stand up and yell 'bravo.' "

"Bravo, bravo," rehearsed Gaye as she stumbled down the aisle.

Shillitoe retraced his steps to the wide mouth and spoke into it until it told him how to get backstage where he would find the chairman.

When the woman with the terrible body odor took the aisle seat, Lydia Wren moved along to the middle of the row. She had accepted, as had Mr. Czolgacz's other pupils, his invitation to have iced coffee with him after the recital. He had mentioned that there would be others on the program, but had done so in such a way as to make it clear that they were simply preliminaries to his appearance.

The mimeographed program told her otherwise. Underneath the listing of Mr. Czolgacz's harp selections it said, *S. Shillitoe, reading from his published poetical works.* Lydia felt a vague need to move back closer to the aisle. But the foul-smelling woman was there and the auditorium was filling up fast. The inertia Lydia had been experiencing more and more lately kept her where she was.

The program also told her that she was a guest of The Silver Horn Society. Studying the members' hairdos and dresses, Lydia placed the organization somewhere near Fifth Avenue and Ninetieth Street. She wondered if any of them could tell she wasn't a Silver Horner, and decided they probably couldn't. She lived twenty blocks down from them and further east, but she had become an obvious type, too—wife of a professional man, children in private school, dabbler in the arts; nothing that would make her stand out in this crowd.

The chairman, horsey, sporting an enormous orchid and nervously doing an abbreviated Charleston, eventually hushed the hall and introduced the first guest. He was an art critic Lydia had never heard of, his subject for today was Suprematism and he had a high roof to his mouth so that all *L* sounds came out like horses' hoofs on cobblestones. Lydia knew little about Suprematism except that it had derived from Cubism and that the "White Square on Black" at the Merivale Gallery was an example of it. Sneaking glances at the attentive profiles flanking her, she wondered how much the audience really understood about what was being said. Most of it sailed over her head and she had studied art for almost two years.

Mr. Czolgacz's harp provided a welcome change of pace. His choice of the Attaignant piece and Dussek's Sonata was, she knew, deliberate. The egotistical snob *would* play things with which his audience wasn't familiar. She could feel the women nearest her relax as he moved on to Bach and she too felt more comfortable with the familiar sonorous sounds.

Czolgacz acknowledged the applause with perfunctory little bows and it was then that Lydia realized her mistake. Hers was the seventh folding chair in from the aisle. To make her move during the applause would incur Czolgacz's wrath for weeks. Waiting meant she'd have to inch her way past the line of chubby knees during S. Something's reading of his published poetry. Not knowing what to do, she did nothing.

The horsey chairman again, this time doing a sort of mambo. Then a tall, rangy, fierce-looking man in a bulky brown tweed suit wavered to the center of the platform, shielded his eyes and peered at the audience as if sighting land. Some handclapping greeted him. Lydia decided to try to get out before it died and half rose from her chair. But the reeking woman on the aisle suddenly stood up and started shouting "bravo." Lydia sat down again and waited, ready to make her escape as soon as she could summon up enough impervious nerve. Then she heard the first line of her favorite poem.

"How do I love thee? Let me count the ways."

He spoke the words with a solemnity which made them ring out more hauntingly than ever before. Then he paused. Lydia wanted to call out to him to go on, to recite the rest of it. "I love thee to the depth and breadth and height my soul can reach." But he wouldn't. He just stood there looking slowly across the rows of women, his eyes gliding past her own for a flimsy second. Then he started muttering and she had to strain to hear.

"That's probably the kind of lullaby you want me to sing. But can't do it. Neither sickly nor feminine. Never found out why, when a woman thinks about love she always starts counting. Nothing against Lizzie, though she probably dimmed old Browning's lambent flame. Can't turn out a poem when you're horizontal. She tried to write poetry. Can't be written. Got to be formed, like a gallstone, only opposite direction. Still, what she did was better than any of you will do if you live to be three hundred and five. Just mention that so you'll know your place."

There was a scraping of chairs as several members of The Silver Horn excused their way past others and headed for the exit. Lydia knew this was her chance to leave, but now she wanted to stay. She consulted her program again. *S. Shillitoe,* and in a footnote, *Mr. Shillitoe is from Indiana.* She cheered him on silently. "Go on, S. Shillitoe from Indiana. This is priceless."

"Shame," said the poet. "Shame that we should have to meet this way, you bribing me to show you some fully dimensioned slides of the real world. Give you lots of credit. Don't know how the hell you can drag yourself through day after night where you are. Cruel of me to tell you about places you'll never see. But that's my reason and the reason of the composers who were just screwed by your banjo player."

Banjo player? Lydia prayed that Czolgacz had heard it.

"And you are paying me one hundred dollars and I am sworn to read to you from my blood. Almost as drunk when I made the deal as I am now. Immoral of you to hold me to it, but that never stopped you. Where was I?"

He looked straight at Lydia as if she was his prompter, nodded at her and continued.

"Right. Facts spread their madness in overlapping circles. Sensation of progress is nothing but currents of air passing between two equal minds holding different information. So you should revive when poetry spins tornadoes through your windows. Why don't you? I don't know. People being more reflective than shadows, makes a shadow wonder about substance. Bedlam's in my pocket, rats are in your beds, welcome all easy-to-spell conditions. Any questions?" He waited as if expecting some. "None? Won't anyone ask me if what is might be preferable to what she thinks it is?"

The woman next to her poked Lydia and motioned toward the aisle. Czolgacz hunched there, impatiently waving at her to come out. Lydia got up.

"Ah!" came the delighted shout from the platform. "One woman not yet lost."

Lydia stared at him in horror. What had he asked that her standing up was an answer to? She felt all the smirking little faces around her and saw Czolgacz signaling her again. Dropping "excuse me" on each lap and crunching on several toes, she stumbled toward him.

"Not that way! Up here!"

Czolgacz seemed unaware that the voice from the platform was aimed at her. Why didn't he hurry?

"Up here, Pocahontas! This way!"

Everyone was looking at her and the exit seemed miles away. She didn't realize she'd been sitting so far down front.

"When the juggler failed to stop the show
She changed her seat to another row
And snubbed agility."

He chanted it in rhythm to her step. Rotten Greenwich Village character making fun of her. How dare he? He probably sold socks at Macy's. As Czolgacz held the door open for her, the socks salesman was addressing himself to the whole audience.

"Looking at your faces, I know you are all sincerely interested in poetry. Or else my fly's open."

Then she was in the lobby with Czolgacz's other students and the harpist was probing them for compliments.

A sudden invasion of Boy Scouts from Harrisburg, Pennsylvania, most of whom wanted grilled cheese, kept Rhoda on the sandwich block an extra hour. By the time she reached the lobby of Da Vinci Hall the women were stampeding from the auditorium.

"Most disgusting thing I've ever heard."

"People like that should be put away."

"He obviously isn't a poet at all."

Rhoda swung her handbag at the last one, but a new wave of women from the auditorium pushed her target out of range. Rhoda turned and faced the tide, rolling and bumping against it until she was through the door.

"When putty and ungainly strings resolved to join in me."

She recognized the line from *Hellebore* but it seemed to come from the acrobats on the platform. Then she realized that the center of the acrobatics was Samson's winter suit. Rollie Butter was clinging to its right arm for dear life, a woman with a big orchid was pulling on the back of the collar and Samson was inside. Another woman in a tight satin dress reached across the edge of the platform and tried to snare one of Rollie's ankles. Rollie jumped out of the way, his mouth and eyes open like he'd stepped into some ice water. Then he saw Rhoda.

"Mrs. Shillitoe! Help!"

Rhoda, already halfway down the aisle, shouted at them to get their hands off Samson's suit.

"An apparition, scratching off the crust of sleep," proclaimed Samson, waving his free hand at her.

The first one she reached was the ankle grabber. Rhoda sunk her fingers into the bulging back and pulled. Regaining her balance, she looked down at her two handfuls of damp satin.

"Not her, you idiot," called Samson.

The ankle grabber had become a contortionist, twisting her head around and pawing at the openings in the back of her dress. Rhoda vaulted up onto the platform.

"So the soul is chased deviously."

"Please, Mr. Shillitoe," panted the orchid lady.

"Tail with snapping teeth."

"Let go of him," ordered Rhoda and tried to pry open the fingers gripping the Harris tweed.

"That's his wife," panted Rollie, still hanging on Samson's arm.

"Oh." The orchid lady let go. Samson, suddenly free of his anchor, spun around like a discus thrower and heaved Rollie into the front row of folding chairs.

"Dear lonely import house," intoned Samson to the empty auditorium.

"Please tell him to stop," the orchid lady begged Rhoda. "The program's over. They'll never let me be chairman of anything again." She seemed about to cry.

"Busy with micrometers. Boasting of tolerances."

"That's enough, baby," said Rhoda.

"Advertising Africans with brogues in haciendas."

"I said that's enough."

"He ruined everything," sobbed the orchid lady. Rhoda felt like sitting down and having a good cry with her. Then the ankle grabber crawled up on the platform.

"Somebody tore my dress."

"Rhoda," said Samson, "this is Gaye."

Rhoda felt jealousy heating her face.

"You been at it again?"

"No, no. Gaye goes back more than a dozen years. She charges."

"Who's gonna' pay for this dress?" screamed Gaye.

"Mr. Applegarth," said Samson.

The orchid lady, crying openly now, was salvaging Rollie from the folding chairs.

"You pimps!" yelled Gaye. "What about my good dress?"

"Rollie," said Samson, "give her two bucks out of my hundred."

"Your hundred?" shrieked Rollie, freeing his leg from a chair. "Do you expect to get paid for what you've done?"

"Look at this. Look at it!" demanded Gaye, tearing the back of her dress more to emphasize the holes. Then she beat at the sides of Samson's head until he grabbed her hands and both of them tumbled to the floor. Rhoda started to pull them apart, then saw Rollie limping up the aisle with the orchid lady. She jumped down from the platform and caught up with them.

"What did he do wrong?" asked Rhoda.

The orchid lady gasped and rolled her eyes.

"What didn't he do?" said Rollie. "He didn't wait for me to pick him up. I spent an hour looking in every saloon on Second Avenue. By the time I got here, he'd emptied the hall."

"He . . . he . . ." The orchid lady was getting her speech back. "He made all kinds of pubic references."

"How long did he recite?"

"He didn't recite a single poem," said the orchid lady.

"How long did he stand up there?"

"When I found your apartment empty, I almost died," said Rollie.

"How long?"

"Half an hour at least, making all kinds of pubic references," said the orchid lady.

"You said a hundred dollars for twenty minutes," persisted Rhoda.

"But he didn't read a single poem," said the orchid lady.

"Everything he says is a poem," said Rhoda, holding out her hand.

"Don't pay her." Rollie started to pull the orchid lady away, but Rhoda clamped onto her arm.

"No!" cried the orchid lady. "I can't go through that again." She produced a sealed envelope with the saw-edged outline of a check showing through.

"It's indecent of you to accept it," sneered Rollie.

"Just look at him up there," said the orchid lady.

"Just look," echoed Rollie. "Portrait of a poet."

Rhoda looked where they pointed. Gaye and Samson had separated on the platform. She had reached her hands and knees and was making an effort to get to her feet. But Samson just sat there, one leg twisted under him, staring blankly.

"He should have help," said the orchid lady.

"I'll say he should," said Rollie, pushing his face in front of Rhoda. "If you want to put that money to good use, you'll give it to a head doctor."

Rollie took the orchid lady by the hand and they moved up the aisle clucking to each other. Then Gaye made it to her feet and stood swaying unsteadily.

"You want me to help you get him home?" she called to Rhoda.

Rhoda said she could manage.

"Don't forget your promise," Gaye said to Samson. He nodded and waved. "I'll see you." She drew in her breath, patted the piece of her torn dress into place and staggered out the door at the side of the platform.

"We have been bluffed too long by poker faces in the crowd," mumbled Samson.

"It's okay, baby."

"Love has never scarred the earth." His voice rose and reverberated through the room. "Love is always chipped from me."

"I know, baby." She watched him trying to roll his leg out

from underneath him. A string of saliva unwound from the corner of his mouth.

"I wonder where all their heads will rest tonight. Or were they just one head on one pillow with one reheated stew of dreams?"

"I don't know, baby."

"Wound's impossible to treat unless the misery's completely frozen. Couldn't do it today. Too many of them. Kept leaking out the sides. But sometimes it's done. Both hands working fast. Whole ancient comedy engraved in the needle's eye."

Above his drunken ranting, Rhoda heard Mrs. Fitzgerald telling her Samson needed a psychiatrist and Rollie spitting out that she should give the money to a head doctor. Instead of the jumbled row of chairs, she suddenly saw Doctor Wren's calm, relaxing office and his steady eyes crinkling a little around the edges. Doctor Wren wouldn't look down his nose at Samson helpless on the platform. He understood what a writer went through when he couldn't write. What else was it he'd said? She heard his comforting voice again as if he was standing right next to her.

"I've had success with that particular problem."

Rhoda looked down at the envelope she still held. Turning, she placed her body between it and Samson and, furtively, she slipped the check into her handbag.

Chapter Six

THE fifth applicant was an altogether unwholesome specimen—round-shouldered, yellowing skin, obviously not a *phallus thaumaturgist.* Doctor Frederic Voegler took one look, then circled the third name on the pad before him. The board was only admitting one new patient to Para Park today and his vote would go to Herman Horvath, the third applicant, who refused to speak at all during his interview. This decided, Voegler let his thoughts drift with his glance along the shiny mahogany table to Oliver Wren.

Voegler did not delude himself about his feelings toward Wren. He detested him. And this had nothing to do with their competing for the presidency of the Parapraxes Society. Voegler acknowledged that Wren was a capable psychoanalyst, probably a little more than capable, maybe even one of the more talented of the Americans. But this was the key word, *Americans.* An American practicing psychoanalysis was like a Viennese playing jazz. No matter how adeptly it was done, it wasn't very good. There was no question about it. If it wasn't for the Europeans in the country, all of American scientific effort would be a century behind—at least. Still, the trend in New York was away from the European-trained analyst to the homegrown variety, just like they were pushing their own champagne. Their champagne! Seltzer water and sugar.

It wouldn't last but, meanwhile, Wren was riding the crest of this chauvinistic wave. He was getting celebrities as patients now, probably charging thirty-five or forty an hour. Voegler didn't resent this so much. Then what was it? His youth? Wren was ten, twelve years younger. His good looks? *Eh!* His wife? Lydia? Yes, above all he envied him Lydia. This was a delicious woman. As Voegler thought of her now, he envisioned himself kneeling before her, slipping off her shoes, raising one of her dainty white feet to his lips and nibbling her sweet, pedicured toes.

He was all the way to her instep before realizing that Wren was staring back at him. Voegler quickly shifted his eyes to Milicent Akers, who was busy taking notes on what the fifth applicant was saying. Probably something Milicent could use in her next book. Voegler thought of his own book on the *phallus thaumaturgist* personality; fifteen years slaving away at it and not even half finished. He was too conscientious. Milicent was turning out a book a year. Trash! But she must be doing all right from them. She hardly ever took patients any more.

Milicent suddenly leaned back and Voegler found himself looking past her to Massey. Massey showed up at all the interviews, studied the applicants and always left before the discussion and voting. This infuriated Voegler. Did Massey think he was too good to exchange opinions with them? Voegler watched him mopping the back of his flabby neck. Massey lived in a constant steam bath. Imagine trying to deal with patients when your own glandular malfunctioning was so obvious. In fact, Massey's whole appearance was repugnant, the small rimless glasses embedded in his fat cheeks, the hair greased down so that his ears stuck out like jug handles and the never-still fingers that looked like they'd been chopped off at the first knuckles. Not that a psychiatrist had to be a matinee idol, but he should present a moderately attractive vista for his patients. Of course, with a lobotomy-heavy practice like Massey's, it probably didn't matter so much.

Voegler turned in his chair so he could see Abelson. Though he'd voted against David Abelson the year before, he had to admit that Abelson had done an adequate job as president. He'd captured Doctor Kropotkin to head Para Park and the reputation of the society hadn't suffered during the year. Still, it hadn't gone up very much either. As soon as Voegler took over the office, it would be another story.

Abelson leaned forward and wrote something on his pad. Voegler couldn't make it out from where he sat. Was Abelson considering this fifth applicant? Surely, several of the others were more interesting. He watched Abelson tear off the sheet he'd written on and fold it carefully. Then Abelson slid it across the table to Wren. In broad daylight! Yet none of the others had noticed. What was this?

Voegler watched carefully as Wren picked up the piece of paper and slowly unfolded it. He waited for a facial reaction as Wren read the message. But there wasn't a twitch in the straight nose, no clenching of teeth registering in the jaw muscles, nothing. This face was too good-looking. That could distract patients, too. The middle-aged All-American boy in his dark gray suit. He probably picked the fabric to match his hair.

Then Voegler caught the exchange. It was very slight, very subtle. Wren, reaching for a cigarette, turned toward Abelson and nodded. There was no mistaking it. He'd nodded. They were agreeing about something. But what? The applicant? If they both voted for the same one, Voegler vowed to raise an official protest. The rules clearly stated that there could be no exchange of opinions until all the interviews were over. He'd call a special meeting of the whole society if necessary. If he hadn't already beaten Wren for the presidency, this would do it for sure.

When the fifth applicant was shown out and Massey got up and left as usual, the meeting was thrown open to discussion. But Voegler didn't participate. His eyes stayed riveted to the slip of paper on the table. Then the polling. Abelson asked for his selection and, without looking up, he named Herman Horvath. He heard Milicent Akers vote for Horvath, too. Then he tensed as Abelson turned to Wren. Now he'd find out who they'd agreed on. The innocent way Abelson asked for Wren's choice. As if he didn't know.

Wren saying "Horvath" was like a kick in the stomach. That made the three votes needed for admission, so Abelson didn't have to announce his own. Voegler remained in his chair as the meeting was adjourned, letting his unexploded protest drain away. By the time it did, Abelson had gone downstairs to the office and Milicent was chattering at Wren out in the hall. Voegler ripped the page of names from his pad and tore it into small pieces. It was while looking for a place to put them that he noticed the folded note still there.

He circled the table with the note as his hub. The election might be closer than he expected. Any indelicate move on his part could throw Wren a few more ballots. Voegler picked up a wastepaper basket and began emptying the ashtrays. But most of the votes were probably in by now. And the anti-Freudian element in the society wasn't strong enough yet to defeat him. Voegler was sure that even Wren wasn't kidding himself about the outcome. Picking up the note, then, couldn't really hurt his chances.

He had unfolded it before he saw Wren standing in the doorway watching him. But it was too late. Voegler had already absorbed the message Abelson had written.

> *Almost all the votes counted. Result certain. May I be the first to congratulate you.*

The first thing that occurred to Oliver upon learning he'd been elected was to call Lydia. But Milicent Akers kept buzzing around him. Her publisher wanted her to write a definitive book on healthy sexual attitudes and conduct. Should she or shouldn't she? As if one more or less mattered. Then Freddie Voegler, happening on Abelson's note, pounced on him, pumping his hand and mixing congratulations with thinly disguised references to the anti-Freudian elements in the society. Oliver decided to call Lydia from the office. He was late in getting back, however, and his afternoon appointments overlapped.

Alben Parker was one of them, in a high state of tension because the stenographic service which typed his play made no reference to its merit. Then young Kimberly Kaufman after almost three months without wetting his bed had done it again. And, following him, Joanna had surreptitiously parried all attempts to make her face her pregnancy. When he left his office at six o'clock, Oliver still hadn't told Lydia the good news.

He started to while they were dressing to go out, referring offhandedly to the election. But she didn't pick it up so he chose to wait a little longer. There was sure to be a right moment during the evening when he could work it into the conversation. "Vacation? I don't know when I'll be able to take one. I'll have less time than ever now that I'm president of the Parapraxes Society." Well, not as clumsily as that. He'd find a way to mention it obliquely so Lydia would know it was meant only for her, and her radiance would extend to him through the noise and clutter of the party.

It should have happened that way, but it didn't. No one asked him about his vacation plans or anything else that would provide a lead-in. What's more, the galloping hostess seemed determined to keep him and Lydia at opposite ends of the room. Three times he heard Lydia describe a recital she attended that afternoon, something about an art critic and a poet. But each time she was getting to the point, the hostess dragged him off to a neutral corner from where he heard the admirers around Lydia burst into laughter.

He asked her how the story ended when they went to bed.

"It's not worth repeating," she yawned. "Just something I used to be sociable."

He would have told her about the presidency then if she hadn't rolled her back to him. He turned off the lamp, determined to tell her at breakfast, proper moment or not.

Naturally, Scott would pick that morning to go on a hunger strike.

"Scott's not eating ever again, darling. I suppose we *could* feed him intravenously or something."

"Eat your breakfast, Scott." Oliver tried not to make it an order.

"Still if he doesn't want to," said Lydia. "A boy of nine has every right to starve."

No undercurrent of concern in her tone at all. But when Deirdre decided to join her brother's movement, an irritability appeared.

"What goes for nine-year-old boys doesn't go for six-year-old girls."

Oliver thought she could have phrased it better. But small criticism. Her patience with the children was remarkable.

The downstairs bell, rung by the driver of the day camp bus, sounded more and more like that of a rescue ship in a fog. Hasty, self-conscious kisses left him with sticky cheeks and the children clattered out. A few seconds to shake their presence from the room, then he'd tell her. But how? Almost twenty hours had elapsed since he found out. How would he explain that?

The New York Times solved the problem. Abelson hadn't said anything about releasing it to the papers, but there he was on page twenty-one. The photograph must have been furnished from the Parapraxes files along with a résumé of his career. The part about his jumping with the paratroopers on D-Day to study their battle reactions sounded a bit too heroic. But his work at Doctor Holland's hospital in Philadelphia was covered adequately, plus his writings on ego aggression and depersonalization and his eleven years of private practice in New York.

All he had to do was act surprised, say, "Look at this, darling," and pretend they were both receiving the news at the same time. No. Though he enjoyed creating little scenes for Lydia to respond to, that would be a lie and they never lied to each other. He watched her going to the stove for the coffee. Why say anything at all? He folded the paper so that his picture was uppermost and laid it next to her cup.

"Oliver?" What was she dawdling over at the stove?

"Yes."

"Let's go to Africa."

"Where?"

"Africa. It's a continent." She pointed out the kitchen window. "That way, I think."

He couldn't suppress the laugh. "And what the hell would I do in Africa?"

"I don't know. You could psychoanalyze all the cannibals."

"Some of my patients are as cannibalistic as anyone in Africa."

"But think of the book you could write. 'I was a head shrinker of the headshrinkers.' Milicent Akers would turn green."

She'd topped him again as she always did in repartee. But this time he was holding the real trump. He watched her face as she brought the coffee to the table, readying himself for the shriek of glee. What was she waiting for? Damn it. Her elbow was planted right on his photograph.

"Don't you have a harp lesson this morning?"

"I'm not going."

"Why not?"

"Oliver," her voice was higher than usual, almost plaintive. "Oliver, I'm a lousy harpist."

"Oh? Failure already?"

"Failure again."

"Mr. Czolgacz said you show a talent for the instrument."

"Hah!" She flung herself up and away from the table. "Like I showed a talent for modern dance, prancing around like a baby hippopotamus."

Her shoulders were rigid. He knew it would take the right inflection to relax them.

"You looked beautiful in a leotard." The inflection seemed right but she didn't relax.

"Then I showed a talent for modern art. Everyone else began with the shape of an egg. I ended with it." She turned to face him and her cheeks were flushed. "And I wish you'd bring that *masterpiece* of mine home from the office. Someday it will drive one of your patients over the brink."

He didn't know if she expected him to laugh at that or not. He'd never seen her this wrought up. What was it? He studied her face as if it would provide the answer. A beautiful face, truly beautiful. The flush was receding, returning her skin to an eggshell white. The soft brown nest of hair wrapped it tenderly. Every part of her had that same fragility, the slight cleft at the tip of her thin nose accenting its aristocracy, the only completely undistorted mouth he'd ever seen, the smooth stem of her body which seemed to bend and react with the slightest change in atmosphere.

In the midst of devouring her perfection, he caught himself glancing at his watch. Had she noticed? She gave no sign, but was this the sore spot? Had he been giving these unconscious indications that their relationship was secondary to his work? In how many ways had he been slighting her without realizing it? He tried to remember the last night they'd had intercourse but the face of his watch kept interrupting. His first appointment was less than twenty minutes away. He had to straighten out whatever was upsetting Lydia quickly or there wouldn't be time for her reaction to the news.

"Come on, darling. What is it?"

"I don't know. I'm so bored."

"But you wanted the children to go to day camp." What a lame rebuttal. If he hadn't been so rushed he never would have said it. But, too late.

"I wish I'd sent them *away* to camp. I'm sick of them! There! Does that shock you?"

"No."

"Well, some of my thoughts would."

This squall wasn't going to disperse immediately. He tried to recall who his ten o'clock appointment was, but couldn't. Whoever it was would just have to wait. He calmly poured himself another half cup of coffee.

"What are some of these shocking thoughts?"

"I can't tell you."

"Why not?"

"Because they're subconscious."

He almost groaned. He wanted to say, "No, Lydia, not you. Don't carry on like some of the spoiled women I have to listen to." But he met her eyes as if seriously considering what she'd said.

"You want to be psychoanalyzed."

"Yes." She said it defiantly.

"And who would you want as an analyst?"

"You."

"You know that's impossible."

"Why?"

"Because I love you."

This time her shoulders did relax. She came back to the table and sat down. Oliver couldn't help noticing that her elbow was smack-dab on his picture again.

"If you love me," she said, "you'll do an extra good job."

"It doesn't work that way. Analysis requires complete objectivity. Freud himself said that when the personal interest of the physician is greater, his authority is less."

"Damn Freud." She purred it sensually.

"That's sacrilege."

"You sound as bad as Freddie Voegler. And all this time he thinks you're one of the anti-Freudians plotting to keep him from being president."

Of all the possible introductions to the news, he never thought it would be one supplied by Voegler.

"Wrong tense, darling," he said.

"What?"

"Plotted, not plotting. Don't you ever read the *Times*?"

It was a chain reaction. She looked from him to the newspaper, to him again.

"You won!" He just had time to put the cup down safely before she landed and pecked him with kisses. The bleak mood was gone. She was a little girl again, entirely happy.

The short walk up Park Avenue and across Seventy-eighth Street gave him a chance to review what had happened.

Lydia said she was bored and she undoubtedly was. This didn't come as a complete surprise to him. He had felt its imminence when he encouraged her to take classes. The painting and dancing were fill-ins, but he'd hoped the music would take hold. Not that he'd expected her, at thirty-six, to become as wrapped up in basic harp lessons as he was in his work. But she wasn't too old to develop a strong interest in it, and some people did start on careers late. That, however, took a tremendous amount of discipline and Oliver didn't delude himself about this. Lydia was not a very disciplined person. He didn't regard this as a fault. To the contrary, it was one of the things about her he found most exciting. Her gaiety and romanticism were ideal counterparts for his own ruminative temperament. But what of the creeping ennui which was fevering American women? Now it had spread to his own home. If he couldn't help Lydia overcome it, how could he justify treating most of his women patients?

As he entered the reception room, Miss Bueler extended a brittle, bony hand and relayed the congratulatory messages. Doctor Holland had phoned from Philadelphia to say he'd heard the good news and would be at the inauguration banquet. Other compliments and good wishes had arrived by phone and telegraph. And the editor of a textbook company wanted a bibliography of his published articles in hope that there were enough for a book. These out of the way, Bueler proceeded to more immediate matters. One appointment canceled because of hives. Bueler added "psychosomatic" under her breath. The new patient at eleven meant his schedule was filled to capacity again. And Mrs. Shillitoe had called three times in the last ten minutes. Oliver couldn't place the name, decided she was probably a reporter and told Bueler to stall her off.

At eleven o'clock, glancing at the memo Bueler had given him on the new patient facing him across the desk, he saw *referred by Doctor Posmanture.* This time he remembered the name and, with it, Mrs. Shillitoe's.

Why would she be phoning him? Could she have seen the item in the newspaper and, by some lopsided reasoning, felt it necessary to add her congratulations? Much more likely, the podiatrist he'd recommended had staggered her with his bill.

The episode of that credulous woman taking off her shoe had developed into one of his favorite stories. Lydia had found it too delicious, particularly the idea that another patient had been misdirected at the same time. Oliver had wondered all week if this was how it had happened and now, at last, was a chance to find out. All he had to do was ask Mrs. Tupperman if she'd been sent to a podiatrist by mistake.

But before he could, Mrs. Tupperman began weeping unashamedly and telling him why she was so unhappy.

It was the slowest hour Leonard Tupperman had ever spent. After dropping Evelyn off he'd circled the block twice without finding a space, then double-parked right in front of the dark blue painted door she had entered. Mrs. Fish leaned forward from the back seat and told him to move the car down the street.

"You've got to advertise where your wife is?" she said, but he didn't answer. She tapped him on the shoulder and started to repeat it but he didn't so much as move his head. She caught on then and left him alone, but every time another car squeezed by and the driver glared at him she shifted nervously.

Good, he thought. Let her stay on pins and needles. My only consolation will be if she gets an ulcer before I do. Leonard tapped his wristwatch and listened to make sure it was still going. Almost twenty-five after. This time at least—it must be the right doctor. Leonard thought of the morning, a week before, when he'd driven them to another building not too different from this one and how he'd felt just like he was feeling now when Evelyn went inside. The old battle-ax in the back seat must have read his mind right through the back of his head.

"Some system," she said. "In my day all the doctors had

shingles with their names and what they did. Now you don't know which is for skin troubles and who's a dentist."

Why beat around the bush? Why say skin troubles and dentist? Podiatrist! That's what she meant. When Evelyn had come running out ten minutes after she went in he couldn't believe his ears. The Doctor Gordon that Posmanture had sent them to was a foot doctor! Leonard still didn't know how much she had told him before finding out. After all, foot doctor's weren't sworn to secrecy the way psychiatrists were. Leonard was sure he'd never forget that drive home with Evelyn crying more than ever and Mrs. Fish demanding he leave her off at Doctor Posmanture's. She knew Posmanture was away on vacation, but she still wanted to go to his office. In the state she was in, she probably would have torn all the diplomas off the walls and the old *nudnick* deserved it.

"I wonder what he does on a first visit," said Mrs. Fish.

"I'm sure your daughter will tell you every word," he answered without thinking.

"Leonard, such a philosophy isn't going to help her."

Help her? He wanted to say that the best way she could help Evelyn was by dropping dead right now. But he remembered his vow to suffer in silence. He would be the chauffeur, the signer of the checks. That was all. When Evelyn came to her senses and realized the whole thing was a waste of time and money, she'd have to admit he'd been generous and considerate as well as right.

Leonard tried to keep his eyes away from the blue painted door and the narrow brick building it hinged on. Inside, in a stuffy room full of books, Evelyn was lying on a worn leather couch and a bearded old man with watery eyes was asking her questions about her sex life; *their* sex life! And she was telling him!

"I hope she don't hold anything back," said Mrs. Fish.

"Shut up!"

"Listen, I don't have to sit here and be insulted." She reached for the door handle.

"Stay here." Leonard made it sound as pleasant as he could and she sat back again.

"Fifteen minutes more," said Mrs. Fish. And a minute later, "Providing he took her right away."

Leonard groped for a train of thought to occupy the last quarter hour and landed on his sister-in-law. Norma. Some Norma, with that bang across her forehead that looked like the moths had been in it and with her hook nose. This was the skinniest, most unattractive woman that ever walked, which wouldn't be so bad if she wasn't nutty too. Ever since she'd arrived from South Bend, Indiana, all she'd done was change her glasses. Whenever he turned around, there she was with a new pair of another color. "Charles likes these," she would say and there'd be another half hour about her husband the optometrist. That galled him, too. None of them lost a chance to say that optometry was a profession requiring a college diploma. They wanted to add that being in real estate didn't require any education, but they didn't have the nerve. If one of them did say it, Leonard was ready for them. He'd offer to put down his bankbooks and stocks and bonds next to Charles's and see who was the smart one. If Charles was such a good optometrist, what was he doing way out in South Bend, anyway? What did he have there? Notre Dame University. Nothing but Catholic football players, so what did they need glasses for? But, in spite of everything, Leonard was glad Norma had come. She was his ace-in-the-hole. If ever Mrs. Fish dared to suggest that he was responsible for Evelyn's carrying-on, all he had to do was point to Norma. Compared to her, Evelyn was a picture of mental health. And he wouldn't hesitate to say it. That would spell finish to Mrs. Fish's bragging about her two fine daughters and how she brought them up all by herself after her Aaron left her a widow. She always said it as if he'd got killed on purpose. And who could blame him?

The blue door swung open and Evelyn trotted out to the car. Leonard got upset at the sight of her swollen eyes but it went away when she chose to sit in the back instead of up front with him. Then, right away, the cross-examination.

"Well?"

"I'll tell you later, Ma."

"What did he say it is?"

"It was only my first visit, Ma."

"Still, he must have told you something."

"I'm not supposed to discuss it."

"He said that?"

"He implied it."

"Not even with your own mother?"

"No."

"Who makes up such rules?"

"I have to go twice a week," sniffed Evelyn, trying to change the subject.

"Did he at least tell you how much he charges?"

"His secretary told me. Twenty-five dollars."

"A week?"

"A visit."

Fifty dollars every week! More than they spent on food. And they didn't even ask him. They acted like he wasn't there. Not until he pulled up to the building and Evelyn was getting out did she so much as acknowledge his existence.

"Doctor Wren wants to have a talk with you," she said and the two of them disappeared into the lobby before he could recover.

Chapter Seven

RHODA getting ready to leave for work sounded like cargo loose in the hold. Shillitoe reached out from sleep for something to throw and touched the ashtray. It rained its contents on him before missing the door.

"How'd that happen?"

Rhoda bustled around him, scooping the butts and ashes off the bed. He was half awake now and his first thought was of money.

"Did it come?"

"I ain't been down to look."

"Then go now, dope."

Her new orthopedic shoes cloppity-clopped down the stairs and he pulled his eyes open. The cracked ceiling blocked out infinity so he shut them again and waited for Rhoda to return. If the check wasn't there this morning he'd go down to *Moot* and take the hundred dollars out of Rollie Butter's hide. He should never have listened to Rhoda. After he recovered from the poetry reading she suggested it would be more diplomatic for her to call Rollie about the money. She had and Rollie told her he would mail the check. That was Friday and this was Monday. So much for her diplomacy.

The cloppity-clop again. His Isadora Duncan was gliding up the stairs like a herd of elephants. Then she came in brandishing the check.

"One hundred even," chirped Rhoda and shoved a pen under his nose. "If you'll endorse it, I'll get Herschel to cash it. It will save you a trip to the bank."

He grunted and scribbled his name where she placed her finger.

"Bye-bye," said Rhoda, transferring some toast crumbs from her lips to his. "There's another letter for you, from—you know."

Yes, he knew. Papp. Didn't the bastard ever run out of stamps? How many payments was he behind now? He tried to figure it out but wads of residue of sleep were wedged between his teeth and a hot poker had been inserted ear to ear. Seven-thirty of an August morning in his forty-second year was no time for bookkeeping. Besides, his unexpected vacation was almost over. Tomorrow he would return to Moscowitz and the carpets of Bataan. This was his last day to complete the pattern which had been dimly taking shape all week.

It was no longer an allegory. The plan for the poem had evolved into something larger and more inclusive. There was too much to be covered to bother with parallels and disguise. Woven throughout would be the basic unity between the poem as force and man as species. But the tough part would be making the voice local yet throbbing from the whole. He had found the way it might be done. Looking down, continent-wide, he'd seen the profile of a placid terrier. With New England the ears and Puget Sound the snout, the retina would be in the dogwood along Lost River and in the wide solid streets of Cob City, Indiana. The inflections of his words were thus justified. As for the words themselves, their being would provide the conflict. They would rise from mongrel throats blistered by sun and gagged by snow to challenge the tyranny of the imported rhythms. And from the battle would emerge another inch toward reality.

Reality! What the hell did he know about reality? Reality was waiting on the table in the other room. Daniel K. Papp was reality. Daniel K. Papp was living proof of the triumph of the practical man. Papp could cite case after case to show that the pure spirit and good in itself were irrelevant and immaterial, that sentiment, humility and charity were what spun the world, and hemlock was too good for anyone who thought otherwise.

The shape of the poem had vanished now. Shillitoe stretched. Did it matter? Damn right it mattered, *if* it was poetry. But how did he know it was? Who ever said that he was a poet? Billy Tyler had said it, but Billy Tyler was dead. And why did Billy Tyler's father publish *Hellebore*? Sentimentality. Chalk up another point for Daniel K. Papp.

Shillitoe sat up to ward off the same old nagging questions, but they came on anyway. Why couldn't he see things ass-backwards like all the Papps saw them? Why couldn't he march out-of-step too? Somewhere in southern Indiana it had happened. A sycamore was pulled clumsily and from its cracked, extracted roots came Samson Shillitoe. Hah! He was pining for parthenogeneric birth as much as everyone else, maybe a little more for he had almost made it. Not the conception itself. His beginning had been the common one of guilt or obedience or the thick bravery bottled in cheap rye. But from that a corrugated white tapeworm of defiance had grown. Was it defiance? And was it his haste to appear or his reluctance that ripped apart the insides of Mary Shillitoe and made death the first act of his life? The Cob City courthouse records wouldn't say. Mary's serene face fading on Ben's mantel wouldn't say. Ben wouldn't say either, finding more sense in the trucks and tractors he repaired than in his son. At the most, two dozen words a year were all Shillitoe ever got from him; and since he'd left Cob City, twenty-five years ago, only half of that appended annually to a Christmas card. He had hoped for contact when he sent his father a copy of *Hellebore*. He'd thought about including a note: *Here. This is more life-giving than your Mary or any other woman.* But he'd mailed it without any explanation and Ben had never acknowledged the slim volume of poems.

Was this why he had written *Hellebore,* to justify himself to Ben? Someday a fussy associate professor would use that for the thesis of his critical introduction to the new edition. And it would be swallowed whole like most lies. No one would ever know why, why he wouldn't accept the Fox Movietone News version of the universe, why the needle of routine had failed to impale his tongue. Not that he himself wouldn't like to know. What had been the gravitational influence toward poetry? Why not a saint, dying in a scented mixture of optimism and surprise? Why not nature's scarecrow, pecked by pedestrians and bleeding straw? Why this everlasting song, clashing with the hoarse, strident creaking of existence? Where had he stumbled on the elephantine lumps of beauty and the succulent passage that delirium had somehow missed?

All of these questions were appropriate, *if* he was a poet. But where was the proof? One little book, that was all. What a Pierian spring! More like a crudded barrel with a leaky tap. Trees made better music talking with their hands. At this rate he'd never make the *Oxford Book of American Verse*. The thought cheered him; no droning into a microphone until out came a long-playing record, no autograph sessions in Brentano's and no interview by one of Time-Life's special breed of eunuchs.

"Tell me, Mr. Shillitoe, how did it happen?"

"Well, you see, 'a little flower is the labor of ages.' "

It was a better explanation than they deserved. But they'd insist on details. How about the day he'd closed the door of Cob City and walked away? The serpent, sick from its balanced diet, demanded experience. What was riding on the wishbone then? A kiddie car to Venus? All the Goldwyn Girls in one private harem? The Chase National Bank? No, he hadn't been that ordinary. He'd been an uncoordinated cube rolling across the rumpled blanket of states and falling into moth holes.

There'd been two years of farm labor across Illinois and Iowa—an introduction to the slope of the prairie, a simple time of sows' ears and silken snatches. Then, on the outskirts of a Nebraska town with the unlikely name of Imperial, he'd hooked onto a wagon of the James E. Strate Show and begun working his way up in the great tradition.

His first assignment was keeping his eyes open for the local constabulary while Queen Shirley Fillipowitz of Wilkes-Barre bumped and ground and made passes at a papier-mâché rhino's head, and whether or not her shuffle ended with the G-string coming off depended on his signal. It was probably the greatest responsibility he'd ever had and he'd only loused up once, in Salina, Kansas. But once was too often. When they pulled out of Salina, Shirley had to be left behind and he was promoted to the numbers board. Eight marbles in a jug and eighty digited holes for them to roll into. The trick was in counting fast, always totaling one number higher or lower than the magic figure which won the portable radio. But his one weak subject had always been arithmetic and after he'd given away the third radio he was promoted again. This time it was to spieling for a walk-through tent with a flea circus, an Oriental contortionist and a seventy-year-old hermaphrodite who couldn't get its social-security status straightened out. That whole summer he'd played with superlatives.

While a Chinaman called Harry
in arthritic pain,
balanced umbrellas on his toes
and prayed for rain.

He picked up his pay in Denver and wandered off again, feeling between the hips of the continent. At every intersection old men held out eight arms each, pointing the ways to heaven, but all were parallel to the horizon and all were wrong. Kitchens and freight yards, orchards and saloons, driving a nitro truck to Tulsa and cleaning up after an embalmer in Santa Fe; it all added up to one of those résumés that verified authors on the dust jackets of their books. Yet it was right for the time and place and collection of events. There was a song in the lungs of the transient labor and the throats of the auctioneers. And once he'd heard it, poetry became the only thing that made sense to him, the only entity to which he could completely sacrifice his personality and feel gain.

Poetry had never been an escape. He had never sought it. He had sniffed and bitten and tasted the decontaminated garbage of waking-sleeping, yawning-staring and kissing-gargling before discarding them. The line of vision had refused to budge, the passion wouldn't be misdirected, boiling and bubbling to an impossible pressure until he'd let some of it out, writing secretly and only for himself. But how was he to define what had tumbled to the page? Whose judgment could he take? No one's, not until the army's tabulating machinery brought him to Billy Tyler. *S* came before *T,* so Shillitoe belonged to the bunk under Tyler; William Makepeace Tyler, foaled in literature, son of a dignified publisher, patted on the head as a boy by the bony hand of Amy Lowell—friend of the family. Billy Tyler seemed to know what poetry was about and Billy had sworn that Shillitoe's was poetry. There were long talks at Fort McClellan and at Leonard Wood and at Mead and on the stuffed *Mauretania* and Omaha Beach and across France until the eighty-eights drowned them out at Nancy. Billy had quoted giants: Homer, Sappho, Ovid, Cavalcanti, Dante, Catullus, Villon, Rimbaud, Coleridge and Goethe and Blake—especially old Blake. He'd begged Billy to quote some more, but Billy just lay there on the road to Metz. And when Shillitoe last looked back, the impervious tread of a Sherman tank was squashing William Makepeace Tyler's sensitive brain.

onto the earth
like afterbirth

That had been the armistice for Shillitoe. While all the others dodged and crawled toward victory he stood upright, marking the design of the puffs and pockmarks and the crazy-legged upside-down cows and sullen roofed villages. He was a poet and he was impenetrable. The fools had mistaken this for bravery and given him a battlefield commission. But he'd never issued a command. He'd still remained apart. Was this why he had survived, because his spirit wasn't there? Or had he been blown to bits in nineteen forty-four and was this whole thing about poetry only the extension of the final second of a random shellburst after which he'd fly apart every whichway?

The questions had sidetracked him again. What did the war have to do with Daniel K. Papp and how many payments he was behind? It all fitted together loosely. It had been Billy that led to his staying in New York to find out what other poets had left for him in the public library. From Hebridean folk songs to Victorian charms, from old Parson Taylor in Westfield, Massachusetts, right up to old Doc Williams pounding out a good measure on New Jersey pelvises; the storehouse was vast and he'd stayed until his army separation pay was gone and he was stranded. Getting a job never occurred to him. There was too much to find out and too much to set down. So he'd reached out to the nearest person for support and it happened to be Gaye gyrating by. He had no compunction about living off her whoring those six months. She was just making a good investment of what other soldiers had given her for years. But one afternoon she brought home a customer when he was right in the middle of a poem and after he'd thrown them out, Gaye called it quits. But she'd been square, even finding him the rooms he was still living in and paying the first month's rent.

There had been visitors. He recalled them more by what they moved in and out than anything else: an exercising bicycle, a spinet, two Dalmatians, several budgerigars and one plywood and sheet-metal box that accumulated orgone energy. Then came Beverly and Daniel K. Papp.

Daniel K. Papp was just a name, spidery and black, thermographed on the best Hammermill bond. But Beverly? Beverly was eternally present, the unforgettable lesson in human duplicity, the undeniable evidence that Homo sapiens were capable of sudden alteration.

He couldn't remember exactly where he met her. It

was one of those dip-your-own-potato-chip gatherings in a crammed room where he rolled along elbows until he was stopped and told he looked like someone else. Beverly snagged him in just that way, as if the brass ring was hanging from his nose. She asked if he was a liberal-progressive and he said sure. Then they sat heraldically, she in a straight wicker chair and he on the floor at her feet. His right palm on the inside of her right knee, she spread her margarine of pity on minority groups. As his index finger passed the double fold of nylon and broke onto the green, she mentioned the famine in Madras and shuddered. He was nearing the cup when the memory of the late Senator Bilbo made her stand up suddenly. Almost broke his wrist. Then the pursuit. Three weeks, three precious weeks of life. She'd paid the tab, boasting of being a television production assistant, and hinting at a hundred and twenty-five a week rolling in. That wasn't what provided the momentum though. Money was sordid compared to Beverly. Beverly was completely fresh, all parts in their original cartons, skin almost translucent, not a flake of dandruff on her. She gave the impression that the insides, too, were smooth and never used. Even on a long date. He could pick her up at noon on Saturday or Sunday and be with her fourteen, fifteen hours and she'd never excuse herself for that military walk to the "powder" room. Brand-new, cellophane-wrapped Beverly. Sarah Lawrence College had done its work well.

He'd tried, harder than ever. Maybe too hard. Then, when he'd been reduced to a disheveled, panting beggar, she sprang the trap.

"I know I'm being old-fashioned and silly, Samson. But I happened to have a puritan mother and whatever she drilled into me is part of my character fiber. I can't pretend it isn't there."

"Beverly. Beverly."

"I know, Samson. I want to, too. But I just can't."

"Beverly. I quote from the best."

"It's no use, Samson."

" 'Sooner murder an infant in its cradle than nurse unacted desires.' "

"I know. I took a whole semester of William Blake."

"Screw your character fiber, Beverly."

"If only . . ."

"Yes? If? If?"

"Never mind."

"Tell me. If what?"

"If we could just go through the formality. A city hall marriage isn't like a real wedding. It only takes a few minutes. No one need know—except, of course, I'll have to tell my folks. Just so our enjoyment won't be spoiled by my stupid medieval guilt feelings. It will only be a formality, Samson."

Simpleton, mooncalf, bonehead. Only a formality. A formality in the hands of a Daniel K. Papp is as good as a bribed judge and loaded jury. Her name, his name and she brought along twenty witnesses. Christ!

He had no alibi. He'd been perfectly sober. His eager hands has signed below hers before they tore the wrappings from the never-opened package. And what did he find? He never expected anything to measure up to what he imagined it to be, but still! If nature grows hair to protect its weaknesses, that first night must have made her weak all over. Overnight the butterfly became a caterpillar. Within twelve hours she sprouted steel wool from her shins and thighs and armpits and six other places, veins swelled on her ankles, the commode started flushing and dandruff snowed down.

He could at least have taken an advance look at her paycheck. A hundred and a quarter, balls! Sixty-eight, seventy-five take-home pay. Television production assistant was a "glamour" job. She wasn't very good at it anyway and after one year of martyrdom for poetry, started going domestic. If he hadn't been working on *Hellebore* he would have spotted the symptoms and taken a few minutes to get sterile. But, as it was, he'd practically forgotten her existence until she floated in with that hatchery halo and cooed her announcement.

"I'm going to name him after President Roosevelt," she added.

"Beverly, Beverly," he reasoned, "we've got to stop passing the buck to babies. We've got to push the human spirit beyond its infancy."

"I don't know why you act like this, Samson. A woman's never more beautiful than when she's pregnant."

"Except when she's throwing up."

"Samson . . ."

"Ssh! I'm trying to remember. There's a way you can abort yourself with a knitting needle."

"Samson . . ."

"What do you want?"

"Don't you think Delano Shillitoe is euphonious?"

The way she raced around the formica table and sling chairs. He'd never known she was so fast on her feet.

"Beverly, Beverly. Just one little left jab in the stomach. Delano will never know what he missed. Stand still, Beverly. It won't hurt. Stand still, goddammit! Where you going, you lousy bitch?"

Where the lousy bitch went was to her lousy parents on lousy Long Island. The furniture stayed behind to be sold later on Second Avenue. The plastic and stainless-steel wedding presents from the girls at the network stayed behind too. But the amoeba of Delano left intact and he'd never been curious enough to take a look at the outcome. He wondered how Beverly accounted for his absence. If she had a pinch of romance, she'd have said he was killed in Korea. If she had any imagination, she'd have added that he was one of the Chinese volunteers. But Beverly was a liberal-progressive and that meant everything explained and nothing described.

"Delano dear. Sometimes older people have disagreements and they decide not to stay married. That's what happened to Mommy and Daddy. But Daddy's refusal to acknowledge your existence doesn't mean he hates you. It means that he really loves you too much."

Maybe it wasn't a complete lie. He didn't have anything against the kid. After all, Delano got rid of Beverly.

Freedom! Euphoria! The weary traveler, freed of his pack, catapults to heights unknown. In twenty days, twenty sleepless days and nights, he completed *Hellebore* and dropped it at the office of Billy Tyler's father. That night a good Samaritan, walking his poodle, found him starved and unconscious in Union Square and he woke up in Bellevue.

They'd found some poems in his coat so it was touch-and-go for a while. Pound was still interned and all poets were suspect. Expediency ruled the day until the God of accident intervened in the person of Jonathan Tyler's private secretary. She'd been ordered to contact him and somehow traced him all the way to the observation ward. Yes, Tyler and Brothers, founded shortly after the first boot touched Plymouth Rock, was to publish *Hellebore* by Samson Shillitoe. The lip-licking tribunal, impressed and disappointed, put aside their ink blots and refunded his clothes.

The book had been printed and, months later, he was granted one minute in the oak-paneled presence of subfusc, dignified Jonathan Tyler. *Hellebore* had sold one hundred and thirty-eight copies said Mr. Tyler, adding that this had exceeded his most generous expectations. The firm had lost over two thousand dollars on the publication which was a more than ample repayment for the friendship Mr. Shillitoe had shown toward his son William. And now would Mr. Shillitoe please stop deluging this firm with his trash?

But that was long after the morning he'd opened the mailbox and had his first sight of the letterhead of Daniel K. Papp.

Shillitoe went into the other room and looked down at the letter on the table. How many payments was he behind? He was tempted to tear up the notice. But there was always the possibility that Beverly had remarried or died.

DEAR MR. SHILLITOE:

Your former wife did not receive a check from you last week.

She also informs me that you have not yet sent the two payments you missed last month.

I trust these oversights have been due to increased business activity on your part and its subsequent rewards and cannot think of any other excuse you could offer. Nevertheless, you are now three hundred dollars in arrears in subsistence payments and that situation must be remedied immediately. Otherwise, we have no recourse but to take proper action.

This may be for the better, of course. The former Mrs. Shillitoe is finding it increasingly difficult to manage on one hundred dollars a week. Considering inflation and the needs of a healthy, growing ten-year-old girl like Delano, the court would undoubtedly grant an increase.

Cordially yours,
DANIEL K. PAPP

An increase! Beverly was tightening the screws again. To hell with her! Not another cent. But how about the threat of proper action? She wouldn't bat an eye; probably be glad to forsake the alimony to see him locked up. Getting mad would be playing her game. *Practical. Be practical.*

Three hundred dollars. He emptied his pockets. Eleven and change left from Moscowitz's advance. There was the hundred-dollar check that Rhoda was cashing, but where could he raise the rest of it?

The same old list was ticked off. He couldn't get any more out of Moscowitz, Rollie had already paid him for the poem he hadn't written yet, Rhoda's mother still refused to open her door when she saw him through the peephole, and his account at the Double-Deuce was beginning to worry Devery. There was no one he could ask.

Gaye! How about Gaye? He'd forgotten her. She'd paid for the drinks the day of the reading; obviously getting some dough from her dirty, certified public accountant. Gaye wouldn't let him down.

He should have been relieved by the thought, but the haze refused to lift. What was it? Something Gaye had said the other day. It became firmer. He'd promised to do Gaye a favor. Yes, he'd said he'd help her hook her Mr. Applegarth and somehow he'd have to keep his word before he could ask Gaye for the money.

Chapter Eight

AFTER the lunch rush Monday, Herschel had enough in the register to cash the check. Rhoda placed the bills carefully in her handbag along with the ten dollars she'd saved from her pay. Only one step remained—delivering the money to Doctor Wren.

It was almost five-thirty when she walked into the familiar reception room. The impetus she'd built up accordioned at sight of the secretary's empty desk. Then, expanding, it pushed her on toward the half-open door leading to the doctor's office. A voice, nice and friendly, made her hesitate. Whatever it said was then answered by another, louder and with a foreign accent. Rhoda placed the first as Doctor Wren's, the other as his patient and wondered if she could go to jail for eavesdropping on a psychiatrist. At that she would have fled, but for the third voice. This she recognized as the skinny secretary's. Rhoda pushed the door a little wider.

The secretary was standing just inside the room. Beyond her, a short man with a thick, square beard sat on the edge of Doctor Wren's desk. Doctor Wren himself appeared a second later and handed the man a drink. This was no patient! Rhoda shoved the door open and walked in.

She was hunched to meet some kind of a blast, an indignant

question about who did she think she was anyway, or a stiff finger directing her out of the room. But Doctor Wren just glanced at her and finished saying whatever he was saying to the foreigner before turning his full attention her way.

"How are you, Mrs. Shillitoe?"

His remembering her name threw her. The guy was just tremendous.

"Could I talk to you a second?" She hadn't meant to whisper.

"Why?"

"Why does anybody?"

"Miss Bueler," he said, "give Mrs. Shillitoe an appointment for next week."

"Your schedule's completely filled."

"The week after then."

"It can't wait," protested Rhoda.

"Mrs. Shillitoe," he said, "we were just about to leave."

"We've got a few minutes," said the foreigner, getting up from the corner of the desk. "Go ahead. Take care of your patient."

"I ain't the patient."

"I apologize, madam." He sat back down again. She had no choice but to talk to Doctor Wren as if nobody else was there.

"It's Samson," she said. "He's getting worse, and if I try to help he gives me this." Rhoda demonstrated Samson's downward chop.

"He gives you that?" The foreigner's eyes were popping at where she'd sliced the air.

"Yeah." Now that she was talking, Rhoda felt easier. "Samson always says we got a perfect sadist-masochist relationship." To avoid any misunderstanding, she added, "I'm the masochist."

"And is he always so violent?" asked the foreigner.

"Not always," said Rhoda. "Fifty-fifty. It's like he's got a split personality, you know?"

She directed the question at Doctor Wren, but he just smiled. She couldn't blame him. The foreigner did look funny perched on the desk, stroking his beard. Rhoda wondered who he was, and Doctor Wren read her thoughts.

"Mrs. Shillitoe, Doctor Voegler," he said. "Doctor Voegler is also a psychiatrist."

Rhoda couldn't imagine Doctor Voegler helping anybody with a problem. He was so loud and jumpy, not calm and capable like Doctor Wren. But it was Doctor Voegler who seemed the most interested in her.

"Samson. He is your husband?"

Rhoda decided he couldn't be too dumb if he guessed that. But she wanted to get Doctor Wren back into the conversation.

"You said you could help writers," she reminded him.

"I'm afraid I can't take any more patients right now," said Doctor Wren. "Doctor Voegler, perhaps you . . ."

"Maybe." Doctor Voegler slid off the desk and started toward her, but Rhoda stopped him cold.

"I got nothing against you," she said, "but it's gotta' be him!"

Doctor Voegler looked at the finger she was pointing at Doctor Wren and his face turned red.

"Madam," he said, "psychiatrists do not compete."

"I'm sorry, Mrs. Shillitoe," said Doctor Wren. "It would be impossible for me to take him. My schedule's overloaded now."

Rhoda had come prepared to argue about money. It had even occurred to her that Doctor Wren might be unwilling to take on a case as difficult as Samson's. But, after all the lying and finagling she'd done—to get this far and be defeated by an overloaded schedule. Rhoda couldn't accept it.

"You've got plenty of patients who ain't nearly as important as Samson," she said. "Drop a couple of them."

Doctor Wren wasn't smiling now.

"And how do we decide who is the more important?"

Rhoda had the answer for this one and she had it in print. The years of carrying the clippings around in her handbag were about to pay off. She took the first and unfolded it carefully before holding it out.

"See for yourself," she said. "This was in the *Partisan Review*."

Doctor Voegler snatched it out of her hand, but lucky for him he didn't tear it.

" 'In *Hellebore*,' " he read slowly the words she knew by heart, " 'Samson Shillitoe proves once again that Americans don't write great love poems. Again and again one finds oneself thinking of how Kemp Owyne or even D. H. Lawrence would have expressed these sentiments. But, in all fairness, Mr. Shillitoe does achieve some success in a few ec-low-goos.' "

"Eclogues," corrected Rhoda. "That's a kind of short poem." She felt like kicking him for lousing up the review with his pronunciation. To make up for it she took out the second clipping and prepared to read it herself. "This was in the Buffalo *Courier-Express*," she first explained. " 'Samson Shillitoe shows in *Hellebore* that he is a tendentious poet.' " She looked up to find them all waiting as if expecting her to read more. They didn't realize how tough it was to get a book of poetry even mentioned in a newspaper. Or maybe they didn't understand it.

"That means he's got a cause," she explained.

"What?" asked Voegler.

"Tendentious," said Rhoda.

"But what is his cause?" asked the secretary.

"Like the *Partisan Review* said. Samson believes in love."

"Oh, I see." The way the secretary's mouth twisted the words made Rhoda mad.

"Aw, get your mind out of the gutter," she snapped.

"Mrs. Shillitoe!" Doctor Wren's tone told her she'd gone too far.

"I'm sorry." Rhoda forced herself to look at the secretary as she apologized. "I take it back. But that's part of Samson's problem." She marched up to Doctor Wren to drive her point home. "Like Samson says, everybody's all screwed up about love, especially on the East Side with their marble coffee tables. No wonder he can't get any writing done. The way some of them throw themselves at him. No shame. Even from good families."

"The case sounds fascinating," said the secretary.

"See what I mean?" pointed out Rhoda. "And she ain't even met him."

Then Doctor Wren started laughing and Doctor Voegler picked it up and the secretary chimed in too. Rhoda tried to smile as if she was in on the gag too, but she couldn't manage it. She felt herself going hot. This wasn't the way it was supposed to be. She had practiced the scene so many times the last few days with Doctor Wren sitting down with her the way he had the last time and discussing Samson intelligently. She had never pictured herself the center of this cackling trio. Rhoda started counting. If they didn't stop by ten, she'd start swinging the handbag. She reached seven before Doctor Voegler came over to her.

"I am especially interested in the *phallus thaumaturgist,*" he said. "In fact, I originated the term in my paper to the Vienna Congress of nineteen thirty-one which was attended by Doctor Sigmund Freud."

"I've heard of him," said Rhoda.

Doctor Voegler's mouth stayed open for a long time. Then he remembered what he was saying.

"The *phallus thaumaturgist*—that is, your husband."

"Samson?"

"Yes. Samson. He is unemployed, am I right?"

"He ain't working now," agreed Rhoda, and Doctor Voegler smiled as if he was glad. "But he starts again tomorrow," she added.

Doctor Voegler suddenly threw up his arms and stamped away. Then Doctor Wren stepped forward. From the way he looked she knew he was going to show her out. She had to do something in a hurry.

"Please help him," she begged.

"I'd like to," began Doctor Wren.

That was as much encouragement as she needed. Rhoda fished the money out of her handbag and waved it.

"How many treatments does he get for a hundred and ten dollars?"

The three of them went stiff. Rhoda wondered what she'd done wrong. She looked to Doctor Wren for the answer, but he turned to the secretary.

"You needn't wait, Miss Bueler."

Miss Bueler practically sprinted out of the room.

"Frederic," said Doctor Wren, "I won't be a moment."

Doctor Voegler bowed to Doctor Wren and her before going out.

"Sit down, Mrs. Shillitoe."

Dr. Wren said it commandingly and she dropped onto the nearest chair. Then he went behind his desk and sat down. He took out a cigarette and Rhoda was out of her chair and flicking his own desk lighter for him.

"Mrs. Shillitoe," he said through the smoke, "you've given me no good reason why I should give up one of my present patients or increase my already too long working day because of your husband."

"Not even those clippings?" she asked weakly.

"Not even those."

She had failed. There was a clear, bright moment when Rhoda saw the whole conversation they'd just had set out like the words in a comic strip. Doctor Wren was absolutely right. She hadn't given him any of all the reasons why he had to help Samson. Quickly she tried to, describing the black moods Samson had been in lately, his drinking and the way he'd carried on at the poetry reading. When Doctor Wren didn't show any alarm, she pulled the neck of her blouse down over one shoulder and pointed to the bruise from the last time Samson clipped her. After that there was no point in holding anything back, so she blurted out her worst fear: that during one of his moods, Samson would make for the gas jets or jump out their top-floor window. Doctor Wren still just sat there looking at her steadily. Rhoda fumbled for other arguments to pile on, repeating things Samson had said to her; mean things to show how unhappy he was and beautiful things to show how he was worth saving. Then she began quoting some of his lines from *Hellebore* and when these didn't change the expression on Doctor Wren's face, she began to cry.

It was the first time Rhoda had cried since she'd been a child, and the sounds she heard herself making, the squeals and the moans and the wheezes, all sounded funny and made her cry that much more. But it was a flash storm and it broke as unexpectedly as it began and when Rhoda wiped the last tears on the back of her wrist and looked again at Doctor Wren she found his expression changed. His eyes were nicer and his mouth wasn't so stiff at the corners. As if aware that he'd been caught offguard, he began flipping the pages of his calendar.

"Mrs. Shillitoe." This time it sounded hopeful. "Suppose I meet your husband once, just once. Let's call it an exploratory interview. And if I feel he can benefit from my services . . ." He ended with a helpless shrug.

Rhoda felt she should thank him and beat it before he changed his mind. But she still had to give him the money. She tried to find the most diplomatic way to bring the subject up.

"What is the usual bite per visit?" she asked.

"The bite?"

"How much does it cost?"

"Well, we try to arrange our fees according to the patient's ability to pay."

"Good enough. So how many treatments does Samson get for a hundred and ten dollars?"

"May I ask why you set this nominal figure?"

"It ain't nominal," said Rhoda. "It's every cent I got."

"Suppose we leave the financial arrangements until after I've talked with Mr. Shillitoe." Doctor Wren stood up. In desperation Rhoda held out the money again.

"What does it usually cost?" she repeated, then took a stab at it. "Ten bucks a visit?"

"Usually it's more."

"More!" Rhoda hadn't expected this. "When Samson had a virus, the doctor charged ten. And he shot him full of penicillin."

"Then shall we say ten dollars a visit, *if* I decide to accept him as a patient?"

Rhoda knew she should be satisfied with that, but she wanted one more assurance.

"Can you straighten Samson out in eleven visits?"

"I don't know," said Doctor Wren.

"But you told me you help writers to write. You ought to be able to do that in eleven visits."

"I ought to," agreed Doctor Wren and his smile made her feel better.

"It's a deal," said Rhoda and as he reached for her elbow to steer her out, she plunked the money into his hand.

"What's this?"

"The hundred and ten dollars."

"You don't have to pay in advance."

"Yes I do," said Rhoda. "How else can we get Samson to come to you?"

Doctor Wren stared at the money.

"You mean your husband will be a reluctant patient?"

"Reluctant!" Rhoda had to laugh and that made Doctor Wren look more puzzled than ever. So she told him the whole thing, about how she'd counted on getting to see him Friday before Samson recovered from his hangover and asked about the check and how his secretary had given her a runaround all day. That was when she'd made up the story about calling Rollie Butter and Rollie saying he was mailing the check. All weekend she'd been expecting Samson to get wise to what she was doing and belt her. But he didn't. Then, right out of nowhere, maybe like the way Samson got his inspiration, she got the idea of pretending the check arrived in today's mail, getting Samson to endorse it and having Herschel cash it. And that was why she had to give him the money before she went home.

"And what will he do when you tell him?"

"He'll come to you and demand the money back," she said. "I'm warning you. He'll make up all kinds of reasons. He's got some imagination. But don't you fall for any of it. You hang on to the dough. That way, either he has to kiss it good-bye or he comes to you for treatment so it won't be a total loss. Now do you get it?"

"I'm afraid I do," said Doctor Wren.

"Good." Rhoda pointed to the money. "You better count it."

"I'm sure it's right."

This took a little while to sink in. Then Rhoda shrugged. "Something new every day."

In the reception room Doctor Voegler was reading *The New Yorker* and pretending he wasn't listening to Doctor Wren telling her to have Samson call Miss Bueler for an appointment. Rhoda took one final look at Doctor Wren, and suddenly she felt sorry for him. What if his nice office got wrecked? Then he smiled again and she stopped worrying. He could handle anybody, including Samson.

Somewhere the bell of a church was ringing six times. Rhoda thought of Samson saying that all church bells in New York were controlled by Irving Berlin. She started walking toward the Lexington Avenue Subway and everything she heard and saw made her think of something else Samson had said. Her steps slowed until she stood still completely. She had done it. Caught up in the doing, she hadn't fully thought about what Samson would do to her when he found out. One hundred and ten dollars. She'd never spent half that amount at once in her entire life. What if Samson just let her have it so hard he killed her and they executed him? Would Doctor Wren keep the money or turn it over to some charity or what? The possible turns and twists the situation could take pounded in her head until she thought it would crack open. Then she spotted the marquee of the RKO Proctor's off in the distance and she hurried toward it.

Chapter Nine

AS the camera salesman leaned over the counter to point out the double-exposure prevention device, Shillitoe resisted an impulse to flick the withered pea of a mole off the top of his high sloping forehead. He saw it ricocheting off the glass showcase, bouncing from the massive automatic enlarger along the ranks of telephoto lenses and finally popping into the open mouth of the woman who was inspecting a camera by squinting through one eye and pointing the damn thing at him.

The salesman droned on about shutter speeds and lens stops and delayed timers. Then furtively, he began trading Shillitoe up. "Now, if you're willing to spend just a little more," and his hand came up with an even more complicated-looking mechanism like a magician's producing a bunch of flowers.

Shillitoe offered no price resistance. The signs in the store window and on all the walls agreed that anyone could have a ten-day free trial of any equipment in stock. Since he wouldn't need the camera for more than twenty-four hours, he might as well get the best one.

He finally settled on a Japanese job that the salesman swore was so simple to operate that spastic six-year-olds could get salon quality photographs with it on their first try. Shillitoe then presented his special problem. He was an amateur member of the National Foundation of Pelagic Fishes, his current project required picture evidence of the mating habits of herring and this blissful activity only took place in pitch-darkness.

The salesman didn't bat an eye. He'd once had a customer who'd faced the same problem with porpoises. He had just the thing. Out came the flash attachment and infra-red bulbs, backed by the salesman's reassuring patter that they wouldn't produce a spark of light that might distract the herring.

Shillitoe found himself captioning the photograph in advance.

"Applegarth in infra-red."

"Applegarth?" asked the salesman.

"A rare breed of herring," said Shillitoe.

The mole tempted him again as the salesman bent over to add up some illegible figures. When he announced that the total amount of the purchase came to only three hundred and eighty dollars, Shillitoe felt he had to react.

"Make it three hundred and seventy-five and I'll take it."

The salesman drifted off to the rear of the store to huddle with the manager. When he pranced back on his toes, he signaled success and waved the little form that had to be filled out: four pages, foolscap sized with six-point type.

"And your last name?" began the salesman.

Ever since he'd been stupid enough to put his right name on the marriage license with Beverly's, Shillitoe had always answered this question with the name of a poet long dead. But since he'd be returning the equipment in the morning he could play it straight this time. Using his own name felt good and he made sure that the salesman spelled it correctly. Mr. Moscowitz was duly printed in as his employer and Rollie Butter as a character reference. But the habits of self-preservation linger. So, when the salesman's ball-point pen hung in midair waiting for him to give his address, Shillitoe recited the serial number on the salesman's identification button and tagged it with First Avenue.

After the signing, which was somewhat more formal than the 1945 surrender of the nation which made the camera, Shillitoe had the salesman load the special infra-red film and arrange all the dials and levers so that they were ready for action. The salesman escorted him out to the street guaranteeing that every picture would come out needle sharp as long as the two images in the rangefinder were perfectly merged. As Shillitoe walked uptown he tried to remember what the rangefinder was.

It was only a little after four o'clock. No sense going back to Gaye's yet. He wandered into Central Park and headed for the zoo. He could practice with the camera on a few of the animals. But the tiger's bored eyes and the gorilla's straggly hair discouraged him. He fingered the key to Gaye's room again and wondered if she had a bottle. No, he'd better stay cold sober if he was to get the two images perfectly merged. He left the zoo and searched the faded grass until he found a shady spot free of manure. Stretching out full length he watched the sky gradually dim.

In the final analysis it was purely a matter of light. Light would change the park from a hiding place for salesmen to a massive mattress for young lovers. Light colored, light distorted, light determined size and shape. Light chased the gray cinereous head of dawn from the window sill and picked the darkness clean. Light sucked the frightened from begrudging rooms and, fading, coupled the Applegarths with the Gayes. And light, infra-red, would make possible the money which would keep Beverly and Daniel K. Papp at bay.

Gaye sat on the stool nearest the cash register, spelling out the backward letters on the steamed window over and over and anticipating Mr. Applegarth's tenpin silhouette.

P-O-H-S. It was Mr. Applegarth's idea for them to rendezvous this way. E-E-F-F-O-C. Gaye never thought she'd fall for such a careful man. Not that he was fussy. Just careful. POHS EEFFOC. Gaye attributed this to Mr. Applegarth being a certified public accountant and to his living in Jackson Heights. But still, how careful could you get? First she had to wait in the

POHS EEFFOC, until he appeared outside. Then he'd follow her home, walk past her building and stroll back. If she heard anyone coming down the stairs, she'd come out again and he'd keep going and make another try in a few minutes. But if the hall was clear, she'd go upstairs and he'd duck inside and read all the names on the mailboxes. Then, when he heard her open her door, he'd gallop up and sit on the bed and have her fan him with a towel until he caught his breath. POHS EEFFOC.

Gaye had often suggested that life would be a lot simpler if she just waited for him in her room instead of bothering to get dressed just to get undressed all over again. But Mr. Applegarth wouldn't listen. In fact, once he got nasty and she decided he might be on the lam from a bughouse and not a certified public accountant at all. There'd been some anxious minutes until she found his name in the directory with the letters C.P.A. after it and the address in Jackson Heights.

He'd told her the truth and she wanted to reciprocate. That night, as they lay exhausted in the hot room, she told him about looking up his name. The bedspring was still busted from the way he jumped up, shaking all over and telling her if she ever dialed the number in the phone book he'd kill her. She wasn't taking that kind of lip, even from him, and she told him so. If she wasn't good enough to dial his pimping phone number he could beat it for good. For a while she thought he was going to. Then he started the my-wife-don't-understand-me bit and told her about his oldest son at Dartmouth who wasn't breast fed because his wife had an abscess and, for some reason, the kid blamed him. It got pretty complicated, and Gaye began to wonder what future there was in seeing Mr. Applegarth. But she didn't send him away. What the hell? Who could tell what would happen? Maybe the little pimp in college would grow up or the wife would croak or maybe Shillitoe would come up with an idea.

The backward letters on the plate glass started getting fuzzy around the edges. Gaye rested her eyes by studying her charm bracelet, the only jewelry Mr. Applegarth had bought her.

She jangled the boot, fish, ball, book, crown and crucifix until the counterman started mopping around her elbow with a smelly rag. Then, looking out the window again and seeing it had turned dark, she twisted her head to read the cashier's wristwatch.

"A quarter to ten," said the cashier as if she knew that Mr. Applegarth had made it clear that if he didn't show up by nine-thirty he wasn't coming.

Well it wasn't the first time he'd stood her up. But she'd been depending on Mr. Applegarth to give her at least a five spot. Without it, how was she eating tomorrow?

Gaye heaved herself to her feet, paid for her three cups of coffee and went out. What now? Two months ago, before Mr. Applegarth entered her life, she'd have managed something. Even a sailor boy with cropped hair and boils on his chin would have been good for a few bucks. But street soliciting after two months with one man was like a first drink after being on the wagon. Besides, there wasn't a sailor or soldier in sight; just the old woman making with baby talk to the dog the size of a horse and the couple yelling for a cab and the big, well-built guy looking in the drugstore window. She watched him. Then he turned around and stared right at her. He was probably waiting for his girl friend with skinny legs and a deep freeze. Still, experience had taught Gaye never to rule out anyone.

As she walked toward him she shook her hand so the charm bracelet jingled. And gradually her hips regained the undulating movement she'd thought she'd forgotten.

Officer Chester Quirk hated his work. When he'd been on duty in the Holland Tunnel, waving his arms at the cars and trucks all day, he was sure any change had to be for the better. He'd prayed for that change and his prayers were answered. Ten men were needed for special duty. The only requirements were that the officers be over six feet tall and unmarried. Single, six-foot-two Chester Quirk was the first to volunteer. It never occurred to him that there might be worse things than the Holland Tunnel. That was what he'd said to Father Keegan when, after making his first arrest, he'd gone to confession. To his surprise, Father Keegan didn't advise him to resign from the force that very day. Instead, he just said that Chester had to objectivize what he was doing. He had to think of his body carrying out a mission in the same way a soldier does during battle. The soldier must only consider whether he is fighting on the side of God. Father Keegan assured Chester that the war against prostitution had the Lord's full endorsement. All Chester had to remember was that it was *only* his body which was solicited by the diseased harlots. It was *only* his body which followed the bloated old streetwalkers up the crumbling stairs to the dingy rooms with the naked light bulbs and cracked washbasins. It was *only* his body which they approached disgustingly! (Father Keegan was so much against sin that his voice cracked.) And, of course, as soon as a prostitute also had her clothes off and took his money, Chester just had to reach for the badge in the pocket of his suitcoat and make the pinch. After all, someone had to stamp out this most predatory of all vices, and the police authorities had shown great wisdom and tact in assigning the front-line assault to unmarried men. All Chester need do was come to confession after each encounter and not withhold any detail, however sordid.

Danger was ever-present though. Chester must never lose sight of the fact that the devil thrived in the whore's womb. Father Keegan cautioned him to keep three allegiances constantly in mind; to God, to the community and to the Police Commissioner. Chester thanked the good Father for his advice and returned to duty more determined than ever to find a nice girl and get married as soon as possible so he'd be ineligible for the front-line assault.

In the meantime, he tried to make as few arrests as he could. He kept away from the bars and saloons where he knew the tramps hung out and when he saw one standing on a corner he'd look the other way. As long as one didn't approach him directly, he was able to rationalize the blank reports he turned in every morning.

This had promised to be another shift of duty summed up with "no arrests" until the old bag came out of the coffee shop. Chester turned away to the drugstore window and studied all the suntan lotions and vitamin pills for enough time for her to get far away. But when he looked around she was hobbling right toward him like she had pebbles in both shoes.

There was no out. When she started fanning herself and telling him how much cooler it was in her room, he had to go along with her. The room was twenty degrees hotter than the street, but at least there wasn't any chipped washbasin and the light bulb hanging from the ceiling had a shade printed with flowers. In fact, the room looked pretty. This made Chester feel guilty again and he tried to concentrate on God and the crummy people who lived in New York and the rotten Police Commissioner who thought up this stinking assignment.

As he took off his second sock he heard the clicking sound from the direction of the closet.

"What was that?"

"What was what, honey?"

She had undressed already and stood watching him. Chester felt himself blushing and wished she'd ask for the money now so he could produce his badge without taking his underwear off. But she just held out her blubbery arms. She didn't even look away when there was the ping and the rattling in the closet.

"Something's in there," said Chester.

"Probably just a rat."

Just a rat. Chester Quirk, born and raised in Brooklyn, hated rats even more than Italians. For the first time since he'd joined the force he felt the need for his revolver, or at least his club. And here he was completely naked.

"You got ten dollars for little me, honey?"

She rolled toward him like a huge wad of baking dough and

took the bill he held out. But, before he could produce his badge, she had him in a headlock.

"Hold it, will ya'?"

She didn't let go, not until the explosion went off in the closet. Then she relaxed her grip long enough for Chester to spring free and grab the brown vase with the ferns in it. Holding this high in his right hand he inched toward the closet and listened.

There was no sound inside. Whatever had exploded must have killed the rat. But it was also possible that it hadn't and the rat was ready to leap at him. Chester's fingers clenched tighter around the vase. He'd probably only get in one blow so his aim had better be accurate. But what if it wasn't? He looked around to gauge the jump to the nearest chair. But the whore was standing on it holding the ten-dollar bill like a fig leaf. The other chair was the one next to the bed, the one on which his clothes were hung neatly. Chester almost put the vase down and made for them. Why not beat it and let the whore clean out her own closet? But the months of training in police school kept him from running away. Besides, he had to make the arrest in order to get the ten dollars back.

There was nothing to be gained by delay. Chester braced himself and slid his left hand to the doorknob.

"Spastic six-year-olds, my ass!"

Chester heard the cursing as he pulled open the door.

Chapter Ten

LYDIA's excitement mounted steadily throughout the day. She concealed it when Oliver telephoned at noon, flippantly offering to bet him that the main course would be either roast chicken—dried up, or steak—too well done. But later, under the dryer at Franchot's, she wished she'd played it straight. If only she'd just said, "Yes, darling, I can't wait." Lydia resolved to make it up to him somehow before the night was over.

Franchot had risen to the occasion with her hair and she knew the lemon chiffon dress she'd found was just right for her. It was quite low, front and back, but her skin could take it. Not a blemish and stretched tight. Oliver had told her that all men hated seeing loose skin exposed. And once he'd remarked that hers was almost too clear.

"Your showing a bare shoulder is more sexy than most women walking around nude."

If this was so, and why wasn't it, tonight she'd be sexier than ever; the Parapraxes Pin-up, the belle of Bellevue . . . She braked her thoughts. *Nothing doing, girl. This is your husband's night to glow. You just smile humbly at everyone and look perfectly adjusted.*

The arrangement was for three of the doctors, Voegler, Holland and Milicent Akers, to meet at the apartment, from where the five of them would go on to the banquet. As Lydia twisted and preened in front of the bedroom mirror for a last-minute inspection she heard Oliver come in. Only one voice with his and *dis mit de accent*—Freddie Voegler.

In the living room, his beard came leaping toward her mouth but she ducked aside in time and it merely scraped her cheek. Then she tangoed around the furniture with Voegler nipping at her heels and Oliver standing there beaming. Was Oliver approving of the way she looked or just anticipating the hours ahead? If only he'd mention her dress.

"I thought Oliver and I should arrive together," Voegler was explaining. "Of course, the election was a slur against the Freudian element of the profession. More than that, it was shameless chauvinism."

"I don't agree." Oliver's tone was quiet but emphatic.

"Regardless," said Voegler, "I wish everyone to know that Oliver Wren and Doctor Frederic Voegler are the best of friends."

Voegler had sneaked up behind her and was arching forward on the balls of his feet to get a better view down her neckline. Lydia swore she could hear lips licking under the beard. She faced him squarely and lifted her arms as if being frisked.

"Take a good look, Frederic. Any chink in my armor? Any visible buds of neuroses?"

Oliver must have detected what Freddie was doing too and glided between them. Lydia was pleased. It was the first time he'd ever reacted to another man's attention to her. Then he spoiled it.

"Lydia feels cheated because she hasn't been analyzed."

All right. If he wanted to play games. She swept around him to Voegler.

"Do I need analysis, Frederic?"

"Everybody needs analysis," said Voegler.

"You see!" She tossed the words at Oliver gleefully. "Frederic, if you really want to prove your friendship for Oliver, you'll take me as a patient."

"Monday morning, ten o'clock." Voegler was dead serious. Did Oliver look annoyed? She thought so, but he wasn't interfering. How deep could she wade in before he'd pull her out?

"It's a date," she said, "unless my husband objects."

They both waited for Oliver's answer. He certainly took his time. Lydia was almost willing to go through with it just to show him. Then he laughed.

"What's so funny?" It was Voegler's turn to look annoyed.

"Nothing doing, Frederic." Oliver put his arm around her waist and pulled her toward him causing the strap to fall from her right shoulder. "Darling." He sounded serious now too. "If I ever detect the slightest indication that you need analysis, I'll take you as a patient."

"You can't!" protested Voegler. "Remember what Doctor Freud said. When the personal interest of the physician is greater, his . . ."

"We know all about that," snapped Lydia, then looked up at Oliver. "You promise?"

"I promise."

Doctor Holland and Doctor Akers couldn't have picked a better moment to ring the doorbell. Then everything was light and frivolous. Milicent Akers' floral dress looked like it would wilt unless sprinkled hourly. Lydia scolded herself for thinking it. Milicent was harmless and fun, soliciting reactions to the title of her new book.

"*The Road Back to Normalcy.*" Milicent announced it ominously.

"The road back?" queried Doctor Holland. "I never knew we passed it."

Holland's sense of humor appealed to Lydia. She waited for him to get a rise out of Voegler. It didn't take long.

"When I came in I thought it was Freud himself standing there. Freddie, you're getting to look just like him."

"So? So?" sputtered Voegler. "Better I should look like Jung?"

Lydia wanted to hug Doctor Holland, or at least to pat the top of his fluffy white hair. What a father image. There she went, using psychiatric lingo again. She was getting as bad as

Miss Bueler. Still, Andrew Holland with his understanding eyes and unshakable calm was what everyone wanted daddy to be. He certainly had been Oliver's guiding light. Oliver never lost a chance to point that out. Even now when they all had drinks in hand and were toasting him.

"I'm very grateful," Oliver said, "especially to you, Doctor Holland."

"Why him?" asked Voegler. "He was your campaign manager?"

Lydia was surprised to hear her own voice answering. "It was Doctor Holland who persuaded Oliver to go into psychiatry."

"It was Doctor Freud who persuaded me," muttered Voegler.

They buried their smiles in their drinks. Then another round and it was time to leave. Voegler appointed himself her escort and insisted she squeeze between Oliver and him in the front of his Jaguar. So the skirt of her dress got creased while Milicent's had plenty of room in the back seat.

They were obviously late arrivals in the banquet room. As they entered, people peeled away from conversing groups and rushed at Oliver. He stood up to the stampede, not with a politician's mechanical smile and handclasp but with individualized greetings and references, after which each steer was turned to Lydia. Doctor and Mrs. Blah-Blah, Doctor and Mrs. Blur-Blur. Oliver with his super-memory knew every name. "You remember Doctor and Mrs. Buzz-Buzz."

"Of course. How are you?"

Lydia felt she should remember some of them. But they all looked strange. *Double-entendre* there. Strange indeed. Why didn't psychiatrists all look healthy like Oliver? Some squinted. Some twisted their mouths when they spoke. Several looked like they'd had their noses bobbed by the same plastic surgeon. One perspired terribly. He clung to Oliver's side after the others started hunting for their place cards at the tables. What was his name? Messy? No, Massey. She didn't like

Messy Massey. As she pried Oliver loose from him, she caught his last words.

"Hope you'll show more foresight than Abelson . . . ridiculous not to open Para Park to psychosurgery."

Was he the one she'd once heard Oliver refer to as "the butcher"? She started to whisper the question to Doctor Holland, but some officious type descended on them and led the way to the speaker's table. This was Abelson, the outgoing president. Was she going to get stuck next to him? Saved. She'd been placed between Oliver and Doctor Holland. She wouldn't be forced to make strained conversation during the one more drink and shrimp cocktail and the . . . *roast chicken!*

She nudged Oliver and nodded triumphantly toward her plate. He looked mystified. Sometimes his memory wasn't so hot either. So there! She felt light-headed and warm. Had she been drinking a lot? She could only remember four. Maybe the place wasn't properly ventilated. No, Oliver and Doctor Holland both seemed comfortable and cool. She decided it was the drinks and resolved not to speak until the feeling passed. *Don't want to say the wrong thing tonight, girl. Keep all teeth firmly clamped when not chewing tough chicken. Mum's the word until coffee arrives.* It finally did, not very hot.

Officious one tapped his water glass with his knife, stood up and started off with "Dear members of the slip-of-the-tongue society." Lydia was sure last year's speaker had started the same way and had received the same volley of laughter. There were many items of business the outgoing president had to cover. She wondered in how many hotel banquet rooms in how many cities at that very moment, sententious people were making committee reports and treasurer's reports and minutes-of-the-last-meeting reports to similar arrays of chair scrapers.

At last she heard her married name. Nice things were being said about her husband. Why not? Even her parents liked him. If she had a pencil, she'd write some of the compliments down. Applause. No time now. Outgoing president was sitting down and Oliver was rising to speak. *Concentrate, wife of new president. Every woman in the room is envying you. Speak splendidly, Oliver. Knock 'em dead.*

"Thank you, Doctor Abelson, fellow members of the Parapraxes Society, ladies and gentlemen."

Not very original. But, at least his voice was mellow and full, a relief after the rasping of the outgoing one.

"My secretary, after typing the notes for this address, told me she approved of what I planned to say. This was the first time I've ever received such approval. And so, one of the many reasons I am grateful for the honor you have bestowed upon me is that you have won me my secretary's respect."

Cute, thought Lydia, but certainly not warranting the guffaws and spots of handclapping. Or was this because she resented the reference to Miss Bueler? Oliver hadn't discussed the speech with her.

"I didn't mean to imply that my secretary is hypercritical of me. Instead, let's say she shares many of the prevailing doubts about our science. No, let's go one step further. Her doubts are greater than most—for our secretaries, like our wives, see daily evidence of our being all too human."

Lydia felt she'd been referred to obliquely, but was still running second to Miss Bueler. But was he right? Was her knowledge of him as a man undermining her respect for his achievements? She studied his outstretched fingertips touching the tablecloth. What a nice hand. But would she recognize it in a pushcart full of hands? How well did she really know him?

"If only we could smear some bulimia or a Ganser syndrome on a glass slide and put it under a microscope. If only we could solve one phobic fear mathematically."

"Hear! Hear!" The Anglophiles were out tonight.

"If only we could," continued Oliver, "we could then wear sterilized white coats and all the cartoonists would have to search for new whipping boys." More applause this time. The audience was with him. "Of course the mathematical approach to emotional problems is a distinct possibility. Another hundred years and it will probably exist. But, for the present, you and I shall have to continue being scientific in the only way we know how. And I'm afraid our fellow specialists working in longer cultivated fields will continue to show ambivalence toward us.

"I want to say a few words about that ambivalence. For example, there are our highly regarded dispensers of justice who, if I may paraphrase, hold life between their lips. They have an occasional need for us. They call upon us for an opinion. 'Is the murderer sane or insane? Never mind the technical mumbo-jumbo. All we want is a simple yes or no.' And, if one suggests, as I have, that every major criminal act is psychotic, then one is regarded as somewhat psychotic himself."

Again the roll of laughter. Lydia looked at the open mouths it came from, trying to find what was so funny.

"Or consider our highly respected and increasingly scientific leaders of industry. Could it be our lack of engineering facilities which leaves them so unimpressed? Or is it simply that there isn't a single psychiatrist on the list of the nation's millionaires?"

More hear-hears this time. The place sounded like the House of Commons. Sir Oliver held up a hand to restore order before going on.

"The official big-business attitude toward our work is that there's nothing wrong with any mind that a lot of money won't cure. But let one of their country club set place a shotgun muzzle to his mouth and we suddenly achieve stature. Incidentally, perhaps one of you could tell me why the wealthy suicidals so often choose this horrible method. Or maybe Doctor Akers will write a book on the subject one day."

A touch of comedy at just the right moment. Milicent acknowledged the laughter and the craning necks with serene aloofness.

"A third example of ambivalence is found in the attitude of the church. Though our particular emphasis on the individual ego has not been declared incompatible with Christianity, our pew is usually regarded with suspicion. I often ask myself why. Certainly we have not invaded sacred ground nearly as much as the space explorers who are out cartographing heaven. Yet we incur much more antagonism. Could it be because, in our exploration of the subconscious mind, we are more apt than the rocket men to stumble onto God?"

Some more applause, but part of the audience had frozen. Oliver had finally said something controversial. Lydia was tickled. But what had he said which could offend anyone? That crack about God? Surely, no psychiatrist could take exception to it. Besides, no matter how much they changed their names, seventy-five percent of them weren't even Christians.

"And so those who are quickest to accuse our work of not being a science at all may in turn be accused by us of exhibiting definite compensation neuroses."

The warm laughter told her he was back on safe ground. *Damn it!*

"Now let me leap over to the other side of the fence." Oliver waited until the room was absolutely still and she saw his jaw muscles tighten. "I believe, and I believe very strongly, that many of us are too intimidated by this deprecation of our right to call ourselves scientists. More and more I come across evidence of psychiatrists playing it safe, confining themselves to those fundamentals of behavioral analyses which are no longer challengeable. And this is a dangerous sign, for our work for the present and during the foreseeable future must be largely intuitive. If we merely keep a neat little file of cerebral symptoms, motor symptoms, sensory symptoms, visceral symptoms, et cetera, et cetera, where do we go from there? The next step will be to hang charts in our offices showing the anal stage in pink, the urethral in brown and the oral in baby blue. And from there it isn't very far to becoming pill and serum dispensers. Too many general practitioners can testify to the emptiness of that fate."

Lydia began analyzing the faces nearest her. Some of them seemed to be relishing the speech. Others appeared uneasy, tine-designing the tablecloth or playing with the paper wrappers of the sugar cubes. Some toes had obviously been stepped upon. *Thataboy, Oliver. Show them they can't buy you off with presidencies.*

"The alternative, of course, is obvious. We must be as insensitive to ignorant criticism as the ignorant critics have always been to progress. The rewards the psychiatrist must seek are the same trophies which have always appealed to the pioneer. And tonight I wish to point to two areas, so far practically untouched, to which I hope the Parapraxes membership and particularly the directors and staff of Para Park will send the first expeditions. The first territory I point to is that of genius. The second is that of evil. With our considerable knowledge of human capacities, these two areas remain virtually a complete mystery. And, since both fools and angels have feared to tread the garrets of genius and the alleyways of evil, I think psychiatrists will have to take on the job. In fact, I think we *must* take it on for I sincerely believe we hold the only possible existing key to genius and evil."

As Oliver paused for a sip of water, Lydia congratulated herself on having been able to follow the speech. She'd expected it to be so highly technical that she'd have to sit through it with a set expression of rapt attention. Instead, she was sure she'd understood everything he'd said. The anal, urethral and oral bit had thrown her momentarily. She couldn't remember which was which. But aside from that she'd held her own. It was just as she was mentally patting herself on the back that Oliver started leaving her behind. Lydia hung on desperately around the first hairpin turns of instinct components and patricidal impulses. But when he continued on to latent orientations and incorporating types that sounded like the original cast of *Antigone* she threw in the sponge. Her face, propped on one fist, made no attempt to hide her adoration. How could one man acquire so much knowledge? *Oliver. Oliver. You make the whole world ignorant. I'm so insufficient for you. Maybe that's why I've been bitchy lately. Why do you bother to put up with me anyway? Any other woman in the world would give anything to change places with me. And you're so goddam handsome, too. Hurry up and get through the speech, darling. I haven't felt so sensy' in ages.*

"And so," said Oliver, "I do not propose that we fill our consulting rooms and Para Park with sadists and surrealists. But I do suggest that we stop shunting them on to state hospitals while we crowd our schedules with minor cycloid and depressive patterns. In the extremes of evil and of genius we may find the spores of mould which, properly isolated and treated, can open new highways into the psyche. My bacteriological analogy is deliberate. Isn't it always the highly contaminated culture plate which leads to the greatest discoveries? And isn't discovery the ultimate purpose of every scientist's life? And aren't we men of science in every sense of the word, engaged in the most vital work of our time?"

The applause beat at Lydia for several seconds before she realized Oliver had finished. Then everybody was clustering around him and shaking his hand. For a while she thought they were going to hoist him on their shoulders and sway out of the room singing "Boola-Boola." Lydia shoved and sidestepped until she was at his side. He was talking to someone she couldn't see, but she couldn't wait until he finished. One hand on his shoulder, she boosted her mouth to his ear.

"Take me home, genius. I want to be evil."

And to emphasize it, she bit the lobe. He chopped his sentence off in mid-air and looked at her, astonished. She tried to wink sexily, but felt it looked like she had something in her eye. No, he got the message and winked right back before turning away to complete whatever he'd been saying. Then, before the next echelon of hands reached him, he sneaked in the aside.

"Just a few minutes, hon, and we'll go."

Lydia hung on to his arm, smiling sweetly at all the women waiting on the periphery for their second-rate husbands to stop fawning over Oliver. *Boy, what they didn't know. Boy, oh boy.*

The maid had changed the bedclothes that morning. *Crisp, cool linens tonight. And no pajamas!*

Chapter Eleven

SHILLITOE waited until the composition of the scene was aesthetically pleasing. Gaye was in the foreground leaning over, the dried apricots at the ends of her dangling udders right off Matisse's brush. Applegarth, much younger than Shillitoe had expected, stood a few feet behind her, sad and sinewy as a Picasso pony. The photograph of them together would make a perfect Christmas Card for the Museum of Modern Art. Shillitoe pressed the button, but not before Gaye straightened up and completely obliterated her boy friend.

Shillitoe remembered the lever which moved the film along and cocked the shutter automatically. He remembered to reach into his pocket for a new infra-red bulb. And, at the same time, he remembered that the camera salesman hadn't shown him how to eject the used bulb from the flash holder. Groping in the dark, he pressed everything on the gadget that moved until there was a *ping* and the bulb fell to the floor. Two years later, it stopped rolling. With Applegarth looking toward the closet suspiciously, Shillitoe backed between Gaye's heavily scented dresses and tried to insert the new bulb into the holder. Gaye was covering Applegarth like a glacier. Just one picture and he could be on his way. But the new bulb wouldn't stay in. Shillitoe moved his foot to apply better leverage, his heel came down on the old bulb and the explosion was deafening. All sirens warned him to run for it. But the ancient tout of the dreamtrack whispered its four words, the same four words that had stretched giraffes and invented the cotton gin and loused up more guys than any other phrase. "Just one more try," it whispered. And for six more tries, the little bulb kept jumping back into his hand instead of catching in the socket. It was then that Shillitoe muttered "Spastic children, my ass" and looked up to see the closet door wide open and Applegarth with vase held high.

Shillitoe, being the less surprised of the two, was able to react first. Left foot forward, right knee up, and down went the vase, Applegarth and all. His clawing of the floor would continue for at least ten minutes. Plenty of time to pose the picture properly.

"Gaye. Come over here and say 'cheese.' "

But Gaye had the window open and was hanging over the sill yelling for help.

"Gaye, for Christ's sake!"

"You!" Looking around, she seemed surprised to see him.

"Hurry up, will ya'?" Shillitoe was trying to figure out how to include the framed quotation from Housman in the picture and didn't see Applegarth groping at the strap of the camera case until too late.

"Let go, Applegarth!"

"That ain't Applegarth," said Gaye. Then she leaned out the window again and yelled, "Never mind. I was only kidding."

Too late. Feet were pattering up the stairs. Shillitoe tried to pull the camera free again. But Applegarth, or whatever he was called, was holding fast with one hand while reaching toward his clothes with the other.

"Under arrest," he gasped. "Prostitution, Peeping Tom, breaking and entering, assaulting an officer."

Shillitoe wasn't listening carefully. So when the badge emerged from the suitcoat pocket, he was surprised enough to let go of the camera. Then someone started kicking in the door.

"Don't come in," called Gaye. "That was only the radio you heard." She was jumping into her clothes like a fireman.

"Damn you, Shillitoe," she croaked.

"Why didn't you tell me it wasn't him?"

"How the hell did I know you were in the closet?"

"Help!" called the cop.

"Come on." Gaye squeezed through the window to the fire escape. Shillitoe right behind her, took one last look back at the camera. The cop still had it in a death grip. Three hundred and eighty dollars. There he was, exaggerating again. It was only three hundred and seventy-five.

Gaye's heels kept getting caught between the metal slats and he had to grab her on the third landing to prevent her going over the side. By the time they reached the alley she was getting maudlin.

"I'm through, Shillitoe. All my expensive clothes and everything."

"Tough, Gaye."

"You know how much I spent decorating that place?"

"Thirty-forty bucks?"

"A lot you know!"

He didn't think it was a good time to stop to argue and started pulling her toward the lights of the street.

"Where are you taking me?"

"We'd better go to my place," he said.

"Nothing doing. You ain't exactly my good luck charm."

A head appeared in the window they'd just left and warned them not to move. Gaye beat him to the street by three strides.

"Any better idea, Gaye?"

"I've got a sister in Metuchen. She won't like it, but she'll put me up."

"Got the fare?"

"He paid me in advance. It'll be enough for two tickets."

"No. Thanks anyway."

"That shill ain't gonna' give up. Not after where you kicked him."

"He'll have to find me first."

"He will."

The downtown bus pulled in at the corner ahead of them and they ran for it. This took Gaye's last wind and it was several blocks before she could speak again.

"Shillitoe?"

"Uh?"

"What the hell were you doing with that camera?"

"Figure it out."

She concentrated all the way to Forty-second Street. Then her forehead uncreased.

"Oh."

"Bright girl."

"You could'a warned me in advance."

"I almost did. But I was afraid you wouldn't look natural."

"Probably. I'm pretty fuckin' modest."

Shillitoe didn't want to talk. He was trying to backtrack events to determine just how serious a spot he was in. Gaye was right. The cop would go all out to find him. How tough would that be? The camera could be traced to the store easily enough and there was that form he'd signed. Good thing he'd given a phony address. The sense of relief didn't last long. He hadn't faked the references. Both Moscowitz and Rollie Butter could tell the cop where he lived. He didn't have a chance. Still, the chase couldn't begin until morning when the camera store opened. By then he could be most of the way to Cob City. But he had to go tonight or never.

He could feel his muscles straining against the inertia of the city. He had sunk deep into the concrete molar with its pus bags and inflammations. Only stark, rampaging fear could free him now. Thought of the naked policeman wasn't impetus enough, but a cell door clanging closed on him was. Lovelace wasn't a good-enough poet to convince him that iron bars didn't make a cage, and he wasn't hanging around long enough to find out. He had always known his escape would be sudden and unplanned. He had never tried to balance his tomorrows symmetrically. Life didn't fall in rhyming couplets. But all the nursery schools taught that it did. And the rabbits were not yet willing to challenge Mother Goose.

Shillitoe looked around at the passengers spaced down both sides of the bus. They reminded him again of the endless variety of sizes and shapes that human features could be mashed into. But, as to expression, they had all the diversity of a crate of grapefruit. All of these twenty-five or thirty on the bus gazed back at him identically; all pasty with temptations memorized, glazed from searching for blossoms in hardware stores. Where was the flame? It had to be there or they couldn't breathe. But where? He'd missed it. Had all poets missed it? Was that why every other piper was followed to the dated gray slabs with only token questions raised along the way? Why wouldn't these faces listen to the bards? Why wouldn't they believe that the battle wasn't with each other but with perspective? Why couldn't they see it? But then, how could they? Their eyes were turned inward so that with every blink the lashes dusted clean the brain. That was the first correction to be made, to turn the line of vision outside the self, against defection and retreat. But why bother? He had no desire to save them. Only salesmen had to pretend to love people. And poetry was not for sale. He didn't have to kiss babies or jump around in a Shawnee headdress or invent lies about human dignity and conscience and inherent goodness. No trying on conceits for him. No boasting of wrist or finger spin. No trying to make a profit out of life. He was a poet! And poetry was forged, as all art was made, through the perfected breathing of the imagination—to be inhaled later by a few other imaginations existing on the same plane. This was his world, not that of the bus with its pneumatic doors sighing the fleshy rhomboids on and off.

Then, from somewhere far off it came, faster than light,

more consuming than fire. If there was such a thing as an Act of God, it had to be this. The words spun in his brain at tremendous speed, falling into formation, modifying each other with a shimmering clarity and building, constantly building, into the muscular shape of things. He had it all, the dimensions of the whole poem. There would be four parts, four peaks, each to be climbed and descended—up and down the gulleys, across the plateaus, every step of the way clearly marked with hard, practical, recognizable objects. It would be a long poem. It had to be to encase everything that had just appeared. The cold carpentry of structure would come later, but right now he had to get back to the apartment and make a beginning.

The bus was crawling. He looked out the window and saw they were nearing Thirty-fourth Street.

"I gotta' transfer to the Crosstown," said the woman next to him.

He slowly saw that it was Gaye, and with her spongy face came memory. Work on the poem would have to wait until he was safe. He had to keep his mind on getting back to Cob City. It wouldn't be long to wait. He'd be there tomorrow, the hundred dollars from the reading paying his and Rhoda's train fare.

"You okay?" Gaye was giving him a funny look.

"Never better," he said. And as she stepped off the bus he called after her, "I'm sorry, Gaye."

She waved to him as the bus pulled away and there were a few strands of remorse over losing her her dumpy room and the cheap dresses in the closet. But at least he'd saved her from a certified public accountant. She couldn't do much worse in Metuchen.

Rhoda wasn't home. That meant she was either out looking for him or staring at a movie screen. What if, mesmerized by technicolor, she had her handbag swiped? The horrible possibility wouldn't go away. Would she be dumb enough to carry a hundred dollars on her? He made the rounds of all the original places where Rhoda tried to hide money—the sugar canister, under the mattress, the chandelier. Yes, she'd be dumb enough to keep it on her. If she waddled in without that handbag, he'd pound her down to four foot three.

Nothing to pack their few clothes in. Rhoda would have to borrow a suitcase from the Fitzgeralds. Fragments of the poem leapt at him from every wall, but he fought them off. This was one time he'd get out of danger first. He changed into his brown suit and began emptying the drawers. The bottom one of the dresser took some tugging. Rhoda had something stuffed in it. Stuffed was right. A mighty pull and every scrap he'd ever scribbled lay at his feet. He sat on the floor and began sorting.

On a paper napkin:

Asmodeus sits next to me,
weeping for widows

When the hell did he ever write that? On the back of one of Daniel K. Papp's envelopes:

some things must be sacrificed
when people move to smaller rooms.
Which will go,
the eagle with a broken wing,
the rusty dinosaur?

And, barely legible, on the torn-off corner of a newspaper page:

Whistler's mother
planted roses in his mouth

And,

there may not always be
descendants
of Montezuma's men

And,

the time of death varies with the dream,
the dying vein compliments the time

And,

we have come a long way
toward ignorance
and all uphill

and thousands more. Most of it was worthless, but he kept any that could conceivably strike a spark someday. The discards he piled in the sink and burned. He didn't think they'd make so much smoke. He opened the window, then went out on the landing to clear his lungs just as Fitzgerald came sniffing up the stairs.

"What's burning?" asked Fitzgerald.

"As the whore said to the midget, 'Keep your nose out of my business.' "

"Wise guy," snorted Fitzgerald and went back down. After the door slammed, Shillitoe remembered that he hadn't asked about the suitcase.

Inside again, searching the closet for a paper bag to put the saved scraps in, he came across the briefcase. He'd forgotten he had it, but there it sat as another testimonial to Rhoda's genius. It was the heaviest, most compartmented case he'd ever seen—for the man who had everything and had to lug it all around with him. Rhoda had presented it to him on his thirty-ninth birthday. At the time he was rolling tennis courts and he was worried about a new threat to his poetry—an evenly tanned one with round, rhythmic Wimbledon aspirations under her snug white shorts. So, instead of chucking the satchel at Rhoda, he'd put it in the closet and never taken it out until now.

The utilitarians had a point. The case was just right for all the scraps, plus the tear sheets of his published poems and the hundreds of those not yet printed. He remembered to throw in his one remaining copy of *Hellebore* and there was still plenty of room for all his socks and underwear. He snapped the case shut and was testing its weight when he heard Rhoda thudding up the last flight of stairs.

His apprehension about the money swept over him again. Would she have it? She sure was taking her time opening the door. Her curly red hair came in first. Rhoda always led with her head. He was sure she looked even more anxious than usual. She'd been robbed. He knew it. Then he saw the worn black leather bag and released his breath.

"You ain't at the Double-Deuce," she said.

He'd been expecting a burst of grievances for not letting her know he wouldn't be home for dinner; then a retrospective listing of all his other lack of considerations since she'd first laid eyes on him. Her flat, dull tone bothered him much more. She was probably sick. Just like her. Never had a temperature in her life, but tonight she'd come down with malaria or something.

"You okay, Rhoda?"

"Sure. Something's burning."

"Not any more."

"You're wearing your heavy suit."

If she made one more acute observation, he wouldn't take her with him.

"We're leaving," he said, and this jolted her head up. "Hurry up and pack."

"Where we going?"

"None of your business."

"It's my business if I'm going there, ain't it?"

"No! Go downstairs and borrow a suitcase." He knew he had to be especially hard on her if he was to get her to go along. One thing he couldn't do was name Cob City as their destination. That would have to wait until the train was halfway across Ohio, for Rhoda had been taught history and geography by Metro-Goldwyn-Mayer. The Lewis and Clark Expedition and the Battle of Little Big Horn were vivid and contemporary in her mind. The vast expanse between California and the west bank of the Mississippi was made up of six-shooters, log cabins and dusty Main Streets with ramshackle saloons. And Indiana was an unruffled pasture with a swimming hole for every little white cottage and Aunt Marthas smoothing their aprons behind every picket fence.

"You going back to Cob City?" she asked.

"Yes, I'm going back to Cob City." Since she'd guessed, he'd be damned if he'd deny it. Then, because she didn't argue, he got defensive. "Don't worry," he said. "You don't have to come along. Never having lived anywhere else, you don't know how this place stinks." Still no resistance. "Well, you coming or not?"

"How we gonna' get there?"

"A train to Indianapolis. A bus from there."

"How much will it cost?"

"Never mind. The hundred will cover it." He was looking right at her as he mentioned the money, so he saw the color drain from her face. "Jesus!" he yelled. "You didn't lose it?"

"No."

"You cashed the check, didn't you?"

"I cashed the check," she said.

What a scare. The dope had shaved another few months off his life. He took his work pants from the closet and folded them for packing.

"Samson." It was a voice she'd never used before.

"What?"

"Can't we wait eleven weeks?"

"Eleven weeks!" Leave it to her to pick such a nice round figure. "We have to get out of here before morning."

"Why?"

"I'll tell you all about it later." He placed his two shirts on top of the pants. "Go get a suitcase from Mrs. Fitz'!"

She headed toward the door obediently, then stopped and faced him.

"Hurry up." He snapped his fingers to emphasize it.

"Samson," she said. "You can run away from here. But you can't run away from yourself."

No. Any line but that. Another time, he would have sent a sizzling left hook within a millimeter of her nose. But not tonight.

"Get the suitcase!" he thundered.

"I haven't got the hundred dollars," she said.

His fear of her losing the money gone, it took a while for this to register.

"You haven't got it?"

She shook her head and spread her feet wide in preparation for the onslaught. Shillitoe looked at her round, vacant eyes, debating how best to reach behind them to her slowly throbbing brain. The calm and understanding parent seemed as good a role as any. He sat down and motioned for her to take the other chair. She backed away from it suspiciously.

"Sit down."

"Hitting me ain't gonna' get the dough back," she said.

"I won't hit you," he promised. "Just sit down."

When she finally did, he enunciated each syllable distinctly.

"You do not have the money?"

"No."

"And how come you do not have it?"

"I paid for something."

"I assume you can take back what you paid for and the money will be refunded." She shook her head. "You mean you don't know what refunded means?"

"Aw, stop talking to me like I'm a kid."

"I'm not talking to you like you're a kid," he said. "I'm talking to you like you're a moron. Now, what the hell did you do with my hundred bucks?"

"I gave it to Doctor Wren."

Suddenly she looked like Beverly. He was afraid to ask, but he had to.

"He's an obstetrician?"

She was laughing. *She* thought it was funny. He almost clouted her, but he caught on in time. She was *kidding* him;

partly on the square, of course. She hoped that, by delaying their departure, she could get him to change his mind. He joined in her laughter, reaching casually for her handbag.

"Naw," said Rhoda. "He's a psychiatrist."

"Oh?" He went along with the game. "And did someone tell you that a psychiatrist could cure stupidity?"

"I didn't spend the money on me." Her laugh was gone, replaced by the cringing, ominous tone of a self-sacrificer. Something was wrong.

He pulled the handbag open and rummaged inside—comb, mirror, keys, two dimes, three pennies and a subway token, a yellowing magazine page and newspaper clipping and a few movie ticket stubs. No hundred dollars. He was about to tear the lining open when she spoke again.

"I paid for eleven treatments in advance."

"You did?" Desperately he stalled off realizing what he knew was so. "Well, let's see," he said. "You wouldn't use my money to pay for Herschel's going to a psychiatrist. And you wouldn't spend it on Mrs. Fitzgerald. And you said it isn't for your own much-needed shock treatment. So, who else is there?"

"You."

He slung the bag hard toward the top of her head. But she ducked and leapt across the room.

"You need help," she said. "Everybody knows it but you."

She jumped expertly behind the chairs and table as he stalked her. Another trick she'd learned from those goddam westerns.

"Samson, going back to Indiana ain't gonna' help. You can run away from here, but you can't run away from yourself."

He just missed with a roundhouse right and skinned his knuckles on the wall.

"It's true, Samson, honest. Doctor Wren's helped lots of writers with your problem. He's terrific. Wait till you go to him, you'll see."

She was within range for a fast one-two, but he didn't throw it. No sense knocking her unconscious before he discovered where to find the bastard who'd conned her. Again he resorted to the monosyllables, pretending to be impressed with her Doctor Wren's qualifications until she supplied the address on East Seventy-eighth Street.

The rest was loud and blurred. He told her to get packed while he went to get the money back. It was when he had the door open that she pointed out that Doctor Wren wouldn't be at his office until ten in the morning. Then he blew up. His slamming of the door made Fitzgerald sound like a ninety-seven-pound weakling. The walls were closing in on him, the escape hatch was narrowing. The odds on the cop catching up with him had jumped to even-money. But, for the present, all he could do was remind her of a few things: that her brain was smaller than a pygmy's gene, that he needed her like he needed a double-hernia, that his only consolation was that she'd never got her mitts on e.e.cummings. They were all things he'd told her before. But this time she knew he meant them and this made her fight back.

She said she'd had enough of being his punching bag. She worked all day and took care of him besides. She called him helpless, ungrateful and mean. He countered with clodhopper and granite-head. She stood up to these, so he added that she was a waitress. This burned her, but not enough. He wanted to hurt her, to make her look as purple as he knew he did. So when she said he was hard up, he said it was nothing a *woman* couldn't remedy. That produced the desired color in her cheeks, even a shade deeper than he'd hoped for. She was hopping now, fumbling for a weapon to retaliate with. And she chose his poetry.

"You think it's so important," she sneered. "To other people poetry is nothing but a hobby. It's a pastime. It's something for sissies."

She realized she'd gone too far and made a dive for the door. The closest movable object was the briefcase. He grabbed it and, swinging it like a hammer-thrower, went after her. She was out on the landing before he got within range.

"Don't you touch her!"

It was Mrs. Fitz' pointing at him from the foot of the stairs with the fireman giving her moral support.

"A hobby, is it?" He swung the heavy case, planning its arc just short of Rhoda's face. All the dope had to do was stand still. But she didn't trust him. Her orthopedic shoes took one too many backward steps and he stood helpless as she somersaulted down, banging from wall to banister until she landed on top of the Fitzgeralds. With all the arms and legs thrashing around he couldn't tell if she was dead.

"We're through, Samson!" She had survived. "You've hit me for the last time. Go on back to Indiana. I don't care."

Her hoarse bleacherite voice drove away any self-reproach. He marched down the stairs into the hail of hissing accusations and threats from the Fitzgeralds. They had reached their feet and weren't going to give way until he growled at them and brandished the briefcase again. Then they stepped on each other getting out of his way.

"Ya' lousy bully," groaned Rhoda.

He vaulted over her still fallen form and continued out of the building.

He had nowhere to go. But there'd been many other nights in all seasons when he'd wandered around the city aimlessly, waiting for the Aryan sun to rise and give direction to his steps. Always the same village sights, the same junkies at their rendezvous points, the same refugees from the Ivy League doing the jazz joints, the same salami and liverwurst in the delicatessen windows, the same bent hawklike grubbers in the newsstands pasted together with the same magazine covers. He was convinced that all hymns to the exciting, turbulent metropolis were composed by advanced cases of St. Vitus dance.

His path was generally north so that morning would find him near Seventy-eighth Street. By then he'd have to have a plan for getting his money back. He tried to think of one now, but the scene he had just left behind kept intruding. Rhoda, fallen and hurt, flickered into Rhoda beaming encouragement into Rhoda cleaning and cooking and lugging him home from the Double-Deuce into the grand finale of Rhoda proffering her love.

Somehow the movies hadn't corrupted this. Her offerings were not the ingenue type, the uvular calisthenics of hungry sparrows (tongue on palate, place! One, two! One, two!), seeking only self to please, alternating hourly when it alteration found. Each side street he walked displayed plenty of these; hanging in doorways like sides of beef, in parked cars crawling down each other's underwear and in basement rooms sacrificing privacy for a breath of air. One Puerto Rican couple, framed by an open window, seemed fairly original so he stopped and watched a while.

No, Rhoda was different from the others. She was a real woman; not the fragile, Emily Dickinson kind of real woman but in the tradition of Pocahontas and Jacataqua and Catherine Blake. Rhoda was incapable of just going through the motions on any aspect of life. Considering how much she concentrated on frying an egg, it was amazing that the intensity of her love hadn't decomposed him. He knew he had shared it with no one and this metachronism was oddly pleasing. The purity of anyone who hadn't been schooled was frightening to most people but exhilarating to him. Rhoda had no preconceived notions, no borrowed attitudes. She responded to everything according to her own senses. True, they were limited senses, poetically speaking, but they were still much more penetrating and reliable than if they'd been corseted by sophistication. If only he'd got around to mentioning these things to her, just once. Then his dart at her womanhood wouldn't have pierced her skin.

It started to rain, as hard as it was sudden, the drops forming sharp arrowheads on the tar paving. In Cob City, a thunderstorm washed clean the humid air. But here, it merely whipped it into a thicker meringue. Island of soot and saliva. He couldn't get away from it soon enough. He hunched his shoulders and splashed on. The wet Harris tweed began to weigh like a suit of chain mail and the briefcase listed him forty-five degrees toward whichever hand carried it. The rain slowed to a steady, all-night tempo. Many saloons and diners offered shelter, but each reminded him of Rhoda in one way or another so he plodded on. He had no conscious destination. But when the street sign numbered seventy-eight, he turned left and a few minutes later he stood before a dark blue door with the number Rhoda had given him. He stared at it, trying to recall its significance. Then, for the first time, the full meaning of what Rhoda had done hit him.

Completely on her own, without even so much as mentioning it to him, she had decided that he needed a psychiatrist. *She* had decided it! She who had trouble deciding whether to see something with Bette Davis or something else with John Wayne. And a minute ago he'd been likening her to Pocahontas. What a likeness. Did Pocahontas take John Smith's beads and trinkets to some high-priced medicine man to buy him a lot of foot stomping and feather shaking? If she had, she'd still be trying to get Captain Smith's rapier out of her rectum. But this was exactly what Rhoda had taken it upon herself to do. What gall! He still couldn't quite believe it. Even if he hadn't needed the money to escape, even if it had been her own money, it would be incredible. But it was *his* money, his hard earned hundred dollars. Of course, she didn't think it was hard to earn. She didn't think it was tough to read poetry to a hallful of intake valves with maternal tendencies. She didn't think anything connected with poetry was difficult. What had she called it? His hobby! His pastime! For a moment he considered retracing his steps and walloping her again.

The rain, stepping up its volume again, dissuaded him. He moved back in the shallow doorway for protection but the slant of the rain had him zeroed in. He wasn't aware of having pushed down on the handle behind him and his suit absorbed another coating of water before he realized the blue door was open.

The streetlamp outlined the narrow hall and the second door which it led to. Inside this one, his hand found the wall switch. The small room he stood in was apparently the cell of a secretary or receptionist. The rug he was dripping on was thick enough for sleep if nothing better appeared. Another door, another light switch and he was in a large office. The couch caught his attention first. It looked spindly but bouncing on it proved this deceptive, and in the dark its seasick fabric wouldn't bother him. He stood up and looked around the room. Some joint. If anyone did arrive in a good mood it wouldn't last long here. He moved to the bookshelves. Several volumes had the name Akers on their bindings—*Anxiety in the Atomic Age, New Hope for Neurotics, Fallacies of Fear*—Alliteration Akers was certainly prolific.

Then, *Sexual Gratification for Married Lovers* caught his eye and he glanced through the chapter headings: "How to compensate for age differences," "Preliminary play," "Frequency and timing," "Accepted occidental positions," "Reaching erotic maturity together." The carefully worded instructions that followed told him he'd been doing everything wrong.

None of the other books interested him. A few were medical, but most were conversation arsenals for the compact liberal majority; handsomely jacketed stuff on anthropology, women, the Dead Sea Scrolls and America's class consciousness. Doctor Wren was obviously a member in good standing of one of the intellectual book clubs.

The cabinet beneath the bookshelves was better, yielding a delightful array of bottles. He had already started on the Scotch when he noticed the Napoleon brandy. Twenty years old! Doctor Wren had some taste after all. Shillitoe took a mouthful and spotted the painting at the same time so he wasn't sure which made him gag. Someone had had a nervous breakdown while holding a paintbrush. What a mess. He moved behind the desk and sat down with his back toward the thing. The desk top before him told him that Doctor Wren was a very orderly man—an expensive pen stand, a silver letter opener with the initials O. W., a desk calendar with notations he couldn't make out, a matching clock which was nearing the face of midnight and, most of all, the machine. The machine was for dictation. He'd seen several like it in offices he'd shampooed but he'd never been left alone with one long enough to experiment. Its controls looked complicated, but Shillitoe had always found that, except for cameras and flash attachments, mechanical aptitude was just a matter of reading signs. So the button marked OFF-ON was turned ON, and the button labeled RECORD was pushed down and, sure enough, the box started humming.

He lifted the microphone from its cradle and didn't have to grope long for something to say. There was only one thing to be said to Doctor Wren.

"You owe me one hundred dollars." Then, in case he hadn't sounded tough enough, he added, "You mercenary bastard." He was going to pile on a colorful opinion of grifters who bled the last penny from working women. But the combination of rainwater, brandy and indignation clogged his throat and his recording wound up in a racking catarrh.

When that subsided and he pressed the next button, a celluloid cylinder jumped out. It took some doing to get it back in. Then he pushed the button marked PLAY, the recorder hummed again and a voice began to crackle.

"File three, three, one, one," it said, "the patient's second visit." It was a solemn and matter-of-fact voice, the kind that droned irrelevant information during opera broadcasts. "Today the patient gave expression to . . . no, strike that. Today it became apparent that a variable pathogenic influence has been exerted on the patient by a single act of deception. Latent guilt has manifested itself in mild hysteria and in attempts to find a scapegoat, casting the blame first on her husband, then on her seducer. The patient has evidenced a degree of pleasure in suffering. This raises the question of whether her deception was an act of ego or altruism. I have asked the patient to have her husband call. It is possible that he has a subconscious desire to reproach his wife by encouraging her infidelity, so I shall try to ascertain any signs of lack of virility on his part."

"You owe me one hundred dollars." He had never heard his own voice before and didn't recognize it immediately, not until it said "you mercenary bastard." He decided he didn't sound too bad, less ponderous than Doctor Wren, but his diction was sloppy. He was also dissatisfied with his wording. He should have recorded a verbal assault to rank alongside *J'accuse*.

Shillitoe took a glass from the cabinet and filled it with brandy. Then he searched the desk drawers until one yielded a full cigarette box, also silver and initialed. One of the drawers had proved to be locked, so he used the silver letter opener to pry it open. The reason for the lock was immediately evident. Dozens of cylinders like the one he'd just played were lined up in neat rows. Each undoubtedly contained similar juicy morsels about virility and infidelity and latent attempts to find scapegoats.

Shillitoe settled back in the desk chair, lit a cigarette, sipped his brandy and began to play the celluloid transcriptions.

Chapter Twelve

MIDWAY in his speech Oliver said that psychiatrists held the only possible existing key to genius and evil. And, as he said the word *key* he remembered that when he left the office he hadn't locked the front door. Oliver took a slow sip of water and went on. The rest of the speech, though, was delivered almost by rote. While Oliver heard his own voice saying the things he'd planned to say, he was seeing his office door ajar, the office itself ransacked, the desk drawers pulled out and the record cylinders containing his patients' case histories gone. He would have to notify the police and, as luck would have it, some snoopy reporter would be hanging around the precinct station and the name Oliver Wren would strike a familiar chord. It wouldn't take much doing for the reporter to dig up the article in the *Times*. What a natural for the tabloid press. NEW PRESIDENT OF PARAPRAXES SOCIETY HAS CONFIDENTIAL FILES STOLEN. Only they'd phrase it more flippantly. TOP ANALYST LOSES ANALYSES, or something like that. And he'd be a laughingstock. Of course, it wasn't too likely that someone would try to break in the one time he failed to lock the door. But it could happen.

Oliver knew he was obligated to his patients to get back to the office just as soon as he could. But he couldn't rush off as soon as his speech was finished. He had to stand there receiving congratulatory comments and making appropriate remarks while each passing minute increased the chances of disaster. Then, out of the blue, Lydia bit his ear lobe. Her teeth were sharp, too. He tried to make rubbing his ear a gesture of contemplation and was relieved when his fingers showed no blood. All he needed right now was a bleeding ear lobe. Lydia's eyes had the moist glow they always had when she was moved. He was glad she'd been impressed by his speech, but couldn't help wishing she'd demonstrated her approval in a less carnivorous way.

The chatter dwindled slowly and it was after midnight when they finally got away. Freddie Voegler always drove too fast. But tonight, with Lydia wedged between them on the front seat, Freddie seemed to slow down in order to be caught by every red light.

"Oliver," said Freddie, "I have a confession to make."

"What's that?"

"When you accepted that new patient today, I couldn't understand it. I thought to myself, could it be that Oliver will take anybody as long as they pay? But your speech tonight makes everything clear. I apologize."

Oliver couldn't follow what Freddie was talking about. He was trying to remember if he had locked the desk drawer with the transcriptions.

"Evil and genius," Freddie said. "Absolutely. A very apt hypothesis. Not exactly original, of course."

"Is too," said Lydia thickly.

"No, darling," corrected Freddie. "Hoffmantle, in nineteen twenty-eight, made the same—"

"Stole it from Oliver."

"Darling, in nineteen twenty-eight, Oliver was only . . . how old were you, Oliver?" Freddie braked the Jaguar as another light turned red. "Anyway, do you think this new one will give you some answers?"

"Which new one?" asked Oliver impatiently.

"You know. The one with the wife with the press clippings. What was his name?"

"Shillitoe."

"Shillitoe," repeated Lydia, "from Indiana."

"No, darling," said Freddie. "This one's straight from Greenwich Village."

"Hoffmantle's a crook," mumbled Lydia.

Oliver noticed that when Voegler moved the gear shift he rubbed his hand against Lydia's knee. That explained the stopping at every light.

"Can't you drive a little faster, Frederic?"

"The streets are wet from the rain."

"So what?"

"So, would you like us to have an accident with what we've been drinking on our breath?"

It was the first time Voegler had ever outreasoned him and Oliver didn't like it. Lydia's chanting "The life you save may be Albert Schweitzer's" didn't help either. Then he realized he had broken one of his strictest rules. He had mentioned a patient by name in Lydia's presence.

"Of course," said Freddie, "if the man is a *phallus thaumaturgist,* you'll be wasting your time."

"Shut up," said Oliver.

"Huh?"

Freddie's hurt surprise made Oliver soften his speech.

"Lydia isn't concerned with what goes on in my practice."

"In nineteen twenty-eight he was eleven," said Lydia drowsily.

When they reached the building, Freddie wanted to come up for a nightcap. But Lydia announced flatly that she was going straight to bed. Oliver begged off too. Then, at the elevator, he told her he had to go to the office for a few minutes.

"You're not going to work tonight?"

"No. I forgot something. I won't be long."

"Sexy-Prexy." She looped her arms around his neck and hung on him. "Love me to bits."

"I'll be back in twenty minutes."

"No!" She shouted it so it resounded through the lobby. He could see the elevator indicator flicking from five to four to three.

"Sssh." He unlocked her arms and tried to get her to stand upright. But she toppled backwards and grabbed on to his lapels.

"Oliver Vincent Wren," she proclaimed. "Do you know I am bursting with admiration for you? What a speech! What a goddam speech! What the hell was it about?"

She began to giggle and he tried again to hush her as the elevator door opened. Frank, the night operator, stood waiting.

"You missed a great speech, Frank," said Lydia. She bowed and made a sweeping gesture from Oliver to the elevator car. "After you, Doctor Oliver Wren."

"You go on up, darling," he said. "I'll be right back."

"Don't go!" She threw herself on him as if he was threatening to walk out for good.

"Stop it." Of all the ridiculous places to make a scene. "Come on now," he coaxed. "Go upstairs."

"Don't work tonight." She tightened her noose on his neck and nuzzled her face against his. Then she bit his ear lobe again.

This time it really hurt and he jumped back out of her clutches. Frank seemed to be enjoying the routine. No doubt the whole building staff would get a full description of it.

"Frank, take Mrs. Wren up." Then, to Lydia, "I'll be back shortly."

He didn't look back until he reached the street door. She hadn't moved. She still stood at the elevator staring after him. She was upset and needlessly. He should have explained why he had to go to the office. But it was too late now. He'd tell her what it was all about when he got back.

As he neared the office, his concern about it seemed exaggerated. The street was perfectly quiet, the neighboring buildings peacefully darkened for the night. The blue door faced him reassuringly, as tightly closed as ever. But he was right. He hadn't locked it. He reached inside to press down the catch and the light from the reception room slashed his eyes. He reached out wildly for an explanation. He had left the light on himself. A policeman, making his rounds, had noticed the outside door open and had gone in to check. Bueler had come back for something. Then he heard the voice coming from the consulting room. His first impulse was to rush outside and telephone the police. But the police could mean publicity. He saw again the thick black headlines making fun of him. There was only one alternative. Oliver moved silently to the consulting room door and inched it open.

Someone was sitting in *his* chair, with his big feet on *his* desk, drinking *his* brandy and listening to *his* voice.

"What the hell are you doing?"

The man turned his head slowly and looked at him. Cocky beggar. He still didn't take his feet off the desk.

"Doctor Wren?"

"Who are you?"

"Are you Doctor Wren?"

"Yes."

"You owe me one hundred dollars."

Furious as he was, Oliver tried to think who he could possibly owe money to. Then he saw the open desk drawer and the jumble of cylinders.

At least they hadn't been stolen. But the relief passed quickly and he felt a tremendous urge to grab the intruder and hit him right in his insolent face. That could mean the wrong kind of publicity, too. A psychiatrist had about as much freedom as a political candidate. Oliver became increasingly aware of his own voice coming from the machine. It was speaking of self-punishment mechanisms, of a patient forcing herself into inextricable dilemmas. He recognized the case history as Joanna Russell's, the transcription as the one he'd dictated after she told him about becoming pregnant from a Negro. He quickly switched off the machine and took out the cylinder.

"Have you found these interesting?" he asked.

"Not very."

There was neither fear nor guilt in the man's behavior. He didn't seem to care that he'd been caught in the midst of an indecent as well as a criminal act. The lack of shame and conscience was a clue. The hundred dollars didn't fit exactly, but Oliver thought it worth a stab.

"Mr. Shillitoe?"

The grained, unshaven face told him he'd hit the mark.

"Mr. Samson Shillitoe, isn't it?"

"That's right."

"Your figure's a little off," Oliver said. "The amount your wife gave me was one hundred and ten dollars."

"You sure?"

"I'm sure."

"Better still," said Shillitoe. "Just hand it over and I'll beat it."

Oliver began straightening up the transcriptions in the drawer. As he bent over to pick up one on the floor he realized how tired he was. It had been a difficult day like all days and the banquet had been an extra strain. He was in no mood for his first encounter with Samson Shillitoe. But the heavyset man in the rain-matted tweed suit wouldn't care about that. Oliver took a more scrutinizing look at Shillitoe's face. Beneath the thick black hair and wide forehead, the eyebrows were heavy, hanging forward and down like awnings, and the eyes themselves were bloodshot. The nose was large and the mouth was too full. Altogether, it could be a sensuous face or a cruel one or both.

"I gave your wife my word that under no conditions would the money be given to you."

"Suppose I use force."

"You may. But you'll find me quite expert at Judo." As if to illustrate this, Oliver grabbed the ankle farthest from him and swept Shillitoe's feet off the desk.

"You would be," muttered Shillitoe.

Oliver picked up his desk calendar.

"How about three weeks from Wednesday at ten-thirty?"

"What for?"

"Your first appointment."

"Cut the crap and give me back the dough."

"Absolutely not!"

Shillitoe stared at him as if first realizing he was serious.

"You need money that much?" he asked.

"No. I just think you need me."

"You're an idiot."

Oliver was surprised to find that the word stung, then decided it was because of its professional connotation.

"Frankly, Shillitoe, I didn't want you as a patient. My schedule's overloaded as it is and I've been neglecting my work at the public clinic. However, certain things your wife told me about you changed my mind."

"What things?"

"Oh, about your poetry. And your being so irresistible to women."

"Flattery won't help you." Shillitoe slammed his hand on the desk top and stood up. He was taller than Wren had thought, and broad, too. If he did try to use force to get the money back, it would be a struggle.

"Give me the dough, Wren. Wash your hands of me. I'll just corrupt you. I'll make you hate yourself, your wife, your children—"

Oliver couldn't resist breaking in.

"How do you know I have any children?"

Shillitoe looked at him appraisingly.

"Your type always has one boy and one girl."

Oliver tried to remember if there was a picture of Scott and Dierdre in one of the desk drawers. Shillitoe stood grinning at him. He knew he'd guessed right about the children. Oliver took the bottle of brandy from the desk and returned it to the cabinet before speaking again.

"As I was saying, I believe I can help you."

"Idiot!"

Again the word rankled. And Oliver waited for the feeling to go before speaking.

"Mr. Shillitoe, you appear too intelligent to stoop to name-calling. But if it helps establish a rapport between us, you may call me an idiot or anything else. Let me say, though, I've had just about all types of patients, the woman who claims I try to rape her, the Southerner who holds me personally responsible for the Civil War, the wealthy kleptomaniac, the exhibitionist . . ."

"And the white girl who's been knocked up by a black boy."

"Yes," admitted Oliver, "that too."

"But never a poet who is irresistible to women."

"That's right. You complete my repertoire."

"Who you trying to kid?" Shillitoe catapulted to the middle of the room and spun around as if modeling the brown tweed suit. "Look," he said, "stick to mending scratches of disappointment and forget about me. One of the rules of a tragic time is that real enemies must never meet in open combat."

"I don't think we are enemies," said Oliver quietly.

"You don't? You who protect what is while I envision what can be? You who find sickness where I find the fierce abstractions of desire? You who make a profit out of human misery while I command the moon and make melodies in a warehouse of gutturals? And you don't think we're enemies!"

In spite of his weariness, Oliver was excited. It was too early to be sure, but Shillitoe could be just the challenge he'd been looking for. The passion was there with no apparent inhibitions. The man had fire, the fire that Alben Parker lacked. Oliver watched him striding about the room continuing to flaunt celestial achievements. Then, when Shillitoe paused for breath, he slammed him back to earth.

"And is that why women won't let you alone?"

Shillitoe considered the question for a few seconds.

"I guess so. They know I'm capable of beauty more real and lasting than theirs, and the bitches can't stand that. But they're cunning little beasts. I no sooner get a few simple words into circulation than one of them pipes up, 'Oh, I've never met anyone like you before.' It never fails. My ego springs to life. Hopes and discontents pour out like she's pressed my tongue with a spoon. And she eggs me on. 'Oh, I could listen to you forever.' Hah! Do you know what a woman means by forever? At the most twenty minutes. Then she moves in, her cholorophylled breath puffing my words back into my lungs. What the hell can I do?"

Oliver's mind had drifted away from Shillitoe's harangue. The mention of women had reminded him of Lydia. He'd told her he'd be back in twenty minutes and more than that had already elapsed. He thought of how she looked, standing in the lobby as he walked away.

"Perhaps we can get started next week," he said.

"You're not really serious?"

"Mr. Shillitoe," said Oliver firmly. "I've heard enough to

know that you have a good mind, alert, inquisitive, alive. There's absolutely no reason for your despair."

"Despair?"

"Yes. I know all about the moods you've been having. Your wife didn't strike me as a person who panics easily. So, if she's afraid of your attempting suicide, you must have given her good reason."

Shillitoe clapped his hand to his forehead.

"What else has that lamebrain been telling you?"

"Mrs. Shillitoe told me you've been unable to write lately, that you've been despondent, that—"

"Women!" bellowed Shillitoe. "From the second you're born they tickle your toes and chuck you under the chin until you laugh yourself sick. Somewhere they got the stupid idea that laughter means happiness. So if a man walks around thinking, they call him suicidal. And you encourage them."

The distortion of the argument fascinated Oliver. Shillitoe was obviously prepared to pounce upon any thread of the conversation and weave it into his own garish tapestry. There was some dissociation in his logic, but surprisingly little considering the pitch he maintained. Watching him posture and gesticulate, the masochistic plating seemed inches thick. And, as was always the case with paranoia, Shillitoe would be able to cite countless and specific instances to prove that the world persecuted all its inhabitants and especially him. But that was all part of the challenge. Oliver was convinced now that he had finally found a patient who would fight him each step of the way and who had the intelligence and resourcefulness to fight well. It would require every ounce of his ingenuity and experience to deal with Shillitoe. The passive technique of sitting and listening often worked even with highly excitable types. But it wouldn't work this time. If he was to get Shillitoe to come to him at appointed hours he would have to dominate their relationship right from the start. He would have to be more open and direct with Shillitoe than Shillitoe was pretending to be with him.

"Sit down, Mr. Shillitoe," he ordered.

"Why?" Shillitoe broke off a diatribe in mid-air.

"Sit down!"

He didn't, nor did Oliver expect him to. But at least he'd been silenced momentarily.

"Mr. Shillitoe, do you have any idea how dull most of my patients are?"

"Of course."

"Then you know that I don't often get a case that's very challenging. I've never treated a real artist, for example. But I've wanted to. I suppose every psychiatrist has wanted to. We all wonder, could we have controlled the rages of Beethoven, the criminality of Rimbaud? Could we have cured Poe of drink or saved Van Gogh's right ear? Probably, more than any other, the riddle of art nags at us. What is this poetry you throw yourself into? Why do you write it? Is it a neurotic catharsis or a kernel of health? These are the questions. But where can we get the answers except from the artist himself? And I needn't point out to you that the true artist isn't easy to recognize in his own time. So all we can do is hope for an accident. Science is very dependent on accidents, you know. Now, bear with me a little longer. Your wife came here by mistake about ten days ago—accident number one. Tonight I left the door unlocked—accident number two. And here you are, the rebel, the man who commands the moon, uncontrollable, dissipated, perhaps depraved—"

"Just a minute!"

"Maybe you're a phony," Oliver went on. "But maybe not. I have no choice but to take the time to find out. And, after all, I have been paid in advance."

He calculated the last line to spring Shillitoe's temper and it didn't fail.

"Give me my dough!"

"No."

He was sure Shillitoe would swing his right fist and tensed, ready to block the blow. But Shillitoe suddenly put both hands over his face and the voice that filtered through them was plaintive and confiding.

"Look, Wren. I'm in a jam with the cops. I need the money to get out of town for a while. Honest."

Oliver had expected a more original story. The fact that this was so worn out, so third-rate melodrama, made him think it might be true. Certainly Shillitoe was capable of inventing something better. But then, Shillitoe might be a step ahead of him, reasoning that a cliché would stand a better chance of being accepted.

"You don't believe me, do you?" asked Shillitoe.

"No, I don't."

"Give me the money anyway."

"That's out of the question," Oliver said.

"Okay." Shillitoe stopped massaging his face and sauntered over to the couch. "Then we may as well get started."

He jumped up and landed on the couch flat on his back. The wrought-iron legs spread under his weight, and for a moment Oliver was sure they would snap.

"Let's go," chirped Shillitoe.

"What do you think you're doing now?"

"I'm waiting for my money's worth."

"Do you know what time it is?"

They both glanced at the clock on the desk. It was twenty past one.

"Look," said Shillitoe, "you fleeced my poor, hard-working wife out of a hundred and ten dollars. Either you give it back or you start earning it right now."

Some of the fatigue had left Oliver, but he wished his mind was clearer. Lydia skipped across it briefly. Twenty past one already. She'd be livid over his staying out. But he'd face that tomorrow. This was more urgent. Oliver moved toward the couch but as he did, Shillitoe flipped over on his stomach and wrapped his arms around it in a fierce bear hug.

"Don't get any ideas about Judo," he warned. "If I get thrown out of here, this goes with me."

"All right." Oliver sat down in his listening chair and waited.

"Is this the correct position?" asked Shillitoe.

"Whatever's most comfortable for you."

Shillitoe rolled over on his side and propped on one elbow. "What do we do now?"

"Just talk."

"About what?"

"Anything you choose."

"Me?"

"Preferably."

"Good. Where should I start? You interested in the prenatal part?"

"I'm interested in all the parts."

Shillitoe turned and lay full on his back, staring at the ceiling. Oliver looked past him, trying not to anticipate what would be said. He knew Shillitoe was trying to wear out his patience with these oblique parries. What Shillitoe didn't know was that evasions often revealed more than direct statements.

"Chapter one," began Shillitoe. "My mother groaned, my father wept, into the dangerous world I leapt."

"I'd rather hear one of your poems than one of Blake's," said Oliver.

"One day a soldier wandered into his garden and Blake threw him out because the uniform ruined the beauty of the flowers. So they hauled him into court and charged him with being a traitor. They had minds like yours."

"Keep talking," said Oliver.

"Don't you do anything?"

"Mr. Shillitoe, do you really insist on starting at this ungodly hour?"

"Absolutely."

Oliver couldn't prevent the sigh from underlining his instructions.

"Then continue talking about anything that comes to mind."

"One hundred and ten dollars," said Shillitoe.

"Feel free to give full expression to any image, no matter how unreal or fleeting it may seem. Remember, nothing honestly expressed is ridiculous or vulgar or obscene. Nothing said here can possibly embarrass you."

The instructions sounded flat and dull to his own ears. He had grown accustomed to saying the same words in the same order to all new patients. Oliver resolved to phrase them differently in the future.

"I can't think of anything to talk about," said Shillitoe. Then, when Oliver refused to break the long silence, "I could tell you about the dream I had last night."

"Go ahead."

Shillitoe wiggled about the couch and finally settled on raising his knees and letting his arms fall over the sides.

"It was the morning of a mighty day," he said somberly. "A day of crisis and of ultimate hope for human nature. Then, a mysterious eclipse. Somewhere a battle was traveling through all its stages. I had the power to decide it. And yet the weight of twenty Atlantics were upon me. I lay inactive. Then, like a chorus, the passion deepened."

As Shillitoe's voice surged on, Oliver's mind stuck to the phrase about twenty Atlantics. He tried to recall where he'd heard it before.

"Darkness and light," moaned Shillitoe. "Tempests and human faces and female forms. There was a sigh, like the caves of hell sighed when the incestuous mother uttered the name of death. The sound reverberated, everlasting farewell, and again."

The incestuous mother was another clue. Oliver tried memory association to place it.

"Farewell," called Shillitoe faintly. "Farewell." Then he opened one eye and aimed it at Oliver. "What does my dream mean?"

"I don't know."

"You don't know? If you can't even interpret a simple dream, I demand my money back."

"You said you would tell me a dream you'd had."

"I just did."

"I'm afraid De Quincey dreamed it first," smiled Oliver. "It *was* one of his opium dreams, wasn't it?"

"I paraphrased it a little," sulked Shillitoe.

"Not enough to disguise it."

"But I did dream it last night." Shillitoe sat up and stretched. "I often dream about things I've read. One night last year, I dreamt most of *War and Peace*. Naturally I overslept."

It was a feeble joke. Shillitoe was obviously grasping at straws now, so there was no sense in prolonging the interview. Oliver got up and went to his desk.

"I'm listed in the phone book under Physicians," he said. "If you'll phone tomorrow, Miss Bueler will arrange your next appointment."

"You're kidding," said Shillitoe.

"I've never been more serious," replied Oliver. "Good night."

"Good night? And where the hell am I supposed to go?"

"Go home." Oliver made it an order.

"You weren't paying attention, friend."

"I thought we were enemies."

"Don't start getting clever," snarled Shillitoe. "You weren't paying attention to what I said before about the cops. My place is where they'll look first."

"Mrs. Shillitoe warned me that you'd make up some story to get the money back."

"Listen," said Shillitoe, "if you won't believe anything I say I'm changing psychiatrists. Give me my money back."

"No."

"You've got to give me the money or get me a place to sleep. All this probing of my subconscious has worn me out."

Oliver studied him a long time before answering. The bravura was fluttering out. Shillitoe's face now looked older and worn. The bulky suit, still damp, was creased and misshapen, the shirt collar frayed, the shoes cracked and their laces knotted in several places. They all contributed to the picture of a man on the run.

"Why do the police want you?"

"It's kind of complicated."

"Tell me about it next visit," said Oliver.

"If the cops get their hands on me, there won't be a next visit."

Oliver hadn't thought of that aspect. The possibility that Shillitoe was telling the truth became a larger factor.

"Let me stay here," said Shillitoe.

"Here?" Oliver looked around quickly for an excuse and saw the record cylinders. "So you can listen to the rest of those case histories?"

"I've already played them all," said Shillitoe.

The utter impudence of the man made indignation futile. Oliver weighed the situation. Shillitoe did look incapable of doing anything but sleep. Chances were he wouldn't disturb anything more than he already had.

"My secretary gets here at nine forty-five," he said.

"I'll be out by nine-thirty," promised Shillitoe.

"You give me your solemn word?"

"So help me."

"And you won't touch anything in the room?"

"I respect other people's property."

Oliver looked again at the drawer filled with transcriptions. The wise thing to do was to take them back to the apartment with him. But, having been asked to display confidence in the patient, he couldn't refuse. It was a risk, but one he had to take. Besides, the transcriptions contained no names, only code numbers.

"All right," Oliver said. "But be sure you're out of here by nine-thirty."

He went to the door to the reception room and Shillitoe started peeling off the damp tweed suit.

"And you'll telephone my secretary for an appointment?"

"Sure."

"I mean it."

"Don't worry," said Shillitoe. "I'll be back. I want that hundred and ten bucks."

"It's only a hundred now," said Oliver. "You've just had your first visit."

Chapter Thirteen

AFTER making it to the window and warning them to stop, Chester Quirk got into his clothes. He was still doubled over when he opened the door and pushed through the people in the hall. But in spite of the pain he scoured the neighborhood for a dozen blocks before giving up and returning to the Station. There he typed "no arrests" on his report sheet with two forefingers, switched to pen and ink and carefully worded a request for immediate reassignment to tunnel duty. Chester knew that, if granted, the transfer wouldn't go into effect for forty-eight hours. And that gave him enough time to track down his assailant.

Chester had one clue, the camera. It was unmistakably a very expensive one, and the sticker on its back told him the name and address of the photography store it came from. The sticker also told him that the camera wasn't stolen property, because a thief would have been sure to remove it. Chester thanked the Lord for giving him the strength to hang on to the camera and began looking through the books of mug shots for the face he'd never forget.

By six-thirty all the faces looked alike. Chester washed his face with cold water, stopped for a cheese Danish and a cup of coffee at the corner Rudley's, then set off for the photography store. The owner showed up promptly at eight, making so much noise unlocking the iron trellis gate covering the door that he couldn't hear what Chester was saying. Chester followed him inside, but the man kept an arm's length away.

"It's a beautiful piece of equipment," he kept repeating. "Maybe you didn't know how to work it."

It was only after Chester produced his badge that the owner listened to him and took the camera to read its serial number. Then he trudged off to a filing cabinet at the rear of the store. The bill of sale he brought back exceeded Chester's highest hopes. Not only did it tell him his attacker's name and address, but also those of his employer and a personal reference. As the owner began a minute inspection of the camera, Chester promised to return the bill of sale as soon as he'd finished with it.

"Some bill of sale," the owner called after him. "Some way to start the day."

Timing was important now and a taxi was the fastest way to cut across town to the address on First Avenue. Chester couldn't sit back and relax as the sign on the back of the driver's seat said. There was a hot, giant searchlight extending from the dull ache in his groin to the dirty rat named Shillitoe. The buildings down each side of the street were dim gray blurs. Shadows of people going to work tightroped along their fuzzy edges. Only Shillitoe's face was sharply defined, so sharply that Chester could see every pore of its rotten skin. The more Chester concentrated on it, the more positive he was that it was a lousy wop who had kicked him.

"What are ya', funny or somethin'?" snarled the cab driver.

"Huh?" Chester tried to look at him but Shillitoe's face was in the way.

"If ya' wan' the U. N. , say 'the U. N.' Don' give me street numbers that was tore down ten years ago."

Chester leaned to look up at the glass façade and almost fell out the cab door when the uniformed guard opened it. He started to say there was some mistake when it dawned on him that there might not be. The strange assortment of characters entering the building hinted that he might have stumbled into something big. Shillitoe could easily be a foreign spy using the United Nations as a cover. What better explanation for why such a seedy character had such an expensive camera? He'd need it to photograph secret documents. Chester racked his brain to figure out how the prostitute fitted into the scheme.

"Eighty-five on the meter," said the cab driver.

Chester handed him a dollar and hurried past the guard, who kept eying his chin. Chester wished he'd shaved at the Station. All the full-grown beards in the lobby made him extra conscious of the light fuzz on his face. He fingered his badge for comfort and wandered around until he found an information desk.

The dark girl behind it had a blob of red paint between her eyebrows. She looked up at him mysteriously.

"Where can I find Mr. Shillitoe?"

"Which section is he in?"

"Dunno'," said Chester.

"Which legation is he with?"

"Dunno'."

The dark girl looked up at him sadly.

"Shillitoe? Shillitoe?" she repeated. "It could be a name of the Middle East."

"I think he's Italian," said Chester.

She opened a huge directory and ran a pointed fingernail down the page.

"He is not with the Italian delegation," she said. "Are you sure he is not from the Middle East?"

"I ain't sure," admitted Chester.

"Perhaps Iraqi," she said and ran her fingernail down another page. "No," she sighed, "not Iraqi. Perhaps Lebanese." Again she consulted the directory and clucked in dismay. "There is no Lebanese Mr. Shillitoe. Could he be from Saudi Arabia?"

"I don't think so," stammered Chester and backed away.

She watched him with those sad eyes until he ducked around a corner. The hollow, bustling sounds in the lobby added to his confusion. The winding stairway in mid-air and the giant xylophone hanging from the ceiling made him feel small and insignificant. A pretty, uniformed guide stopped and told him the tours didn't begin until ten o'clock. Somehow, when she said this, the place no longer seemed secretive and mysterious. Chester concentrated with all his might and concluded that Shillitoe had given the camera store a phony address.

He consulted the bill of sale again. W. Moscowitz of Acme Carpet Cleaning and R. Butter of Waverly Place could both be bum steers. If they were he was dead. But there was only one way to find out. The Acme address was closer and easier to get to by bus.

"Shillitoe?" asked the fat Jew, Moscowitz. "How do you spell such a name?"

Chester spelled it out as it was lettered on the bill of sale.

"What kind of *mishugah* name is that?" asked Moscowitz.

"I think it's Middle Eastern," said Chester.

"And you think I'd let him work for me? An Arab yet? What's the matter with you? You haven't read the papers for twenty years? A member of the Irgun I ain't. But Benedict Arnold I ain't either."

"I don't know where he's from," said Chester. "He's a tall guy."

"Everybody works for me is short," said Moscowitz.

"He said he worked for you."

"I'm responsible for what some Arab says?"

"Maybe he knows you," persisted Chester. "He's dark and he's got a big nose."

"So!" screamed Moscowitz. "That's why you come to me.

You think only people of Jewish faith have big noses? Go look at a picture of Abraham Lincoln. And don't come in my store with your anti-Semitic remarks. I don't care if you are the police. Out! Out!"

By the time Chester reached the address on Waverly Place he was afraid that everything on the bill of sale was false. But the dingy narrow stairway with the loose bannister raised his spirits. It had the right kind of lousy smell, and the cardboard sign that read MOOT MAGAZINE looked like a blind. He tapped on the door, ready to call out "Western Union." But he couldn't hear anyone inside. He pounded on the door heavily. Still no sound. He stepped back to propel himself at it when a floorboard creaked overhead and a door upstairs was opened.

"Who is it?" The voice was high and sleepy.

"I'm looking for R. Butter," he called.

Slippers clacked on the stairs and a guy with light hair peeked over the bannister. His robe was black with big white and yellow flowers, and he had nothing on under it.

"Oh, hello," he sang out, pulling the robe closed and coming down the rest of the stairs.

Chester felt uneasy and made his questions short and snappy. Did Mr. Butter know a Mr. Shillitoe? Yes, he knew the beast, unfortunately. Did Mr. Butter know where Mr. Shillitoe lived? Yes, if one could call that living.

Then he supplied the address. Chester shook Mr. Butter's hand and kept thanking him for his valuable assistance until he got his hand free.

"You're entirely welcome," smiled Mr. Butter. "If there's *anything* else I can do for you, I'll be here all day."

Whenever Rhoda moved she hurt all over. But she still would have gone to work if it hadn't been for her right ankle. She'd twisted it when she landed at the foot of the stairs and, in spite of Mrs. Fitzgerald keeping the cold compresses coming all night, it went right on swelling. Though Rhoda made several tries, she couldn't put any weight on it. So, finally, she asked Mrs. Fitzgerald to call Herschel and tell him she wouldn't be in.

Mrs. Fitzgerald was having a regular field day. Samson's clobbering her was just what she'd predicted. And being able to play nurse again had really gone to her head. Rhoda kept telling her to go downstairs and get some sleep. She wanted to think about what had happened. She wanted to go over every word of the fight in her mind just to make sure Samson had made worse cracks than she had. But Mrs. Fitzgerald kept gabbing about people who'd neglected sprained ankles and wound up with amputated legs. Even when she went down to telephone Herschel for her, she was only gone long enough for Rhoda to get to the part where she told Samson she didn't have the money. Then Mrs. Fitzgerald was back fussing around again until her dopey husband came out in the hall yelling for his breakfast.

Rhoda hopped from the bed to the kitchen and heated a kettle of water. Cold compresses might be okay for a hangover, but Rhoda's mother had always soaked anything swollen in hot water and Epsom salts. Rhoda had barely immersed her foot in the steaming pail when there was a light knock on the door.

Her first thought was of how hurt Mrs. Fitzgerald would be to see what she was doing. But Mrs. Fitzgerald wouldn't knock. It was Samson who was out there, rapping so gently because he was ashamed of what he'd done.

"Okay, come on in," called Rhoda, putting on a scolding look. This was set so firmly that she wasn't able to remove it immediately when the door opened and the big, good-looking young guy with the crew cut came in.

Rhoda was used to aspiring writers coming around to see Samson. They'd read a poem of his in *Moot* or the *Antioch Review* or someplace or even have come across a copy of *Hellebore* and they'd want to talk to him about poetry. Though she'd never said it, she'd always thought Samson was wrong to throw them out. She knew he didn't think that poetry was something you could talk about. But, still, manners were manners.

"You want Mr. Shillitoe?" she asked.

"Yes." The young guy kept fidgeting and looking at the bedroom door.

"He ain't here," said Rhoda. "Besides, he won't talk to you. He never discusses his work."

"Where can I find him? It's important."

"You're wasting your time," said Rhoda. "He'll just tell you to go home and work on your poetry."

Knowing how sensitive young writers could be, she'd tried to let him down easy. But she must have sounded too sympathetic or done something to give him the wrong idea. Why else would he suddenly run into the bedroom?

"Hey! Get out'a there."

He came out like she said, but she didn't like the way he looked at her. Rhoda reached for the pail. If he had any ideas he was going to swallow a lot of hot Epsom salts. Then she saw the badge he held out.

It didn't scare her. If anything had happened *to* Samson, the cop wouldn't be looking for him.

"What did he do?"

"Nothing."

"You picked a dumb time for a social call," she said.

Then he explained about having good news for Samson. He wouldn't say what it was but kind of hinted there was money involved. Rhoda thought of the last letter she'd seen from Daniel K. Papp. The shyster was getting real nasty. The only possible chance of Samson paying what was owing would be an unexpected inheritance or something. And if he did get a sudden windfall, he'd have to let her off the hook about the hundred and ten dollars.

Rhoda had a pretty good idea where Samson was. It was almost nine-thirty, so a million-to-one he was parked on Doctor Wren's doorstep waiting for the office to open. She was about to say this when she noticed the cop biting his upper lip. Samson always told her to watch people's faces. If they were tense, he always said, be careful. And if this guy's wasn't tense, nobody's was.

"I don't know where he is," said Rhoda.

"But where could he be?"

"I ain't got the faintest idea."

As usual, Samson was right. The cop started making with the threats if she didn't tell him. He had good news for Samson all right—like cowboys loved Indians.

"You got a search warrant?" demanded Rhoda.

She could tell by his stalling that he didn't.

"Then get off my premises." She stood on her good foot and picked up the pail. She didn't put it down until she could no longer hear his steps on the stairs.

When Mrs. Fitzgerald came in, Rhoda was all dressed except for her right shoe, and her eyes were teared up from trying to get that on. Mrs. Fitzgerald tried to pull the shoe out of her hands until Rhoda sent her flying by letting go of it. Then Mrs. Fitzgerald kept yammering behind her as Rhoda hopped down the stairs one at a time on her left foot. Every stair practically killed her. It felt like all the blood in her body was being pressed into her bad ankle, and on one hop when the bare, swollen foot banged against the wall she yelled out loud.

At each landing she almost gave up. All the apartments in the building except theirs had telephones and she could call Doctor Wren from any of them. But every apartment also had at least one pair of big ears and one big mouth. Rhoda thrust out her chin and hopped on.

The nearest place with a phone booth was the cigar store. Rhoda was halfway to its red La Primadora sign when she looked back and caught the cop ducking behind a garbage truck. She hadn't figured on his tailing her. The trick now was to get to the phone booth and make the call before he could come in and trace who she was talking to. Luckily, she'd called Doctor Wren's office so many times she knew the number by heart and wouldn't have to look it up.

By the time she got inside the store, Rhoda's whole left leg was rubbery and numbing. She paused to recharge her strength and looked out to see how close the cop was.

The jerk was way back at the front stoop with Mrs. Fitzgerald! Rhoda almost laughed. If Mrs. Fitzgerald knew how she was helping Samson by waylaying the cop, she wouldn't be standing there jawing at him.

The phone booth was only four or five more hops away. But something about the way Mrs. Fitzgerald's head was wagging and the crew cut nodding back kept Rhoda from moving. Then, as the cop started writing in a notebook, it all started coming back to her. She remembered the pain of the long miserable night and the sinking sick feeling that her life was coming apart. She remembered Mrs. Fitzgerald's face poking at her and asking over and over about why Samson had hit her. And as she watched the cop pocket his notebook and take off down the street, Rhoda remembered how she'd given Mrs. Fitzgerald *all* the details.

Now it all depended on Doctor Wren. If only he was in his office to answer the phone. And if only Samson was there so Doctor Wren could warn him before the cop showed up. Rhoda's hand trembled as she deposited the dime and dialed the number. Then the ringing began.

Chapter Fourteen

LEONARD TUPPERMAN stood staring at the dark blue door. He had tested the handle and found it locked, so now he had an excuse. He had gone to Doctor Wren's office just as they'd made him promise he would. Was it his fault if the doctor wasn't in? "What was I supposed to do?" he'd ask Evelyn and the old bloodsucker. "You want I should stand there waiting all morning while my business goes to hell?" What could his mother-in-law say to that? Plenty. "Did you ring the bell?" That would be the first thing she'd ask. And if he admitted he hadn't, she'd look at the ceiling and flap her arms. "He's never heard of doorbells," she'd say. "Evelyn, unscrew all the light bulbs. With your husband, candles are still the newest rage."

Leonard punched the button next to the door and heard it buzz faintly inside. He pushed back his shoulders, adjusted the knot of his tie and pulled the handkerchief a little further out of his breast pocket. He wanted Doctor Wren to see right away that he was dealing with a neat, self-confident man of the business world who would put up with no nonsense. Leonard knew how important a first impression was. That was the mistake he'd made with Evelyn and her mother. If he'd put his foot down right from the start he'd have spared himself all the heartburns. Now it was too late. Last night proved that. He'd sworn never to set foot in their Doctor Wren's office. For three days and three nights he'd sworn it. But as soon as he'd walked in the door last night, he'd known his time was up. Evelyn couldn't even look at him, let alone swing the ax herself. Her wonderful mother had to do it for her.

"You have an appointment tomorrow morning with Doctor Wren." She made sure to say it just as he was swallowing.

After he'd stopped choking on the smoked salmon, he'd refused point blank. In spite of all their screaming and begging and arguing, he'd held out until two o'clock in the morning. So, what did it get him?

On the other side of the door a telephone began to ring. Gradually, Leonard's shoulders resumed their slump. No one was answering the phone. No one was there after all. Now that he'd rung the bell he really had a leg to stand on. He turned to scoot back to his Buick. "And how many *times* did you ring?" He could hear Mrs. Fish's cross-examination. "Once? Did you hear that, Evelyn? Once! And you can just imagine how hard he rang. You'd need a magnifying glass to hear it."

Leonard pressed the button furiously and, this time, the buzzer sounded much louder. Then his heart stopped. The telephone was still ringing, but now there was another noise. Someone was fiddling with the door. Leonard tried to straighten his shoulders again, but they wouldn't go back. He tried to look cool and calm, but his whole face felt full of novocain. He watched, petrified, as the door handle turned.

Leonard had a clear picture of the psychiatrist in his mind. He'd overheard Evelyn enough times telling her mother and her zombie sister about how handsome he was. Even allowing for her crazy ideas of what was handsome, the unshaven lummox with the baggy suit was all wrong.

"Doctor Wren?"

"No," said the lummox.

He went back inside and Leonard didn't know what else to do but follow. It was the telephone on the desk in the small office that was ringing. As they went through, the lummox said, "Aw, shut up" and knocked it off its cradle. Then he went on into the big room. Leonard decided he was a janitor. Now he had proof that he'd been there. He wondered if the janitor would write out a note to that effect. There was plenty of paper strewn all over the desk. If he could just get one piece and write the note himself the janitor would undoubtedly sign it, especially if he gave him a few cents for his trouble. Leonard started to make his offer and reached for a sheet of the paper. Lucky he had fast reflexes. The way the janitor's fist came down, it could have broken all his fingers.

"If you could spare a small piece," said Leonard, but the janitor ignored him. "You work for Doctor Wren?" The man shook his head and went on writing. Watching him, the suspicion grew larger and larger until Leonard had to ask, "Are you one of his patients?"

"What?" The bloodshot eyes focused on him as if seeing him for the first time.

"Are you one of his patients?" repeated Leonard.

"In a way."

"What's wrong with you?"

"Nothing," said the lunatic. "What's wrong with you?"

"I'm not a patient," said Leonard defensively.

"Don't be smug!" The lunatic snapped his fingers under Leonard's nose. "It could happen just like that."

Leonard jumped back from the snapping fingers toward the door. He'd been foolish to antagonize this man. The best way to deal with a lunatic was to be friendly.

"My name's Tupperman," he said.

"Mine's Swinburne," said the lunatic.

"Do you know when Doctor Wren will be here?"

"What time's your appointment?"

"I don't have one."

"Gotta' have an appointment," said Swinburne. He seemed to forget Leonard's presence again and started reading over and crossing out some of the things he'd been writing.

"The doctor told my wife to have me stop in," said Leonard, and suddenly Swinburne was pointing at him with his right finger and pounding his left palm against his own forehead.

"Three, two, four, one," he muttered. "No, that was the pregnant dame. Three, three, two, one was the bed wetter. Wait a minute. It'll come to me. There was the queer, the playwright, the embezzler." Leonard was at the door again when Swinburne smiled happily. "Three, three, one, one," he called.

"It was nice meeting you," said Leonard.

"Hold it!" Leonard stopped dead in his tracks. "I think you'd better wait."

"You know what he wants to see me for?"

"Don't worry," said Swinburne cheerfully. It was easy for him to be cheerful. He was nuts.

"Maybe Evelyn's got something serious," said Leonard.

"Evelyns never get anything serious." Swinburne leaned back in the swivel chair thoughtfully and bit a pencil in half. "I think he called it a variable pathogenic influence," he said.

"How do you know what he called it?" asked Leonard.

Instead of answering, Swinburne pulled open a desk drawer and rummaged inside. Then he held up a little roll of brown plastic.

"What's that?"

"I think this is your wife," said Swinburne. But when Leonard reached for the piece of plastic he held it out of his reach.

"Let me have it," demanded Leonard. "It's my wife."

"Providing she's number three, three, one, one."

"How should I know what number she is?"

"We have to be sure," said Swinburne. "You wouldn't want to hear confidential information about another man's wife, would you?"

"Sure," said Leonard.

Swinburne gave him a reproving look. "What's Evelyn like?" he asked.

"About this tall." Leonard adjusted the flat of his hand at the point of his nose. "And plump." He racked his brain for an identification mark. "And she's got a birthmark right here," he said, pointing to the bottom rib on his right side.

"You're a big help," said Swinburne, again moving the roll of plastic away as Leonard lunged for it. "Wait a minute." He seemed to have an idea. "How many times has she been here?"

"Twice."

"And she's got mild hysteria?"

"It ain't so mild," said Leonard.

"And she blames you?"

"For everything."

"It must be her," said Swinburne and, with a grand gesture, he presented Leonard with the plastic. Leonard examined it carefully. Not knowing what else to do, he ran his fingernail across its grooves.

"Dope! You'll scratch it. Here." Swinburne took it back, shoved it in a machine on the desk and pushed a button.

"You owe me one hundred dollars, you mercenary bastard," said the machine.

"That's me," said Swinburne, switching it off. "I had it in backwards." He reversed the roll of plastic and turned the machine on again. Sure enough, a voice was saying the numbers three, three, one, one.

"Today," it went on, "it became apparent that a variable pathogenic influence has been exerted on the patient by a single act of deception."

"What did I tell you?" bragged Swinburne.

"Latent guilt," said the machine, "has manifested itself in mild hysteria and in attempts to find a scapegoat, casting the blame first on her husband, then on her seducer."

Having listened to all the cylinders, Shillitoe was bored with Wren's carefully modulated voice and all the antiseptic descriptions of piddling little problems. So, as little Tupperman glued his ear to the dictation machine, Shillitoe started gathering together the manuscript he'd been working on all night. The pages formed a thick wad. He'd made a strong beginning to the poem. Now he had to find another quiet place and keep going. He was trying to think where when he noticed that Tupperman's face was turning a strange color.

"I have asked the patient to have her husband call," said the machine. "It is possible that he has a subconscious desire to reproach his wife by encouraging her infidelity, so I shall try to ascertain any signs of lack of virility on his part."

"I guess that's why he wanted to see you," explained Shillitoe.

"You owe me one hundred dollars, you mercenary bastard," said the machine.

Shillitoe reached over to turn it off, but little Tupperman got to it first, punching all its buttons fiercely until the cylinder shot out across the desk. Tupperman pounced on it.

"He's going to ascertain my . . . my . . ." The last word wouldn't come out. "She's trying to kill me," he yelled. "She and her mother and her screwy sister."

"Don't take it so hard," said Shillitoe. But little Tupperman wouldn't be soothed.

"My business, my insurance, everything!" he screamed. "That's what they want. That's all I mean to them. And she, she, she, she . . ." As if to cure the stuttering, Tupperman flung the cylinder to the floor with all his might and started jumping on it with both feet. Shillitoe watched in amazement as each jump seemed to take the little man closer to the ceiling.

"How's this for a sign of virility," Tupperman called out boastfully. Then he grabbed his left side and slumped across the couch. Shillitoe went over and shifted him around to a sitting position.

"Some life," groaned Tupperman. "Everything she wanted, I gave her. A diamond wrist watch she wanted, a full-length mink coat she wanted, not a jacket but full length. Then she wants a psychiatrist so I give her a psychiatrist. Did I ever complain about the twenty-five dollars a visit?"

"Twenty-five!" said Shillitoe. "He's only charging me ten."

"Ten?"

Shillitoe wasn't sure the little man would win his fight for breath.

"Got to get home," wheezed Tupperman. "Car outside . . . I'll give her . . . sneaking behind my back . . . a prostitute yet . . . are you satisfied, now, Mrs. Fish?"

"Who's Mrs. Fish?"

"Buick . . . out front . . . help me."

Shillitoe looked at the stack of paper containing the beginning of the poem. Tupperman was in no shape to drive, but taking him home meant more time wasted.

"Please," begged Tupperman.

Cursing his own softheartedness, Shillitoe dragged him outside to the car.

"Very grateful," Tupperman slobbered. "Do you a favor someday. Get you a good deal on an apartment. How many rooms you need?"

"One's enough," said Shillitoe. "But I've got to have it today."

"You've got it. We'll throw out Norma. You take her room."

Shillitoe was ready to concede that justice hadn't deserted the world completely. He'd done a good deed and was being rewarded for it just like the Boy Scout manual said. Tough shit for Norma, but she couldn't need the room as much as he did. Indeed, things were beginning to look up. Segments of the poem lay in the brief case beside him and the Buick was about to move him another lap ahead of the cop. He started the car, but a cab pulled up. Wren or his secretary or his first sucker of the day was arriving. Shillitoe looked to see who, then dove under the steering wheel.

"Drop something?" asked Tupperman.

Shillitoe peeked over the bottom frame of the windshield. The cop who wasn't Applegarth was only a few feet away, going from the cab to the blue door. The cab started up and Shillitoe, still low in his seat, drove after it.

"Look out!" yelled Tupperman.

The cab had stopped to pick up a passenger. Not enough time to hit the brakes. Shillitoe shut his eyes and aimed the Buick at the narrow alley between the cab and the parked cars, waiting for the crunch of metal. When it didn't come, he looked to Tupperman for a compliment on his driving skill, but Tupperman's teeth were chattering too much for him to speak.

Shillitoe slowed to turn up Fifth Avenue and, glancing back, saw the cop still waiting at Wren's door. The bastard had made good time. Shillitoe told himself he'd grossly underestimated his pursuer. No, it wasn't that. He'd expected the cop to get from the camera to Rhoda. His mistake was in overestimating Rhoda.

Rhoda! Shillitoe recalled having had kind thoughts about her the previous night. When was he going to learn that any woman, no matter how much on his side she claimed to be, was against him? Rhoda might be the best of the lot but she was still a member of Predatory, Inc. Worse than that, she belonged to the American chapter. To her ancient appraising mechanisms, forged of a million years of laundering and broth stirring, had been added all the refinements of capitalistic technology. She'd been spared the liberal arts courses that the Beverlys had, but she was still a woman. Women! In and out, swell and discharge, blunt-headed monsters impersonating the tide, acrid nipples filleting the young so that none would rise above the chimney tops of home-sweet-home. Just as all the perfume in Paris couldn't fully hide the odor nature had bequeathed them, nothing could counteract their unholy bent to get night and day tidy and shipshape. Treat them equally and they tear you apart. He must never forget that again. He must never lose sight of Rhoda's ultimate purpose. She was determined to make a husband out of him. He could be an errant stud and sow a few wild oats. But every day with her brought him closer to the ninth reel when he was supposed to see the light just before the light went out forever and "The End" appeared prophetically on the screen.

As he backed into a parking space on Riverside Drive, Tupperman regained his voice.

"Shouldn't inflict such relatives on a friend," he kept apologizing. "But I need you for a witness. Remember every word we heard on that machine. They'll call me a liar, but you back me up, won't you?"

The lobby Shillitoe followed him into was the standard imitation Versailles. The hall on the eleventh floor was thick with clashing breakfast odors. And the heavily bolstered and cushioned living room with the beige wall-to-wall carpet was still stupefied from last night's television shows.

"Evelyn! Don't try to hide from me." He could hear Tupperman invading the other rooms. "Evelyn! I know everything. Come out and look me in the eye."

Shillitoe finally found him in the bathroom, searching for Evelyn behind the shower curtain.

"Which room is mine?" he asked.

"They've all left," cried Tupperman. "They knew I'd find out the truth. They know I'm smarter than their fancy doctor. Don't forget to tell them what you told me. Tell them he only charged you ten dollars a visit. I'll get a refund if I have to sue. *Sssh!*" He cocked his head and his ears stiffened. Somewhere in the apartment a door was opening. Tupperman raced toward the sound and Shillitoe went after him.

The boy with all his joints in the wrong places kept staring at him while answering Tupperman's questions. Evelyn, it seemed, was with Gramma and Auntie Norma. Shillitoe swore that if the lunk didn't aim his leaky eyes somewhere else, he'd kick him.

"Go outside and play," ordered Tupperman.

"I just came in," complained the snotty kid.

"Then go play in your room. And keep the door closed."

The deformity gangled off, turning to look at Shillitoe once more and stumbling over his own feet.

"That's my son," said Tupperman proudly.

"Which room can I use?" persisted Shillitoe.

Tupperman led him to a small bedroom.

"If any of Norma's stuff is in the way, throw it out," he said. "And when she comes back, we'll throw her out."

Shillitoe pulled a chair over to the vanity and pushed the bottles and jars aside to make work space.

"How could *she* find a seducer?" asked Tupperman. "So many pretty girls are walking around."

Shillitoe shrugged and found the place where he'd finished writing. Minutes later, snatching at the loose thread where he'd left the poem, he was dimly aware of Tupperman going out of the room. Then he caught the thread and swung high above himself and time and distortion. The first part of the poem dealt with the struggle to speak naturally. To dramatize this he was using dialogues between the expanses of narrative, snatches and glimmerings plucked from off-guard tongues lapsing into authentic rhythms before regaining the starched, unwieldy sounds they'd been taught to make, sounds like the charivari coming from the other room.

Shillitoe clung to the words unraveling from him. A unit was forming, a design emerging from the rubbish-bin odds and ends, from the nondescript phlegm of bitten lips, discarded blind third eyes and soaked explosives. The words welded the structure, cadenced on the paper, to the traffic and the machines and the dense, unresolving mass of particulars. Images from the past came alive, flickering up like dilated hooded cobras to the fakir's flute. It was *right.* He knew it was. The painful ease had no jagged edges, no splintered bones. The only flaw was the harshness of the voices crowding in on the scene and ripping apart its texture. Shillitoe put down his pencil and listened. One voice was Tupperman's. The others belonged to women. He went to shut them out, but before he could close the bedroom door, Tupperman rushed in.

"Come on." His voice was high and wavering. "I told you they'd say I was making it up. You tell them what you heard."

"Maybe she isn't three, three, one, one," said Shillitoe. But Tupperman wasn't listening. He was running back into the battle with new accusations. There'd be no peace until victory was his.

By the time Shillitoe gathered up his manuscript and reached the living room, Tupperman was again retreating. A white-haired wisp of a woman was whirring at him like an eggbeater, whipping out an endless list of crimes he had committed as a husband. Tupperman turned to Shillitoe beseechingly.

"Mr. Swinburne, tell them! Tell them what you heard with your own ears. Don't hold anything back."

The white-haired bantamweight turned to him, the taker-on of all comers sizing up her next opponent. Shillitoe sidestepped around her and the other two women came into his view. One was a rake with glasses that looked like two swordfish were fencing across the bridge of her nose. The other was roly-poly, and obviously the errant wife. Though her back was to him, he could see every layer of her fat shaking in shame.

"A bum!" snorted the old woman. She shoved her face right up under his and sniffed, her sharp little beak wrinkling to match the rest of her skin. "You pick up a bum and give him a few dollars to back up your lies. Your heart's as black as the ace of diamonds!"

Shillitoe was about to breathe on her to prove his sobriety when he heard the yipe. Roly-poly had turned around.

"Evelyn! What's the matter?"

Evelyn tried to answer her mother, her mouth opening and closing rapidly, but no sound came out. Then she collapsed on the beige carpet like a parachute and Tupperman and the two women were patting her cheeks and rubbing her wrists.

Shillitoe headed for the front door, but the goddam kid barred his way.

"I know who you are." As Shillitoe put his hand over the goofy face and shoved it aside, it went on talking. "You were here to clean our carpets."

The midmorning glaze covered him. Inside, the neglected coals of the poem were turning black. He tried to think of a quiet place where he might gently fan them back to life. The public library reading room would douse the fire completely, and the park along Riverside Drive was filled with New York's happy children—happy as divinity students with the clap. Even from where he stood he could hear their squeals as they played self-consciously under the supervision of mammies, Northern style (time and a half for singing spirituals).

Reluctantly, he let the poem slip from his mind. It was time to plan beyond the immediate hour. He couldn't be sure how far behind the cop's meaty hand was. Soon, Daniel K. Papp would set another arm of the law into motion against him. There was no sense in returning to his job. Tabs were probably being kept on Moscowitz. No chance of returning to Rhoda either. Every road was blocked, except the one to Cob City. Ben might not be overjoyed to see him again, but he couldn't refuse shelter. And in the rooms above the garage he could work undisturbed.

Cob City had to be his destination and the sooner he started toward it the better. He emptied his pants pocket and counted the coins. Forty-eight cents. Hitchhiking meant living on salted peanuts and the generosity of whoever gave him lifts for the next twenty-four hours. His stomach rumbled at the prospect and he realized that almost that much time had already elapsed since his last meal. Still, in the past, he'd gone as long as five days without eating. He started walking downtown, figuring that the entrance to the Lincoln Tunnel would be the best place to thumb the first ride. For several blocks the sun taunted him through the gauzy air and the briefcase banged a bruise below his knee. How much inequity could a man stand? There he was, starving, doomed to beg his way homeward while the hundred dollars, *his* hundred dollars, earned unforgivably by degrading that most precious to him, was nestling in Doctor Wren's alligator skin wallet. That hundred dollars meant an air-conditioned railroad coach. It meant food, no matter how burnt and toughened in the dining car kitchen, and coffee brewed from the waiter's sweat, sloshing the sides of the cup. It meant a shave and his suit pressed downstairs in the terminal at Indianapolis. It meant walking, not crawling into Ben's garage.

Shillitoe ducked into the nearest drugstore and looked under "Physicians" in the phone book for Wren's number. He couldn't give up the money without one more try. As the line buzzed he took hope. After a night's sleep, Wren might have a change of heart. Or Rhoda might have contacted him and called the whole thing off.

The secretary's voice, chilly and constipated, insisted on trying to give him an appointment. As Shillitoe called it names, it became even more austere. Doctor Wren was not there but he had told her that Mr. Shillitoe would probably call. How about Thursday, the nineteenth at four o'clock?

"Up yours!" Shillitoe hung up and tried to pull his next move out of his scalp.

The open telephone directory gave him the idea. Two numbers were listed opposite Doctor Oliver Wren, one belonging to his residence on Park Avenue. Shillitoe dialed this one and spread his thumb and forefinger inside his mouth to sound like a professional man. The voice answering this time was also lifeless, but softer.

"This is Doctor Arlington Robinson," said Shillitoe. "We are trying to locate Doctor Wren. It is an emergency." He was prepared for the woman to suggest that he call the doctor's office. "We did," he said. "But there is no answer. Meanwhile, one of the doctor's patients is dying from the consumption of seventy-three sleeping tablets. Would you have any idea where Doctor Wren could be?" At last he'd got a rise out of one of Wren's harem. The woman sounded completely unnerved. "We are stomach-pumping like mad," said Shillitoe. "But where is Doctor Wren?"

She wasn't sure. But she thought the doctor had said something about the interviews being held today. He had to deposit another nickel before she found the address and telephone number.

"Good news," said Shillitoe. "The patient is up and doing a soft shoe."

The address she'd given him was back across town. Shillitoe debated whether to spend fifteen of his remaining twenty-three cents on a bus, then voted against it. By the time he reached the square white building with PARAPRAXES SOCIETY on its polished bronze plate, his throat was parched and a pinwheel was spinning at the base of his skull.

The next obstacle was the receptionist. He began to extemporize a new emergency, but when he mentioned Doctor Wren, she just pointed her pencil at a stairway and said, "Third floor."

Count on the Parapraxes Society to have the steepest steps in New York. The last fourteen were taken backwards and sitting down, the two-ton briefcase hoisted behind him one step at a time. Then there were two more, only the door; and, inside it, three men and two women hunched in large leather armchairs.

"Is Doctor Wren here?" asked Shillitoe.

None of the five acknowledged him, but a muscular, tattooed gorilla bounded up behind him with a pad and pencil and asked his name.

"Chaucer," said Shillitoe.

"First initial?"

"*G*, of course."

"Just have a seat, Mr. Chaucer." The paw gripping his arm and leading him to the empty chair seemed unnecessarily firm.

"I have to see Doctor Wren."

"Don't worry, you will," grinned the gorilla and planted himself solidly in front of the door.

Doctor Lothar Massey dabbed the already damp handkerchief along the back of his neck, then used it to conceal a yawn. None of the five applicants were of any interest to him. The first four had been depressives, one manic and three involutional, and though the one being interviewed now was a schizophrenic, the schizophrenia was chronic. What Massey was looking for was just the opposite; frequent, but short, periods of catatonic excitement plus an indefinite pattern of hallucinations.

Doctor Lothar Massey knew that performing prefrontal lobotomies was not the way to become famous. Moniz had gained himself a place in history that way, and Freeman and Watts and Fiamberti and maybe one or two others. Of course, they had all operated almost exclusively on chronic cases and, except for Fiamberti, they had all performed it the old way, through a small burr hole on each side of the skull. But refinements and perfections never got the attention of first efforts, however crude the first efforts may have been. Not that the use of the transorbital leukotome was any longer unique. It was merely that control data was still insufficient on transorbital surgery performed on the acute schizophrenic. This was the essential area of scientific knowledge to which Massey had decided to devote himself. He had made that decision more than a year ago, thirteen months to be exact. Thirteen months during which he had performed numerous lobotomies, but only three on acute schizophrenics, and the results from these three were of little value. The first two patients underwent extreme transitions in behavior, one of them lapsing into a somewhat vegetative condition. Massey had then concluded that seven centimeters was too deep an insertion to make in the orbital plate. On the third patient he reduced it a centimeter and the reaction was much more encouraging. However, the patient lost sphincter control and on the sixty-third day following the operation had an epileptic seizure.

Massey was now convinced that the answer lay in five centimeters. True, this deep an insertion could produce varied and sometimes strange effects on non-schizoids. But his scientific instinct told him it was the cure for acute schizophrenia and he was determined to substantiate this instinct with a body of case reports. This, he was discovering more and more, would not be easy. Ideally, two thirds of the patients would have to be men. And in a matriarchal society, increasing in conformity daily, catatonic excitement in the male was becoming almost as extinct as the dodo.

The interview room of the Parapraxes Board was one of the many places where Massey carried on his search. To date it had rendered him nothing. His colleagues seemed to handle only mild depressives and melancholics. At least these were the only patients they ever presented for admission to Para Park. Massey took off his rimless glasses and rested his eyes, writing off today's session as another complete waste of time. Then, the fifth applicant was excused and the sixth was ushered in.

"Mister Chaucer," announced Arnold, the attendant from Para Park. And, tilting his head in turn toward each doctor seated around the table, he introduced Abelson, Voegler, Wren, Milicent Akers and, almost as an afterthought, Massey.

Massey hardly noticed the slight. He was watching Oliver Wren. Wren had jumped to his feet when the applicant was shown in. Massey shoved his glasses back on and took a closer look at the man with Arnold. He almost said "ah" aloud. This wasn't another one of the sulking carcasses they'd been questioning the past two hours. This was a wild wolf of a man, scurvy, unshaven, ready to lash out; Dempsey off the freight car, the chain gang escapee stumbling from the swamp.

"I want to see you," the applicant stormed at Wren.

"Sit down, please," said Arnold, pushing the man toward a chair, and not too gently.

Massey could have told Arnold this was a mistake. You don't push someone who might be an acute schizophrenic unless you're willing to risk a severe reaction. Massey nodded in satisfaction as the fist crunched against Arnold's eye.

"That's all, Arnold!" Wren quickly took over the situation before the fight could get out of hand.

Massey noticed Arnold muttering something toward the applicant before he went out. But Chaucer just made an obscene gesture.

"A point of order before we begin," said Wren. "There's been a slight error. The applicant's name is not Chaucer, but Shillitoe. First initial, *S*."

Massey saw Voegler throw Wren a knowing look as all the doctors made the correction on their notepads.

"Now, Mr. Shillitoe," began Doctor Akers, "we'd like to ask you a few questions about yourself."

"Some other time," snapped Shillitoe.

"We only want to help you," said Abelson.

"Help me?" snorted Shillitoe. "My wife's been in an accident. I don't have a place to live. My ten-year-old daughter doesn't know where her next meal's coming from. And he won't give me back my money." The accusing finger pointed at Wren again, turning all the heads toward him.

"Mr. Shillitoe has a tendency to exaggerate," smiled Wren.

"You going to return that hundred bucks?"

"All right," said Wren, "after you answer some questions."

"You heard him. You're all witnesses." Shillitoe was elated now.

"Tell me," grunted Voegler, "do you like people?"

"Which ones?"

"Let me put it another way," broke in Abelson.

"I'll do my own putting," said Voegler. "Now, Mr. Shillitoe, let us pretend you are in the middle of the ocean. A big wave strikes the ship."

"Which ship?"

"Any ship," conceded Voegler. "Say, the *Queen Elizabeth.*"

"I went overseas on the *Mauretania.*"

"All right. A big wave strikes the *Mauretania* and one of your fellow passengers is knocked overboard. But so is something else, some material possession very precious to you."

"Something I'm writing?"

"Good, good," said Voegler. "A manuscript you have been working on for many years. Now which would you save, it or the passenger?"

Massey could see that the applicant was becoming absorbed in the problem Voegler posed. It had obviously appealed to one of his hallucinations.

"Well?" Voegler was getting impatient.

"Who did you say this other guy was?"

"Just a fellow passenger," said Voegler. "A hypothetical person."

"A *hypothetical* person?"

"Why don't we make him an actual person?" smiled Doctor Akers. "A real man is drowning."

"Who?" asked Shillitoe.

"What's the difference, who?" exploded Voegler.

"Doctor Voegler," interrupted Milicent Akers sweetly, "why don't we suppose that the passenger is an average man, John C. Jones from ah . . . Pocatello, Idaho? He's married and has ah . . . four children."

"All right," said Voegler, glaring at the applicant. "So, would you save him or your manuscript?"

"Neither," said Shillitoe.

"Neither?" Now Milicent Akers was upset. "Are you sure you wouldn't save your writing?"

"My writing exists, independent of me. It has to stand by itself and it has to swim for itself."

"And you definitely wouldn't save your fellow passenger?" asked Abelson.

"John C. Jones," added Milicent helpfully.

"Save him? Save an average man? You want me to deny him a spectacular death so he can go on being average until his average arteries harden in an average way. The poor bastard would never forgive me. Neither would his wife and . . . how many kids did you say he had?"

Perfect, thought Massey. The fantasies were there all right, and the quick temper and rough impatience were obviously due to an oversensitive thalamus. Massey wished Milicent Akers and Voegler would wind up their silly analagous questioning. They didn't begin to understand the patient's sickness. Abelson was more wary, but actually just as dense. Wren was keeping out of the interview completely. Shillitoe was obviously his patient. How else would he have known the man's real name?

"Tell me," said Voegler, "this flippant tone I detect in you. You do not take us very seriously. Psychotherapy does not impress you."

Shillitoe started picking his fingernails. The questions were obviously beginning to bore him.

"Isn't that so?" Voegler wasn't to be put off.

"Never thought about it," said Shillitoe, puffing up his cheeks and releasing the air with a popping sound. "I suppose you've been pretty clever."

"Thank you." Voegler almost managed the smile.

"The names aren't bad. Who thought of them?"

"What names?"

"You know, schizophrenia—sounds like a skiing resort in the Swiss Alps, or get thirty miles to the gallon with the new twin-carburetored Dementia Praecox, or Melancholia by Claude Debussy. No wonder the idiots come to you. They want to be called pretty names."

The leg pulling was so broad that even Voegler caught on and lapsed into silence. None of the others was willing to break it.

"How about my money now?"

"If you'll wait in the next room," began Wren.

"None of that. You promised." Shillitoe turned to the others at the table for support and they all had to assure him that Wren would keep his word before he'd go outside with the other applicants.

Massey decided to wait in front of the building for Shillitoe to come out. He wasn't sure yet of the best way to approach him, but he had to convince him that his hope lay in psychosurgery. The discussion of the applicants began, the same old pompous chatter. Massey headed for the door and had reached it before Abelson spoke up.

"Mr. Shillitoe brings to mind Oliver's very splendid speech of last evening."

The others clucked in agreement. Massey spun around and looked at them. Could they seriously be considering Shillitoe for Para Park? This possibility had never occurred to him. Massey went back to his chair and retrieved his pad listing the names of the six applicants. He couldn't remember which was which. But any of the first five would fit in at Para Park with its therapeutic schedule of long hikes in the woods and watercolor painting. Massey chose the second name on the list.

They all stared at him when he voted. He never had before. Wren announced that he was abstaining because Shillitoe was his patient, then solicited the others' ballots. Massey drummed his fingers on the arm of his chair, concealing his anger as each of them voted for Shillitoe. Three votes. That made it official.

There was only one other chance now. Massey wiped the back of his neck and lingered behind until Voegler, Abelson and Milicent Akers left.

"Oliver," he said, "remember, last night, I mentioned the possibility of opening Para Park to psychosurgery?"

"You know we have no surgical facilities."

"With the transorbital leukotome, none are needed. I use a local anesthetic. The whole procedure only takes a few minutes."

"We have no cases requiring prefrontal lobotomy." Wren started to shoulder past him.

"But we have. The man we just admitted. What can Para Park do for that kind of anterior thalamic radiation?"

"I have every confidence that the man will respond."

"To what? To infantile questions about his dreams and his parents?" Massey immediately wished he'd been more cunning.

"There may be occasions when a lobotomy is justified." Wren chopped sharp the ends of each word. "But *only* when everything else has failed. I repeat, we have no such cases at Para Park."

Oliver was still in a rage when he entered the room where the applicants sat waiting. The incredible nerve of Massey, trying to get those link sausage fingers on *his* patient. Massey knew it was his patient. Oliver had made that abundantly clear. He needn't have abstained from voting, either. He had the right to vote for admitting his own patient to Para Park. And he'd wanted Shillitoe admitted. It was the only chance to continue his treatment.

The visit from Officer Quirk that morning had made that

evident. Oliver realized he should have thought of Para Park then. But he hadn't, not until Shillitoe walked into the interviewing room and he'd recovered from his surprise. Then, as the interview progressed, the idea seemed better and better. Shillitoe's behavior confirmed Oliver's initial impression. His answers were neither devious nor furtive, but there was a skewness to them. It was as if they were arched from another level and just happened to slant accidentally across the plane of reality.

The applicants were looking at him, all with faces of hopeful expectancy, except of course for Shillitoe. Oliver wished he'd thought out what to say before entering the room. This was his first unpleasant task as president of the society. He wondered how Abelson had phrased the news to the rejected applicants.

"The one opening at Para Park has been filled," Oliver said. "You may apply again any time after an interval of six months. Mr. Shillitoe, will you come with me?"

As he went down to the office on the second floor, Shillitoe stayed on his heels. Oliver sat down and found himself staring at the framed photograph on the desk. A fat woman and three fat children were grimacing at him. Abelson's brood. Oliver wondered if the picture frame belonged to the society. One of the photographs he'd taken that summer of Lydia with Scott and Deirdre would just fit it.

"Quit stalling." Shillitoe held his hand out, palm up.

There was nothing to do but plunge. Oliver began a favorable description of Para Park.

"Jesus! Is there nothing you won't do to keep my money?"

Oliver began again, pointing out that the customary weekly charge to a patient at Para Park was two hundred dollars, but that Shillitoe could be one of the few special patients who were admitted free.

"Bargain day at the looney bin. No thanks. Just give me my hundred."

Oliver felt his face flushing. The archaic and ignorant reference to a mental institution would never cease to irritate him. There was an impulse to take a hundred dollars from his wallet and get rid of Shillitoe for good. The board would have questions. They'd want to know why he'd presented one of his patients for admission if the patient didn't want to be admitted. But he'd just tell them the truth.

"It's up to you," Oliver said. "But I'm surprised you don't jump at the chance under the circumstances."

"What circumstances?"

"I had a visit from a police officer this morning."

"I know it."

"Of course, you may be able to elude him. But he didn't think so. And he had quite an imposing list of charges, housebreaking, resisting arrest, assault, theft—"

"I didn't steal anything."

"It was something about buying a camera on credit and giving a false address. Apparently, that's considered theft. Still, you may prefer the conditions in a prison to having your own quiet room at Para Park."

Mention of the quiet room seemed to elicit a spark of interest. Oliver hastened to elaborate. Shillitoe could have his own room with a desk to write on, even a typewriter if he wished it. The food was edible enough, the hours would be his own and there were plenty of recreational facilities available. Doctor Vera Kropotkin who was the director of Para Park would make few demands.

"For instance?" Shillitoe was suspicious again.

"For instance, you'll be expected to keep your own room and belongings clean and you'll have to attend a group therapy session twice a week."

"Come on, Wren. What's the catch?"

"The catch," said Oliver straightforwardly, "is what I told you last night. I happen to have a scientific interest in your behavior. That's the one other demand on you. I'll be visiting Para Park every Saturday and I'll want you to give me an hour each time I do."

"No thanks. I'll take my money now."

Oliver's offer had sounded so logical and generous to him that he couldn't believe Shillitoe was refusing. He was going to argue further. But the calloused palm thrust out at him seemed symbolic of Shillitoe's whole nature. Bitter as it was to swallow, there came a point when it was best to admit defeat.

"Well?" The hand came closer.

"As I promised," sighed Oliver, "I'll return the money . . . to Mrs. Shillitoe."

"To me!"

"It will be waiting for her at my office."

"She can't come over for it." Oliver could almost see Shillitoe's mind racing to find a reason. "I thought I told you, Rhoda had an accident last night. Fell down a whole flight of stairs. Broke her leg, poor kid."

"When she telephoned me this morning, she said it was a sprained ankle." Oliver couldn't resist piling it on. "She also told me how it happened, *and* she asked me to hold on to the money until she came for it."

"It's my money!" Shillitoe pounded the desk top until everything on it was jumping. Oliver couldn't take his eyes off Abelson's picture. The children seemed to be leaping up and down, taunting him about bungling the situation. *Daddy would have handled it better. What if Shillitoe is a great poet? How many chances like this come along? Why don't you abdicate?* Then the pounding suddenly stopped.

"You sure the cops can't touch me if I'm in that place of yours?"

"You're not subject to legal action while there," said Oliver.

"How about if someone gets a court order?"

"What kind of court order?"

"I'm just asking," said Shillitoe. "Let's take a hypothetical case."

"John C. Jones?" Oliver congratulated himself. He'd finally made Shillitoe smile.

"That's right. Suppose there's a court order against him for something like not paying alimony."

"It couldn't be enforced while he was at Para Park."

The admission papers took but a few minutes to fill out. Then Oliver took Shillitoe downstairs to where Arnold waited in the station wagon. Arnold's hostility toward the patient was still very much in evidence, so Oliver called him aside.

"I don't have to remind you," he said, "that the people in your care are ill. They're not always responsible for their actions. You mustn't bear them any grudge." Arnold shuffled sullenly. Another time and Oliver would have continued to reason with him. But he was already late for his luncheon appointment. "In other words," he said severely, "no rough stuff. If I hear of any you'll be fired immediately, understand?"

"Yes, Doctor."

Oliver watched the station wagon drive off. Then he went back upstairs. He'd have to be a few minutes later for lunch. He owed it to Doctor Kropotkin to call and brief her on the new patient.

Chapter Fifteen

WHEN Oliver asked her if she'd like to go along, Lydia thought he was trying to make amends for Monday night. Not until they stopped for gas and he suggested that she drive did it dawn on her that the invitation was therapeutic, and this made her madder than ever. He was behaving as if *she* was in the wrong, as if the strained formality between them all week was *her* fault. So her driving the Thunderbird was supposed to release her tension, was it?

"We're not in that much of a hurry, hon."

Her foot obediently eased up on the accelerator, then rebelled and pushed down again. She could feel Oliver watching her critically as she swung out and past the green convertible and the Nash Rambler and the dusty, overladen heap with the grubby children watching her from its rear window. Oliver always said that speeding was neurotic. Oliver also always said that she was so well adjusted. She'd make him retract one statement or the other.

"Please slow down."

"Chicken."

But she did, until the speedometer hovered around the sixty mark. It wasn't because he'd asked her to. Part of her longed for an accident. Several times during the week she'd deliberately crossed streets against the light, almost daring the cars to hit her. She saw Oliver gently lifting her crushed body, tearfully begging her to forgive him for Monday night. But there was that other part of her, the part that old Siggy Freud called the narcissistic mechanism or something. This painted different pictures, horrible portraits of her burned and disfigured. It was this that made her dodge the onrushing traffic at the last moment, and it was this that had really slowed the car. If Oliver was such an astute analyst he'd realize that instead of doing the damn self-satisfied deep breathing.

"The country air smells good," he said.

Country air. They'd hardly passed New Rochelle. Chitchat, that's all it was. Strangers-on-a-train talk, as if nothing was wrong. That was just how he'd acted Monday night. Why did she keep thinking *Monday* night? It had been Tuesday morning, twenty minutes to three, Tuesday morning, when he'd come home. And she like a lemon had waited up. He had to go to his office for a few minutes. Sure, Lydia believed it. Lydia the sucker believed everything he said. Over two hours, her anger turning into worry and almost to frenzy as she watched the clock on the night table. She'd started to dial the office several times, but something had held her back. Then she'd heard the front door and just managed to put away the candles she'd arranged in the bedroom and jump back under the sheet before he walked in. She hadn't feigned sleep, though. She'd just lain there glaring at him. A lot of good that had done. He'd hardly noticed her. His mind had been somewhere miles off, high on top of his oral, anal and urethal mountains.

"Sorry, hon. I got tied up."

That was all, when he should have smothered her with apologies and pleaded for her forgiveness. But no. He knew good old Lydia wouldn't mind. Lydia would put up with anything. But not this time. She'd hardly spoken to him since and this was Saturday—five days of being ignored. And he needn't think the freeze was over just because she'd agreed to go along to Para Park.

Lydia tried to justify having accepted the invitation that morning. For one thing, she'd never been to Para Park and she was curious about this place that she'd heard so much about. For another, it *was* Saturday. No day camp for Scott and Deirdre and the prospect of chasing around after them in Central Park all afternoon wasn't exactly thrilling. But neither of these was the main reason. Her main reason was that she'd thought it was his way of making up to her for what he'd done.

"Next exit, hon."

Hon, hon, yes hon, no hon. When was it he started calling her hon? If she could place it, she'd know precisely when they began drifting apart. Lydia slowed the Thunderbird and turned off the Merritt Parkway. Oliver directed her. Left at the second traffic signal, then a narrow road to a narrower one winding off and up to the right. The heavy trees overhung the road, shutting out the sun. The air was cooler here and quieter. One car passed them coming the other way. Then the Thunderbird hummed alone, climbing higher into the rarefied atmosphere surrounding dear, old Para Park.

"Here we are."

Lydia was sure he was mistaken. The sleepy white house with blue shutters at the end of the snaking driveway was a private home, not a mental institution. But as they neared it, she saw the inmates loitering about the grounds. Poor, pathetic creatures. Still, if one had to blow one's top, this was a more pleasant place to blow it in than most.

"Good morning, Arnold."

Arnold was anthropoid and all in white. He opened the door and Oliver got out. Lydia sat gripping the steering wheel, determined not to budge until Oliver or Arnold or somebody opened the door on her side. But Oliver seemed to have already forgotten her presence. Typical. He was back with his first love now and she didn't count.

"The place ain't been the same since he come here." Arnold was trying to whisper but he was so perfectly developed he couldn't mute his voice.

"What exactly has he done?" asked Oliver. Lydia wished one of them would say who the he was.

"What ain't he done?" croaked Arnold. "Most of the time he's sittin' there writin'. Anybody so much as coughs, he throws things. A real violent psychotic, I tell ya'."

"Have you been bothering him?"

"Me?" Arnold was highly offended. "Never. The only thing, I figure he should be gettin' a little sunshine instead a' bein' cooped up alla time. So one day I took all his paper away and told him he hadda go outside 'n paint like everybody else."

"And?"

"He went okay. But later on I see he's got the canvas out a' the frame an's writin' on that. So when I took that away too, he starts complaining 'bout diarrhea an' when I go to see what's keepin' him in the john, he's written up half a roll a' paper."

"From now on," said Oliver, "when he wants to write, let him write."

"But that ain't all." Arnold was obviously presenting his complaints in an order of increasing importance. "Ya' know the group therapy meetin's. Well, they ain't meetin's no more. They're lectures. He goes soundin' off about everythin' and he keeps tellin' the worse cases how healthy they are. Like that Herman Horvath, you know, the guy that don't talk at all."

"Does Herman talk to . . . ?"

Lydia couldn't make out the name. She let go of the steering wheel and slid over to the other seat in order to hear better.

"Not a pipe outa' him," said Arnold, "but he keeps following the guy around like he's his slave or somethin'."

"There's nothing wrong with that." As Oliver failed to get upset, Arnold became more desperate.

"But how about the new ripple bath we got?" he asked. "Ain't it supposed to be for all the patients? Only he says it stimulates him an' now he wants to sit in there alla' time doin' his writin'."

"Suppose we let Doctor Kropotkin handle that."

"Her!" Arnold glanced back over each shoulder, before letting the big cat out of the bag. "She's taken in by him. Honest, every chance she gets, she's in his room. If you ask me, they're havin' a extramarital relationship."

"Thank you for the report, Arnold."

"You gonna' get rid of him?"

"You can go back to your duties now." Lydia recognized Oliver's tone as the one he used to spank the children when they got out of hand. She watched Arnold stampede off toward the four ungainly people trying to keep a badminton bird in the air. The muscular torso looked anything but spanked. Oliver had made himself an enemy.

Wonder of wonders! He'd remembered her existence and opened the car door.

"I have to see Doctor Kropotkin and one of the patients," he said. "I'll be tied up for a couple hours."

"Let's see," calculated Lydia, "two hours Oliver Wren time is about thirty-six hours daylight saving time."

He looked at her blankly.

"Oh, you mean the other night. I'm sorry about that. I got tied up." She looked around for a rock to hit him with, but he went blithely on. "There's plenty to occupy you, a good library in the house, or maybe you'd rather stay outside."

"I think I'll take a ripple bath," she said drily, but he had already turned toward the entrance to the house.

"I know it isn't necessary to mention it." He apparently decided it was necessary and turned back to her, lowering his voice. "But don't hesitate to talk to any of the patients. They're all . . ."

"Harmless?"

"They like company."

"Of course," she said. "*That's* why you brought me along."

The sarcasm fell flat against his back as he walked away. Lydia waited until he disappeared inside the house, then slammed the car door as hard as she could. The badminton players stopped swatting and pivoted toward the noise and one of them stepped right on the shuttlecock. As he held it up mournfully for the others to see, Lydia hurried off in the opposite direction.

The evenly mowed carpet of grass dipped gracefully from the back of the house to a border of woods. Here and there a tree provided a splash of shade and, carefully centered, a variety of flowers were interwoven in a small rock garden. Lydia started toward this, but changed direction as Arnold came out of the back door of the house leading a group of women. Each carried a partly filled-in canvas while Arnold himself lugged a stack of painting easels. These were distributed and as the women set them up around the rock garden Arnold peeled off his T-shirt and slacks and made like Rodin's thinker. Lydia was reminded of her own art classes and her painting in Oliver's office. The line dividing her from the women at the rock garden wasn't thick enough to brag about.

Lydia suddenly became conscious of the sun. Its intensity was the kind that always murdered her skin. The house offered shelter, but she didn't want to risk barging into Oliver right now, not until she'd simmered down a little more. The badminton players had found a new shuttlecock and didn't seem to bear her any grudge. As she came around the house two of them waved. Lydia waved back and, skirting their court, made her way across the front lawn to where a row of deck chairs was shaded by two large and overlapping elms.

Only one of the chairs was occupied. Lydia didn't know whether to take the one nearest it or farthest away. Ordinarily she would have sat in the farthest one. She didn't like people near her, particularly when she felt warm and sticky. But avoiding the little man who was stretched out reading might make him think she was repelled by him because he was mentally ill. Lydia set a faint, friendly smile on her lips and lowered herself onto the deck chair next to his.

He glanced up from his book but made no effort at conversation. Lydia decided it was up to her to speak first. But what could she say? The remarks which leapt to mind—"Isn't it nice here?" "Have you been here long?"—were immediately censored. Everything had the wrong connotation in this place. She thought the book might be one she'd read and, leaning forward to swat an imaginary insect from her chair, she peeked at its cover. *Hellebore.* She couldn't even pronounce it, let alone discuss it. She sat back again and, as the man turned a page, she caught a glimpse of the strangely staggered type. Poetry!

"Good book?" she asked.

She was aware of having sweetened her voice, as if speaking to Deirdre about *Winnie the Pooh.* But if the man thought her condescending he didn't show it. He just nodded and turned the page. Lydia inclined her head casually, trying to read the bottom of the page nearest her, but the man's hands were shaking and the words wouldn't stay in focus. It was something about sunlight and beauty and Apollo. Lydia tried to remember the Greek gods she'd learned about in high school. Was Apollo a good guy or a bad guy?

She couldn't remember and the more she tried to distinguish him from Zeus and Cronus and Jupiter the more her head ached. Then a tight cramp began a counterpoint in her stomach and she had to lie back and close her eyes. When she opened them a few moments later the white house had grayed and the blue shutters had grown ominous and the carefully trimmed grounds appeared funereal. Before her was most persons' private version of heaven: a rock garden and painting and badminton and, in the basement of the house, undoubtedly a woodworking shop. That was the terrifying aspect, that all these goodies weren't confined to places like Para Park. The people outside, at least everyone she knew, were all following the same pursuits. Here stood a capsule version of their Utopia, peaceful, bland, secure. Here was everything she herself had settled for. The needle charting the graph of her life had jumped a few times: when Paul Caldwell whom she was engaged to crashed on a training flight; homecoming day at Berkeley when she was one of the Queen's ladies-in-waiting at half-time in front of sixty thousand people; the garden wedding in Santa Barbara; giving birth the first time, then Deirdre's, much more troublesome and painful, and that was about it. The needle quivered now and then, marking occasions like Oliver's election. But did all the zigzags on the graph add up to much more than the little shrieks of glee from the badminton players as points were scored in their meaningless game? From any perspective, her days totaled nothing. She was an insignificant speck merely going through the motions of living and there was absolutely no intelligent reason why she should just keep going on and on and on.

Lydia put her hands on her temples as if physically to lift herself from her depression and from deep within her pulled a long, anguished sigh. The silent man turned to her and he looked concerned. Some company she was. Again she floundered for something to say.

"Do you know what the ripple bath is?"

Now why had she asked him that? The man put down his book and began flapping his hands. Her face must have shown him that his pantomime wasn't getting through, for he gave up the gestures and pointed toward the lower left window of the house.

"I understand," said Lydia.

This time the insect near her ankle wasn't imaginary. She sprang from the chair, then felt silly as she always did over her fear of crawling things as the silent man bent over and flicked the bug to the grass.

"Thank you." Straightening and smoothing her skirt helped her regain her nonchalance. "I think I'll take a look at that ripple bath," she said. "I've heard so much about it."

When the car drove up, Vera Kropotkin broad-jumped to the window and everything in the room shook.

"It's heem," she said, "and he brawng his vive."

Shillitoe stopped writing and went to see who he and his wife were, but Vera misunderstood his intentions and collapsed his ribs again. Then she unlocked her arms and pushed him away.

"Net now, Semmy. He vill be vanting me." Her Brobdingnagian buttocks crashed against his table, chair and bed on the way out.

On the driveway below, the gorilla was talking earnestly with Wren and a slim ivory elbow was propped on the open car window from inside. Shillitoe completed the woman in his mind: long chin, tinted hair, going to loose fat. He had to throw away the sketch when she stepped out. Delicate stuff this, sinuous and elegantly slim. Fragonard could have used her if she stood straighter. The spine was too loose, as if she was hanging on a clothesline in a crosswind. But under the gold clinging blouse and a full white skirt there were possibilities. Too bad she had never been tightened and solidified to command her acre of air. Still, he had to concede that Wren had better taste than he'd given him credit for.

Shillitoe went back to the small table and the poem. It was growing, agonizingly but sure. He told himself to feel more kindly toward Wren. Wren had got him into this dump and everything had worked out fine. The gorilla was a nuisance, but two-ton Vera Kropotkin kept him at bay. Vera herself had become a minor problem, marching into his room at all hours and getting him in her bone-crushing embraces. But he was willing to endure some interruptions and it was important that he keep Vera on his side until the poem was finished.

Meanwhile, the ripple bath was coming in handy. Like all oversized women, Vera made a fetish of delicacy and would never come into the bathing room while he was in the tub. So, the last couple of days, he'd taken to sitting in it for hours at a time and writing there. This would work out fine as soon as he perfected the technique of holding the paper clear of the surging water. The ripple bath had been designed to relax, but it had just the opposite effect on him. The undulation of the water invigorated him; its rhythm, steady and predictable as a Spenserian sonnet, giving him an adversary on which to vent his natural beat.

Three parts of the poem were practically done. As each new part joined the others, Shillitoe could feel it swell in strength. Another week or so and the fourth part would be written and the complete poem could stand alone. Thrust and proportion; it had both. There were still a few inarticulate passages where he'd reached higher and farther than ever before. These would need some carpentry before they took their places in the overall scheme of devastation and beauty. But most of the images held their shape as he read them over: the white cross on the untrodden beach, the wanted posters profiling great men, the hoarse battalions of senators, the dreams projected by fat grocers and shriveled matrons on sweat-walled cells of night. And the entirety would mash down the guck and glue of mangled dates so that the worms squirted out in every direction. Some of the little fabrications might escape, but not the big one; not the sham tuxedo that man could only hope to control his hate, but never his love. It was this that had swaddled the centuries. How could no strong voice have protested that it was just the other way around? Love was the concoction that could be hewn, each man his own sculptor. Hate was nothing more than the hobby of lazy souls. How they'd scream if death was ever evicted from the spice bin. But they always did when some vision which took no account of them happened to spill a crumb of light on their misery.

He wrote on. The gulls were ugly, foraging promiscuously, sucking in rind with pulp, stool with seed. But once with the moon cool and the bay ruffling its sheen they rose from their cliff sanctuary and arranged their wings in a glorious pattern. It was a more important beauty than the rich coat of the pompous parrot or the falcon's grace because it had the glow of artlessness and the power of possibility. It was only in splintered fractions such as this that the unimagined was ever revealed. The fraction proved passions existent in every countenance, and those who connived their faces into rapture and vaunted their imprisonments and probed the crackerjacks of day for lead toys—they would never know this because they were fools.

"Fools" made him think of Wren. He wondered how long Wren would keep Vera Kropotkin away from his door. Expecting her resounding footfalls at any moment spoiled his concentration, so he stuffed what he'd written into the briefcase with the rest, grabbed a pad of blank paper and headed for the ripple bath.

The contraption still amused him. It hung like a double shell of a canoe two feet off the floor and its formidable bank of dials and levers glowered at him as if rejected at Los Alamos. Shillitoe turned them on, the water coursed out of a dozen openings and the tub rocked port and starboard.

He set the thing into high gear and was unbuttoning his shirt when ivory elbow swept in. Seeing him, she fell back against the door frame as if pinned there by an arrow through her left shoulder. Shillitoe looked down at himself to see what had caused her violent reaction, and by the time he looked up she had recovered.

"You can use it first," he said, "but don't dawdle."

Her glistening little mouth opened and closed twice before anything came out.

"I was . . . the ripple bath . . . I was curious."

"That's it," pointed Shillitoe. The thing was making too much racket, so he swaggered over to it and hit the button which stopped its rocking. "Would you like a demonstration?"

"No. Don't let me disturb you." She started backing out, but something about him was magnetizing her. He followed the aim of her soft brown eyes and wound up at the blank paper in his hand.

"Do you write poetry?" she asked.

"Christ! Is it that obvious?"

"No." Why the hell was she so beet-faced? "I mean . . ." What a tongue-twisted broad; antithetical to her husband, unity of opposites and all that marriage counseling crap. "I mean," she finally got out, "I've heard you talk about poetry."

"With no visible effect," he said.

"I'm afraid I didn't understand it."

"Don't be afraid."

He waited for her to scram, but she gave no indication of going. He took off his shoes and she still hung there. Probably the progressive type who took a leak while hubby sang "On the Road to Mandalay" in the shower.

"I'd like to understand poetry," she said.

"Doubt it," he growled. "You live in the house of Mercury with the orators and thieves and traders. Mine is a different world."

"The world of Apollo?" Now why did the sweet fragrant bitch say that? There might be hope for her after all. He hadn't realized he'd said it aloud.

"Hope for me? I'm quite happy, thank you."

"Bullshit!"

"It's not bull—" she couldn't quite say it, but trying to had straightened her spine. "Everybody knows I'm not a discontented person."

"Everybody's always wrong," said Shillitoe and took off his shirt. She didn't let her line of sight sink below his Adam's apple. Progressive, all right.

"Never mind me," she said. "How about you?"

That was it, the amateur psychologist coming along with her professional man to look at all the poor, demented people. Florence Nightingale was in Connecticut, and she wouldn't go away until he performed.

"What would you like to know," he asked, "the thickness of the mattress on which I was heaved into being, the special formula of Spanish fly I was weaned on, the exact temperature of the melting pot that boiled my bubble of conceit over its rim?" The angel looked like she was going to take notes. "You see," he added pompously, forgetting he wasn't wearing a shirt and having nothing to brace his hand on for a Napoleonic pose, "my first words were a perfect heroic couplet. By the time I was six I had seduced my nurse, three spinster aunts, Bessie, Essie and Tessie, and a census taker who happened to walk in without knocking. Now take off, will you? I've got work to do."

He held the door open for her but she went into a trance and sat down on the rim of the tub. It tilted under her ninety-eight pounds and the seat of her skirt got dunked. But instead of the screech he expected she came up with a smile.

"True to form Lydia," she said. "So much for poise."

"You don't need it."

"What does that mean?"

"The voice at Montfort, Lady Agnes' hair, the viscountess' throat. Where'd you hear me sound off about poetry?"

"Da Vinci Hall."

He groaned. One of those. He should have known from her nose, upturned at the tip from sniffing culture. And she'd dabble; writing her confessions, ceramics, painting. The last clicked. She was probably responsible for the nightmare on Wren's wall. He had to find out if he'd guessed right and asked her.

"That's one of mine," she said. "What do you think?"

"Puke."

He hoped she'd put up a token defense. But her shoulders drooped and she nodded.

"Guess what I've been doing lately," she said.

"What?"

"Promise you won't laugh."

"I promise."

"I've been taking harp lessons."

He burst out laughing and was surprised to hear her joining in.

"Nothing like a divine avocation," he said.

Her laugh snapped off and with it went her whole length of backbone.

"I'm so bored," she whimpered.

He'd seen this plaster mask three times before, twice on soldiers nailed to sprays of flame, once on a drowning man in the frothy water of Morro Bay. Pretensions and paraphernalia had relaxed their grip and she was floundering, desperately sucking in last globs of air before her momentum fizzled into stone.

He talked fast, pumping out dithyrambs to bring the pale rose back to her cheeks. Her gallows complexion warned him back to fundamentals. So he fanned the cards, matching gratitude to inequality and sympathy to pain, picking out the sadistic song of sentiment with one finger until she could hear it unmistakably, demonstrating with the everyday that progress was illusion, that popularity was scorn, that the optimist despaired and the approving merely surrendered. For a while she lingered, then his words began to fasten their splints around her flaccid spine.

"Right," she chirped faintly. "I'm joining Apollo."

"You sure you want to?"

"Positive."

"You'll be virtually alone. You'll lose all your so-called friends."

"Who cares?"

"You'll be accused of overthrowing all right and decency."

"Where do I sign up?"

"Not so fast," he cautioned. "You've a lot of toxin to get rid of first, chimeras and cobwebs and pressed corsages and honeymoon stickers and all the other stagnant little compartments dividing up your soul."

"Okay. Tell me what to do."

"I just did," he sighed and began all over again. Why did she have to be so goddam dumb? This time he practically drew diagrams, A being the pinnacle of truth, B being a lady of gilded virtue and line A-B representing the imagination. "Nothing is real but the imagination," he said, "and the closest most people ever get to imagination is love."

"Ah, love," she inhaled deeply, "tell me about love."

"Can't," he admitted. "The lips extract more from a kiss than they can say. What's love to your everybodies? Cool perfume condensing overnight into wrinkled thighs and lank strands of hair. Still, it's their only net profit. Delicate stuff, love—thin, ragged orphan, belted and strangled by button-fumbling hands. Where is it hiding in you? The fruit is never bitter as the skin. Come here. What child is hiding inside? Is she soft? Is she fair? Let her be beautiful, for human beauty proportions my dreams."

He hadn't meant to command her to come closer, but he had and there she was and her moist lips were slightly parted just beneath his own.

"Don't stop," she said. "I love the way you phrase things."

The familiar line hit him like a stopped-up drain and he jumped backwards.

"What's the matter?" She was after him. "What did I do?"

"Never mind." He tried to put the ripple bath between them. "I'm not getting dragged into any dungeons today. Take your clammy tentacles somewhere else."

He'd unfastened his belt and zipped open his pants when she caught him full in the face with a roundhouse right. He drew himself up indignantly and the pants sagged around his ankles.

"Now why the hell did you do that?"

She didn't answer. She had turned away, her mouth pressed against her hand. She'd probably stubbed a finger when she hit him. Good. Then he saw her shoulders trembling. Why did children always start bawling when they hit someone else?

"Cut it out," he ordered, but the trembling increased. "Come on, you're shaking more than the goddam ripple bath." The kidding didn't work any better. Nothing else to do but walk up behind her and still the shoulders with gentle hands. "Please don't cry," he said. "Please. I can't bear to see anyone cry."

Shillitoe's empty room and the briefcase bulging on the table presented too great a temptation to resist. This turnabout was fair play. Oliver sat down and carefully assumed the pose in which he wished to be discovered, his feet on the table and the handful of manuscript he'd taken from the briefcase on his lap. It wasn't a comfortable position, but anticipating Shillitoe's entrance made up for that. Then, both the discomfort and the anticipation faded as he began reading.

Each man has a season marked in red,
three weeks of blisters and a month of flame,
like all convulsions
unpredictable
and better coped with at an early age.

That was obscure enough. But it got steadily more so. Several pages amounted to a potpourri of just about anything: pieces of menus, church sermon announcements, garage repair bills, laundry lists—some of the items being more graphic than Oliver had ever thought them, but they hardly seemed poetry or even the material from which poetry was made. One sheet of paper did present some doggerel that rhymed. But this, on closer scrutiny, turned out to be a parody of a Burma-Shave ad, and pornographic at that. Other pages proved equally difficult. Several were torn off the roll of toilet tissue

Arnold had mentioned and the scrawling on them was barely legible. Oliver pressed on, covering almost half the manuscript before allowing himself any conclusions.

The first person, the "I," was noticeably absent throughout. Also, nowhere had he found any mention of the biology of living, the eggs and the fruit and the spawning. One piece, about there always being a waiting list for well-douched ruts, seemed to sum up the attitude behind the omissions. Shillitoe's bitterness had made him reluctant to make more grist for the frightening twentieth-century mill. He had withdrawn. But why?

Some eyes cannot see
colors in air;
blues of bruised delusions,
limes of fear

Shillitoe was obsessed with colors and with shapes. In fact, he seemed only concerned with the way things *looked.* This was certainly a key. The obsession could be likened to that of the *voyeur,* substituting the eyes for the penis. *Voyeurism* usually resulted from having witnessed one's parents in the sexual act as a child. This was a line to pursue. There were other indications too; the assumed superiority, the standing back from the world and examining it instead of competing in it. The main arena of life was as forbidding to Shillitoe as his parents' bed had been.

always outside,
too big,
discarded by conceit
for little reasons
unidentified

The lines as much as confirmed it. Another possibility struck Oliver. Shillitoe's boasting of his sexual prowess could be nothing but wish fulfillment. After all, his wife was rather plain, and he wasn't a man that most women would find attractive.

Oliver leafed on through the stack of paper, alert now for any allusion to himself or to psychiatry or to Para Park, for any reaction at all to the reality of the present situation in which Shillitoe existed.

do not confuse the difficult
with suffering

Then, after several words impossible to make out,

to be sad is easier
than going
MAD

Oliver thought the lines revealing. These and others could springboard questions for him during his hour with Shillitoe.

Oliver's right foot had fallen asleep and he had to stand up and hobble around the room until the circulation was restored. This made him conscious for the first time of the room's small dimensions and airy whiteness. It wasn't the best atmosphere for the session with Shillitoe. Remembering that Doctor Kropotkin had volunteered the use of her office, Oliver picked up the manuscript and went downstairs.

The main hall was deserted, but from the east wing came a clatter of kitchen noises and the mashed-potatoes smell that cafeterias always seemed to have. Fortunately, the thick oak door of Doctor Kropotkin's office shut out both. Oliver took in the room, decided against talking across the desk and slid two chairs over to the window. He put the manuscript on the desk and was about to set out in search of his patient when he noticed Shillitoe's file folder. Doctor Kropotkin had undoubtedly got it out and forgotten to give it to him. But it wasn't a serious oversight. The folder's contents were of little interest. The physical report was excellent, though Doctor Kropotkin seemed to have given Shillitoe a more thorough examination than was customary. And the registration card just told Shillitoe's address in New York and the facts of his birth. Doctor Kropotkin hadn't filled this in completely either. The city of birth wasn't given, only the state of Indiana. This nagged at Oliver. He had known Shillitoe was from Indiana but couldn't remember how he knew. Shillitoe hadn't told him, and he couldn't recall Mrs. Shillitoe having said anything about it.

Shillitoe wasn't one of the badminton players in front of the house. Oliver thought he might be the man watching him from the deck chair until he got close enough to see it was Herman Horvath. Then Oliver went around to the back lawn and was about to interrupt Arnold's modeling when he thought of Arnold's complaint about the ripple bath. Even if Shillitoe wasn't in it, he wanted to inspect the new equipment.

Oliver heard the splashing before he pushed open the door and leaned inside. Shillitoe had taken over the ripple bath, all right. Through the steaming mist that hung in the room Oliver could see him, face down in the tub, cavorting like a baby whale, his broad shoulders emerging rhythmically, shining and dripping before descending again into the gyrating water. Oliver was about to call out to him.

"That's an odd place to practice the breast stroke."

But he never said it, for Shillitoe rose from the water again and this time he soared higher than before so that Oliver could make out the other head tucked against him and the painted fingernails digging into his back.

Oliver drew back behind the door. But, before it secreted him completely, Shillitoe's face came up again and his eyes as he shed water, looked right at him. Oliver stood motionless, toying with the notion of treating Shillitoe to a dose of his own tactics by barging in on the lovemaking as brazenly as Shillitoe had invaded his private records. And while Oliver weighed the possible consequences of such an act, he stared at the narrow gap in the doorway and, gradually, he picked out the trail leading in the direction of the tub, the shoes and the white skirt and the gold blouse and the delicate underclothes. And then he remembered who had told him that Shillitoe was from Indiana.

Chapter Sixteen

WHEN Mrs. Fish got to the apartment with her news she found Evelyn dragging around the kitchen and Norma in the guest room packing.

"She's leaving?" she asked Evelyn and Evelyn began to cry. Ever since the blowup, you asked her the time and she started dripping. Mrs. Fish went into the guest room and closed the door.

"You're leaving?" she asked Norma.

"Obviously," said Norma, all uppity-puppity.

"You had a fight with Evelyn?"

"We haven't exchanged two words."

"So why are you packing?"

"I just spoke long distance with Charles," said Norma stubbornly. "He's leaving tonight for the optometry convention in Indianapolis and he insists I meet him there tomorrow."

"Charles *insists?*" scoffed Mrs. Fish, but when Norma just let the gauntlet lay there she shifted to a weary shrug. "Some people never can rest until they're dead, and others can go running off to conventions."

"At the Claypool Hotel," added Norma. The way she said it told Mrs. Fish that her mind was made up. Not that Mrs. Fish was sure she wanted to argue. Norma had been some help, filling her in every morning on what went on after she left the apartment the day before. But Dana could do the same thing, and Norma's presence did give Leonard a few extra bullets of ammunition.

"What time's your train?"

"Three-thirty from Grand Central."

Evelyn's appointment was for four. She could just make it.

"I'll tell you what I found out on the way," said Mrs. Fish, throwing all her weight on the lid of the suitcase until Norma clicked the latches.

The cabdriver was the race track kind, switching lanes and jamming in front of everybody else, so Norma was holding on to the seat instead of listening to her.

"Hey, Barney Oldfield," said Mrs. Fish. "You're trying to win a loving cup?"

That made him slow down and Norma paid more attention. But still she seemed mopey. She didn't even say it was astounding how Mrs. Fish had tracked down the Acme Carpet Cleaners. Not much it wasn't. Private eyes wouldn't take on a case without more clues than she'd had to go on. Sure, Dana recognized Swinburne the tramp as the one who'd cleaned the rugs, but he didn't know where he came from. Evelyn wouldn't tell her anything. All she did was faint and cry. And Leonard was even less composed. So, reluctant as Mrs. Fish had been to take matters into her own hands, there was no other way. Yesterday with Dana out playing and Evelyn napping, she sent Norma up to the butcher shop and headed for the desk drawer in the breakfront. Discovering how much or how little Leonard had paid for various things waylaid her several times before she found the receipt from the Acme Carpet Cleaners on Ninth Avenue. She would have gone there right away, except she couldn't leave Evelyn alone, and by the time Norma got back it was too late to go downtown. But that morning she had set out with blood in her eye.

The refinement of the proprietor pushed her off balance. A perfect gentleman, Mr. Moscowitz, in fact, a little reminiscent of her Aaron.

"Swinburne!" he said. "I ain't got no Swinburne."

This had been a real fast ball. Lucky she hadn't accepted it as final and took a roundabout route. Certainly, a business kept records, so who did the records say had shampooed the carpets of Mrs. Tupperman?

"When were they done?" asked Mr. Moscowitz.

Mrs. Fish estimated it as six or seven weeks previous.

"I make no adjustments after thirty days," said Mr. Moscowitz. Then he brought out a spindle with what looked like invoices from every day since he'd opened his doors and pulled one out like it had germs. "I should have known," he gasped, both hands holding his heart. "Why did I even bother to look it up? What did he do now? No, don't tell me. I don't want to hear. He stole the silver? He insulted the woman of the house?" Mr. Moscowitz covered his ears before asking the next question. "He molested the maid?"

Though she was the injured party, Mrs. Fish had found herself comforting him. What else could she do? The longer she lived, the more she found that she was the only one who had any self-control. Whoever said it was the Age of Anxiety had never spoken a truer word.

Then Mr. Moscowitz calmed down enough to tell her who the man was. Shillitoe? Even when he spelled it out, it didn't sound like a name.

"Whatever he did," warned Mr. Moscowitz, "don't get mixed up with him. Let the police take care of him. They're already out looking for him and they got guns."

A gangster! That explained the name, or so she had thought. He was a Sicilian, a member of the Mafia if she ever saw one.

"That's what hurts," moaned Mr. Moscowitz, "when it's one of our own."

"Shillitoe?"

"What else? Otherwise, wouldn't I turn him over to Sing Sing myself?"

"A Jewish gangster?"

"Say, it happens. And so much damage one bad apple can do. Remember Murder, Incorporated, with all the Bugsies and No-Noses? *Mentsch!* Everything Gershwin accomplished, they spoiled."

Mrs. Fish had remembered Murder, Incorporated very well. Mr. Moscowitz was a wise man. The police could handle Shillitoe better than she could and more power to them.

"But why would Evelyn have an affair with a criminal?" asked Norma. The first time she'd opened her mouth during the whole story and she had to ask such a question.

"I've got to draw diagrams for you?" said Mrs. Fish. "It never occurred to you that it isn't like Evelyn to cry and faint all the time? You don't even recognize the symptoms when your own sister's been raped by a convict."

"I suppose it's conceivable," said Norma.

"Nothing was conceived," hissed Mrs. Fish.

"Shillitoe doesn't *sound* Jewish," said Norma. "Maybe he changed it from Shapiro."

"Even if it is conceivable," argued Mrs. Fish, "at least it won't be a goy."

So many people were in Grand Central, she could hardly breathe. You'd think they'd open the gates and let the people on instead of making them all rush at the last minute. Meanwhile, anybody shoved her, got shoved right back. Mrs. Fish again told Norma to give her love to Charles and to kiss the twins for her. There was nothing else to say, so she studied the giant color snapshots that Eastman Kodak always had up in the terminal. Such a smiling, happy family. The father was nice-looking, the mother was freckled but sort of cute and the children seemed very healthy, if not so intelligent. This was other women's families, not hers. All over the country, fathers and mothers and children sailed boats together and picnicked together and pushed each other on the swings and laughed all the time. Not in New York, of course. But in the rest of America people knew how to live. Eastman Kodak changed the pictures often, so they couldn't have much trouble finding contented families to photograph. It was a good thing, too. If they ever took big colored pictures like that of Leonard and Evelyn and Dana and put them up in the station, everybody would cash in their government bonds.

As the gates were finally opened, Norma kept telling her not to come all the way down to the platform. Mrs. Fish reluctantly gave in and they clung to each other crying good-byes and suddenly thinking of things to say until the surge of passengers pulled Norma away. Mrs. Fish glued her eyes to the turquoise glasses until they disappeared in the heads bobbing down the tunnel. Then she hurried to the Lexington Avenue Subway.

A mother's intuition had again proved to be a remarkable thing. Yesterday when Evelyn asked her to call up Doctor Wren and cancel the appointment, Mrs. Fish had said she would. But her intuition kept her putting it off. Now she knew why. Doctor Wren could be the best psychiatrist in the world, but he had to go by professional ethics. He couldn't look in Leonard's drawer and track things down the way she had. It would probably take him months to learn from Evelyn the things that Mrs. Fish would tell him in the next hour.

Norma slept fitfully. And each time she woke, before she identified the clacking train wheels, there was a horrible moment when she thought she was still in New York and he was standing at the foot of her bed looking at her. As soon as it began getting light she struggled into her clothes and managed to push the roomette bed up into the wall without ringing for the porter. Then she looked out the dirty window at the flat landscape and the monotonous telegraph poles.

Norma had planned to stay in New York for three weeks. She had made that clear to Charles and that was undoubtedly why he'd been surprised at her calling long distance and her decision to meet him in Indianapolis. She had also told her mother how long she was staying, so she'd never expected to get away after only twelve days without making a full explanation. But her mother was too busy playing detective. All she cared about was Evelyn. On the way to the station with her mother claiming that Evelyn had been raped, Norma had almost said,

"Who couldn't be?" But she hadn't, and now nobody would ever know.

Of course, last night was partly her own fault. She'd always suspected how Leonard felt about her. And as the emotional strain he was under increased, particularly the past four days, the looks he'd given her had become more frequent and more obvious. She should have left that day Leonard brought the man called Shillitoe home and Evelyn as much as admitted everything by fainting. Her mother might never have forgiven her for deserting her own sister at such a time, but it would have been better than compounding the crime.

Every time Norma thought of it, she wondered what the end would have been if she hadn't been such a light sleeper. Or if she hadn't had the presence of mind not to move or open her eyes wide. If she had been Evelyn she would have screamed and caused a scene. But she had always been the cool-headed one. So, as he stood at the foot of the bed eying her, ready to pounce on her, she did the cool-headed thing. She raised her tongue to the roof of her mouth and began to snore. It had worked with Charles for years and it worked with Leonard. He backed slowly away from the bed as if being pushed and, a second later, she heard the door close.

Norma was still impressed at her own quick thinking. If only Evelyn had as much resourcefulness. Norma told herself to be fair. The man who had assaulted Evelyn didn't look as easy to put off as Leonard was. Besides, being wanted by the police already, he probably had nothing to lose. Norma could see the criminal's face clearly, both full-front and in profile, as it undoubtedly appeared in post offices all over the country. It was a frightening face and she was still thinking about it when she stepped from her Pullman car into the steaming terminal and started along the platform. So, when she thought it was him leaping out of the coach right in front of her, she told herself her preoccupation was playing a trick.

The resemblance, however, was too striking to be so easily dismissed. Norma trotted past the passengers and porters ahead of her, then swung around and took a full look at him. He had the same passionless, killer's eyes, the same degenerate leer. Then she recognized the heavy brown suit he wore. Two men might look alike, but they both wouldn't be wearing Harris tweed in this weather. And the briefcase! That cinched it.

Norma spotted Charles waiting behind the railing and could tell from the way he was smiling at her that his hemorrhoids were bothering him again. Her plan was to tell him to grab the man in the brown suit and hold him until she found a policeman. But Charles kept pecking her forehead above the yellow and brown spectacles which were his favorite pair, and the more she pointed and whispered "Him! Grab him!" the more he asked "Who? Where? Who?" and pecked again until the criminal was halfway across the station. Norma shoved her overnight case and luggage checks at Charles, told him she'd meet him at the Claypool later and rushed off in pursuit.

Wherever the criminal was heading, he didn't seem in much of a hurry. He walked clear around the Circle, doing slow pirouettes every once in a while and throwing back his shoulders and slapping his chest with both hands. Once, as he did this, Norma was near enough to hear him say "Hot shit." Then he went down Illinois Street to the bus station.

She stayed two places behind him at the window but the woman between them sneezed just as he asked for his ticket. It sounded like he'd said, "One way to Cob City." Norma grabbed a timetable from the rack, trying to find out if there was such a place while keeping one eye on him. There it was, between Bedford and Jasper, and there he was, disappearing under the sign, BARBER SHOP—MEN'S ROOM—SHOE SHINE. When he didn't come out after fifteen minutes, Norma decided she'd done all she could and it was time to relinquish the responsibility.

It came to eleven words the first time she wrote it out, so she tore up the blank and phrased it another way.

MAN NAMED SHILLITOE ENROUTE BY BUS TO COB CITY INDIANA

The woman who counted the words could at least have looked at her. You'd think she'd want to see who was sending such a wire to the Chief of Police of New York City.

Chapter Seventeen

THE bus ground its way out through the fortification of the city, past the shrill single syllables and exclamation points, the SALE! SAVE! EAT! GAS! DANCE!, past the silent, contradicting cemetery and pillbox motels. Then the land burst into view.

Shillitoe couldn't sit still. He'd forgotten what color was, the earth and sky of partridge tan and frosted blue; the green —not the slurping, dockside eastern green but the confident green of growing, unflustered by scalds of grain and the plowman's corkscrew claws. He slid open the window and sucked in the air.

"Fertilizer!" The fat woman bulging over the armrest between them held her nose.

"There's the soil for love." He banged her joyfully on the elbow and stuck his head out the window. Everything staring back at him asked why he'd stayed away so long. Lean, burnt men told him by their stance that they'd seen more of life from their silos than he had in all his wanderings. The voices jostling for his attention inside the bus were similarly rooted and sure.

"Wreck the other night. That bend there."

"Ummm."

"Fella' from up 'round Logansport."

"Ummm."

"Lickered up some an' got over the white line."

"What'd he hit?"

"Big trailer job. Saw the headlights an' thought they was two motorcycles. Tried to drive plumb between 'em."

Good old Hoosier humor, macabre to the sentimental slobs who couldn't understand leverage. Those who dealt with life never made too much fuss over it. That was for the professional sufferers, complaining over every breath while praying to live forever. But he had found the unacknowledged clause of death. One sweet kernel of time he had run away and, while sniffing strange vats of air, had glanced back and seen that his absence left no space. No one cared that he had gone, so he was able to return. He was going home, home to the garage. The twist of the platitude made him chuckle out loud. The only thing needed to complete the setting was a little mood music. Shillitoe began singing, "When the moon is shining bright along the Wabash," and when the fat woman lurched down the aisle to another seat he was able to spread out more comfortably.

Casting his mind back over the intervening years he arranged the sights in the order they would appear. But the bus slowed and abruptly turned and dipped and when it straightened its course again it was on a new four-lane highway. Except for filling stations, precisely spaced, it passed nothing but other vehicles. Martinsville, Bloomington, Bedford and the in-between villages Shillitoe had counted on seeing again were but names lettered in reflective glass beads on gray metal signboards.

The bus, head down, hustled on toward Evansville. The driver assured Shillitoe that it would stop at Cob City because a rest stop was mandatory every two hours. So Cob City, once proudly flanking the main road, was now reduced to a urine trough. Speed had been served, speed and the maxim that the shortest distance between two points was in the avoidance of all character. Progress had once again stretched tight its cordon and pushed back all distractions, back out of sight beyond the dirt cliffs lining the highway. No wildflowers, no loafing cows, no limestone quarrys, no apple trees, cherry trees, pear trees, neither rye nor clover to decorate the way of the itinerant bus.

Uterus clutcher! Shillitoe pulled himself clear. Yesterdays were the worst kind of quicksand. There he'd been carrying on like one of the hernia cases who'd played soldiers in wartime movies, surviving on the memory of good old Pop's corner drugstore and the strawberry marshmallow sundaes with whipped cream and chopped nuts and all that made democracy worth fighting for, yum-yum, and it's a good thing we saw our dentists twice a year or we'd never be able to pull the pins out of hand grenades with our teeth.

The anesthetists and slide rule boys had been here and that was that. So Cob City had undoubtedly had its face lifted to match that of every other profit-bearing oasis. The streets would be straightened and pressed flat, the houses deloused, the Courthouse Square frilled with neon and appliance stores and steatopygous teen-age girls. And Ben's garage, his home-sweet-home, would look like a miniature contagious hospital with a drill team of interns leaping out to service whatever drove up. That was the pattern. Just as the nation's rivers found their way to the sea, so its human sludge wended to the twin cesspools of New York and Hollywood to hide in furnished rooms and Anglo-Saxon names. There, everything was seen wrong, all the silt from the belly of the land was collected and dehydrated into teaspoons of instant feces to be disseminated across the country as fashion and entertainment and education. This was one reason why every head was spinning, from trying to adjust what it was told to what it could see. And, meanwhile, the dispensers waved the stars and stripes and proclaimed their undying patriotism and filled their lives with African carvings, Berlitz languages and chopsticks.

So what? So antennas on all Cob City roofs would be sucking illiteracies from the sky. Manifestations came and vanished, affecting little. Only the surface of Cob City would be altered. The underlying rock would not have changed in proportion;

one part hope to thousands of ignorance and calculation. It was the same ratio he'd found everywhere since leaving Cob City and winding up at Para Park.

Para Park! Crusher Vera and push-ups Arnold and silent Herman now seemed remote. But it was only yesterday when he'd sneaked out the back door, threaded his way through the woods to the main road, walked to Stamford, caught the train to Grand Central and bought the one-way ticket to Indianapolis. There'd been time to kill in the station and he had a pestering urge to call Herschel's luncheonette and say good-bye to Rhoda. He told himself he just wanted to rub it in, to let her know he had his hundred dollars in spite of her and was heading home. But he knew that wasn't the reason. Hard as he'd tried to preserve his fury toward her it had disappeared. He wished she was going to Indiana with him. Just listening to a conversation between her and Ben would justify her fare. He wanted to call her in the hope that she would ask to go along. But she might show up at the station with the cops. She'd almost turned him in once already and he was too near freedom now to risk it. Still, he wished she knew that he bore her no ill feelings. Bad as her intentions were, things had worked out. Not only was the poem growing and healthy but he'd stumbled onto a new experience. In the ripple bath yesterday it had almost lived up to a virgin's expectations. Installed in every American home the contraption might even save the family unit. Shillitoe tried to recapture the exact ecstatic sensation but, whenever he almost had it, Wren's face intervened again. At first yesterday, Shillitoe had thought some septic pocket of guilt was projecting Wren's fierce visage. But apparitions disappeared in a puff of smoke, not by jumping back behind a door. Shillitoe's conditioned reflexes had taken charge and as soon as diplomacy allowed he left ivory elbow soaking in the tub.

He did consider the option of waiting out the situation, but not very seriously. If Wren had bellowed and charged in and slugged him it might have been possible to stay. But delayed action bombs were too tricky. Beware the contemplative man who had to undergo a complete physical before making a chess move. His were the cruelest tortures.

Shillitoe had known he had to run. But he couldn't have gone far without Herman. Good old Herman, the only man who spoke less than Ben, was waiting in Shillitoe's room. Somehow he seemed up on the latest turn of events, pulling off a shoe and handing Shillitoe a folded, smelly hundred-dollar bill. Then Herman kept pushing him toward the back stairs. But Shillitoe refused to leave until he'd written the note. This was addressed to Wren, explaining that the long-overdue debt had been bought by Mr. Herman Horvath and that Wren was to return the hundred dollars *plus interest* to Mr. Horvath *immediately*. Herman read it over and nodded. He'd heard Shillitoe sound off in the group therapy meeting about how Wren robbed him. He understood.

The bus slowed again and turned off the highway, retching and climbing into the north side of Cob City, the gingerbread side where the boy Samson had tread softly in spite of his hardening convictions. At Para Park, the designer of these houses would be branded with a royalty complex. Each of the three-storied frame structures had a mysterious tower, each an engraved pediment and heavy, dripping cornices. Shillitoe could recall having stood outside one of them, toeing the edge of its untouchable lawn and watching a party silhouetted on the bay window. He could only have been six or seven then but the pitiable figure of himself in awe and envy still hurt. He'd partly made up for it a little later when, at maybe twelve or thirteen, he'd led a pimpled patrol into the backyard of the same house to watch the rich undress and discover Kipling's truth for themselves.

He had always thought of the north side as far from the Square, but the bus proved him wrong. Children were taught other than linear measurements. The Square! The focal point of all energy and time, the beginning of all distance, the anchor of all planets. The county courthouse still rose up as the apex of Cob City and (he blinked twice to make sure) there were the same old men draped in the same positions on the Liars' benches outside. Which one would they be telling—probably about the day it was so hot that all the popcorn in the field popped and the jackass thought it was snow and froze to death.

He'd guessed right about the neon and the new stores and the young girls' haunches. The cars slanted into the curbs now instead of alongside, and, at first count, there were seven saloons where there'd only been six. But more remained than he'd expected: Jack Bloom's shoe store and the Cob City Trust and the Grand Hotel with its ersatz Doric columns and the miserly Hinskin Brother's Pharmacy which still hadn't changed its window display and, there flaunting its mud-brown masthead, the inexhaustible emporium of J. C. Penney. But all were so much smaller, shrunken to half by the inch he'd grown.

The three taxi drivers sizing up the passengers reached for his briefcase at the same time like tap dancers finishing their routine, but he shook them off. Now that he was back all hurry and urgency departed. The present contracted into a substance to be tasted and touched and lived in, not through. It took him over an hour to walk the mile to the garage. Every few steps, something would spike his eyes on a memory and he would turn slowly, walking backwards until it disappeared or something else caught him. The road ran parallel to the meandering Lost River, past rolling fields of mint, dry-brushed against the hills. This was uncorrupted ground. Nature had been good to it, stopping the coal veins and sulphur springs and salt licks far enough away to keep out the impresarios. He stopped at the leftover ferry landing and remembered the boatmen singing Creole songs they'd learned in Vincennes. He put his ear to the ground and listened for the buffalo that had first stamped out the road. He walked out on the covered bridge and made sure it hadn't lost its boom to his hello.

Then the sign, loquacious as Ben himself:

GAS
CABINS

He'd been wrong to think the garage would look like an infirmary. It was white enough, but it was still the same old three partitions holding up the living quarters above with the box of an office and rest room pasted on one side. The Esso pumps were the same, too. More boyhood memories. How he'd waited for the day when he was first allowed to fill a tank. What would Para Park say to that? "The insertion of the pump nozzle is an obvious symbol." Shillitoe couldn't decide which was worse, wallowing in the treacle of the past or regarding it as a disease.

The big change, of course, was the row of cabins. There were three of them, enlarged outhouses—shutters down and all screens from the waist up—on the ridge behind the station. Though solid enough looking, they gave an impression of stages and particles. Shillitoe was sure Ben had built them himself.

As usual, the first sight of Ben was of the soles of his heavy shoes, then his white socks and the blue overalls slightly bent at the knees. The cars were much lower, but he still hadn't installed a lift or pit, managing somehow to squirm underneath. Shillitoe squatted alongside the canvas envelope of tools and waited. The banging stopped occasionally and Ben's hand would reach out for a pliers or wrench or different hammer. But his face stayed beneath the beaten-up '53 Dodge and the sun burned steadily hotter and the juice of homecoming began to dry. Before it could fully evaporate, Shillitoe slid all the tools out of their sleeves.

Ben's hand again, first sure, then groping, refusing to believe itself. He wriggled out, shielding his eyes, then raising them up Shillitoe like a tourist's up the Washington Monument. Shillitoe stood straight and still, glad he'd shaved and cleaned up in the bus terminal. Had he seen a twist of welcome in the gaunt hawk-face or had the reflection from a hub cap played a sardonic trick?

"You've come back," said Ben.

"Looks that way."

"Hungry?"

"Sure."

"Go on up," said Ben, "and put some coffee on while I wash up."

That was Ben's quota of talk for the year. Shillitoe watched him trudge across the gravel to the rest room. What was wrong? It was more than the shriveling and that the sinews were gone. The texture of the face was thawing, dissolving in a way he'd seen before. The cancer somewhere in Ben was well advanced.

Shillitoe took it slow going upstairs. Source of a first effort:

Rooms, like burly uncles,
shrivel as we grow.
The rug out in the rubbish bin
once was a plateau

The parlor had been papered recently but the pattern was of the same abnormally bright fruits and flowers. The maple-limbed mail-order furniture hadn't budged, but something new had been added. It was the slender binding of *Hellebore* on the mantel, peeking out between the Bible and the 1938 World Almanac—a position of honor second only to that held by the photograph of Mary. Shillitoe went closer to look at her.

Eighteen years a virgin,
eighteen months a bride,
eighteen hours your mother,
and I died.

Her face had less beauty than he'd ever admitted. Her hair at the sides narrowed her forehead and her teeth protruded a little. He was still studying the picture when Ben came in.

"Sorry," Shillitoe said. "I didn't put the coffee on yet."

"Ain't changed much."

As Ben rattled around in the small kitchen, Shillitoe went to the alcove. Nothing remained in it but the lumpy iron-railinged bed and the straight wooden chair; no clothes he'd outgrown, no tarnished trophies, no scraps of early writing.

And days are made from what we save
And dreams from what we throw away

Tourists would never pay a dime to see the cramped quarters where the poet Shillitoe was formed. He tossed his briefcase on the bed, sending up a fur of dust, then joined Ben at the table.

The eggs were greasy, the roll returned to raw dough as it touched his tongue and the coffee was dense with grounds. If Rhoda had come along she'd have hustled Ben away from the stove and saved all their digestions. But he was hungry and managed to get it down as Ben sat watching him.

"You in trouble?" Ben finally asked.

"Sort of."

"You right or wrong?"

"Who the hell knows what's right and what's wrong?"

"Still talking that way."

"And always will."

A car pulled in below and honked. Ben winced in pain as he got up.

"Safe here," he said. "Get some sleep."

The exhaustion which had been spreading over Shillitoe sealed his eyes as soon as he sprawled on the bed. Twice they fluttered open. The first time the window of the alcove was black and he heard footsteps and whispers outside. Young, luggageless lovers were fumbling toward the cabin assigned to them. Old Ben, pimping at his age. He hadn't turned out so badly after all.

The second time he was awakened he blinked at morning light and heard a rough voice blunting itself on Ben's stingy replies.

"Indianapolis got it on the teletype and passed it on."

"Did?"

"The New York police sent an inquiry on him."

"Did?"

"And one of the taxi boys recognized him getting off the bus yesterday."

"Did?"

Shillitoe went to the window and moved the curtain aside. The beefy character had his feet widespread and his thumbs hooked on the back of his belt. The black Ford idling nearby filled out the sketch. Small-town sheriff. He looked familiar.

"Wouldn't want to take Samson in, Ben. Hate to turn over an old buddy to those New York sheenies. But he can't stay in Cob City."

"Can't?"

"Look, Ben." The voice of the law had extended its generosity and now returned to duty. Shillitoe recognized it. Wesley Zimmerman. He always was a fart face. Old buddy, like hell.

"I can't have him right on my doorstep," said Wesley. "What if the State Troopers found him? How would I look? You tell Samson to get a move on."

"Where?"

"Anywhere, long as it ain't here."

Wesley had almost reached his Ford when Ben answered.

"Nope."

He retracted his steps and shoved his jaw at Ben.

"If he ain't gone by morning," he announced, "I'm takin' him in and wirin' New York for instructions. And I can close up those cabins of yours, too."

"And Mrs. Zimmerman can see my register."

Ben said it flatly, as if carrying on the sheriff's train of thought, but the wind wheezed out of big Wesley and he hardly had the strength to slam the door of the Ford before he skittered it away.

Shillitoe waited until they were washing up for lunch before asking Ben about the register.

"What they do's their business," said Ben. "But everybody takes a cabin, signs the book."

"And how many times has Wes Zimmerman signed it?"

" 'Bout once," answered Ben, wiping intently between his fingers before adding, "a week."

"What is Mrs. Zimmerman, besides unsatisfactory?"

In as few words as possible, Ben explained. Wesley Zimmerman had been elected on the Republican ticket and his father-in-law was party boss of the county.

"That's the way, Ben!" Shillitoe slapped him between the shoulder blades, producing a hollow sound. It was as if the ribs had loosened and been restrung on wires.

"Don't have to go away because of Wes Zimmerman," Ben said.

"I've come back to stay," said Shillitoe.

He had dug right in that morning, cleaning up the shed and waiting on the few customers who stopped for gas. Ben still hammered away under the Dodge, but seemed in no hurry to finish it. By noontime, Shillitoe knew that Ben's income derived less from the garage than from the cabins. After lunch he went up and swept these out, turned their sheets over and made the beds. Then he walked back into town.

No welcoming signs or bright bunting, but the streets waved their remnants. He seized on these, anxious to make a bridge of familiar objects to span the years. There had been the icehouse, there the dry cleaner fronting for the bookies, there the carvers still chipped scrollwork on a block of oölitic stone. In that candy store on Rush Street he'd deliberated over a future of licorice or peanut brittle. Into that lofty, stuccoed house on the corner of French and Marshall he'd dragged, hurting, helpless and resigned. And, after he'd refused to cite name or place, grinning Doctor Grantham had broken the inflamed, swollen innocence between a wooden mallet and towel-wrapped dictionary. What better seed for a love of words? Another day, another year, and half of Cob City clucked around the Grantham house as the heroin-heavy doctor was carried to the special car which would speed him to the Federal hospital in Lexington, Kentucky.

Shillitoe strolled on. The tar road heated the air until it danced, rising in torrid grace up the narrow flue between the trees. The citizens he passed moved slowly, steadily, certain they would last the day. Having been from this place he quickly regained the stride. It hadn't mattered that he'd scurried around. Character was formed in the first three years. If it hardened in a ghetto there was always the terror. If it hardened here there was always assurance. He had a point of departure and those who didn't could search all the ports of the world without finding as much as he'd gulped in to replace his first outraged scream.

He passed the library, a square ivy hive listing slightly toward its ballast of violence and passion, and went on to the high school. On its caked and cleated practice field he had learned the thrust toward vulnerability which sprung him from Gaye's closet. Inside, the corridors were sour with accumulated adolescent breath, the desk lids monogrammed and blackened around the dry inkwells, and the slate blackboards belatedly wished him a nice summer. Here a poem had been held the opposite to manliness. But the state insisted on a minimum memorized and he'd had to stand, rocking from foot to foot, mumbling some aloud; of a garden being a lovesome thing, of a cabin of clay and wattles and of not knowing where the goddam arrow fell to earth. Snorts and titters and goosings. But there'd been other lines that couldn't be cackled away.

Fat black bucks in a wine-barrel room

I strove with none; for none was worth my strife

And Richard Cory, one calm summer night,
Went home and put a bullet through his head.

They'd affected him. That was impossible to deny. And Miss Ada Jennison had touched him too by chanting Shakespeare in her quivering soprano and talking rapturously of a lover named Dusty Evsky. But the nourishment she'd served wasn't seriously bitten into until that calm summer night when Miss Jennison went home and joined Richard Cory.

Teacher spinning on a rope
Doctor self-prescribing dope

I hear America singing!

The ends of the bridge were joined now and firm. The intervening years had furnished him with compass and catapult. Everything else he needed was here. The heads of all those who'd delayed his return bobbled forgotten in the moat below until he stood before the Invicta Theatre. The paste-bubbled posters showed a pansy stalking some fluff with a bowie knife while she waited so openmouthed he could see all the way to her ovaries. MURDER IN HIS HEART! SIN ON HER LIPS! Rhoda would have liked this one; probably sit through it six times. If she'd come with him, she'd have worn a trench from the garage to the Invicta's little glass box-office booth.

He was still thinking about Rhoda when he turned around and bumped into Wesley Zimmerman. It was a stationary moment. Wesley, his eyes darting about like two flies on a moose turd, couldn't make up his mind whether to run or reach for the handcuffs ringed to his belt. Shillitoe decided to take the initiative.

"Whatcha' say, Wes?"

Wesley wasn't saying anything. He just squirmed there like a bludgeoned tuna.

"Don'cha' remember me, Wes?" Shillitoe realized as he asked it that he'd lapsed into Hoosier singsong. Meanwhile, Wesley was still staring, refusing to commit himself.

"Longfellow," said Shillitoe. "Don'cha' remember your old buddy, Hank Longfellow?"

"Huh? Oh, sure." Wesley extended a pudgy hand, pulling it back as soon as Shillitoe touched it. "Wha'cha' say, Hank?" And he galloped off.

Shillitoe felt better for the encounter. Ben's register had obviously vetoed the request from the New York police. Shillitoe hadn't given that matter any thought but, watching Wesley duck around the corner, he thought about it now. Who could have sicked the cops onto him here? Beverly knew about Cob City. He'd been dumb enough to laud it to her. But Papp couldn't have taken his proper action so fast. The only other possibility was Rhoda. Would a rejected woman stop at nothing?

She'd lost though. She'd lost for good. He was safe in the arms of county politics and a sheriff's libido. Not as warm arms as Rhoda's, but less treacherous and exhausting. Shillitoe started back for the garage, walking faster as his mind returned to the essential. Poets fought for minutes and he'd just won himself a stackful. The wheel was spinning, the flame leaping, the blaring insistence wouldn't be stilled.

Ben called out something to him, but he didn't hear. He had discordances to unload and new debris to weave into the poem. He took the steps two at a time, ran into the alcove and dumped the contents of the briefcase on the bed. Then, thrashing through the papers again and again, he refused to believe that the poem wasn't there.

Chapter Eighteen

OLIVER wished he'd made the luncheon date with Doctor Holland for a day earlier or a day later or for any other day but this. He knew he could neglect to mention the board meeting and that Doctor Holland would never give it a thought. Besides, Doctor Holland wasn't on the board of Para Park and, except as a courtesy, had no right to attend.

But Oliver didn't want anyone ever to be able to question the slightest aspect of his handling of the case. So he extended the invitation and Doctor Holland said he'd very much like to sit in.

Oliver had called the special meeting of the board as soon as Doctor Kropotkin notified him of Shillitoe's disappearance. He wanted to get the case out of his own hands and into theirs as soon as he could. As luck would have it, though, Milicent Akers was in Vermont putting the finishing touches to her latest book and couldn't even be reached by telephone, and Abelson begged off coming in from his one week with his family on Fire Island, and even Massey was off somewhere attending a conference on psychosurgery. So it was the day after Labor Day when they finally assembled. Shillitoe had now been gone almost two weeks.

For some reason, probably that they hadn't yet fully relocated from their recent trips, none of the members seemed much concerned. Oliver reiterated the fact that this was the first time any patient had left Para Park without being officially released, then called for a report from Doctor Kropotkin.

All he wanted was an objective recital of events and her own impressions as a psychiatrist. After all, the patient had been in her care for almost a week. Anything she'd observed would be pertinent. But Doctor Kropotkin merely stammered some irrelevancies about Shillitoe seeming to be happy at Para Park.

"Happiness is not a psychiatric term," Oliver reminded her. "Could you be more specific?"

"He vass functionink," said Doctor Kropotkin. "He vass identifyink. He vass relatink."

She let out an audible sigh of relief when Oliver thanked her and she was able to sit down.

Arnold was much more to the point. He repeated the same complaints he'd made to Oliver, about how Shillitoe had disrupted the group therapy sessions, how he'd spent all his time writing junk and how he'd monopolized the ripple bath. Mention of the bath stirred up that scene again and Oliver calmly noted the slight racing of his pulse and moist cracks of his palms. Such physiological reactions would keep him double-checking on his objectivity until he was no longer involved in the case.

Arnold, with a tactfulness Oliver had never accorded him, omitted his suspicion about Shillitoe's relationship with Doctor Kropotkin. A slight prodding would have brought it out, but Oliver saw no point in it. Arnold's conflicting testimony had damaged Doctor Kropotkin enough. Anything more would force her resignation and, though the woman was obviously incompetent as a psychiatrist, she seemed an able administrator and that was what the position at Para Park required most.

It was obvious that the others hadn't awakened to the significance of the case. Oliver hesitated to introduce the third report. It would be wasted while the board members were in such a sluggish frame of mind. He thought of making a sudden noise by shouting or hitting the table, anything to arouse them. But that wouldn't activate their interest. They simply did not share his involvement with the patient. He almost snorted aloud. That was the understatement of the year. They could *never* share his involvement. They could never know *everything* Shillitoe had done. But they could be told most of it.

"I think it is essential," he said, "for you to know something of the patient's behavior before he was admitted to Para Park." Oliver did not elaborate on the facts. He presented them chronologically and dispassionately, beginning with Mrs. Shillitoe's fear of her husband attempting suicide and ending with Shillitoe's uninvited appearance before this very board. In between were the items that gradually roused the members —Shillitoe's stealing a camera and attacking a policeman, Shillitoe's beating his wife so badly that she was unable to go to work the next day and Shillitoe's breaking into his office and listening to his recorded transcripts. This last, of course, was only half the story, but he couldn't very well tell them that Shillitoe had repeated the information from one of the transcripts to the patient's husband. Oliver still hadn't fully recovered from Mrs. Fish's visit and learning of the almost unbelievable coincidence. And he'd suspected Shillitoe of sex boasting!

The board was interested now. Oliver sat back and waited, wondering who would ask why this information wasn't presented when the applicant was interviewed. Massey probably. Or Abelson. No, Voegler spoke first.

"Doctor Kropotkin," he said. "Did you give him a Wasserman?"

Doctor Kropotkin's slack jaw told everyone that she hadn't. "Ve neffer do," she finally managed to say.

"It is then my fault," announced Voegler. "When the man was interviewed I realized he was a *phallus thaumaturgist.* He should never have been admitted to Para Park."

"You voted for him," said Massey.

"Never!" denied Voegler. "Most certainly not!"

"Yes you did." Massey's heavy breathing made it an accusation.

"I demand," sputtered Voegler, "I demand we get the minutes of that meeting."

"They're not necessary to this discussion," intervened Oliver.

"I would never vote to admit a *phallus thaumaturgist* without a Wasserman first," insisted Voegler. "Haven't I always maintained there is a high correlation between the *phallus thaumaturgist* and the syphilitic? And such a disintegration of behavior as we've just heard described, doesn't that frequently accompany the fourth stage of syphilis?"

Oliver could see Doctor Holland grinning and resented it. Not that the vehemence of Voegler's protest wasn't a bit too much. And Freddie's claiming he hadn't voted for admitting Shillitoe was ridiculous. Oliver clearly recalled that he himself had abstained and that Voegler, Milicent and Abelson had rendered the three necessary votes. But Doctor Holland couldn't know that. What so amused him was Voegler's harping on his pet *phallus thaumaturgist.* But it was possible that Voegler had stumbled onto something. After all, Shillitoe obviously slept with any woman who'd let him. So it wasn't unlikely that he'd contacted a venereal disease. Oliver thought of the black specks of the spirochete distending under the microscope and envisioned them being passed from Shillitoe to Lydia. And from her to him? No. He hadn't so much as kissed her since that day.

"May I interrupt?" asked Doctor Holland.

"The board welcomes your comments," said Oliver.

"I'm afraid I haven't any comments yet, not until I know much more about the case than I do now and, perhaps, not even then. But I'd like to hear more about the 'junk' that the attendant referred to. What exactly was the man writing?"

This was the ideal moment to introduce the third report, but Voegler had to jump in and ruin it.

"He thinks he's a poet," he said.

Holland's eyes twinkled as he turned to Voegler. "A poet? An artist? Well, well."

"Well, well, what?" asked Voegler suspiciously.

"I was just thinking of something your friend Sigmund once said."

"Doctor Freud!" corrected Voegler. "He wasn't Sigmund to me and he isn't Sigmund to you."

"Very well," conceded Holland. "But didn't Doctor Freud once say that psychoanalysis must lay down its arms before the problem of the artist?"

"The man isn't an artist," said Voegler. "He's a syphilitic."

"But we don't know that for sure."

"Besides, Doctor Freud stated explicitly that art is a manifestation of anal eroticism."

"Yes, he frequently contradicted himself."

The argument was about to get out of hand and Oliver wanted to stick to the subject of art.

"I have been very concerned with the question Doctor Holland has raised," he said. "Both in my capacity as Mr. Shillitoe's private doctor and when he was at Para Park I realized that any treatment had to include the possibility of his being an artist. If his writing was poetry, one set of factors applied—if it wasn't poetry, another. The problem was not an easy one, even if my literary knowledge was much greater than it is. I might add that none of his writing was readily accessible to me. At the time Mr. Shillitoe left Para Park, however, I happened to have borrowed from his room and without his knowledge, a sizable portion of manuscript he was working on. This, Doctor Holland, was the 'junk' Arnold referred to. I apologize for the unfortunate choice of that word and trust that the board members will not be influenced by it in any way."

"Can we see the manuscript?" asked Milicent Akers.

"I've taken the liberty of doing something I thought more expeditious," said Oliver. "I asked one of my patients, a prominent author of poetic drama, to suggest an outstanding authority on poetry. The person he named is one I'm sure you've all heard of." Oliver, pausing to give the name proper reverence, wished he hadn't called Alben Parker's dramas poetic. "X. O. Waterfall," he said, and though the others looked impressed, he decided to make sure.

"Mr. Waterfall, as you know, is probably the foremost anthologist of poetry in the country as well as being a poet in his own right. In addition, he is presently a professor of English at Princeton University and regularly contributes essays and criticism to several national publications. I have never met Mr. Waterfall. But I have spoken to him on the telephone and he agreed to read and give us his opinion of Mr. Shillitoe's writing."

Oliver didn't add that Miss Bueler had been unsuccessfully trying to contact Waterfall for several days and that he'd sent a telegram yesterday to remind the *great man* of this appointment. As he opened the door Oliver had a sudden, sinking certainty that the anteroom would be empty. But Arnold was there, engrossed in the newspaper comic strips. And, across the room, eying this disdainfully, a white-haired, stiff-collared and delicate little man who had to be X. O. Waterfall. Delicate was right. As Oliver escorted him in and introduced him, he could almost see a tremor passing through Waterfall's body. This was explained after the poet took a folded sheaf of typewritten pages from his inside coat pocket and pressed out its two creases on the arm of his chair.

"I am not very adept at extemporaneous speaking," Waterfall said, "so I wrote out what I wished to say. I'm afraid it never occurred to me that there would be ladies present. It just never occurred to me, and I'm afraid I've included a few quotations from Mr. Shillitoe's writing which are, shall we say, now inappropriate. If you'll allow me a few minutes, I'll make the deletions in my text."

Doctor Akers rose to her feet protesting and Voegler joined her, demanding that the report not be expurgated.

"Ve are medical peeble!" thundered Doctor Kropotkin and Mr. Waterfall shrank smaller than ever.

"As you wish," he agreed. "However, please note that any obscenities are Mr. Shillitoe's, not mine." He smoothed out the typewritten pages again and began to read in a quiet, unforced voice which was surprisingly easy to listen to.

"When I received Doctor Wren's request, I had never heard of Samson Shillitoe. I inquired about him among my graduate students at Princeton and one of them, a rather untidy youth, was not only familiar with his work but rather unstinting in his praise of it. I pass on this information to you to make it known that Samson Shillitoe has at least one admirer and, I suspect, more.

"By the time I received the handwritten manuscript from Doctor Wren, that same graduate student had supplied me with a considerable body of Samson Shillitoe's published efforts. Among these was one bound volume, entitled *Hellebore,* published—I must confess, to my surprise—by the respected firm of Tyler and Brothers, and consisting of one hundred and twenty-six pages of untitled poems of various lengths on the twin themes of love and death. It is undoubtedly unnecessary to add in my present company that the title, *Hellebore,* refers to the ancient name for a certain plant which was thought to cure madness.

"The other published works of Samson Shillitoe at my disposal were poems printed in various journals which we refer to as 'little,' 'quality' or 'literary' magazines. I counted seventy-three of these, published over a period of the past twelve years. As to the publications, some were responsible but most were of the more transitory journals often deemed 'arty.' Of the latter, the one which seemed to publish Samson Shillitoe with the most frequency was a magazine called *Moot.* It is one I have never read and which my better students judge as rather esoteric.

"I will make no specific criticism either of *Hellebore* or the other published work for the simple reason that I have not been asked to. However, I did feel it necessary to study them so as not to base my judgment of Samson Shillitoe's talent on the one manuscript which Doctor Wren provided. After all, even Shelley had his *Queen Mab,* didn't he? But let me say now that there was little discrepancy between the manuscript and the published work, so that my opinion of the manuscript can be accepted as a general evaluation of the writer's ability.

"The handwritten manuscript I was given bore no title. From this point on, for the purpose of clarity, I shall refer to it as 'the poem.' Careful examination of the poem has led me to conclude that in its entirety it will consist of four parts, though the sections I received fall into but three subdivisions. The construction of the poem is a familiar one. Poets in all ages have found it convenient to divide long works into four parts. *Endymion* leaps immediately to mind or, to give a more recent example, Eliot's *Four Quartets.* Four is a good symbolic number. There are four seasons, or man's life can be separated into the four stages of childhood, youth, middle years and old age. I could also present the parallel use in symphonic construction, but I'm sure that isn't necessary. The point I wish to make is that Samson Shillitoe is employing an established overall format. Though he has not subtitled his parts, I don't believe it would be too amiss to call Part One, 'discovery,' Part Two, 'exploration' and Part Three, 'exploitation.' Following the pattern I mentioned before, Part Four would then be the equivalent of winter or old age, say, 'destruction,' or, if the writer chooses to end on a hopeful note, he might try 'redemption.' But I promised not to conjecture about the part of the poem I haven't seen.

"Of what I *have* seen, perhaps the most favorable characteristic I can point to is a certain raw vitality. Indeed, it seems at times as if the very paper will explode with a bang as when one punches a blown-up bag. My metaphor is not intended to imply that Mr. Shillitoe is full of warm air. In fact, he often goes to unnecessary extremes to prove the contrary. He literally strips himself to the bone to show that he conceals nothing, palms nothing and, what is more pertinent, borrows nothing from the acknowledged masters of his medium. Though I detect some admiration for William Blake, Shillitoe will have none of Blake's lamb, nor even of Shelley's skylark. Shillitoe only once ventures away from the human image and then, of all living creatures to extol, he chooses the sea gull. In fact, if sea gulls are all that Shillitoe can see in the sky, one is tempted to quote Dante, *'O frate, l'andar su che porta?'*"

Waterfall paused, as if expecting laughter. When it didn't come, he cleared his throat and muttered, "Or, 'Brother, what is the use of going up?' " Then he again buried his sharp, veined nose in his report.

"Of course, when one refuses to learn from the great poets of the past, it is always possible that one is not capable of learning. This is not very likely true of Samson Shillitoe. Though he exhibits little evidence of a formal education, I would guess that he has traveled and read widely, though in the opportunistic manner which Robert Graves described as 'proleptic.' Shillitoe's is an undisciplined and fragmentary knowledge. But his lack of scholarship, instead of making him humble, seems to have given him a pronounced confidence, if not an Olympian conceit. Not having the classical grounding which reveals shades of gray, he sees only blacks and whites. Not knowing the philosophers' scale of comparison, he insists that everything he sees and hears and feels is absolutely true. Throughout the poem there is not a solitary note of hesitation or doubt. He does not make a single qualification. This would be tolerable in a work of Augustan purification but Mr. Shillitoe's manuscript doesn't fall into this category. A charitable verdict would be that he is engulfed in the same haze of innocence that so limited the Romantics. Such a pronouncement, however, involves the emotional maturity of the work and you are better qualified to judge that than I. My concern, as I understood it, was not to be with what Samson Shillitoe had to say but with whether or not he said it poetically.

"I think not. Of course, as Coleridge so aptly pointed out, one cannot expect a long poem to be all poetry. But even after making that concession to Mr. Shillitoe, I believe he fails. That does not mean I find no virtue at all in his work. There are some striking lines. When describing the sensation of waking from a nightmare he says, 'Sleep, sleep, before the pillow's dampened thread slinks back inside the silent ear.' I rather like that. But this knack for imagery can also be put to bad purpose. For example, when Shillitoe derides those American poets who are openly indebted to English poetic heritage as 'Magdalen's Foreign Legion,' and in another reference, equates their writing with 'rat's feet embroidering the edges of the Thames.' Not only is the jargon unfortunate but such insularity of sentiment has no place on the international plane of poetry. However, to remain completely fair, Shillitoe's strong regional identification does occasionally pay a small dividend. Take the phrase, 'Apaches in the alleys keep us walking on the street.' The image is peculiar to America and is cleverly applied to present-day conformity. As we stand at the new frontiers of the space and nuclear age our shapeless fears loom up as did once the war-painted, fierce Apaches. So, more and more, we stay to the brightly lighted and broad main thoroughfares we know. At least, that is my interpretation of the lines.

"There are others, perhaps a dozen lines in all, which I consider meaningful. When Mr. Shillitoe refers to the lack of direct communication between people, he employs the simile, 'like fenceposts in Montana snow.' This, I think, is rather good. You see the drifts with only the tops of the posts sticking out, each seemingly isolated. Yet you are aware that concealed by the clean, untrodden snow are the connecting wires, barbed and strong.

"But a dozen effective lines do not make a poem. One wishes constantly that Mr. Shillitoe would stop and define what poetry is to him. In that way we might better be able to follow what he is attempting to do. But he seems not to care. Only once does he allude to poetry itself, when he says, 'The lie makes work for poetry, while liars play the games.' This you will notice is consistent with my previous remark about Mr. Shillitoe's private version of truth. One is reminded of Keats' statement that the only means of strengthening one's intellect is to make up one's mind about nothing. But Mr. Shillitoe appears to have made up *his* mind about everything. This is to be pitied because Mr. Shillitoe is not totally barren of talent. If he confined himself to poetry, he might even be deserving of some encouragement. If only he could learn from Mistral that form alone exists. If only he could accept Lord Bacon's advice and not try to use poetry to subject the soul to external things. But Mr. Shillitoe seems determined to stand apart and forge a new poetry. And, since poetry cannot be divorced from the warp and woof of all life, he has taken on himself the task of formulating a new philosophy, a new religion, a new politics, a new version of history and even at times a new language. I need not here concern myself with his special brand of atheism, anarchy and metaphysics. As Valéry so ably put it, 'Poetry is made with words.' So I will just comment briefly on one way in which Mr. Shillitoe abuses language.

"Throughout the poem there appears what can only be described as latrine hieroglyphics. These become most obnoxious in the second part where Shillitoe deals with what he calls 'the bullshit of history.' Again he confines himself to our national history claiming that every poet has to clean up his own mess. Some of the references are indeed unforgivable. For example, when he speaks of George Washington as the father of our country, the o in country is deleted, I am sure deliberately—for in a prose passage following this line Shillitoe tells an outlandish story about our first President dying of a stab wound inflicted by his gardener who found Washington in bed with his wife. 'Diggin' in her cabbage patch' is precisely the offensive wording used."

Oliver thought of the cuckolded gardener coming upon his wife with Washington and a curtain descended over Waterfall's voice and the rapt faces of the board members. All Oliver could see and hear was that damp, steamy room and the bucking aluminum tub and the two of them wrapped together so tightly. A lowly gardener wouldn't hesitate to attack the most esteemed man in the country if he found him making love to his wife. Why hadn't he done as much? Why hadn't he rushed in and dragged Shillitoe from the tub and hit him and hit him and hit him until his face was smashed and broken and his mouth gushing blood? Why hadn't he even gone in and confronted them? Why had he turned his back and sneaked away?

Oliver knew very well why. Shillitoe was his patient. It was as simple as that. If he had let his temper override his concern for his patient, if the role of husband had superseded that of doctor, then he would no longer have the right to regard himself as a man of science. Actually, he was proud of his behavior. He could not imagine any situation ever trying him as strenuously as that of the ripple bath. He would never again worry about his ability to maintain a detached view toward any case he undertook.

The test, though, hadn't completely ended. Every time he looked at Lydia he was tried anew. Sentiments and responses he'd never had coursed through him. Since he'd been sixteen or seventeen he'd known that intercourse while bathing was not an uncommon practice and he and Lydia had often kidded about it. But they had never done it, and now he wanted to. He wanted to very much. Whenever he heard her splashing in the bath, he could hardly restrain himself. But he knew that if he instigated it so soon after what had happened, she might guess why. Besides, a stationary, porcelain tub wasn't the same as a ripple bath.

There were other cravings and Oliver carefully noted them. He wanted to embarrass Lydia. At a cocktail party the night before, watching her standing a bit apart with that immaculate demureness she always assumed, he'd wanted to strip her bare in the center of the room and let all the men present gawk at her. He wanted her to be so destitute she had to dance at a cheap roadhouse or take to prostitution. He wanted to bloat her with another baby and this time insist on witnessing the delivery. Most of all, he wanted to seduce her over and over and over. But he was afraid to touch her, not because of the spirochete but because he was afraid to do anything which might jog the balance of his self-control before he completely disposed of the case of Samson Shillitoe.

Now that was almost accomplished. Oliver again reviewed the events of the past two weeks to make certain his professional ethics hadn't shown the slightest flaw. Had he endeavored to prejudice any member of the board against Shillitoe? To the contrary, he had bent over backwards to do just the opposite. As president of Para Park, however, he did have his responsibilities. He didn't want Shillitoe's leaving to reflect improperly on Doctor Kropotkin or other members of the staff. That was the main reason for today's meeting. Having Shillitoe's manuscript evaluated had been an afterthought. But, after making such a strong speech about genius and evil, Oliver felt open to the old charge of his practice not living up to his preaching. The board members knew that Shillitoe wrote and one of them might ask why Oliver was giving up so readily on a possible genius. This could be avoided if a literary authority asserted that Shillitoe was not in the genius class. On the other hand, Oliver knew that X. O. Waterfall might declare Shillitoe an artist. One moment, as Waterfall quoted lines which impressed him, Oliver was sure he would. The next, as Waterfall assailed Shillitoe in sarcastic terms, Oliver observed his own feeling of relief. It was no use trying to deceive himself. The case would be disposed of much more easily if Waterfall concluded that Shillitoe's writing had no merit.

The complete silence dug into Oliver's thoughts. No one was speaking and Waterfall was patting his pages into a neat pile. Abelson seemed to realize the report was finished at the same moment and began to applaud. But suddenly aware of doing it alone, he pretended to be swatting at a mosquito.

Oliver sat forward and appealed to the committee for questions. They looked back at him vacantly and he guessed that their minds had wandered during Waterfall's reading just as his had. Only Doctor Holland appeared alert and Oliver was now glad he'd asked him to the meeting after all.

"I'd like a little clarification," said Holland.

"Proceed." Waterfall sounded like he was addressing one of his graduate students at Princeton.

"The purpose of your report is to tell us if the behavior of Samson Shillitoe is to be evaluated on the basis of his being an artist."

"So I understood," said Waterfall.

"Can we assume from what you've said that you do not consider such special consideration warranted?"

"I thought I made my opinion exceedingly clear," said Waterfall with a tolerant smile.

"You did," agreed Holland. "But since this is a sort of verdict, we would avoid any possible misunderstanding if you'd say yes or no."

"Yes or no, what?"

"Do you believe Samson Shillitoe to be an artist or, more specifically, a poet?"

"No."

"Thank you." Holland waved his hand to signify acceptance and started to sit down. Oliver had seen his mentor in action too often. He knew Holland was far from finished.

"By the way, Doctor Waterfall," said Holland, standing up again.

"*Mister,* not Doctor."

"I'm sorry."

Waterfall was flustered and Oliver knew Holland had tagged him deliberately.

"I'm afraid I don't read as much poetry now as in the days of my youth," said Holland.

"That's your misfortune," countered Waterfall.

"I'm sure it is," said Holland. "I must also apologize for not being familiar with your poetry, sir. I did understand Doctor Wren to say that you write poetry as well as criticism, didn't I?"

"I have published a considerable body of poetry."

"But"—Holland stabbed his forefinger toward the ceiling exactly as Oliver had seen him do hundreds of times before—"but Samson Shillitoe has published poetry, too. At least, so I understood you to say. So, do I gather that the publication of poetry does not necessarily make one a poet?"

Waterfall fidgeted with the pages of his report and sighed patiently before answering.

"I referred to Mr. Shillitoe's manuscript as 'the poem,' " he said, "because, as I explained, I thought it would simplify matters. But I was careful to refer to his published efforts as his work or his writing, never as poetry."

"They are definitely not poetry?"

"In my opinion they are not."

"He is not even a minor poet?"

"You must realize that *even* a minor poet is a superior creative person."

"Yes or no, please, Mr. Waterfall?"

"Shillitoe, in my opinion, is not a minor poet. No."

"Thank you." Again Holland made as if to resume his seat, but as soon as he saw Waterfall relax he shot his next question. "How about your efforts?"

"I beg your pardon?" Waterfall was wearying now.

"Are your published efforts poetry or mere writing?"

Oliver felt he was going too far and hastened to intervene.

"Doctor Holland, I presented Mr. Waterfall's qualifications before we heard his report."

Holland turned slowly to face him and Oliver knew the penetrating look was intended to make him uneasy.

"I know you did, Doctor," said Holland, "but we are being asked . . ."

"The *board* members are being asked," corrected Oliver.

"That's right." Holland always appreciated being picked up on an error. "The board members are being asked to accept Mr. Waterfall's literary opinion of Shillitoe's writing. Therefore, I submit that the board should also hear not *your* opinion of Mr. Waterfall's writing but Mr. Waterfall's opinion of his own writing. For all we know, he may judge his own work as something less than Shillitoe's."

Oliver knew Holland was enjoying himself. Waterfall, meanwhile, kept looking dazedly back and forth between them.

"Would you mind answering?" asked Oliver gently.

"I've forgotten the question," said Waterfall.

"Do you consider your work to be poetry?"

"Of course," said Waterfall.

"Minor poetry or major poetry?" Holland was really twisting the knife.

"I am prepared to let posterity decide that," said Waterfall with quiet dignity.

Oliver felt the little man regained some stature with that and hurried to thank him for his enlightening report and accompanied him out to the anteroom.

"I didn't expect an inquisition!" Waterfall was obviously upset.

"I should have warned you," Oliver apologized. "Psychiatrists are in the habit of asking impertinent questions."

"They certainly are." Waterfall had refolded his report but

was having difficulty fitting it into the inside pocket of his suit-coat. Then he remembered to return the manila envelope bulging with Shillitoe's manuscript.

"We're all very grateful," repeated Oliver, but Waterfall still didn't leave.

"Shall I send my statement to the society or to you?" he finally asked. Oliver was glad he did. A bill mailed to the society might raise a question of procedure. The budget didn't allow for any outside reports. Neither did his own, actually. But it was worth paying three hundred dollars to insure his objectivity toward Shillitoe.

"A statement isn't necessary," said Oliver and wrote out the check.

Re-entering the meeting room, he met a silence that seemed sudden and unnatural. Someone had been holding forth and the angles at which the members sat told him it was Massey.

"If there is no other business—" began Oliver.

"I was just wondering," broke in Voegler. "This bringing in an outsider with a formal report and everything. Is this a precedent you're setting?"

"No."

"What I mean is," said Voegler, "why so much fuss over one patient?"

Oliver suspected it was a digression, but he still had to meet it seriously.

"I established that before," he said. "Shillitoe is the first patient ever to leave Para Park without being released."

"So we've got to take an hour to hear about poetry?"

"I think we're avoiding the basic issue," said Massey. "The basic issue is not that one patient has spurned Para Park. It is that there are some patients, of whom Shillitoe is but an example, on whom the treatment offered at Para Park is ineffective."

"Yes," squeaked Milicent Akers. "We were talking about that while you were out of the room. Doctor Massey thinks this case called for psychosurgery."

"Hindsight," grunted Voegler.

"I recommended psychosurgery when the patient was first interviewed," claimed Massey. "Isn't that so, Doctor Wren?"

"Yes," admitted Oliver. "But couldn't this wait until our next meeting?"

"Why not take a vote now?" challenged Massey. "All the members of the board are here."

"A vote on what?"

"On my motion."

"What motion?" asked Oliver testily.

"I move that Para Park be opened to psychosurgery."

Oliver was going to argue, but the others did it for him, questioning, qualifying, drawing out statistics and percentages and reversion ratios, then demanding guarantees.

"In other words," summed up Abelson, "the results can be as different as the individual patients."

"Not with acute schizophrenics."

"That's only your opinion," taunted Voegler.

"I can prove it!" Massey dabbed the back of his neck and offered his final compromise. "Let me demonstrate with one transorbital lobotomy. And I will perform this only on an acute schizophrenic who has failed to respond to your other treatment at Para Park."

It was a stupid motion. All the patients at Para Park were responding well, and who was to decide if one of them wasn't? But no one raised any further objection and, as president, Oliver had to call for the vote.

"Yes," began Massey.

"No," barked Voegler.

"No," echoed Abelson.

So the whole discussion had been in vain anyway. What was Milicent waiting for?

"Doctor Akers? How do you vote?"

"I think . . . yes," she said.

"Two and two," counted Massey.

Oliver looked to Doctor Holland, then remembered that

Holland and Doctor Kropotkin were not members of the board.

"It's up to you," said Voegler.

Oliver wished they'd all stop drilling holes toward him with their eyes. The room was suffocating enough without their hemming him in.

"Well?" Massey kept drumming his stumpy fingers.

Oliver refused to be rushed. What was the basic issue again? He had to boil it down to fundamentals. It would be easier if the air conditioning hadn't gone off. No, the ribbon on the window unit was still fluttering.

"Yes."

Oliver heard his voice say the word. He wanted to cancel it, to think some more, but the others were asking for adjournment and he complied. As he stood up, the back of his suit stuck to him and his shirt felt like it needed wringing out. If only he could go back to the apartment and shower and shave instead of having to lunch with Holland at the club. Any day but this.

In the cab, Holland kept the talk light and easy. Oliver knew this technique too and was waiting for the carefully timed question when it did come.

"Haven't you taken an unusual amount of interest in this man?"

"Which man?"

"What's his name, Shillitoe?"

"No more interest than I take in any patient."

"Admirable."

"Thank you."

Holland waited a full minute before his next thrust.

"You're sure you've no special interest?"

"What does that mean?"

"I'm not sure exactly."

"Then you can't expect me to know, can you?" Oliver sat forward, away from the hot leather seat of the cab. The combination of heat and fumes made him nauseous and he had to breathe through his mouth. Why the devil did they have to go all the way downtown to the club when any of a half-dozen nearby restaurants served better food?

The lobby of the club was especially cool as if to justify itself. Oliver never drank at midday but when Holland suggested it, he followed him into the small bar. The single Scotch was just what he needed and the slight lightheadedness would wear off during lunch. The unidentifiable music was soothing, too, mingling with the subdued conversations in the rooms.

"Another round, please."

It was Massey looming up out of nowhere. But at least he didn't gloat over the meeting. Just small talk, trout fishing and golf and his new Mercedes, until he noticed the envelope.

"I'll bet that's the poetry we've been hearing so much about." And, when Oliver nodded, "Any objection to my borrowing it for a few days?"

Oliver couldn't think of any and slid the envelope along the bar toward him.

"Send it to Doctor Kropotkin when you've finished," he said. "She has the patient's home address." He turned to go into the dining room, but Massey restrained Doctor Holland.

"A little riddle," he said, hoisting the envelope as if weighing it. "Suppose a passenger on a ship fell overboard and so did this. And suppose that man Shillitoe was standing at the rail. From what you heard today, which do you think he'd try to save?"

"I have no idea," said Holland.

"Take a guess," persisted Massey.

Holland threw Oliver a quizzical glance before answering.

"The passenger?"

"Maybe," said Massey. "Or maybe neither one. But I think he would try to save the poetry."

Chapter Nineteen

THE letters from Daniel K. Papp had been arriving with increasing frequency. Rhoda placed each new one at the bottom of the neat pile on the table so they'd be in order. In a way she was glad the letters kept coming. Each time she saw Samson's name typewritten on an envelope she felt that, officially at least, he still lived there.

The postcard was another story. One side was a mess, full of crossings out and "not at this address." As far as she could tell, the card went someplace first, then went back to the sender, then was forwarded to Samson in care of Rollie Butter and Rollie had readdressed it properly. She figured this out while eating her breakfast and it was only after she had done so that she turned the card over.

Dear Customer:
The camera you returned contained a roll of partially exposed film. It has been developed and printed and you can call for your photographs any day before six P.M. *(Nine* P.M. *on Saturdays.)*

Before her conscience could get started on her having read Samson's private mail, she decided that the postcard was just a come-on gimmick. They made up any old lies to get people into their stores so they could sell them on having a picture taken or something.

Still, doubt throbbed in Rhoda's head all day. There was one chance in a million that the camera store was on the level. And they couldn't *force* her to buy anything. And she had nowhere else to go when she finished work.

The clerk who dug the brown envelope out of a box full of brown envelopes did ask her if she needed any fresh rolls of film. But he didn't try to sell them very hard and Rhoda felt ashamed of having suspected the store. She didn't feel as much ashamed when the clerk soaked her a buck sixty-five, and her suspicions came back bigger than ever when she found the envelope full of blank strips of celluloid. She was about to turn right around and get her money back when she noticed the dark rectangle on the end of one strip of film and, at the bottom of the envelope, the picture. It was only about an inch big so she had to hold it close to her eyes and it was pretty dark and fuzzy, but she still recognized the woman!

Plodding out of the store, Rhoda called herself every name she could think of. No wonder Samson always said she was a lunkhead. If she wasn't stupid like he said, would she have paid a buck sixty-five for one little picture of his woman with nothing on? And when she found him at Da Vinci Hall dead drunk with that woman, would anyone but a dope have believed it when he said there was nothing going on between them? They were rolling all over the platform, but Samson said there was nothing going on between them, so she believed it. Boy, sometimes even she was amazed at how dumb she could be.

The insult which hurt the most, though, was the shape of the woman in the picture. Rhoda had heard Samson say a thousand times that he couldn't stand dumpy women. He always said it in quotation marks because Lord Byron, whose real name was George Gordon, had said it first. But, anyway, every time Samson said it, Rhoda had laid off the dessert. She wasn't dumpy, but she was pretty solidly built and, if she wasn't careful, she could blow up. But even if she ate nothing but desserts she could never look like the woman in the photograph. This was the dumpiest woman that ever lived. And Samson had taken a picture of her without a stitch on. So much for his taste. He was a hypocrite. He probably preferred dumpy women all along and only pretended that he didn't because he wanted to sound like Lord Byron.

Rhoda wasn't sure what hate felt like. Samson always said she wasn't capable of it. But if the thoughts she was having now weren't hate they would certainly do. They scraped against her insides like sandpaper and there was a painful feeling across her chest like she'd swallowed a coat hanger. She'd never hurt so much in her whole life. She was poisoned with hate and Samson had done it.

Seeing Mrs. Fitzgerald coming out of their building, Rhoda almost dove into the Double-Deuce. Then she saw the man with her, a big well-dressed salesman type with one of those leather portfolios under his arm. He had Mrs. Fitzgerald busy talking and Rhoda decided it was a good chance to scoot upstairs and burn the picture and film.

"Oh, here she is now," said Mrs. Fitzgerald. "This gentleman was looking for you."

"I don't want any," said Rhoda and went inside.

It wasn't until she was on the top landing digging out her key that she heard the footsteps following her. If her hand hadn't been shaking with anger she would have been inside with the door locked before he got there. But she was still trying to fit the key in when he started up the last flight of stairs.

"I told you I don't want any," she called down, holding the railing with one hand and shoving the other one against the wall to bar his way.

"I'm not selling anything, Mrs. Shillitoe."

Rhoda drew an invisible line two steps down. If the face came above that it would get her shoe planted in it.

"I want to speak to you about your husband."

Rhoda suddenly had him pegged.

"Daniel K. Papp," she said.

He stopped on the fourth step from the top and looked down over the bannister as if checking to see if he'd come the right way.

"I thought your husband was Samson Shillitoe."

"So?"

"But didn't you just say Daniel K. Papp?"

"He ain't here anyway," said Rhoda.

"Daniel K. Papp?"

"Samson."

Granted her hunch about who he was had been wrong but, compared to him, she was fast on the uptake.

"Suppose we begin again."

"Okay," sighed Rhoda. "What's your spiel?"

"Spiel?"

"Don't you understand anything?" she asked.

"I'm afraid you're confused."

"*I'm* confused."

"I mean, you think I'm someone else."

"Look, I'm dead." She went to the door and this time the key went straight into the hole. But he was right behind her.

"Beat it," she said.

"It will only take a minute."

"Beat it!"

"I've been waiting for over an hour."

"One . . . two . . ."

"Doctor Wren will be very disappointed."

The name still had a magical effect on Rhoda. Just hearing it relaxed her as much as two Anacin. And in the light of the apartment, after the man followed her in, he didn't seem so mean-looking.

"I'm afraid I haven't introduced myself," he said, sinking down in Samson's chair. "I'm Doctor Massey."

Massey was uncomfortable. He had no stomach for this cat-and-mouse, bedside manner, hand-holding piffle that so many of his colleagues rejoiced in. They wanted to be called scientists but they wouldn't stop acting like some hybrid of priest and playboy. He was one of the few real scientists in the entire Parapraxes Society. He knew his tools, he knew his technique and procedure and he could predict the results sixty percent of the time. That was science. Not the cajoling and coaxing of this stupid woman who had acted as if she wasn't even going to let him enter her shabby two-room tenement.

He wished she'd sit down. Her towering over him added to his discomfort. Not that she was tall; only five foot three or four. But the one chair in the room which looked big enough to hold his two hundred and eighty pounds had proved deceptive. The damn thing didn't have any springs so that only the thin lumpy cushion separated his trouser seat from the floor, and the arms of the chair had caught him underneath the shoulders like crutches. He wondered if he'd be able to get out of the contraption without assistance. Mrs. Shillitoe might have to get one of the neighbors to help pull him out. All in due time, however. He could do his explaining from where he was.

Oddly enough, she didn't go white and pull the hysteria act that women so often did under the circumstances. Her thalamus was obviously sluggish. Even when he told her some of the remarkable achievements of the new treatment available to her husband, she didn't seem to care. This encouraged Massey to take a stab at getting her signature straight off and he unzipped his case and produced the three copies of the papers.

As she took them the first hesitation appeared. She shook her head at his proffered pen, lowered herself slowly onto one of the wooden chairs flanking the table and mouthed each word as she read.

"It's a standard form," said Massey. But her concentration made her deaf to him. There was nothing to do but wait. He lurched slightly to one side and managed to slide his hand down to his back pocket. Another lunge and he had his handkerchief and was able to wipe the perspiration from the back of his neck.

Twenty minutes later she finished the last line and looked up at him.

"Well?" he asked, smiling reassuringly.

"I don't understand a word," she said.

"Let me explain." He tried to hoist himself from the chair

but got less than halfway up before his elbows gave and he plopped down into it again.

"Don't bust the chair!"

"Let me explain," repeated Massey, clenching his teeth. How the hell could he speak to her as a scientist while caught in this tiger trap?

"So?"

"It is very simple. In cases of this kind, we like to have the consent of the patient's spouse before beginning treatment."

"Why?"

"It's strictly a formality."

"I don't want anything to do with him," she grumbled.

"I can understand your feelings," consoled Massey.

"How do you know?"

"What I mean is, the spouse of a mental patient endures so much that there is often a desire to wash one's hands of the whole thing."

This seemed to strike a responsive chord inside her. She looked down at the papers again and flipped the corner of them with her thumb.

"Tell me one thing," she finally said.

"Gladly." Massey braced himself to meet any of several questions which required delicate answering.

"What's a spouse?"

It took him a while to rearrange his thoughts.

"A spouse is a husband or a wife."

"So why didn't you say so? You doctors. It's like those prescriptions that nobody can read but you and the druggist."

"I'm sorry, Mrs. Shillitoe. I—" Massey cut off his apology because she was holding out her hand and he realized she was waiting for his pen. He uncapped it before handing it to her and she lowered her head to the form and, with a sudden flourish, licked the nib. A filthy habit, the gesture of a peasant before making an X. It was bad enough when done with regular ink but the chemical effect of spittle on the special indelible, quick-drying ink in his fountain pen was grotesque. All he could do was toss his handkerchief to her, but she batted it aside and ran to the kitchen sink.

After she came back, gargled and wiped clean, he had to refasten her mind to the papers. But now she didn't seem so ready to sign them.

"Why didn't Doctor Wren tell me about this himself?"

"He's a very busy man."

"How come you've got so much time?"

"I don't have, Mrs. Shillitoe. I'm here because I'm interested in your husband's condition."

"I ain't," she scowled. "Not any more."

"But perhaps you will be after he's received proper care and returns to you a different man."

"I ain't taking him back."

Massey wondered why she glared at her handbag as she said it. "That's up to you," he soothed. "But still, as a humanitarian, you want him to receive all the help he can."

The chin which she'd been thrusting toward him seemed to recede a bit. She turned to the papers again and ran her finger down the top one until she found what she was hunting for.

"It says 'surgery.' "

"A technical term," explained Massey.

"It ain't so technical. I know what it means."

"What I meant was, in medical terminology, many things fall under the heading of surgery which you might not consider surgical. For example, the extraction of a tooth."

"You call that surgery?"

"Yes."

"And here I've been telling people I ain't never been operated on."

"In fact," said Massey, "the treatment offered Mr. Shillitoe doesn't amount to much more than having a tooth pulled."

He criticized himself for not having drawn this parallel sooner. That's what people like Wren did. They put everything into terms that the most ignorant could understand.

"You sure it won't hurt him?" Her voice had suddenly lost its pugnacity.

"Positive," said Massey. "As I pointed out, it's like having a tooth pulled."

"I had one pulled that hurt like hell," she said. "This one here." She pulled the side of her mouth back to her ear and pointed to an empty space.

So much for putting it into simple terms. Massey changed back to the role of scientist, carefully explaining that most pain was in anticipation and that since her husband need not know of the treatment in advance he need not anticipate it.

"Besides," he added, "under a local anesthetic, the patient doesn't feel a thing."

She seemed to be examining his logic on the point of his pen. Then, after several minutes, she touched it to the bottom of the form again.

"How much is this surgery gonna' cost?"

"Nothing."

"You sure Doctor Wren thinks it's the best thing?"

"It was he who made it possible."

This was the added note of reassurance she needed. Her nose descended alongside the pen and she carefully wrote a square, legible signature.

"Would you sign all three copies, please?"

When she had, the mandatory papers taunted him from well beyond his reach.

"Mrs. Shillitoe?"

"What now?"

"Please help me up."

She placed both feet against the base of the chair and hoisted him to his feet with surprising ease.

"I always have to do that for Samson," she said, and the memory saddened her face.

Massey tried not to look too eager as he scooped up the forms and pocketed them. He was anxious to escape from the stuffy room but he wasn't quite finished.

"Where can I find Mr. Shillitoe now?"

"You mean you don't know?"

"I'm afraid I don't."

"Then how can you give him treatments?"

"I hoped you'd tell me where he is."

"I ain't got the slightest idea," she said. "And I never want to see him anyway."

The chin was thrusting out again and her belligerence seemed real. She probably *didn't* know where he was. But what she didn't know today she might know tomorrow. As he took back his pen he held out his card.

"If you should hear from your husband, will you call me right away?"

"Why you?" she asked. "He's Doctor Wren's patient."

"Then will you call Doctor Wren? By the way," he added, "there is a manuscript which Mr. Shillitoe was working on."

"I ain't interested in poetry any more."

"I just thought I'd mention it. If your husband should want it, will you tell him it's at Para Park?"

"Para Park," she repeated, as if memorizing it.

Out on the landing, with the door closed behind him, Massey found a dry patch on his handkerchief and mopped his face and neck. Then he patted the pocket holding the signed papers. From below a stench was rising. His unerring sense of smell identified it as cabbage being boiled and he was about to start down into it when he caught the odor filtering from the room he'd left. He sniffed several times but couldn't place it. Whatever Mrs. Shillitoe was cooking was something he'd never before encountered. It smelled just like burning celluloid.

Chapter Twenty

ONCE again, conclusive proof that companionship is debilitating. Honeymoons produce more pains than passions. The presence of another provokes infected cells just as attentive adults bring out the worst in children. The healthiest man, as well as the strongest man, stands alone.

This time Ben provided the evidence. In the days following Shillitoe's arrival, the black edges of his cancer doubled their speed. It was as if his muscles had barely staved off the onslaughts of the disease until reinforcements got there, then collapsed.

Shillitoe took over the garage work, and Ben, while providing simple instructions on the automatic transmissions and power stuff, handed him the tools. But even this seemed an agony, the fingers that used to be so sinewy now loose and trembling so that the tools as often as not slipped from them. Once when this happened their avoiding glances caught, each informing the other that he knew what was happening. After that, Ben confined himself to straightening up their rooms and the cabins and to dismal attempts at meals. For a while he tried to conceal his own lack of appetite. But when even dry toast produced convulsions, he dropped all pretense of eating and only sipped weak tea. Then one morning he was no longer able to rise from his bed.

Running the place shouldn't have been too much for one person. There were few repair jobs and only one or two cars an hour stopped for gas. But these always seemed to pull in when Shillitoe was up cleaning out the cabins and he'd have to race down. Then, too, Ben required some looking after. By nightfall Shillitoe was fairly worn out. But then he had to stay in the office until the last cabin was taken and his register signed. It was a brand-new register, Woolworth's best, blank and innocent. Ben had started him off with a clean slate before dragging upstairs for the last time. At least, Shillitoe thought that was his motive until the morning he found the office had been broken into.

"Wes Zimmerman," Ben called from his bed. "Know the sound of his Ford. Was a little before three."

Shillitoe was sure the cancer had reached Ben's brain.

"Now why the hell would the sheriff break in?"

"The register," Ben said.

After that, Shillitoe was aware of Wesley Zimmerman's frequent visits. The black Ford would appear at various hours of the day or night. Often as not, he wouldn't hear it arrive and was sure that Wesley cut his motor down the road and coasted in. Once, coming out of one of the cabins and spotting the sheriff's car below, he hurried down and surprised Wesley in the office. Another time he found him rummaging in the toolbox. In both cases Wesley coughed and hawed and blustered and fell over his own feet getting back to his car. In both cases the Longfellow routine was preserved and Wesley sang out a "see ya', Hank" before pulling away. Shillitoe knew that once the sheriff got the old register in his mitts that would be dispensed with. He kept meaning to ask Ben where it was, but every time he remembered to, Ben was asleep.

The thing that was getting more obvious every day was that the place needed a woman. Shillitoe knew the chores that weighed him down would be duck soup to someone like Rhoda. Looking up at the cabins, he often visualized her whizzing through them with broom and dustpan. He also could train her to operate the gasoline pumps and perhaps even change tires so that most of his time could be free for thinking and writing. When he daydreamed of this he always wound up cursing his clumsiness. If he had handled her properly, Rhoda would now be there with him.

He did try to find a replacement. There were trips to the cafés and diners in Cob City and a methodical appraisal of their waitresses, followed by a number of test runs. But most of those under fifty were clapped up or already supplementing someone's pay, and the dozen or so who weren't had that temporary look. There was no dedication in the way they set down a pork barbecue before him. Once they had their rings and inflated abdomens they'd be retiring from service.

The most promising candidate in Cob City was Lucy-Jo; stringy, except for her thighs which flapped against each other when she walked, and bent forward at the waist from carrying heavy trays. No inspirer of sonnets, Lucy-Jo, her steeply receding chin emphasizing her startled eyes, her skin of permanent German measles. She didn't gab, though, and she'd never heard of self-expression. Given enough time and patience he could make something of her. But he remembered it had taken him months to beat all the confusion out of Rhoda and funnel some clear fluid into her. And Rhoda had been an especially eager and tireless pupil. Shillitoe's most generous estimate for enlightening Lucy-Jo came to the better part of a year, and that was too long. Besides, in her best moments Lucy-Jo didn't even come close to Rhoda's muliebrity.

Beneath all these other concerns lay the major one. The days were falling by, never to be recovered, and the fourth part of the poem wasn't written. Shillitoe had made constant attempts, writhing, straining, exhausting attempts, always late at night after the last drooly kid or fussy clerk or windy salesman signed the register and led the shadow hovering on the other side of the screen door up to cabin number three. The sounds had been favorable, crickets harmonizing with the rips of passing cars and deeper rends of the trucks, the coughing, spewing, dilatory freight trains of the Monon tracing the edge of town, and the sporadic shrill giggle or basso groan trickling down from one of the three outposts of bliss. Shillitoe would stare out of the office window at the black perimeter of night, burning to tattoo the poem on its shell. But he couldn't and he knew why. The fourth part of the poem was not an entity in itself. It had to follow freely and consistently from everything that preceded it. But the first three parts were not there. Shillitoe had tried to reconstruct them, to write them again. And pieces had come back, lines here and there so clearly engraved on his memory that he had only to transfer them to paper. But the bulk of it would not return. It was existing independently at Para Park; not fully independently, for it had to be aware that something was missing—even though, like a Manx kitten or blind baby, it couldn't know what. *He* knew, however, and with knowledge came obligation. He had released three-fourths of a poem to life, a deformity of sorts that couldn't incubate to full size. What hope was there for a stunted effort in a world where giants had difficulty surviving? More than that, what of the fourth part of the poem, still undelivered? The last of the Siamese quadruplets wanted to join the others and was kicking hell out of his prostate gland.

Though he delayed as long as he could, he never deceived himself. He knew he had to set foot on the plague spot once more. It needn't be for long. With luck he could be in and out of New York within a matter of hours. The first thing he'd do would be to contact Rhoda at Herschel's or at home and let her know he needed her. The most expeditious approach would be to mouth some of the string-orchestrated slogans she'd learned from Hollywood and which the combined efforts of all the great men who'd ever lived could never offset. But desperate as he was he doubted if he could stoop to that. Of course, it was very possible he wouldn't have to. A straight presentation of the facts of Ben's condition might do it. In spite of all his teaching, Rhoda still salivated at news of an impending burial. It occurred to him that he could tell her just as effectively by phone, but he reminded himself of how Rhoda regarded Indiana. She might take weeks to get typhoid, tetanus and antitoxin shots before venturing west of New Jersey. It would be faster and easier to go and drag her back by the hair. But he knew this was rationalization. The truth was that Rhoda was a secondary trophy of his trip. The first prize was the missing parts of the poem. If he didn't go after them right away, he still would have to eventually. And the longer he delayed, the greater the chance that some drudge of a cleaning woman at Para Park might throw them into the incinerator.

When he told Ben he had to go back to New York, Ben looked as if he'd been expecting it. Shillitoe explained that he'd only be gone for two days at the most, depending on plane schedules. But Ben's eyes didn't believe him. There was no avoiding them. They'd protruded more and more as his face shrank beneath them, and now they glistened like two rich stones, emerald or jade, set in a wax mold.

Shillitoe decided he couldn't leave Ben in this shape and called the Cob City Hospital to send out its best man. There was enough in the office till to pay him and for a full-time nurse until he got back with Rhoda. This meant hitchhiking to New York instead of flying, but he could still get there and back in a few days. It seemed the only solution, so when Ben rallied his lifelong distrust of doctors, Shillitoe found himself in the unique position of defending them.

"They're not so bad," he said. "In the last eight hundred years they've figured out four or five cures."

The doctor didn't take long before squeezing his face into sympathy and making oblique references to malignancy. Shillitoe gave him the alternatives: enough morphine to divorce Ben from pain, or—if he was more human than professional—an overdose of any of several things would do. The doctor, as expected, picked the morphine and hurried away. But the nurse he dispatched was a good choice. One look at Emma Cathcart, broad, starched and efficient, and it was clear Ben was in good hands.

Shillitoe lettered a CLOSED sign, locked the office and went up to say good-bye. He thought of asking Ben not to die until he got back because Rhoda had always wanted to meet him.

But looking down at the incredibly emaciated body on the bed, he suddenly got mad—not at fate nor microbes nor any divinity, but at Ben. He wanted to tell Ben off for being stupid enough to get cancer. He wanted to explain to him why it happened. Sure, silence was more eloquent than speech, but Ben had carried it to extremes. No man could keep sopping up dregs and never unloose any in return. Ben had shown he could take it. Big deal. What kind of accomplishment was that? He'd played right into the hands of his time; the midcentury male, effecting nothing and letting everything be done to him. And now his reward, this ignominious death that befell every majority statistic. If only Ben had once struck back. If only he'd inflicted other scars besides the son he'd wreaked at the universe. But hell, he probably hadn't even got himself laid since Mary died. It was as late to reprove him for everything else as it was for that. But there was one thing he wanted to know.

"Ben, I sent you a book. Did you ever read it?"

A long, long time before Ben nodded.

"What did you think?" asked Shillitoe, wishing immediately that he hadn't. What difference did it make what Ben thought? He'd signaled that he read it. That was enough. Why dig for praise? What the hell did Ben know about poetry?

Shillitoe slapped Emma on the buttocks and walked out. He was halfway down the stairs when Ben's answer reached him. It must have taken all the air in Ben's dwindling lungs to propel the words.

"Made no sense to me."

Chapter Twenty-One

"HARD astern!" called Chester Quirk, swinging his arm. "Port! Starboard! Abandon ship!"

These were all the nautical commands he knew, so he shouted them again and again into the roaring tunnel. Sometimes a driver noticed him yelling and guiltily slowed down. Then Chester had to wave his arm that much faster.

Commanding his battleship only got him through a small part of his daily shift. Most of the time Chester used baseball. He had learned that the average pitcher who went the route in a nine-inning game threw the ball between one hundred and seventy and two hundred times. So, each day in the Holland Tunnel Chester pitched the equivalent of three double-headers. The passing drivers never knew that the fingers at the end of his swinging arm were dishing up curves and sliders, and even an occasional knuckler.

Chester had invented rules, too. If a bus passed as he let go his pitch, it counted as a single. A sports car was a two-bagger, a taxi a triple, and a red-white-and-blue moving van a home run. Everything else was an out. A further refinement was memorizing the lineup of the team the Yankees were facing that day and pitching carefully to each batter's weakness. Hirschberger up next. Keep it low and breaking at the knees. Pontiac! A pop up to second. So much for Mike. Al Smith? He'd never hit a good knuckle ball yet. Hah! A Studebaker! Side retired. No hits, no runs, no errors, nobody left on base.

There was also a dream and Chester had it daily. One of the cars going by would be a new black Cadillac limousine and the cigar-smoking executive in the back would happen to look out just as Chester came down with his fast ball and Nellie Fox struck out. The man would look amazed, lean forward and bark something to his chauffeur. There'd be no cars behind the limousine, so the chauffeur would be able to grind to a stop. Then the man would jump out, climb up on the catwalk and embrace Chester.

"Never saw a delivery like that," he'd yell. "The Yankees need you today. Doubleheader against Chicago. Ralph Terry has a sore arm so you're pitching both ends. Eighty thousand bucks a year, plus a cut of the World Series dough and whatever you can pick up by saying you eat Rice Crispies and smoke Camels!" Dizzy Quirk! Dazzy Quirk! Big Train Quirk! Pride of the Yankees! Everything he is he owes to his training in the Holland Tunnel.

Chester always got a grip on himself at this point and ran to the callbox to check in with Sergeant Jago at the Manhattan Exit. He was afraid that someday he might not cut off the dream in time and they'd drag him out of the tunnel screaming. But it was a chance he had to take. If it wasn't for the baseball, if he saw the cars as cars and the tunnel as a tunnel, he'd start screaming right now.

Another thing bothering Chester was the kidding he'd been getting from Jago and the others. When they found out that he'd requested transfer from what they called "Prostitute Patrol" back to tunnel duty, they really went to town on him. Of course they didn't know why he had requested the reassignment. If they ever found out, they'd ride him so much he'd have to leave the force. It was a good thing he'd made his request vague and hadn't reported what had happened that night. *That night.* No matter where his train of thought began, it always wound up at that night with Shillitoe kneeing him. If it hadn't been for that, Chester knew he would still be sauntering around Times Square or Central Park or East Seventy-ninth Street instead of pitching six full games a day in the crummy tunnel.

If only he could have caught Shillitoe. The *if* was still there, nagging him. In fact, the only time it had ever left him was the morning after, that morning he saw Doctor Wren. Doctor Wren had told him that no good could come from locking Shillitoe up and Chester had promised to think about that. But he never had. After he left Doctor Wren, the desire for revenge came back as strong as ever. It was okay for Doctor Wren to talk about some people not being responsible for what they do and how Chester had to understand the pressures and the motivations and all that. It was easy for him to tell Chester not to arrest Shillitoe because Shillitoe was a nut. But when some nut kicks you in the nuts, what are you supposed to do, laugh?

Still, Doctor Wren had taken the time to talk to him and he had made him feel better for a little while. That was more than Chester could say about Father Keegan. No doubt about it. Father Keegan wasn't interested in his problems any more. When he'd been on special assignment, Father Keegan never hurried him in confession. He'd wanted the details on every arrest Chester made. But now, when Chester told him about the un-Christian feelings he had toward Shillitoe, Father Keegan just droned something about love and charity and sent him on his way.

Chester looked down at his right hand and saw that it was going white from gripping the rail. To get some circulation into it, he reared back and let fly his high, hard one. Robinson whipped his bat around and a lousy Austin Healy went by. Man on second, nobody out. Chester rubbed his sleeve against his eyes, then leaned forward to see who was coming up next. The zero on the back of the player bending over the bat rack wasn't listed on the White Sox roster. Then he picked up the resin bag and came toward the plate swinging three bats and Chester recognized him. Shillitoe! No wonder he hadn't been able to find him. The louse had been hiding in the Chicago dugout. Chester started down from the mound, but the umpire stepped forward and called out, "Play ball!" Okay. He wouldn't do anything to hurt the team's pennant chances. He'd play ball. Chester shook off Howard's sign. The hell with Robinson on second base. Let him steal. Chester took a full windup and his fast ball zoomed right at Shillitoe's head. It was the fastest pitch Chester had ever thrown, untimeable, unduckable. And just as it had always happened in the dream, there was the black Cadillac stopping alongside him.

Chester was leaning over the railing to see if the man inside was smoking a cigar when the silence of the tunnel enveloped him. Only then did he see that the two lanes of cars were stationary. Chester went into the booth and picked up the phone.

"They're stopped in my section," he reported.

"No kiddin'," rasped Jago.

"Anything you want me to do?" asked Chester.

"Sure. Come out here and make like a bus axle. What a place to fall apart. Tell me it ain't true, Quirk."

"What ain't true?"

"What I heard about you. You didn't really ask to be sent back here, did ya'? Come clean. What're they punishin' ya' for?"

Chester didn't answer. He just waited until big Jago tired of razzing him and told him to feed the traffic into the outside lane. Then he walked back along the catwalk, calling out to the drivers to merge into one line. Blue-and-cream Chevvy, white station wagon and black Volkswagon, Lincoln, Dodge, Plymouth, Mercury—they were nothing but vague colors and shapes. So were their occupants. Chester was too busy to pay attention to any of them and he never would have stopped to look in the cab of the moving van at all if it hadn't been red, white and blue. His first thought was that the bus wreck had saved him from giving up his initial home run. His second was that the face staring at him from alongside the driver was one he'd seen before. But it wasn't until the guy wrenched the door open and started running up the tunnel that Chester remembered when and where.

Shillitoe had a good head start to begin with. Then Chester was boxed in by a Corvair crossing into the outside lane, and by the time he'd hurdled that, Shillitoe had stretched his lead to almost eight car lengths.

"Stop! Halt or I'll shoot!" yelled Chester, but his threat rebounded weakly from the curved walls as he remembered that he didn't have his revolver on. He might have continued the chase, falling farther and farther behind, if Officer Danilewski at Station Eight hadn't called out to him.

Chester vaulted up onto the catwalk and rushed to Danilewski's booth. The breaks were with him. Jago was still on the phone cursing out instructions.

"Suspect in brown suit," panted Chester, "heading for Manhattan exit."

"Get off the phone, Quirk," ordered Jago.

"Stop him!"

"Look, Quirk. I got a busted bus on my hands."

"He may be armed."

"Quirk, will ya' . . . Hold your water. I see him."

Chester slammed down the phone and renewed the chase. The traffic had begun to move slowly but with all the cars in one line, the lane alongside the bridge was clear. Head back, arms up and pumping, Chester sprinted with all his might just as he had in the high school intramural hundred-yard dash at Randall's Island when he'd come in fifth. But his police shoes became blocks of concrete fastened to each foot and a cramp spread across his chest and by the time he reached the incline where the daylight streamed into the mouth of the tunnel he was sucking painfully for his second wind. For a while it seemed like it wasn't going to come and his eyeballs rolled up into his forehead. Then his lungs expanded, his vision returned and he saw big Jago with his powerful arms wrapped around the struggling Shillitoe.

At any other time there would have been a crowd gathering. But with the tow truck arriving and the passengers from the bus complaining to each other and all the horns tooting and beeping, no one seemed to notice what Jago was doing. Chester slowed to a walk as he neared him. There was no mistaking the face in the vise of Jago's arm, but it didn't hurt to have positive identification.

"What's your name?" Chester had to shout above the noise.

"Thomas Tickell."

"It's Shillitoe, ain't it?"

"Milton. Johnny Milton."

"You gonna' book him?" asked Jago.

Chester hadn't thought about that. Booking him would mean charges and explanations. Resisting arrest—how? Assaulting an officer—where? You never could tell with a nut. The guy might make a full confession about the whole thing in the streetwalker's room and everything. Besides, Doctor Wren had said that jail wouldn't solve anything. Chester put his mouth to Jago's cauliflower ear.

"Anybody in the lockers?"

Jago's whole beefy face creased as he winked knowingly. Then he twisted Shillitoe's arm up behind his back until the nut was prancing on his toes and steered him toward the door in the concrete wall.

It was dead quiet inside, hard to believe so much confusion was going on not thirty yards away. Jago broke the silence by tossing Shillitoe against the metal lockers. Shillitoe bounced along the row until the corner stopped him, then crouched in it like a scared rat.

"What'd ya' say your name was?" asked Jago.

"Coventry Patmore."

The voice gave him away. Chester hadn't recognized it outside because of all the racket. But hearing it now brought everything back—the humiliation of writhing on the floor naked while this nut and his old bag ran down the fire escape, the wild-goose chase all over the city from the U.N. to practically being thrown out by the dame with her foot in a bucket and every stinking miserable minute he had to spend in the damn tunnel.

"He's the one," Chester said.

"Want me to hold him?" rasped Jago.

Chester shook his head and walked slowly toward the nut. He raised his fists, planning to shoot the left into the stomach and the right to the jaw.

"Watch it!"

Jago's warning was too late. Chester was able to block the left coming at his stomach, but the right caught him on the jaw and spun him around. When he righted himself Jago was behind Shillitoe, holding him in a full nelson. Chester cocked his fists again and moved in and again he was just about to throw his left when Shillitoe seemed to sit down while Jago held him in mid-air. Then the shoe kicked out toward him found its mark.

As Chester clawed the cement floor, he heard the banging of the metal lockers. Gradually, their olive green replaced the fireworks and there was big Jago looking like he'd just finished a juicy steak.

"What did this bastard do, Quirk?"

"He's a Communist nut," gasped Chester.

"Maybe I was too easy on him."

Chester struggled to his feet and looked around until he spotted Shillitoe under one of the wooden benches. From his position he could have been asleep. But he was groaning and trying to raise his head. One strenuous effort got it several inches from the floor and the way it stayed there made Chester mad. He went over and jammed his foot down on it, not expecting the head to make such a cracking sound when it hit the floor.

"Jesus!" Jago grabbed him roughly, and almost tore off his arm. No wonder he was the heavyweight wrestling champion of the force. "Not so it shows, ya' dumb jerk. You want to make investigations? Look at his nose."

The nose had the smudged imprint of Chester's heel and was pouring blood. Chester felt sick. He wanted to kneel down and staunch it.

"This is the way ya' do it," said Jago, and thudded his heavy shoes into Shillitoe's ribs. Every kick produced a slighter spasm and Chester prayed that Jago would stop before the body on the floor didn't move at all.

"Take over, Quirk. I better see what's doing outside."

Then the locker room was completely still and Chester was sure Jago had purposely left him with a corpse on his hands. He wanted to run all the way back to his station in the tunnel. They'd have to prove he'd done it. It was Jago's word against his and every man on the force knew Jago's reputation.

Chester would have fled then if Shillitoe hadn't groaned. At least, he thought he heard a groan. Since being back on tunnel duty, Chester wasn't always sure of what was real and what he was imagining. He got down on his knees and stuck his head under the bench so that it rested on where Shillitoe's heart was supposed to be. Then he held his breath and listened. The thumping wasn't very loud, but it was there. Chester dragged the body out, propped it into a sitting position, shifted around behind it and lifted it to its feet.

"Now we're even," he said. "Okay?"

The head hung loosely, the eyes stayed closed and the mouth didn't answer. Chester put Shillitoe's arm around his own shoulders to make it look like he was supporting a drunk.

"You're getting off easy," he said.

Outside, the tow truck was hoisting the front of the bus and the file of cars was going by in one lane. But several truckers were in no hurry and had pulled off to one side to watch what was going on. Chester staggered under Shillitoe's weight to the nearest truck. It was small, but the back was only half full and the driver wasn't around. Chester dumped Shillitoe, headfirst, over the tailgate and walked away quickly into the tunnel. According to his watch, there was a little over an hour of arm waving before he'd be relieved and could go to confession.

Finale of the *Ziegfeld Follies.* Straight up, astride Pegasus, rising on a greased sunbeam. No vibrations, no lighted instructions to smoke or not to smoke, no plastic stewardesses with shaved shins and mint Life Savers. Only the white feathers of the saddle-down. Shillitoe was just about to tell Pegasus that in future he'd never travel any other way, when the screeching tumultuous eagle swooped down and lifted him from his mount. Its claws pulled aside his curtain of skin, its beak chipped at his pain. Eagle, hell! He'd recognize Beverly's nose-cone anywhere. And she'd traded in her breasts for jet engines. Not a bad idea. She hadn't got much mileage out of the old ones. But he'd never before noticed her resemblance to a Messerschmitt. The bitch had probably strafed him all the way from Normandy to Pilsen. That's where he'd made his mistake. If only he'd unscrewed her navel, her fuel tank would have fallen off.

"Ya' can't even park for two minutes wid'out some drunk crawlin' inta' the truck."

Shillitoe placed the accent and flavor before opening his eyes. Where else did self-pity sugar every word? And where else did suffering meet such dull eyes as those of the three crass Boeotians staring down at him? The scummy eagle of a Beverly had dropped him right on New York.

Getting to his feet was like gathering up a bag of kindling wood. His arms and legs were disconnected from their sockets. All his insides below the waist had been shoveled out. He was afraid to look down at himself, certain that splintered bones protruded from his sides. The three men moved back to give him room. Haulers of some kind and they deserved every sore on their tails. Exception. Wonders never ceased. One of them had taken courage and was holding out a hand. Shillitoe grabbed for it to keep from falling, but it was quickly withdrawn and, on his knees, he found he'd been given a two-bit piece.

"He'll just spend it on booze."

Typical. Here charity was dollars and cents. Just mail in your contribution to heart fund, lung fund, dystrophy fund, sclerosis fund—and for orphans in less fortunate lands across the sea. You needn't touch them and all money donated is tax deductible and the giver reserves the right to insinuate graft and malpractice. Shillitoe tried to heave the coin back at them, but his arm wouldn't obey and the quarter rolled away.

"Beat it, bum!"

No strength to argue, and no reason to try. Their hours were their penalty. He stumbled off, doubled over, holding his knees to keep them from buckling. When he did try to straighten up, the cords digging into his stomach wouldn't give and he had to twist his head sideways to see where he was going.

Flat, blackened, hollow building after building; some windows opened and more blurred by grime, so they made a crossword puzzle. Eighty-five across—a warehouse street somewhere in the Twenties and what looked like Tenth Avenue up ahead. The light and shadow told him it was midafternoon. Where to go, the apartment or the lunchroom? His bed beckoned, but the knifing and tearing within him warned that once he lay down it would be difficult to rise. The picture of the steep flights he'd trudged up so many times decided him. He turned toward Herschel's.

Somehow he managed to drag himself up the two steps of the bus and to a seat. But each bump it hit, every time it stopped and started up again, he almost cried out. He knew his only hope for maintaining consciousness was to separate his mind from his broken carcass, to pry it free. It was slow going, like picking apart a knotted shoelace with frozen fingers. It was easier to quit or scream or beg someone else to do it. It was hopeless. Nothing was giving way. Then, a loose end. He should have thought of it sooner. The poem. It opened its unfinished mouth and swallowed his torn flesh and rattling bones. By the time he pushed open the door of the lunchroom, he was almost able to stand upright.

It was empty with the hush that follows a holocaust. The glasses were still steamed from being washed, the plates were stacked evenly, the counter wiped clean, the ammunition at the sandwich block ready for the next onslaught. Somewhere in the back, behind the swinging doors, a pot clanked against a pan. Round one. Shillitoe thought of another day when he'd wearied of watching the sniffing, shoving hopefuls at Stillman's Gym and went out for a cup of coffee. Good things come from minute particulars. From coffee and circumstance arose Rhoda. Not Mona Lisa even with the benefits of his imagination. But perhaps Velleda as Corot painted her. It was the only time a woman had looked at him without taking inventory. Historians would probably label it love at first sight. But it wasn't. There'd been no conjunction of mind, no opposition of the stars. It had merely been the collision of a tired genius and a ripe vegetable.

The pan hit back at the pot, drawing him toward the kitchen. Then he saw himself in the mirror behind the counter. No wonder no one had taken the seat next to him on the crowded bus. He pulled a paper napkin from the container, spit on it and wiped off his nose and mouth. But this started them bleeding again and he was still trying to clot the blood when the swinging doors from the kitchen were pushed open and Rhoda waddled in with a high pile of saucers pinched between her chin and interlaced fingers. She was almost to him before she saw him. Then she stopped dead and the saucers didn't and she had to run forward to keep them from billowing away from her.

"How many you busted today?" he asked, waiting for the porky look she always gave him when he teased her. But she clattered on by him and eased the pile of saucers on top of the sandwich block.

"You want anything?" She asked it without turning around.

"What the hell you think I'm here for?"

"I mean, you want anything to eat?"

"Just you."

He reached across the counter to squeeze her but she slapped his hand away.

"Nothing doing! You think I'll take you back no matter

what. But not this time." She was looking at him now and she couldn't keep her eyes off his nose so he knew it was bleeding again. "Who slugged you?" she asked maternally.

"Never mind," he said. "Tell Herschel you quit and let's go." He hadn't meant to do it that way. He'd planned to tell her where he'd been and about Ben and how they both needed her. But his swelling mouth made talking an effort and inside him the mains had burst and he was sure his stomach was a ditch full of blood. "Hurry up," he snapped.

"Maybe that's the way you talk to your girl friend," said Rhoda hotly, "but not to me."

"What girl friend?"

"You know what I mean."

"I never know what you mean."

"I suppose you got more pictures of her in your wallet."

"I haven't got a wallet."

"Or tacked up on your wall."

"What wall?"

"You think I'll put up with anything."

"Aw, for Christ's sake."

"Don't you swear at me."

Her obstinacy had tightened the rack and he had to lower himself onto a seat at the counter.

"And don't play sick."

"I'm not playing," he said. "Come on, lunkhead."

"Don't call me that."

"I always call you that."

"Not any more, you don't."

She stood there, bristling, unbudgeable, a suffragette chained to the sandwich block.

"This is your last chance," he warned. "I'm going back to Indiana tonight."

"I've heard that one before."

If he could have reached her, he would have belted her with a downward chop.

"I mean it," he said.

"So who's preventing you?"

"Stubborn, ungrateful bulge."

"Then what do you want me for?"

"I don't!" It came out between his thickening lips before he could stop it. The way she folded her arms told him it was no use retracting it. "I just came back for something I wrote," he added. "I thought you might have it."

"You took all your stuff with you."

"Nothing came in the mail?"

"Sure. Lots of things, all from Daniel K. Papp."

"I'm talking about my poem," he roared. "Did they send it back?"

Then it dawned on him that Rhoda didn't know about the poem. He wanted to tell her about it. She'd be pleased to know that it was three-fourths done. It would be some reward for the few piddling sacrifices she'd made.

"Maybe that's what he meant," she said.

"What who meant?"

"The doctor. He said your manuscript was at Para Park. Is that the one?"

"That's the one." He thought of the distance to Para Park. He could never make it. But Rhoda looked in the pink.

"Get it for me," he said. "It's just a few miles past Stamford. I'll draw you a map."

"Are you kiddin'?"

"You can make it up and back in a few hours."

He couldn't believe she was standing there snorting at him.

"You've got a nerve," she said.

"I'm asking you to save a poem."

"I don't care about your poem."

"Goddam, ignorant . . . !" The tempest in him subsided momentarily as he noticed the apron of her uniform. Mustard, ketchup and mayonnaise had splashed an interesting pattern there. Then he raised his eyes to her face, so set it could have been painted on a balloon. "Helium head!" he yelled, then scanned her precious sandwich block for another charge.

"You've got as much soul as your lousy chicken salad. *You* don't care about my poem. And who are you to care or not to care? And what the hell do you care about? Okay, forget it's a poem you're going after. Make believe it's an autographed picture of Jack Holt."

"Jack Holt?" she chortled. "Boy, are you behind the times!"

He was so weak that when he threw the napkin container she was able to catch it easily. She had their total strength now. She was his only chance.

"I have to finish the poem," he said. "Get it back for me." And when she didn't move, he added, "Please."

There! It was done. He had begged sincerely for the first time in his life and the bitter fumes of it smothered his pain and fogged his sight. He could barely make out Rhoda reaching into the pocket of her apron. Then with the same paroxysm of disbelief with which a soldier first sees his jagged wound, he saw the ten-dollar bill she had placed on the counter.

"Go 'way, Samson," she said. "Leave me alone."

He shoved to his feet and lurched a few steps before he could right himself. The spikes of pain were driving back, greater than before. He wanted to leap over the counter, to ball up her money and ram it down her throat until she gagged. But the unfinished poem was waiting helplessly, a basket case thirty miles away at Para Park. Sixty miles up and back and, battered and bleeding as he was, no motorist would give him a lift. And even if some hidden cache of strength enabled him to walk, it would take the rest of the day and most of the night just to get there and his return to Ben would be delayed that much longer.

The huge, polished surfaces of the cyclotron were coming together, the whole of his pride hanging between them. And if the wheels and gears and levers in their holy turning did shudder from any resistance, it was perceptible only to him. He snatched up the bill and didn't look back until he was outside.

There was a taxi and a train and another taxi. But the journey was made through gusts of rage and he knew none of its particulars. All the contempt he had hurled at fools avalanched back on him. Fools seldom made the same mistake more than twice, but he'd made his dozens of times. Everything he'd ever witnessed had verified the unalterable nature of women. Yet he had gone on betting on scratched entries time and again. So he had elevated Rhoda's spirit, had he? So he had infused some beauty and dignity into her colorless life. Sure. That was why she galvanized into bronze when he asked her to do him a small favor. There would have been nothing wrong in being deluded by this conceit if he'd just used and discarded her as he had the others. Rhoda would have been willing to pose for him and flattered to become an unidentified she when he needed her for imagery. Not her waddling walk, of course. It was more like a night of rolling thunder than one of cloudless chimes. Not her grace, either; anything but glad. Nor did she offer love-crumb eyes, nor green asphodel, nor anything but the lineaments of gratified desire. She was a clear mirror, though. She could have been his waterfowl, his cuckoo, his Grecian urn, his ecstasy's spittoon. But he had to go and be generous and let her put her clothes on and get into the act, peeking over his shoulder and ready to preen at the sight of her name. He might have gone that far, too, if she'd had any name but Rhoda. But she wasn't responsible. She would have been content to unwind her life in a stupor. He was the one who had awakened her when, in any halfway decent anthology, the long chorus line from fair Margaret to Annabel Lee showed that the proper women for poetry were dead ones. So much for regarding Rhoda as different—as more than another gnarl in the long, winding intestine passing man's rhapsodies, like excrement, on toward eternity. Heterosexuality never gave up, though. Even when he'd left the lunchroom, he'd stopped and looked back through the window, reluctant to believe that she wouldn't change her mind and come running after him. But she hadn't so much as waited until he was out of sight. She was already at the pay phone on the wall, dialing, probably anxious to find out when the main feature began.

He had the taxi driver drop him at the beginning of the driveway and as he limped up toward the house he forced his thoughts to the task ahead. The house was completely dark, but the quarter moon set it in a chiaroscuro with the lawn and trees. He kept to the blackest areas, afraid a sudden yellow patch in one of the windows might spotlight him. He knew the poem could be anywhere inside, but the most likely place was Vera Kropotkin's office and that meant entering the front door. He went toward it, sealing in his breath to preserve the silent air. But some of the leaves had already fallen to September and crackled under his feet. If the noise awakened Vera and she gave him one of her hugs, his ribs would be beyond repair.

He had reached the front steps when he heard the window upstairs slide open. There was nothing else to do but look up and try to calm whoever had seen him. Herman! Shillitoe, relieved, almost called out a greeting to good old Herman waving down at him. Instead he waved back, but this made Herman gesture all the more. Shillitoe could hear him gasping heavily. Then the voice which he had never heard speak croaked out the one word: "Run!"

Simultaneously, the clamps hit both his arms. Arnold was on one side of him, a twin gorilla in white on the other, and both seemed determined to finish any dismantling the cops had left undone. Shillitoe tried to squirm free, but he had nothing left. All he could do was hang limply, making them drag him into the house while he howled curses at the mothers who spawned them and the gutters that allowed them to grow.

In the entrance hall, the lights flooded on and Vera Kropotkin loomed up before him. Hope coursed back. Vera would chase away the gorillas and find him a place to rest. Vera would prove that not every woman was ungrateful. Vera would give him back the poem.

"Forgiff me, Semmy."

She pouted it at him like a farewell kiss. Then she pushed

up his sleeve and the point of the hypodermic needle pierced his skin.

Chapter Twenty-Two

SINCE becoming an atheist at the age of eighteen, Frederic Voegler had carefully forgotten all the Biblical teaching he'd received in his youth. But one phrase had resurrected itself to haunt him the past three weeks. "Ask and ye shall receive." He had to admit there was an occasional truth in the opiates after all.

Something else had recurred to him at the same time. It was a story a patient had told him many years before. It was odd that of all the thousands of incidents related to him, this particular one should have remained so eidetic.

This patient had been plagued by a type of insufficient sexual initiative which was almost the diametric opposite of the *phallus thaumaturgist.* There was no lack of sexual appetite. It was just that, with the single exception of his marriage, the patient had never successfully pursued a woman. He consistently put women on too high a pedestal. The story that had lodged so firmly in Voegler's mind proved that.

It had happened when the patient was a freshman in college and had taken to idolizing one of the coeds from afar. When it came to beauty, she was everything he'd ever dreamed of. Then one night, in a rash of impetuous courage, he telephoned the girl and asked if he could escort her to a dance the following Saturday night. To his amazement she accepted.

The big night arrived. The young man bought a more expensive corsage than he could really afford and took the girl to the dance in a taxi though it wasn't more than fifty yards from her sorority house. Throughout the evening he examined each word he was about to say before saying it. When they danced, he held her an arm's length away, his right hand barely touching her back for fear of leaving a welt on her lily-white skin. He performed unnecessary amenities cheerfully, certain that he was the envy of every fellow student in the hall. When the dance ended he was going to call another taxi and thought she was the most considerate person alive when she said she'd rather walk. He'd drawn out the walk, loitering over the short distance to enlarge every precious moment, and when they finally reached the sorority house he pretended not to notice the other couples necking all over the porch and lawn. He'd wanted to apologize to the girl for them, to let her know he would never engage her in any such base activity. And while he was fumbling for the most tasteful way to phrase this, she leaned forward and whispered in his ear.

"Don," she asked, "do you like fruit?"

"Why, eh, ah, . . . sure," he stammered.

"Then take a bite of my ass. It's a peach."

It was this scene and especially this line that had kept recurring to Voegler the past weeks. He, unlike his patient, was far from lacking in sexual initiative. But so far as his behavior with Lydia Wren went, he was just as bad. The pedestal he had always kept Lydia on was of his own making. There was nothing virginal or untouchable about her. After all, she was married with two children. And the harsh truth of the matter was that while he was secretly wanting her more than he'd ever desired any woman, other men were helping themselves. At least, unless Arnold was a diabolical liar, one other man had.

It was too much to live with. Voegler knew he'd never again have a peaceful night's sleep until he remedied the situation. And that was why, much as he wanted to witness the lobotomy, he had to forego it.

The timetable he had laid out was as precise as a field marshal's. The operation was scheduled for eleven. Wren would have to leave not later than ten o'clock to be at Para Park by then. The two children were back at school. The only other bottleneck had been the maid. It was really too much to hope that she'd be off the day of the operation. He'd asked anyway and Wren had looked at him curiously until he improvised the explanation of needing a cleaning woman once a week for his bachelor apartment. When Wren said his maid had Thursdays off, Voegler inwardly rocketed with joy. But outwardly he shook his head in disappointment and said he wanted someone to come in Mondays.

There was still one unknown quantity. Lydia could be out. He didn't think she would be so early in the day. But it could happen. Voegler prayed that she'd made no appointment earlier than a luncheon date—which he'd make her forget about easily enough. Then he remembered his atheism and renounced his prayers. Lydia's not being home was a mathematical chance with which he had to contend.

Voegler trimmed his beard carefully and fluffed it with the back of his hand to bring out all its silvery luster. The lime cologne was sprinkled on the back of his neck. He examined all his white shirts and put on the one with the best laundered collar. The selection of his tie was made with an eye to Lydia's obvious taste for subtle shades. Finally, at exactly ten-fifteen, he inspected himself approvingly in the full-length mirror fastened to his closet door. Then, for no accountable reason, he thought of his father presiding over the family as it sat down to dinner at the round table in the house in Salzburg. No one could touch a soup spoon until the head of the family said grace. Voegler thought of the incantation, simultaneously translating it into English in his mind. "For what we are about to receive, may the Lord make us truly thankful." Not this time. There'd be no mystic rites before this meal. For what he was about to receive, he had waited much too long.

Lydia hadn't conducted a systematic search for the book. But, somehow, she kept finding herself in the Village and every time she passed a bookshop she just happened to drop in. The clerks weren't very courteous. Most of them wouldn't even bother to look when she asked if they had any poetry by Samson Shillitoe. But Lydia was positive there was a book in existence, the one the silent man in the deck chair had been reading. So she'd browse over the shelves herself.

The dusty, weathered bindings made her aware of how little poetry she knew. Arnold, Dryden, Wordsworth, Pope, Gray, La Fontaine; they were all names she regarded as great poets, but she actually knew next to nothing of the body of their works. Lydia made up her mind to begin reading poetry again. It had given her many stimulating moments in college, particularly during her junior year when she'd been all involved in Gerard Manley Hopkins. She had been silly to let her interest lapse. But it wasn't too late to renew it and the first thing to do was to get someone who knew poetry to tell her what to read and in what order. The only person she knew, however, who would be able to advise her was Shillitoe. And she couldn't very well ask him without first becoming familiar with some of his work. Regularly convincing herself that this was her only motive, she continued her search and eventually in a small shop on Fourth Avenue, she found the thin volume snuggled alphabetically between SHELLEY: POETICAL WORKS and SPENSER: FAERIE QUEENE.

There wasn't a chance to read any of it in the cab going home because the driver was one of those grievance collectors who never stopped complaining. Then Scott and Deirdre tumbled into the apartment two minutes after she did and they insisted she be the audience for their puppet show. After that there was the new game Oliver's mother had sent them—spin the tin arrow and move your plastic space rocket so many squares forward unless you land on green, in which case you go into orbit or on red, which returns you to Cape Canaveral and you have to start all over. Lydia wondered what kind of imbeciles thought up these things.

When she heard Oliver come in, she excused herself from

the game despite Deirdre's shrieks that she was only two squares away from the moon. Lydia had remembered leaving the book of poetry in the bedroom. Oliver might see it and think she was prying into his practice or something. She slid it into her lingerie drawer just before he walked in.

There was no chance to get to the book that night. They didn't go out, but neither did Oliver go into his study to work. He seemed nervous and restless, continually getting up and adjusting the volume of the hi-fi, and when at last he turned it off and spoke to her, his voice sounded strange.

"I have to go up to Para Park tomorrow morning."

It was a perfect opening for the favor she'd been wanting to ask him. She'd thought it over from every angle and the more she did, the better it seemed. Oliver couldn't claim it wasn't worthwhile or beneath her or anything like that. "Oh," she said vaguely. "Will you be taking the car?"

"No. I'm driving up with Doctor Massey."

"Want me to come along?" It was a silly question—Lydia had asked it without thinking. But still, it didn't warrant the disgusted look he threw her or the steam he put behind his "no."

"Oliver," she said, "there's something I've been meaning to talk to you about." There it was, out in the open. No turning back now. She wished he hadn't switched off the hi-fi. Mahler's Ninth would have made her request sound insignificant.

"Go ahead," he said, and his hands fumbled slightly as he took out a cigarette. She hadn't noticed his getting so jumpy. He *was* overworked.

"I've been thinking." She found it easier to look at Modigliani's "Little Girl in Blue" than at him. "You know I have too much time on my hands. And you're always saying how mental institutions are understaffed."

"Yes?" He wasn't giving her any encouragement at all.

"So, I thought I might be able to help out one or two days a week."

"Where?"

"I thought Para Park."

"And just what would you do there?"

"I'm sure I could make myself useful."

"Useful?"

"I thought you'd think it was a good idea."

"I do," he said. "Not at Para Park, though. We don't want anyone accusing me of nepotism, do we, darling?"

"I don't mind." She said it flippantly, but couldn't crack his serious expression.

"No, not Para Park," he repeated. "But all the hospitals in the city need volunteer personnel. Why not Bellevue?"

"It's such a depressing place."

"Then it needs your brightness all the more." He was smiling now. "They may have you carrying bedpans for a while, but it's *useful* work. I'll see if I can arrange it."

"But I had sort of made up my mind to Para Park."

"Why?"

"I don't know," she said. "I guess I took a fancy to the place."

"I'm sure you did."

She didn't want to leave it at that. She wanted to discuss it some more, but he put on the eleven-o'clock news and the room filled with international problems, none of which seemed as formidable as what she'd got herself into. She'd really done it this time. She'd never been inside Bellevue but its dingy hulk left little to the imagination. Oliver had sure picked a great way to be helpful. But she'd asked for it. She should have known from experience that he wouldn't give carte-blanche endorsement to any plan of hers. He always had to improve on it a little first. Bellevue! Some improvement.

At breakfast she was afraid he'd get right on it and start making arrangements. But he seemed to have forgotten the matter. At least, he didn't mention it. His nerves were better, too. He was patient and expansive with the children and even walked them out to the elevator when the school driver rang the bell. Then it dawned on her that his suggestion about Bellevue was just his way of dissuading her. He'd probably figured that hospital work would be too hard on her but didn't want to say so for fear of making her feel incompetent and useless. How tactful could a person be? Lydia felt warmer toward him than she had in weeks and with this feeling came the first nasty itching of guilt. She wondered if he'd be terribly hurt if he knew. Of course, he'd never show it, but he probably would be. Men had such a knight-in-shining-armor attitude about these things. Oliver might even regard it as meaning he'd failed her as a lover. He never had, not as a lover; only once in a while in the timing of his attentions. But all the talk and magazine articles and books about technique seemed to make men self-conscious just as they made women curious. Until three weeks ago, she'd swallowed some of it herself. But she had an alibi because before then she had no basis on which to compare Oliver. There'd been plenty of close calls before her marriage, of course. But how much she'd got involved or aroused had always depended more on her mood at the time than on anything her partner did. She couldn't even except Paul Caldwell. Apart from Oliver, she'd loved him more than she had any man and when she learned he'd been killed, her first regret was that she'd denied him that last night of his furlough after letting him undress her.

But now that she'd made love with someone besides Oliver she was sure that all the talk about technique was exaggerated. The circumstances might vary, that was all. Like that wild bathtub with the water pulsing out from everywhere. That was novel, all right. And there'd been a few other differences. Shillitoe didn't nibble the way Oliver did, and he hadn't kept asking her if she was enjoying it the way Oliver did. But there was one difference which was the main one. Oliver had always taken the initiative. He refereed over their bedroom activities. But Shillitoe had gone on preaching away as if he was much more interested in what he had to say than in her. Why not admit it? She had really seduced him. She had wanted to demolish that pose of his, to bring him down to size. And she'd done it too.

She didn't think she could make Oliver understand why she had to do it, or that the whole thing resulted from a haphazard collection of incidents and frustrations that could never accumulate again. Nor would he ever admit that what took place between her and Shillitoe wasn't nearly as intimate as the relationships he had with his women patients every day. The only thing to be accomplished by telling him would be that he'd be hurt. And this was something she'd never forgive herself for doing.

"I told Massey I'd be waiting in front of the building."

She walked him out to the elevator just as he had done with the children and raised her face for him to kiss her good-bye.

"I may be a little late."

No kiss, not even a peck on the cheek. The presence of the elevator operator had never intimidated Oliver before. And no matter how preoccupied he was, he could at least have squeezed her arm. As Lydia walked back into the apartment, she couldn't recall when Oliver had last kissed her. This was going too far. He knew enough about physiology to know that this was unhealthy for both of them.

She made up her mind to have it out with him that night. Pouring herself another cup of coffee, she blocked out the conversation that would take place. She'd begin by saying she had taken a leprosy test and it had come out negative. He'd ask her what the hell she was talking about and she'd come right back and ask him why he'd been treating her like an untouchable. Lydia was inventing an appropriate apology for Oliver to make when she remembered the book in her dresser drawer.

The bedroom was stale and rumpled and Oliver had left a swastika of yesterday's socks on the floor. Lydia told herself to tidy up the place and shower and dress before looking at the poetry. But she opened to the first page just for a little peek and she was still sitting on the edge of the bed in her pajamas and robe a half hour later when the doorbell rang.

Frederic Voegler at the door made too sharp a contrast to what she'd been reading. She told him Oliver had left, but he kept teetering there as if about to dive into a swimming pool.

"Maybe he stopped at the office, Frederic. Why don't you try there?"

"I don't think so." Freddie ducked under the arm holding the door open and made the middle of the foyer in one bound. "You are alone, darling?" he asked.

"Not any more."

He looked alarmed before waking up to the fact that she meant him. Then his chuckle got lost in his beard.

"For a moment I thought my plans aft ganged agley."

While she was trying to figure that out, he marched into the living room. Lydia shut the hall door and went after him.

"What plans?"

"As if you didn't know, darling."

"Frederic, I'm busy."

He looked at the book of poetry she still held.

"That's busy?"

"I'm studying." His eyes traveled up to the neckline of her robe. "I was just going to get dressed," she said.

"Lydia." He trotted toward her and she just managed to skirt aside and put the love seat between them. "What is it, darling?" he asked with a pained expression.

"That's what I'd like to know."

"I am too eager, eh?"

"What do you want, Frederic?"

"And you are too blunt." He perched on the love seat and reached for her hand, but she pulled it away. "Suppose we talk a little first," he said.

"I told you I'm busy."

"Just a little."

"About what?"

"You."

"No thank you."

"Why are you suddenly afraid of a little talk? It wasn't so long ago you were begging me to analyze you."

"I was just trying to make Oliver jealous."

"That's a healthy relationship." The way he said it made her furious.

"Shut up," she snapped.

"What did I say?"

"If you want to discuss my marriage, discuss it with Oliver."

"Oliver knows how I feel, just as you do."

"I don't know what you're talking about. Now please leave."

"No."

She couldn't believe he had said it. She had never seen Freddie be anything but agreeable. But if he had to be handled like a little boy, Scott had given her plenty of experience. She sat down, opened the book of poems and read the same line over several times.

"Are you ignoring me, darling?"

She didn't answer or look up, but she could sense his walking toward her and her nerves tightened. He veered off, though, before reaching her and when she sneaked a glance he was standing at the window.

"It must be a very engrossing book," he said. When she didn't reply, he went on. "I was reading an interesting book too, just last night. Some very remarkable statistics about the women in this country. Unbelievable! In such an enlightened day and age, in such a progressive culture, still more than sixty percent of the married women have never experienced the orgasm."

Lydia was tempted to spike his guns. A simple retort would do it, a mere question as to who conducted the survey. But she maintained her silence.

"And even the thirty-eight percent who think they have," he said, "most of them have never had a real orgasm. They've only experienced a clitoral stimulation. You don't confuse that with proper sexual gratification, do you, darling?"

Lydia turned the page and struggled to fix her mind on the first line of the next poem.

"Unbelievable," repeated Freddie. "And worse than that,

to think that ninety-three percent of the adult women of America have never practiced fellatio."

Lydia wished she had something besides the book to heave at him. What a low bastard, trying to titillate her and hiding behind statistics. She'd fix him. She'd remember every single word including his percentages and relate it all to Oliver.

"Don't you find that unbelievable, darling?"

There was a strong odor of lime, then his breath on the back of her neck. She made a casual yet quick movement away from him, but he was after her.

"Why are you so restless, darling?"

"Frederic, go away."

"What are you afraid of?"

She parried his grabs several times before he managed to hold both her arms with one hand. His fingers dug into her with a strength she'd never guessed he had.

"Frederic," she squirmed, "let go of me!"

"Don't be sophomoric, darling."

"You're hurting me!"

"We are only two nervous systems reacting to each other."

She learned backwards to avoid his kisses and his beard tickled the skin of her throat. Lydia wanted to laugh. Their stances and dialogue were straight out of a drawing-room comedy. It was the moment for her husband to walk in and discover them and sock Freddie on his well-padded jaw. She looked toward the foyer, but Oliver wasn't there. Then Voegler pushed his free hand inside her robe and between the buttons of her pajama top and she sobered to the seriousness of the situation.

"Stop it!" she gasped. But Voegler was beyond listening to orders or threats or admonitions. She could see the side of his face and neck inflamed and hear him panting as he wrestled her toward the couch. The hand inside her pajamas was squeezing her left breast painfully. She was frightened now, but all her trying to pull and twist away merely tore a button off.

"Lydia, I love you. I've loved you for years."

He almost sobbed it and her stiffened body began to relax.

What difference did it really make? It would be an experience, perhaps pleasant, at least amusing. One more man would ply her with compliments and caresses and would melt from her touch. What was one more? For a moment, she balanced on the rim of resistance.

"I will make you forget every other man."

That did it. Of all the corny lines. The code book came back, brandished by her mother and skinny aunts and round-shouldered clergymen and Deans of Women. And with it came a flash of strength which sprung her free from Voegler's grip. He turned toward her to get a new hold, but something in the way she drew herself up to full height and pulled her robe together made him stop.

"If you don't leave immediately," she said, "I'll tell Oliver."

He must have realized he'd gone too far. But he still tried to save face with a supercilious smile.

"You wouldn't do that," he said.

"Wouldn't I?"

"No," he smirked. "You don't want he should have Massey do a lobotomy on me too."

The struggle had somehow left her unusually clearheaded. At any other time she would have dismissed Voegler's remark as undecipherable. But now she had a sudden instinct toward its meaning.

"You'd better explain that," she said.

"I have to run along," he mumbled and started past her. This time she did the arm grabbing.

"Who did he have Massey operate on?"

"No one, darling."

"Tell me or I'll tell Oliver what just went on here."

"I swear to you," he cringed, "Massey hasn't operated on anyone."

"But he's going to, is that what you meant? When? Is it this morning? Is that why they went to Para Park?" She shouted the questions without waiting for him to answer. "Who are they doing the lobotomy on? Who?"

Voegler turned away and pressed his lips together like a prisoner of war being tortured. But she saw him look down at the book which had fallen to the floor and a hundred fragments suddenly fitted together.

"When?" she pleaded. "At least tell me when."

"It's scheduled for eleven."

Voegler padded behind her as she rushed to the bedroom, but remained outside the door.

"I thought you knew about it, darling," he whined. "When I saw his name on the book you were reading, I thought you knew all about it. Otherwise, I never would have mentioned it. I mean, I didn't say that Oliver was doing anything wrong or unethical. I mean, I'm sure Arnold made up the whole thing about seeing him see you."

Lydia heard only part of his ranting. A fierce, hysterical siren was howling in her brain. The scatter rug between her closet and dresser kept getting longer, her hair was knotted so she couldn't pull the comb through it, and the zipper of her skirt caught and her blouse wouldn't fasten. Then, when she picked up the bedroom phone and dialed the garage it seemed that the ringing would go on forever. But at last it stopped and a voice growled hello and she screamed at it to get her car out right away.

Chapter Twenty-Three

WHATEVER was in the blue pills canceled all direction, and with direction went all sense of time. Shillitoe had no idea how long he'd been heaped on the bed. Assassins came and went, washing him, feeding him, sliding the pills down his tongue and bracing him along the hall to the toilet. From somewhere came word that he'd been through all this before, dribbling and wetting while hairy hands stitched the cries on his lips and pressed the tears back into his eyes. But there was a difference between infancy and this. Now, as each pill weakened and slowly retreated from him, memory returned—lifting first the widow's veil thick with grief, then the thinner mosquito netting until, finally, there'd be the cameo clarity. Ben would be waiting for him, the poem would be waiting for him, all the unfinished landscapes would be waiting for him to get to work. But before he could, another blue pill and the sudden sinking into the thick, sedated mud, and another piecemeal awakening to find himself still chained by cobwebs.

One compensation—the pills deadened the pain in his body, toning it down to a dull fugue by a tortured Hungarian. But how much could be sacrificed for relief from pain? Certainly not this total separation, not this guillotine leaving him seeing the sun and hearing the rain but unable to feel the weather. He looked down at his fingers and toes, commanding them to move, and from the sluggishness of their response came panic.

Once he'd seen the great Thurston insert metal plates in a sawed wooden box and slide the half with the woman's head away. But Thurston's magic was only a carpenter's compared to that of the pills. These milked the will from his marrow and stuffed them into his skull. He, who'd never been able to confine an idea to his brain, was now reduced to thought without action and opinion without touch. This, he told himself, was the natural state of most men. Maybe even worse. Maybe this was what it felt like to be a critic.

He groaned then, a mournful sound muffled in the blanket of helplessness and, as if in answer, two assassins came in and propped him up. He was able to walk. The springs and hinges worked as long as they gave him a start and supplied the route. It wasn't to the toilet this time. They turned him the other way, then kept their hands off except for helping him down the stairs. Warm light poured from an open door and he wanted to go toward it, to let it thaw out the cold numbness. But they turned him again, through a different door to where the others waited stiffly like cabinet members welcoming a visiting head of state. He tried to raise his arms, to relax them with the old Tecumseh greeting. He wanted to say, "I have come in peace. Give me back my poem and there shall be no more fighting." But there was righteousness in their faces and duty in their stance and his clumsy tongue was unable to shape the air before it left his mouth.

He didn't see the table, draped in white, until his escorts aimed him at it. The welcoming committee stepped back as he walked the plank. No tickertape. No roses. Not like that morning he'd walked into the concentration camp outside Sonneberg and the skeletons in tight, bleached skins had clapped their hands. This bunch was well fed. The one with the garden on her head could be the Burgomaster's wife. No, he'd seen her before, the day they'd cross-examined him. The faceless flab next to her too. And there was Vera Kropotkin and Wren and a gross Caliban with glasses cutting into his blubbery cheeks. Caliban was draped in white too. Why white? Rabelais said for gladness. Melville said for death. And Caliban, helping to lift him onto the table and stretch him flat, cast another vote for Moby Dick. It was his damp, glistening face that kept blocking out the ceiling, and his festered breath that carried the speech.

". . . TO ALLOW US PSYCHIATRIC OBSERVATION OF THE PATIENT DURING THE OPERATION, I WILL USE A SHALLOW PENTOTHAL ANESTHESIA . . ."

Palms clamped his temples, followed by stings on each side of the bridge of his nose. The paralysis seeped in like spilled gravy, lightening his head to a block of balsa wood. All he could think of was that the fourth part of the poem wasn't done. Only seconds remained now for summing up. Not enough for writing down. Not even time to find the rhythm. His conclusions had to be stated raw.

> "WHILE WE WAIT FOR THE PENTOTHAL TO TAKE EFFECT, LET ME BRIEFLY EXPLAIN WHAT I AM GOING TO DO. AS WE ALL KNOW, ANTERIOR THALAMIC RADIATION IS A TWO-WAY CONNECTION BETWEEN THE PRE-FRONTAL AREA AND THE THALAMUS. AND, OF COURSE, IT IS THE THALAMUS WHICH PRODUCES EMOTIONS FOR OUR IDEAS."

Ideas? Ideas are spooks we chisel from things that look familiar; from puddles in summer, milk in saucers, the pod and the rock, girls giggling their names, hailstones like apostrophes . . .

> "WITH OUR INCREASED KNOWLEDGE OF THE LOCAL FUNCTIONING OF THE FRONTO-TEMPORAL COMPLEX WE CAN NOW DIRECT THE PATH OF THE LEUKOTOME SPECIFICALLY."

. . . a screen door and a barber chair, trumpets, trowels, stumps, crickets and a crocus bulb, sessile leaves and Virginia creeper . . .

> "WITH THIS PATIENT WHO HAS SHOWN EXCESSIVE PSYCHOMOTOR ACTIVITY, I DO NOT THINK IT NECESSARY TO ABLATE ANY CORTICAL TISSUE. I WILL JUST CUT THE WHITE MATTER OF THE FRONTAL LOBE BILATERALLY . . ."

. . . black bishops on a chessboard, a Bantu's teeth, the pitch of a bassoon . . .

> ". . . IN THE PLANE OF THE CORONAL SUTURE . . ."

. . . buckram to touch, gravestones mottled by rain, the poem —especially the poem.

> ". . . WHICH PASSES JUST ANTERIOR TO THE TIP OF THE LATERAL VENTRICLES."

You who swab the decks of evidence, remember this! The bloodier the corpse's trail, the less need for your sympathy.

Never mind my epitaph. Scalpels are clinking and misery awaits your verdict. Dear passive loiterers, the solution to all your problems eludes you because of its simplicity.

"Now I elevate the left upper eyelid . . . and now I insert the leukotome into the superior conjunctival sac. It's essential to keep the shaft in the plane of the nasal bone . . . and the point must be directed against the most convex spot of the orbital plate. Do you feel anything, Mr. Shillitoe?"

What the hell do you think I've been doing all these years?

"Can you hear me? Try to speak."

Nothing doing. Never tell off a headhunter when the point of his spear is against your brain. All this way to fall victim to acupuncture. Byron at least succumbed to exposure and Shelley to the leaping bay. By the way, are there plans for a memorial to me like the one old Percy Bysshe has at Oxford? I saw him sprawled bare-assed beneath that dome while a guide forgot to mention his being expelled and the literature-loving tourists gaped at his dactyl. The sculptor didn't even have the decency to give him a hard-on.

"Now I drive the point of the leukotome through the orbital plate to a depth of four centimeters from the upper eyelid. Then I draw it laterally in the same plane . . . and then I return it to its middle position and drive the point in one more centimeter. Mr. Shillitoe. Mr. Shillitoe!"

Don't bother me. I'm adding up the score. For every forest mowed and stream poluted, there is a new temple of art. That's our tragedy, that the moth is pinned and classified on a Latin tab instead of fluttering. All things must continue to move. After the millionth kiss, her mouth should continue to wrinkle. How many times must I say this?

"At the depth of five centimeters, I move carefully toward the midline . . . until parallel to the ala of

THE NOSE . . . THEN I GO LATERALLY TO APPROXIMATELY THE SAME ANGLE . . . AND ELEVATE THE LEUKOTOME UNTIL THE SHAFT IS AGAINST THE FLOOR OF THE FRONTAL FOSSA. THERE!"

How many times must I say it? In the thicket of canceled dreams, the verb remains obstinate. Movement gives phenomenal insight. Beauty is an interplay. The quickest hands weave the tallest men. Must another million dinosaurs crouch in your waxworks before you're able to see this? Will you go on scraping away all personality until the land mass lies like some albino slab?

"THEN I WITHDRAW THE LEUKOTOME QUICKLY AND WITH A STERILE SPONGE I APPLY PRESSURE TO THE UPPER EYELID. ANY QUESTIONS?"

Two. How come the fittest don't survive? And why are your races always won by the tortoise?

"I'M SORRY THE PATIENT HASN'T SPOKEN . . . OBVIOUSLY A LOW RESISTANCE TO PENTOTHAL. BUT MAYBE IT WILL WEAR OFF A LITTLE AS WE REPEAT THE SAME PROCEDURE ON THE OTHER SIDE."

Again the horrible internal sound, a fingernail on slate, a bent spike pulled squeaking from his rough box. Again the prowling steel turning sour against the thin bones. Again the hollow crack as his concentration failed to stem its path.

But this time a scream, fat with agony, unbelieving and irrevocable. Shillitoe thought it must have come from him, but it was too shrill and as it came closer it had a grain of lilac and a weight pressing on his chest.

"WREN! GODDAM IT! GET HER OUT OF HERE!"

Chapter Twenty-Four

THE girl toasting her an English muffin looked familiar to Mrs. Fish. Girl? She was thirty if she was a week. But where had she seen her before? Mrs. Fish was sure she'd never been in this luncheonette. Still, so many of these places looked the same and this one was just around the corner from Doctor Posmanture's office. It was possible she'd stopped in once without remembering.

The English muffin was burned around the edges and the girl wasn't exactly a philanthropist with the butter, but Mrs. Fish didn't feel like arguing.

"Lay my mind to rest," she said. "Where do I know you from?"

While the girl stood racking her brain, Mrs. Fish read the "Rhoda" embroidered over the pocket of her smock. Obviously done with a machine. Then somebody called out, "Bacon, L and T down!" and the girl spun around and bent over the sandwich board again.

"When you get a chance," said Mrs. Fish, "a chocolate phosphate, not too sweet."

It was plunked down in front of her a few minutes later and there was a good inch between the bubbles and the rim of the glass. But, by then, Mrs. Fish was too deep in her thoughts to care.

She had counted on something developing from the medical checkup. Anybody else would have found at least a little bit wrong, too much sugar or a few anemic corpuscles in the blood. But not Posmanture. "Perfect!" he'd said. "You could pass a physical for the Marines." Such a comedian. Another time she would have told him a few things. But she just couldn't be bothered. Lately, if the truth be known, she couldn't rise to many occasions. Maybe it didn't show up on Posmanture's fluoroscope, but these past weeks had collected their toll from her.

Her decline had started that afternoon Norma left and she went to see Doctor Wren. Up until then, in spite of all the twists and turns, Mrs. Fish had still felt in control of the situation. And, at the beginning, she congratulated herself for taking Evelyn's appointment with Doctor Wren, especially when he confirmed her suspicion that Leonard had never been to his office. Such an office! Such a calm, dignified man, even when she told him that her Evelyn had been raped. It was a pleasure to talk to him. But, as she went on with how Leonard had made up a story about hearing a record right in that very office, Doctor Wren seemed to change. And when she said the name Shillitoe, the bottom fell out.

All of a sudden he didn't want to hear any more. All of a sudden he had decided to turn the case over to another doctor. His explanation didn't hold so much ice, either. Mrs. Fish couldn't see why his having had contact with the raper should disqualify him from treating Evelyn. If anything, it should make him more suited. But the psychiatrists had all kinds of rules about such things and Doctor Wren wasn't breaking any of them. The only concession he made was telling her that Shillitoe was now in a mental institution where he belonged. Then he had his secretary make Evelyn's first appointment with Doctor Reznick who, he said, was excellent with this type of case. Excellent with rape? How specialized could they get?

Evelyn also hadn't been too happy with the switch. In fact, the whole neighborhood must have heard her yelling.

"But he specializes in cases like yours," said Mrs. Fish.

"What kind of cases?"

"You know what I'm referring to."

"No, I don't."

Mrs. Fish was afraid that the word rape might set off a new explosion and searched for another way to say it. *True Confessions* always said "ravaged," but even that sounded too strong.

"I'm talking about what begins with the letter R," she said.

"Doctor Wren said I'm repressed?"

"No, no, no."

"He told you there's something wrong with my reflexes?"

Mrs. Fish realized that the guessing game could go on all day.

"Listen," she said. "It's nothing to be ashamed of. You weren't the only one that maniac attacked before they put him away."

It was then that Mrs. Fish discovered just how sick her daughter really was. Before then, she'd had her doubts. She had never been able to see how anyone who was ill could maintain an appetite like Evelyn's. And she'd felt more than one reservation about the whole thing with the couches. But when Evelyn refused to admit she'd been attacked, Mrs. Fish realized how seriously her mind had been affected. And when Evelyn started saying that she had encouraged the carpet man, Mrs. Fish knew she was up against something over her depth. How could she argue against such raving? This required an expert like Doctor Reznick.

Evelyn kept her first appointment with him, but she wasn't too impressed. She said he didn't act as interested in her as Doctor Wren did and that he wasn't as smart. As if the smartest Gentile could be as smart as the dumbest Reznick. But Evelyn had gone back, eight times already, and after the third visit she was a new person.

"The fact that my subconscious desires came into play is beside the point," she announced. "To all intents and purposes, I was the victim of a criminal assault."

Had the psychoanalysis stopped right there, Mrs. Fish would have had no complaints. If nothing else, it shut Leonard up. After all, he couldn't blame Evelyn who only weighed a hundred and forty-three for not fighting off an assaulter who must have weighed over two hundred. He had to start showing Evelyn sympathy even if it killed him. But the psychoanalysis didn't stop there. According to Evelyn, Doctor Reznick said her neurosis went much deeper than this one experience and he was going to peel back the layers until he got to the roots. And while he was peeling, she had to busy herself with constructive compensations.

That started the sculpturing. Then, on Evelyn's fifth visit, Doctor Reznick decided that she and Leonard should do a constructive compensation together and recommended the jazz music. It never occurred to Doctor Reznick that a mother could also use some compensation. No, it was very obvious that he was trying to ignore her existence. Otherwise, how come Evelyn was making clay heads of Dana and Leonard and even the *schvartzeh* maid, but never once asked her own mother to pose for her? And why jazz music? So there'd be such noise from the victrola and from Evelyn and Leonard fighting about Bixes and Bunks and Satchmos that she couldn't get a word in. The handwriting on the wall was clear. There was a campaign to get her out of the picture. She was no longer the head of the family. Doctor Reznick had taken over.

So this was what it all came to. For this her parents had run from the Cossacks and been stuffed on a boat like cattle and cried when they saw the Statue of Liberty. What did the inscription on the statue say? "Give me your tired, your poor." Why? So their grandchildren can all go *mishugah?* For this her mother and father had spent years in the sweatshops with the piecework. For this they had *kvelled* when she married Aaron the roofer. She'd done a little *kvelling* herself. Aaron wasn't Sir Galahad, but he had his own business, and her marrying a notch up was part of the democracy she believed in. Even when he'd been killed, she still believed. Who dies from falling twelve feet off a garage roof? Only her Aaron. But she still believed. There was the future and the challenge of taking care of her two teen-age daughters and getting them married well.

If she'd been selfish like some women, she would have looked for another husband for herself. She would have gone to a *shatgun* and had him include her in his ad in the *Daily Forward.* But she wasn't thinking about herself and what would become of her after her daughters left. She was thinking only of them.

And this was her reward—Evelyn attacked by a sex maniac and becoming more of a stranger every day—and Norma? Mrs. Fish wasn't too confident of Norma's state of mind either. Ever since she'd gone back to South Bend there'd been letters making insinuations about Leonard, and there was that piece about her seeing the raper in Indianapolis and notifying the police when all the time he was locked away in an asylum. These were what a mother got for her devotion. This was what it didn't say anything about in the Declaration of Independence, that all the mothers would be replaced by psychiatrists. Was this what Washington and Jefferson and Lincoln were fighting for? Was this God's sense of justice?

For a moment, Mrs. Fish thought that God was answering her question, but it was only the girl, Rhoda, behind the counter.

"You want anything else?"

Mrs. Fish saw that all the customers were gone except her. She knew the girl wanted her to pay the check and leave but she had nowhere to go and no one to talk to.

"Want anything else?" repeated the girl.

"No," said Mrs. Fish. "I never wanted much. But I expected a little more than what I got."

"Something wrong with the phosphate?" asked the girl.

"Never mind," said Mrs. Fish.

"Was it too sweet?"

"I'm talking about life, not phosphates."

"Oh," said the girl and took away her plate and glass and thirty cents.

"You struggle and you skimp and you plan, for what?" asked Mrs. Fish.

"Only fools try to make a profit out of life," said the girl.

"I'm not asking for a profit," said Mrs. Fish. "Thanks to my Aaron's insurance, I've never had to beg. But what am I supposed to do at my age, live all by myself like a hermit?"

"No man is an island," said the girl.

"Not that I ever interfered," said Mrs. Fish. "I just wanted them to have all the pleasures I denied myself."

"Martyrdom is always phony," said the girl.

"So with all their Sunbeams and Westinghouses, are they any more happy?"

"It's better to wear out than to rust away."

"America!" snorted Mrs. Fish.

"Advertising Africans with brogues in haciendas."

"I don't know about that," said Mrs. Fish. "All I know is that nothing makes sense any more."

"That's the way the world ends," said the girl.

"How is that?"

"Not with a bang, but a whimper."

"Maybe you're right," said Mrs. Fish.

"I didn't make it up," said the girl. "It's T. S. Eliot."

"I don't know him."

"He steals a lot."

"Who doesn't?" asked Mrs. Fish.

"But he's still a pretty good poet."

"He is?"

"Do you read much poetry?"

"Who has time to read?"

"You should find time," said the girl. "It's difficult to get the news from poetry, but men die miserably every day for lack of what is found there."

Mrs. Fish didn't understand a word of what the girl was talking about, but she still had the feeling that this was the most intelligent conversation she'd had in a long time. She wanted to pursue it further, but somebody called out, "Rhoda" from back in the kitchen.

"Take care of yourself," said the girl and went off to see what they wanted.

Mrs. Fish waited a few minutes, hoping she'd come back. That remark about ending with a *chrex* instead of a bang was bothering her. Somehow, it seemed to sum up her position. Was she going to make some commotion with the time she had left, God willing? This was the decision she had to make. And, once faced, it didn't take her long to make it.

Mrs. Fish placed a dime tip conspicuously on the middle of the counter and went out into the busy street. She was anxious to get back to her small apartment where she could make the phone call in privacy. Before she called, however, she wanted to remember exactly what Mr. Moscowitz had said.

"I never got married again because I wanted to keep my life simple. So now look!"

Yes, those were his words. Mrs. Fish thought of all the stains on her carpet; where she had spilled some furniture polish, where Dana had dripped the cream soda and where Leonard with his twelve thumbs had knocked over a full glass of iced tea. But she wouldn't give the job to Acme unless Mr. Moscowitz promised to come and supervise it personally.

Rhoda stayed in the kitchen until the old woman left. She didn't want to talk anymore. All it did was prove how much she'd been affected by many years of Samson and poetry and how impossible it was for her to return to the superficial level of most people's conversations.

The place being completely empty upset her even more. It was just like this the last time she'd seen Samson, all beat up and asking her for help. She'd been steamed up enough to let him limp out but, after she called Doctor Wren, she ran out to find him and say she'd get his poem back like he asked. If only he'd hung around outside for a minute. Whenever she thought about how mean she'd been to him, she went hot and cold and there wasn't a night that it didn't jab her awake. But there was no use crying over spilled milk. Rhoda knew now that she had to have Samson back and this certainty excited her. She could hardly wait for when he'd again be spouting off at her about everything and pretending to get sore when she didn't catch on right away. The possibility that this might never take place, that she might never see him again, did occur to her. But there were things that reassured her, like her knowing where Samson was and the reports she was getting from Doctor Massey.

Rhoda hadn't liked the idea when she'd called Doctor Wren to ask what was happening and his secretary told her Doctor Massey had taken over her husband's case. But Doctor Massey didn't sound as bad as he looked and whenever she phoned him, which was once a day, he talked to her himself, instead of palming her off on his secretary. And he always told her that Samson was progressing nicely. Still, it was two weeks now and, since the operation wasn't any worse than having a tooth pulled, Samson could do the rest of his recuperating at home.

She had said that to Doctor Massey yesterday and the more she thought about the answer she got the less sense it made. What had her signing those papers to do with it? Maybe Doctor Massey hadn't understood her, or she hadn't made her point plain enough. But this afternoon when she called, she'd really spell it out for him. She wanted Samson home—period.

Chapter Twenty-Five

"YOU have to be there!" Alben Parker shook with insistence and his voice shot up a whole octave. "Don't worry," he added. "I'll pay you for your time."

The jibe was delivered with the total contempt that only

homosexuals could muster. For a moment, Oliver was tempted to let bitchery rule the hour and accept the offer. An hour and a half each way to Philadelphia, plus three hours at the theatre; six hours times fifty. It would make up what he'd paid X. O. Waterfall.

"That remark wasn't necessary," Oliver said. "I just think I can be of more help to you when the play opens in New York."

"An opening night in Philadelphia is worse than on Broadway. Things never go right and everyone comes down hoping it's a turkey."

As Parker piled on reasons for wanting him there, Oliver thought of once having looked forward to the opening night in New York with Lydia sitting beside him. How much had changed since then.

"All right," he said. "I'll take the six o'clock train tomorrow and meet you at the Schubert Theatre at a quarter to eight."

Parker looked almost disappointed, as if he'd wanted Oliver to refuse so he'd have one more excuse for histrionics at the out-of-town opening.

"You don't have to if it will put you out."

"Not at all," said Oliver. "I'll be there."

"Before I forget." Parker held up the small ticket envelope for him to see before placing it on his desk. "I mean it about paying you for your time," he said at the door.

"I didn't know I appeared so mercenary," smiled Oliver.

"If it sounded like that, I'm sorry." The disdain was gone now, replaced by an effeminate rationality. "But, after all, you will be there in a professional capacity."

"We'll see," said Oliver. He knew he'd never charge Parker for the time involved in going to the tryout. But he also knew it would make Parker feel better to think he might. Anything to relieve the pressure on him until his damn play was running.

Oliver went to his desk and sat down, momentarily at a loss. Usually he made use of the spare minutes between appointments by looking over the file of his next patient. But the next person to come in would be Doctor Holland and Oliver didn't want to anticipate why Holland had insisted upon seeing him today. It might have nothing to do with Para Park. And if it did have he wanted to meet it unprepared and unrehearsed.

Oliver opened the envelope Parker left. Two tickets! Parker, in spite of the remark about his attending as psychiatrist in residence, had assumed he'd bring someone. Lydia? A short time ago, nothing could have kept her away. But what would she say if he asked her to go along? The same reply he'd received to everything he'd said for thirteen days, that same silence and hollow stare.

"Doctor Holland is here."

Holland didn't wait to be escorted in, coming past Bueler with his quick, short strides. There was nothing portentous in his handshake. But was his expression less puckish than usual?

"I got in early, so I stopped and saw Lydia." Holland said it just as they sat down. "She doesn't look well, Oliver."

"Did she talk to you?"

"Why shouldn't she?"

"She hasn't been herself lately."

Holland filled his pipe as if waiting for a better answer. What did he want, a retelling of the whole thing? He'd undoubtedly heard it all from Abelson and Milicent and the others who'd been there. But one of the participants might be able to supply more details—was that it? Why had Lydia gone to Para Park? Was it true she had burst in on the operation and thrown herself on the patient or were the stories exaggerated? Had she really turned on him like a screaming wildcat, and what had she actually been accusing him of? The eyewitnesses didn't catch every word. But, most of all, what had happened after he'd got her out of the room? And what had been said on their drive back to the city? And what had been going on between them since? How they all must be dying to know.

"But I didn't come here to discuss Lydia," sighed Holland.

"Why did you want to see me?"

"Among other things, to give you hell."

"I can do without that right now." It came out ruder than Oliver intended, but Holland seemed more concerned with finding some matches. Then the interminable sucking on the pipe until it was lighted to his satisfaction.

"Nevertheless," said Holland, "a little hell is what you're going to get. Why did you have to go and write that letter?"

"That's my concern."

"Unfortunately it's mine too. The Parapraxes Society doesn't have a committee to consider presidents' offers of resignation. So the membership appointed one and made me the chairman."

"I didn't know," said Oliver. "I thought they'd just accept it."

"You don't know your colleagues, my boy."

"Then I suppose you want some information."

"No."

Oliver felt let down by the finality with which Holland said it. In a way, he did want to explain what had happened. So many times that which could be rationalized to oneself didn't stand up when verbalized.

"The committee has finished its investigation of the matter that prompted your letter," Holland continued. "What a botch."

"You mean the lobotomy?"

"I mean the whole case. What kind of morons do we have working up at that place? When they bathed the man, they saw the bruises on his side. They said so. But it never dawned on any of them to tell Doctor Kropotkin."

Oliver was conscious of the division within himself, of the part of him that wanted to hear no more and the part that leapt up in curiosity.

"I haven't been in touch with Para Park since the day of the operation," he said. "You'll have to bring me up to date."

"The man must have been kicked by a mule."

Holland shifted to a straight medical report. Shillitoe's right kidney and three ribs on the same side had been badly bruised. They had unquestionably been that way before the operation, but none of the attendants saw fit to call attention to the swelling and discoloration. They only did so three days after the operation, when the enuresis began and the urine stains on the bedsheets included spots of blood. Luckily, none of the ribs was broken and the swelling responded to ice packs. Kropotkin had also taken a spinal tap, but there was nothing significant in the chemical and cell content.

"What burns me," concluded Holland, "is Massey playing the wounded party. He claims the reaction is entirely due to the injured kidney and that it prevents him from proving that his operation was a complete success."

"But I thought the enuresis didn't appear until after the lobotomy."

"It didn't. But Massey contends that the lobotomy wouldn't have produced it if the patient hadn't been injured internally. I'm afraid he has a point."

"What's your opinion?" asked Oliver.

"I don't know."

"Similar reactions have been reported on other cases of transorbital surgery."

"And they've also been reported on kidney injuries," countered Holland. "Between us, I'd blame that leukotome of Massey's. But, then, I'm old-fashioned."

"So we'll never know."

"Not in this case. But Massey demands another chance to prove himself."

"At Para Park?"

"That's what he wants," said Holland.

"But there are no other patients there requiring surgery."

"Massey doesn't agree. He's found one. Herman something."

"Horvath," supplied Oliver.

"The one who doesn't talk."

"It's out of the question!" Oliver slammed his hand on the

desk to stress it. "A lobotomy on Horvath would be disastrous."

"Well, that's up to the board members," said Holland, and there was no mistaking his meaning as he added, "but I think an adamant stand by whoever's president could influence their decision."

Holland's pipe had gone out and Oliver watched him drawing the match flame deep into the bowl. What was the term Holland had used, "a botch"? Even that was an understatement. Oliver remembered the last time he'd seen Holland, when Professor Waterfall read his report. He'd thought then that he was rid of the case, and now it was more complicated than ever. Would it go on entangling him in its millions of strands until he could think of nothing else?

"I imagine Voegler will be made president," Oliver said, trying to make it sound like a good idea.

"My committee reached a unanimous decision," Holland couldn't resist inserting a long pause, "to ask you to reconsider."

"I can't." It was too abrupt, so Oliver expanded it. "I can't carry out the president's duties at Para Park while . . ."

"While Shillitoe is there?"

"Yes."

"Is that the only reason?"

"It's reason enough."

Holland flicked open his pocket watch and looked at it thoughtfully before speaking again.

"He should be gone by now." Then, seeing that Oliver didn't understand, "One of the attendants is driving him to wherever he lives."

"But who discharged him?"

"Massey." Holland appeared to think about that. "I suppose it's not quite official procedure, but it seemed best."

"Massey discharged him!" Oliver was indignant. "In the condition the patient's in?"

"The enuresis is still as incontinent, but it hasn't shown any blood for several days."

"But there was to be a postoperative study. Massey was to give us a full report—optic perceptions, motor functions, ideational improvement or impairment, sociability, everything." As Oliver kept protesting, his train of thought shot ahead. Why question this turn of events? He should be relieved. Except for excessive urination, Shillitoe was all right. And even this reaction probably wasn't due to the lobotomy. So no harm had come of it. He could prove this to Lydia. Holland would verify it and she'd believe Holland.

"It was too soon for a full report," said Holland. "So we settled for an inconclusive one."

"Based on what?"

"Just a few tests, sorting and reflexes."

"And?"

"Remember your professor from Princeton?" Holland waited for his nod before going on. "Suppose he was wrong. Suppose Shillitoe really is a poet. After all, if a poet doesn't react to life as other people do, it figures that he won't react to lobotomies the same way either."

"How has he reacted?"

"He hasn't. Except, possibly, the enuresis. And one other little thing." Holland appeared to be troubled. "Did Shillitoe ever strike you as farsighted?"

"No," said Oliver. "Is he?"

"Not exactly. But his depth perception seems a bit off. Misjudges distances, that sort of thing."

"I suppose Massey blames that on the kidney, too."

"No. For once he's stymied."

"So he discharges the patient."

"It was his patient," said Holland.

"But didn't anyone on the board object?"

"No. The board was rather anxious to drop the case. Besides, Mrs. Shillitoe wants the patient home with her. She called Massey yesterday and insisted."

Oliver sensed there was more to it. He couldn't see the Shillitoe woman overriding Massey's judgment.

"But she signed the papers for the operation," he said.

"I know," shrugged Holland. "Massey reminded her of that yesterday. That's when he found out that Mrs. Shillitoe isn't legally Mrs. Shillitoe."

Oliver didn't know whether to groan or laugh. Everything about the case had gone wrong, but this extra twist made it a mockery. All their careful formalities and committees and admission boards, all their rules and regulations—and the one relationship which should have been most obvious had escaped them. They had gone ahead on the signature of that slow-witted woman, not one of them guessing that she would have too much working-class morality to confess that she was just Shillitoe's bedmate of the moment. So Shillitoe was still a question mark and Lydia was in a state bordering Herman Horvath's and Massey hadn't proved a thing. There had to be a devil somewhere tangling the strings with fiendish delight. Oliver caught himself about to give up. Taken one knot at a time, no snarl was inextricable.

"I retract my offer of resignation," he said, and Holland nodded as if expecting it. Oliver searched the situation for his next move. As president he'd make sure that Herman Horvath was protected. He'd keep Massey far away from Para Park. What else? Oddly enough, Oliver couldn't think of anything. It was all straightened out, except for Lydia. But what was he going to do about Lydia?

"Lydia?" asked Holland.

Oliver hadn't realized he'd spoken her name.

"You know about what happened during the operation," he said.

"There was some talk," admitted Holland. "Something about her walking into the room by mistake and being upset at what she saw. But everyone understands. To the uninitiated, a lobotomy must look like some medieval torture."

Holland stood up as if they'd covered everything.

"Don't go yet," said Oliver. It was said in desperation and Holland looked surprised. Oliver hesitated. He kept telling himself to let Holland leave. Holland had made it perfectly clear that everything was all right now, that there'd been less gossip than he'd thought, that nothing had really changed. If necessary, he could seek his advice another time.

"Yes?" Holland still waited.

"Don't go," said Oliver. "I need your help."

Then Holland sat down again and it started to gush out, all of it, and it was only with great effort that Oliver was able to keep it dispassionate and precise. One idea kept intruding, that they were seated in the wrong places. Holland should be behind the desk and he in the patient's chair. And each time he thought this, Oliver checked on his detachment, making sure his tone belonged to a consultation between doctors.

In this tone he spoke of Lydia's increasing lethargy and loss of self-confidence, of her withdrawal from outside interests, from the children and from him. He mentioned Lydia's frequent requests that he analyze her and his once promising, though in jest, that he would if he ever thought it necessary. Then he told of the night last week when he'd fallen back on that. He had gone into the guest room which Lydia had taken over and reminded her of his promise and said he was willing to try to help her professionally. He'd even assumed her not answering to be consent and sat down next to the studio couch she was lying on and began instructing her. It was then she'd made the only acknowledgment of his presence since he'd quieted her screams at Para Park—and it was the most terrible laugh he'd ever heard.

Oliver hesitated and quickly reviewed what he'd said. Aside from the worse kind of generalities, he'd only filled Holland in on the beginning and the end. None of it added up unless the essential factor was known, the essential factor that Lydia was convinced he'd used his position to wreak a vicious revenge. Oliver still didn't know where she'd got that notion or what had prompted her driving out to Para Park that day.

But he did know that entwined in her indictment of him was her own guilt over being seduced by Shillitoe. Oliver debated whether his explanation to Holland need include the details of the ripple bath. But, having gone this far, he decided to go all the way.

"It was about a month ago," he began. "A Saturday. I took Lydia along to Para Park."

"Don't tell me any more," said Holland abruptly.

"But it's something you should know about."

"Not from you. If I'm to help Lydia, I prefer to hear it all from her."

Help *her?* Oliver had so firmly resolved himself to relate the incident that he wasn't able to give up on it immediately, not until he'd caught the full import of what Holland had said. Holland had misunderstood completely. He'd thought he was being asked to take Lydia as a patient.

"I'm afraid . . ." Oliver started to correct him, then faltered. Why not? Whom could he trust more? What better person was there to help Lydia? And was there really any alternative? Lydia had shown no signs of coming out of her depression in almost two weeks. He, himself, had been totally unable to establish any contact with her. But Holland had stopped to see her, and, apparently, she'd talked to him.

"Of course," said Holland, "you know I haven't time for an outside patient. And anyway, you couldn't expect me to commute. But, based on the few minutes I spent with her this morning, I assure you she'll be better off at my place."

Holland's place. Oliver saw the two-story building in Philadelphia and remembered the two years he'd worked there. He thought of the worn linoleum and sagging chairs in the lounge, of the inadequate library and laboratory, of the narrow halls mingling the air of sickness from the pathetic little rooms, and of the unremembered occupants who so greatly outnumbered the staff.

"Would you guarantee me one thing?" he asked.

"What?"

"That you'll treat her yourself."

Holland seemed to go over his entire schedule before replying.

"Yes. I'll manage somehow."

But something was missing. Here they sat making arrangements as if Lydia would willingly do whatever they decided. Hadn't he told Holland that she wouldn't even speak to him? Holland seemed to think of this at the same moment.

"There's the matter of getting her to the hospital. Can you handle that?"

Then Oliver remembered the tickets.

"I think so," he said. "I'll have to pretend to be taking her to Philadelphia to see a play tryout. If it works, I'll have her at your place tomorrow night."

Chapter Twenty-Six

SHILLITOE tore open the envelope Vera Kropotkin handed him and didn't follow her out to the station wagon until he'd made sure the parts of the poem were all there. Vera was impatiently scuffing the gravel of the driveway and looked like she was going to make her "back-to-society" speech. But she settled for a handshake that stopped the circulation in his fingers, slammed the station wagon door for him, and waved sadly as Arnold turned on the ignition.

Arnold wasn't in a communicative mood either, so the drive was made in silence except outside Mamaroneck and once on the Hutchinson River Parkway when Shillitoe had to ask him to pull off the road. By the time they stopped in front of the building, his bladder was threatening again. It was a toss-up between the bathroom upstairs and the one at the Double-Deuce. Upstairs was closer, so he raced into the hall and almost stepped on the ferret perched on the bottom stair.

"Mr. Shillitoe?"

"Gangway!"

"One of your neighbors said you were expected today."

The paper was slapped into his hand as he ran by. It didn't seem like he'd make the apartment and when he saw the Fitzgerald's door inching open, he almost settled for their coconut welcome mat. But he held on and was in the bathroom before he realized that one of the things he'd bolted past in the other room looked like Rhoda.

"Herschel gave me the afternoon off," she called out.

So she knew they were letting him go today. It looked like everyone knew, except him. He wondered if Rhoda had played the long-suffering wife during his captivity. Probably. It was a roll she'd been coached in by the film makers for years; smiling bravely through the wire partition on visiting day at Alcatraz, smiling bravely into the teeth of a death rattle, smiling bravely at the photograph of the bravely smiling Lieutenant, then continuing to write the V-mail letter and never once mentioning that their baby, born since he was sent to Guadalcanal, had strangely small feet and slanted eyes. Ah, there was a plot. But if Rhoda was playing it this way, he'd spoiled the whole thing by not coming in on crutches. It didn't matter that he was pissing like Old Faithful. That wasn't the kind of wound that gained audience sympathy.

He washed his hands slowly, trying to make up his mind what to do with her. No inspiration, so he soaped his face.

"Where's the goddam towel?"

He'd barked it without thinking, but it made no difference. From the servile quality of her "sorry" and the sounds of her scurrying around, he knew she was prepared to take his mightiest blows and keep smiling.

"Here you are, baby."

He groped toward her voice, caught a piece of the towel,

then a piece of her. Instantly, she was all over him, patting him dry, kissing him, fondling away his last reserve. He had the sinister idea of paying her back by working her up to a boil, then walking out. But no one deserved that much cruelty. Besides, since they'd pried into his brain he'd had a growing dread of just how much damage had been done. There'd been no rumor of poetry, but it was too early to tell if they'd killed it for good. The other possibility wasn't as bad, but it worried him. And there was no time like the present to find out.

It was the same as ever. Judging from Rhoda's response, maybe even better. Or else she was just starved. Relieved, he fell off to sleep and when he woke up coffee was percolating and she was dressed and standing over him with the envelope.

"You left this in the john."

"It's the poem."

She looked at it reverently, but not enough to make him forget how she'd refused to get it back for him.

"Hands off," he said.

"What about this?" She waved the paper the ferret had given him.

"What is it?" He waited while she stared at it. "Well?"

"It's a degree."

"Degree?" He snatched it away. "Dope, don't you know the difference between a *G* and a *C*?"

"A decree?"

"Yes, a decree." He couldn't figure out why the ferret had given him a copy of the decree that fixed Beverly's alimony. Then he found the threats at the end. He was to be in court at ten o'clock Monday, and if he wasn't the police would be sent to bring him in. Any property he owned could be sequestered. That was good for a laugh. Then there was a bunch of whereases, all of which came to the same conclusion: up to three months in jail if the amount was less than five hundred dollars, at least six months if it was more. He sat up and fumbled into his clothes, trying to remember how many weeks it had been since he'd sent the last postal money order to Beverly.

Rhoda couldn't remember either, but she thought the answer would be in the pile of letters from Daniel K. Papp. He opened the one with the latest postmark and immediately landed on the important words. Eight weeks! Eight hundred bucks! Six months or longer in the jug. Beverly must be licking her chops at the prospect. Well, blow all the Beverlys. Long before the court sent the cops around, he'd be back in Cob City.

There was a sinking sensation as he reminded himself that Beverly knew about Cob City. But it passed quickly. Beverly knew about Cob City, but she didn't know about hard-up Wesley Zimmerman. And as long as good old Wesley was sheriff, all inquiries from Papp and the New York court about him would be stamped ADDRESS UNKNOWN. There was the future danger of Wesley not getting re-elected. But in solidly Republican Cob City that wasn't very likely. What's more, Wesley would always have his boyhood pal, Samson Shillitoe, campaigning tirelessly for him.

"I've saved twelve dollars," said Rhoda. "And I haven't touched the hundred and ten that I got back from . . . you know."

As she brought it to him, her face was screwed up in higher mathematics.

"Six hundred and seventy-eight," she recited. "Where you going to get that much?"

"Don't worry about it."

"But you gotta' be in court Monday."

"Wrong as usual," he said. "Didn't you ever hear of a moratorium?"

"Where they burn dead people?"

"That's close enough," he sighed. "Now, watch!" Taking the letters from Daniel K. Papp one at a time he tore them into little pieces and, swinging into a Morris dance, he scattered the confetti around the room. Rhoda, on her hands and knees scooping it up, suddenly pointed at him and shrieked.

"Not that one!"

He hadn't noticed that the envelope in his hand was different from the others.

"That came last week," she said.

It was postmarked *Cob City,* but he didn't recognize the penciled handwriting. The signature of Mrs. John Cathcart at the bottom of the ruled pulp paper didn't register either, not until he noticed the "Emma" in parenthesis beneath it. His high spirits sank with him into the chair and the pain knifed between his eyes again as he began to read the letter.

Emma had taken a whole paragraph to explain that she knew where to write him because his father gave her the address. She seemed as reluctant to get to the point as he was to find it. But there it was.

Your father passed away about two o'clock this morning.

He read the sentence over several times to crank up some emotion, but all that sputtered within him seemed wrong. There was annoyance at the *passed away.* Ben never did anything that sneaky. He'd died. No, even that wasn't accurate. He'd finished the dying he'd been doing most of his life. The vague clocking of his departure also angered Shillitoe. It seemed a judgment of Ben's stature. No one had bothered to note the exact minute. But this was quibbling. Actually, he felt no ache at Ben's death.

He didn't suffer any toward the end.

Another saying that had become a necessity because people wanted to believe that everything inevitable was painless. They were getting their way too. Soon there'd be a shot in the ass at birth that lasted a hundred years and the vegetables would have bested the animals for good and all. He couldn't help wishing Emma was lying, that at about two o'clock Ben had risen from his bed of cancer and let out a war whoop that cracked the bell in The First Methodist Church. But he knew it hadn't happened that way. Ben's last words were that *Helle-*

bore made no sense to him. He wasn't much better than most; his single virtue that he talked less.

The anger was gone, the anguish had never come. Shillitoe's only remaining thought was the one that the bereaved denied most hotly—how had the death affected him? Would Ben's emblamed carcass be turning to cracked shellack and thickening its stink each day until he got back to bury it? Emma seemed to have anticipated this.

> *Mr. Ponder was here from the Masons and he says your father was paid up in full and they'll take care of the funeral. It will be this Thursday afternoon unless you say different. But I guess you'll be here before then.*

This Thursday was last Thursday. Ben had been buried a whole week. At least Para Park had spared him that ceremony. But it might have been an experience he could some day weave into a poem. He'd attended funerals in the Cob City cemetery often as a boy, attracted by the arrangement of the mourners and the clergymen's tales of woe. The first shovelfuls of dirt on the coffin lid made interesting sounds and the pompous romp might have taken on a new depth of significance when Ben was the center of it.

> *One more thing. Sheriff Zimmerman was here as soon as he heard the news. I don't know what he was after. But he searched the whole place till he found it.*

Then grief swarmed over him. There was no mistaking what the *it* was. His secret weapon, his impregnable fortress against the army of Beverly and Papp, the most precious shacking-up register in the history of civilization—and *it* was gone!

"Sonofabitch!" he wailed.

Rhoda, scrambling eggs at the stove, turned her head around.

"Bad news?" she asked, all ready to pour cheer on whatever he said. But when he didn't answer she assumed it wasn't too bad and went back to the frying pan.

The deep armchair boxed in his frustration. He called to Rhoda to come over and hoist him out.

"In a sec'," she said.

"Right now!"

Still doing sufferance, she obeyed, then trotted back to her goddam eggs. He walked over to the window and looked down at the street. The numbers chalked in the hopscotch squares gave him the final tally. Eight hundred bucks, and he had one hundred and twenty-two. It was no use going back to Cob City now. Wesley Zimmerman would be waiting with open arms and it would be nothing but a fast round trip. Other escape hatches briefly opened. Carny life again? It wasn't what it used to be. The sea? The cruddiest tramp steamer now demanded identification papers. Mexico? All the *si señor* shit could louse up the measure of his poetry, providing the brain pickers hadn't already removed it. But he'd have to take off for somewhere by Monday.

Something else rasped at him and he forced it into the open. *All property will be sequestered.* It wasn't laughable now. As Ben's sole son and heir, he owned the garage and cabins. That changed everything. His doing a disappearing act would lead the bloodhounds to Wesley Zimmerman and Wesley wouldn't fail to mention Ben's place. He could beat them to it by putting the garage and cabins on the auction block himself. They'd bring enough to pay Beverly up to date and keep him out of jail. For what? To squander time earning all the alimony payments yet to come? Like hell! He'd served a ten-year sentence. It had to end sometime.

"Lunch!" piped Rhoda.

"Shove it," he growled.

She came over to him, her sex making it impossible for her to think that any mood of his didn't involve her.

"Samson." She'd almost acquired a dulcet tone. "Samson, I don't blame you if you're still sore for what I did." He tried to guess which of her stupid acts she meant. "But I want you to know I didn't mean what I said about poetry. Honest I didn't.

I know it's the most important thing in the world. No kiddin'. You should'a heard me quoting it to a customer the other day."

Somehow, she'd hit on the right thing to say. His face as he turned to look down at her must have shown approval.

"And there's something else," she beamed. "I'm ready to go to Cob City whenever you say."

The irony of it took him down a few clouds. But she didn't seem to notice.

"Samson, now will you do me a favor?"

"What?"

"You know, what you always do when I've done something dumb."

He knew what she wanted, the fake punch. He'd never realized it meant so much to her. But he couldn't summon up the false fury that was part of the game.

"The eggs will get cold," he said.

"Come on," she pleaded. "How long does it take to throw a left?"

He contorted his face until it felt menacing and snarled at her while she held out her chin. He decided on a left hook, aiming it carefully to sizzle within an inch of her shining cheek. But something went haywire. His fist landed full on her right eye and she went out cold.

Chapter Twenty-Seven

LYDIA walked to Madison Avenue and Seventy-sixth Street and went into the First National City Bank. Then the calm determination which had taken hold faltered for the first time. She had forgotten that it was Friday and there'd be long lines of people cashing their paychecks. But she waited one out and the teller was diplomatic enough to write down the balance and slide the paper out to her instead of saying the amount out loud.

She went to one of the glass tables before looking at it. $704.63. It was less than she'd expected. But Oliver never liked to maintain too large a balance in their joint checking account. This was what he called their miscellaneous self-indulgence fund.

Lydia divided the total by two, hesitated over the odd penny before deciding not to take it, then wrote out the check to *Cash* and joined the line again. Her calmness had returned now. She was actually going through with it. But, though there was a satisfaction in secrecy, she couldn't help wishing that Oliver knew what she was doing. What had he said last night, that she had to start functioning? He'd have to eat those words when he found out about this, and about her daily phone calls to Para Park, and how she'd got Shillitoe's address from his publisher when told he'd been released, and how she'd been doing research on psychosurgery in Oliver's own study.

It was the terrible sentence in one of his books that originally prompted the calls. *Cerebral hemorrhage within the first week is the most frequent cause of fatalities.* Lydia knew if that happened she just wouldn't be able to live. And each morning when she phoned Para Park as a nameless friend of Mr. Shillitoe, that sentence pounded in her temples until the woman with the foreign accent said he was doing very well.

That same book contained a heartless listing of adverse effects sickening to contemplate. But she'd forced herself to memorize them and with each went hideous before-and-after photographs. She saw the exuberant Shillitoe lying inert and without initiative. She saw him eating ravenously, his once gaunt frame now obese. And she saw his spontaneity replaced by silly childishness. These were what the book said could happen, while stressing the many months required for readaptation to society and the importance of the right care during convalescence.

"Three hundred and fifty-two dollars and thirty-one cents." As the teller counted it out, she wondered how much convalescent care it would buy.

Returning to the street, Lydia held back a wave to an empty cab. She had withdrawn her half of the self-indulgence fund, but she wasn't indulging herself today. Much as she hated the subway, she walked back to the station on Lexington Avenue. The filthy platform and the two oily haired delinquents looking her over were part of her punishment. Again she wished Oliver could see her now. If his remark about her functioning had been aimed to spur her to action, he was getting more than he'd bargained for. But it wasn't only the one remark. It was the whole change in his manner last night.

Before then, he'd been careful. He'd treated her delicately, and she was sure she hadn't imagined the self-incrimination in his voice. But last night he got annoyed when she didn't answer his questions about the children and what she'd done during the day. That was when he said she had to start functioning. And when she lay back and closed her eyes, his voice got hard.

"We're going to Philadelphia tomorrow," he said. "Be ready by five."

She still hadn't answered, but she'd opened her eyes and they must have demanded an explanation. That was undoubtedly why he'd left the two tickets to the play on the cabinet where she'd be bound to notice them. They'd tempted her, too. Why deny it? Oliver had a strict rule about her not knowing who his patients were, but he'd dropped several hints that one of them was Alben Parker. Lydia guessed that Oliver had helped him with his new play and she'd looked forward to seeing it. What's more, she'd never been to an out-of-town opening. She wanted to go. But she wasn't ready to go anywhere with Oliver.

Her feelings toward him were not as unbearable now as during those first days. Then, whenever he came near her, she thought of that room with Shillitoe helpless on the table and all of them hovering around while the sweating, bull-necked one forced that horrible instrument into his eye. How could Oliver have taken this kind of revenge? How could he pretend that anyone capable of writing such poetry was insane? But these questions gradually began to lose their force. Even reading and rereading Shillitoe's poems didn't strengthen them. The book on psychosurgery had made everything unbearable again. But now the feeling was almost gone and she couldn't revive it.

Perhaps Oliver had sensed this. Perhaps that was why he'd shifted his approach and ordered her to go to Philadelphia with him. He didn't really care that she loathed what he'd done. Just so long as they showed a united front. Maybe she'd have to go along with the pose eventually, for the sake of the children, but not yet. Not until she saw the results of the operation herself, and then only if they were as favorable as Oliver's book claimed they usually were. But, whatever, she wasn't going to Philadelphia today. After seeing Shillitoe, she'd look around the stores on Fifth, then have dinner out and not get home until after eight. It was a small self-denial but better than none, just as the money she'd withdrawn was inadequate but better than nothing.

Lydia was fully prepared for the street Shillitoe lived on. In fact, she would have been surprised if the buildings were less crumbling or the children playing on the sidewalk more nourished. One leering monster with scabs on both knees and elbows was hitting a frail little girl with a stick.

"Stop that!" As Lydia shouted it, the women in the windows and doorways turned to her. She was only wearing a simple black suit, but in this neighborhood it felt too dressy. These people would enjoy her getting into a fishwife's brawl with the kid's mother. No one came to his rescue, however, and he ran off, the little girl trailing after him. Law of the cave and gutter. The frightening thing was what they would grow up to be and that Scott and Deirdre would have to live in the same world.

Lydia hurried on, suspecting in advance that the number she sought was where the woman sat on the stoop glaring at her. The woman didn't slide over to let her pass and there was barely room to get by and hardly enough light in the musky hall to make out the names penciled on the mailboxes. Shillitoe was on the last one, Apartment H. Lydia started toward the stairway and stumbled over a package propped against the wall.

"Who you looking for?" The woman on the stoop was watching her like a hawk.

"Mr. Shillitoe."

"He ain't home."

"Do you know when he's expected?" It was a natural thing to ask, yet it sounded pretentious here.

"I haven't the slightest idea." The woman seemed anxious to prove that she could sound pretentious too. "Are you a social worker?"

"No. Just a . . . friend."

"A friend of *his?*" The woman looked more than skeptical.

"Do you know where he might be?"

"You're sure you're not a social worker?"

"Positive." Lydia felt she should cross her heart.

"You wouldn't be from that asylum he was in?"

"As a matter of fact, I am." As she said it, Lydia knew the lie would get results.

"Then you might take a look in the Double-Deuce."

Lydia followed the aim of the woman's finger to the corner saloon.

"In there?" she asked. She wondered if she might get the woman to go over and summon Shillitoe for her. Maybe if she paid her something.

She was about to make the offer when a fireman's helmet stuck out over a window ledge above and the beet-red face beneath it yelled, "I'm hungry."

"Okay. Okay." The woman got wearily to her feet. Reaching the hallway, she stopped and turned back to Lydia.

"If you find him," she said, "tell him this package came for him."

There seemed nothing else to do but to go on to the corner. The windows of the bar were filthy, revealing only her own reflection, so she walked slowly past the open door and looked in. One person was inside with the bartender but he was facing the other way. Suddenly she wasn't sure what Shillitoe looked like. Then, penetrating the noises of the street, through the traffic and screeching children, she heard his voice. It reached out through the doorway and pulled her inside.

"Let's see how much you remember," he was saying to the bartender. "What was the best year of all?"

"Eighteen hundred an' nineteen," said the bartender.

"And why?"

"Cause both of 'em was born then."

"Who?"

"Melville an' Whitman."

"Devery, there's hope for you yet." He finished what was in his glass and slammed it down on the bar. "Drinks for everybody," he said.

"There's nobody here."

"Nobody?" Shillitoe turned to verify this, scanning the whole room before coming to her. The bartender saw her at the same time and both seemed waiting for her to speak. She didn't know how to begin. Should she call him Samson? Could she say "Mr. Shillitoe" after what had happened between them?

"Do you remember me?" she asked.

"Ivory elbow," he said.

"I'm Lydia Wren." She was sure he knew the rest but said it just in case. "Doctor Wren is my husband."

"What you drinking?"

"Nothing, thank you. Unless I might have some water?"

The bartender went off as if he kept it hidden for special customers.

"Lydia," said Shillitoe. "Yes, it would be."

She studied him, alert for the symptoms listed in the book. Was it inertia that made him lean against the bar, or was he drunk? One thing was certain. If anything, he was leaner now. The danger of obesity hadn't materialized.

"How are you?" It sounded so casual, but she didn't know how else to ask.

"Never worse," he said, and before she could ask him to be specific he ran off to the men's room.

Alone at the bar now, she was fully aware of the strangeness of her being in such a place. She looked at the photographs Scotch-taped to the mirror, grimacing Neanderthals in threatening stances, a Spanish dancer with her swirling skirt leaving little to the imagination, and several nudes. The bartender came back, saw where she was looking and sheepishly placed down the glass of water.

"Have you known Mr. Shillitoe very long?" she asked.

"Umm." Real talkative, this one.

"Is he drunk?"

"Naw. He's only just starting."

"Perhaps you could tell me." His mouth set as if he'd die first. "Does he seem any different to you?"

"Different from what?" he asked.

"From how he used to be."

"When?"

Yes, when? She started to say, "Before the operation." But the bartender might not know about that.

"Oh, a month ago," she said.

"What d'ya mean, different?"

"Does he seem more restless, or careless, or tactless? Has he been saying profane things? Or being vulgar?"

"Sure." Her heart sank before he added, "But that ain't anything different."

Then Shillitoe was next to her, ordering another drink.

"Nothing doin'," said the bartender.

"A double bourbon," said Shillitoe, "and I'll dedicate a poem to you."

"Uh-uh," said the bartender. "You owe me a small fortune already."

"How much does he owe you?"

They both looked surprised at her butting in. Then, while the bartender rang open the cash register and added up what was on the scraps of paper he took out, Lydia pressed the money into Shillitoe's hand.

"Sixty-eight dollars and . . ." The bartender stared in disbelief as Shillitoe peeled off the bills. Then Shillitoe held the rest out to her.

"It's yours," she said.

"Why the hell didn't you say so before I paid him?" He flipped through the money. "And what have I done to deserve this?"

"Don't you believe in artists being subsidized?" She'd rehearsed the line, expecting he'd ask why she was giving him the money. But she hadn't thought it would make him laugh.

"What's so funny?"

"Nothing." He shook his head as if to rid it of humor. "I thought, maybe I was being paid for something else."

"What else?" As she asked it she suddenly knew.

"Come on," he said. "Where are the strings?"

"No strings."

"Over three hundred bucks for one dip in the tub? Christ, I've been wasting my talent."

It was vulgar, just as the book said. But the bartender could be right. He might have been like this before.

"There's something I must know," she said.

"Here it comes." He winked at the bartender.

"Please," she said. "Could we talk alone?"

"Nope." The bartender had started to inch away. "Devery, stay right here and protect me!"

She had no choice but to pretend the bartender wasn't there.

"Since . . . since what happened to you," she said, "do you feel less energy or initiative?"

"I'm not sure," he smiled. "Let's hunt up a bathtub and find out."

"I'm serious," she insisted. "I have to know."

"Why?"

"It's important to me."

"Devery," he snapped, "I asked for a double bourbon." He waited until the bartender served him before turning to her again. "Go home," he said, "and tell hubby to do his own paying off."

"He didn't send me here."

"Beat it."

"He didn't!" She couldn't keep her voice from rising. "And that isn't his money. It's mine!"

"Thanks," he said. "It can lop three months off my stretch if they catch me." He emptied the jigger of bourbon in one gulp, then started past her. But she moved in front of him and blocked his way.

"I haven't spoken a word to him," she said. "Not since what they did to you."

"Excuse me." He tried to push by but she didn't let him.

"Don't blame him entirely." she said. "I'm the one who's really responsible."

"Will you get out of my way?"

"What if the situation had been reversed? What if it had been your wife?"

"Don't have a wife." He shoved her aside so roughly that she hurt her hip on the edge of the bar, and by the time she turned around he was going into the men's room again. She had her next argument ready to hurl at him when he came out.

"It's possible he believed he was helping you."

"You want the truth?"

"Yes." She steadied herself for whatever it might be.

"Okay," he said. "The truth is that it was a pleasure meeting you last time and if I didn't need your money I'd keep it anyway."

"That's no answer to what I said."

"What did you say?"

"He may have believed he was helping you, at least consciously."

"Look," he sighed. "Your husband settled for a piece of my brain. What the hell will it take to satisfy you?"

"I don't know," she said. "Would a little forgiveness be asking too much?"

"Till pity is become a trade, and generosity a science that men get rich by."

"I don't know what you mean."

"Devery," he said, "tell her what it means."

"I forget," mumbled the bartender.

"I go away for a few weeks and look what happens."

The bartender looked relieved when two truck drivers came in and he hustled off to serve them.

"Suppose you tell me what it means," she said, trying to make her smile encouraging.

"Jesus!" he groaned. "Is there any conceit like a good-looking woman's? You really think you're the reason they chopped me up. You really think that empires rise and fall between your legs."

"I've just suggested the opposite, that he was trying to help you."

"Help me?" He went up on his toes as he bellowed it. "Sure! All history is a story of poets being helped—racks, dungeons, brain operations."

"Put a sock in it!" called one of the truck drivers.

She sensed there was going to be trouble.

"You were saying?" she asked, trying to distract him. But he walked stiffly to the end of the bar and as soon as he was within range of the truck driver he swung.

The driver didn't duck, but the punch missed him by a foot and the momentum of it carried Shillitoe out the open door. She heard the crash and ran outside to where he was sprawled over the garbage can. He wouldn't let her help him up, but when he started down the street he didn't push her away.

"What can I do for you?" she asked. But he was watching the monster who was now whipping the little girl with a piece of rope.

"Save your strength, Gregory," he called to him. "You haven't got a chance." Then his sweeping gesture took in all the people on the street. "Look at them," he said. "Look at them bloating and bulging, trying to breed their way out of here. What will they produce? First the merchants, then the legal minds, then scholars without scholarship, then the ologists like that thing you're married to. All that effort in the wrong direction. I could save a few of them. It's not my purpose, but if I had a couple of years to work without interruption, I'd bust up some of their gods. Length and stress, that's all it takes. Only two issues. How long can you survive? Where will you throw your weight? That's all."

They'd reached the front of his building and he turned to go inside. She was confused now. She wasn't sure why she'd sought him out or what she wanted from him.

"May I come in?"

"We only have a shower."

"Don't you think that's worn a bit thin?"

He didn't reply. He just ran into the hall and took the stairs two at a time. She started to follow, when she saw the package leaning against the wall. She checked to make sure it was his name lettered under the rows of stamps, then carried it upstairs. By the time she reached the top landing her arms ached and all the tars and nicotine of years were clogging her breath. She staggered through the door he'd left open just as he came out of the bathroom.

"This is yours," she said, holding out the package.

"More gifts for the fertility symbol?" While he tore off the brown paper wrapping, she leaned weakly against the wall taking in the room.

It wasn't what she'd expected. She'd thought it would be a jumble of books and manuscripts with vivid, original paintings and marks of the genius in every piece of furnishing. It had none of that, just the reverse. It was so scrubbed and sparse it seemed vacant. But it was right. Quickly she realized she'd expected the cliché when everything about him should have told her otherwise. The place he lived in was as uncluttered as his writing. And, strangely enough, the room appealed to her. Its very barrenness showed her how much that she had gathered around herself was useless and ornamental. Yet, it was his way of living that she had always feared. The times she'd driven through these neighborhoods she'd always been thankful she didn't have to live in such squalor. But she'd walked down the street below and nothing had happened. She'd been inside one of the saloons that she'd always regarded as on the lowest depth of existence and it had been as safe as anywhere else. Now she was inside a tenement and there was nothing to be afraid of. How many people were hanging on to jobs they hated and things that made them miserable just because they were afraid of having to live like this? And all the time there was nothing to fear.

She wanted him to know what she'd discovered. She wanted to tell him she wasn't like the people she knew. She wanted him to believe this. And she wanted him to make love to her, to have that triumph over Oliver. But as she stepped toward him he let out a roar.

"He took the wrong one!" he shouted. "He took the *new* one." He started leaping around the room, hugging what had been in the package with both arms. It looked like a cheap ledger of some kind.

"I can go back," he crowed. "I've got them by the balls. Zimmerman for Sheriff!"

"What is it? What's happened?"

Instead of answering, he opened the ledger and pointed to one of the lines. She saw the handwritten *W. Zimmerman and guest* before he slammed the book closed and jumped some more.

"Ben did it! He must have got Emma to mail it before he died." Then he saw her puzzled look. "Don't you get it?" he said. "I can go back."

"You're leaving here?" She didn't intend to sound disappointed.

"Damn tootin'."

"When?"

"Right now."

"Take me with you."

She hadn't meant to say it, but as the words hung between them she didn't want to take them back. And while he stood there considering it, her mind quickly supplied reasons. The book said he needed many months of the right kind of care. She could take care of him. She owed him that. But she didn't deceive herself. She wasn't being completely selfless. It was a way out, an escape from living out long years of pretending with Oliver.

"You sure you want to come along?"

"Yes, I'm sure." As she said it, there was a thudding on the stairs outside and a moment later, a woman with a black eye came in.

The shouting that followed seemed to be coming from a great distance. Lydia's head ached and her body felt empty and weak. She lowered herself onto one of the chairs at the table and tried to concentrate on what was going on between Shillitoe and the woman with the husky voice. The woman kept making side glances at her and saying it was a good thing she got the afternoon off. And he kept telling the woman to shut up and get her things together. Lydia couldn't understand why he said this, not until she heard him say something about an extra bed in the alcove over the garage and the woman insisted that they needed it. *Ménage à trois!* It was fitting that it struck her first in French. She wasn't the only one he planned to take with him. And he'd never said a word about it. Did he really think she'd be a part of anything so disgusting?

She remembered the children then. She remembered Oliver too, and all the interests they shared. Then she saw the cockroach crawling across the floor and the filth and sordidness of the room closed in on her. She must have been out of her mind coming here. And to think of running away with this crazy loon. Yes, he was crazy! Oliver had been right about him. Oliver was right about everything.

She reached the door, but they'd stopped shouting at each other and Shillitoe was right behind her.

"Where you going?" he asked.

A good question. Where *was* she going? She looked at her watch. A little after two. Enough time to get home and bathe and collect herself and be looking her very best.

"To Philadelphia," she said, and fled down the stairs.

Chapter Twenty-Eight

THE jets sang, the runway dropped and the plane rose and curved slowly until it pointed toward Indiana. Shillitoe finished reading the second part of the poem and went on to the third.

Men marry what they do not fear
(percentages
and pimpled brides)
touch, fail multiply

"It doesn't say to fasten your seat belt any more." Rhoda fussed with his buckle until the straps fell loose. "Gee! Look down there." She was practically on his lap, craning to see out the small, round window, and he had to shove her back into her seat.

to fractions
that communicate
like fenceposts
in Montana snow-
drifts hiding contact.
frozen.
forgetting
what they mark
and why—

"I knew you were just kidding," said Rhoda, breaking the cadence. "I knew you didn't mean it about bringing her along."

He kept his eyes on the poem, knowing that if he so much as glanced at her she'd go on jabbering until they landed. It was no use correcting her anyway. He'd never been unnecessarily unkind to Rhoda, so why start now? He wondered if ivory elbow also thought he'd been kidding. Better if she did think that. A clean break took more than she'd ever have. There was a bitter leftover though. He'd talked too goddam much. He should never have given her a glimpse of light without being sure she could take a full dose. Now she'd be lame, tripping over delusions every day with no broom to sweep them aside. For her own sake he should have powered her into coming along. He might have too, if Rhoda hadn't busted in at exactly the wrong moment. But he couldn't blame Rhoda for that, nor for balking at his idea. After all, Catherine hadn't agreed either when old Blake wanted to add another woman to the fold. Catherine had just sat there and bawled. Rhoda's fighting back was one up on that.

It was a defeat, but a minor one. And in the long run, Rhoda would be the loser. Now she'd have to take care of the station and cabins all by herself. The thought of the place made him reach down and touch Ben's register alongside his leg. It was still there in all its solid reassurance. And the poem was on his lap. And after buying their tickets he still had over three hundred in his pocket. And his bladder had been holding for almost an hour. What more could a man ask? As he inventoried his situation he felt there was a flaw. But he couldn't find one. Barring a plane crash, he'd made it. From near total surrender, he'd rebounded to a setup more ideal than he'd ever dared hope for. There'd be a small but sufficient income with Rhoda taking care of all customers. There'd be no more bloodletting for Beverly, no more time wasted at meaningless labor, nothing to dissipate his strength. For the first time in his life he was completely independent with poetry his only care. Then he remembered what was wrong, the one undetermined factor. Was he still a poet? Or had they sliced out the tissue on which all his plans depended?

"I know where I saw her," piped Rhoda.

"Who?" She'd caught him off-guard. Now there'd be no shutting her up.

"That old lady I told you about. The one in Herschel's." He concentrated on reading the poem to squeeze her voice away. "I just remembered. I was coming out of Doctor Posmanture's office and she was going in." He concentrated harder. "I didn't know who else to go to," she said.

The poem was as right as he'd thought it was. He read on, stumbling occasionally over a rough spot, then being swept on by the heavy surge of rhythm. The devastation was complete, the judgments inevitable. As far as he'd gone, he'd left no loopholes, no thin flanks of high-sounding campaign speeches. But what of the fourth part?

"I don't know how it happened," she whined. "And with everything going on, it didn't seem like it'd been three months."

Three months since when? Before he could ask her, the rumbling began. There was one voice, one isolated drummer on the dunes . . .

"I figure the end of March. That's why I said we're gonna' need the alcove."

One drummer, making the canticles sound hollow . . . sifting, thumping, shaping sand into new melodies . . . coaching the bud of instinct to play by itself.

"And Doctor Posmanture told me I gotta' start taking it easy. You ain't sore, are you, Samson?"

A tug, a whisper, of uneasiness. Something was screwed up. But the plane was steady. He tracked the blinking danger light and came to Rhoda's glow. Her mouth was still flapping, but she was drowned out by the turmoil inside him—swelling, buffeting him, stretching his skin until it screeched. Then the fourth part of the poem broke free, its wild wind carrying him higher and higher. And the words, like hard-brined fists of fire, beat back at the sun.